SEASONS OF TRIUMPH • BOOK 2

FOR THE LOVE OF
TRIUMPH

SEASONS OF TRIUMPH • BOOK 2

FOR THE LOVE OF
TRIUMPH

BRITTANY KOOI
CORINNE FREEDMAN ELLIS

chalice
stories

Print: 9780827211490
EPUB: 9780827211506
EPDF: 9780827211513

ChalicePress.com

Printed in the United States of America

For my family, whose chaos, love, and support mean the world. I love you more than fancy words can convey! Thank you. BK

For everyone whose care, love, and gentle (or not-so-gentle) nudges make me a better pastor, writer, mother, and person. Thanks especially to my family, whose support is everything, and to my coauthors, who dreamed up such a beautiful world and invited me to come play in their sandbox.
CFE

Table of Contents

Prologue

The unmarked police cruiser quickly ate up the highway. Morgan smiled each time the driver of whatever sedan or SUV was in front of them finally looked in their rearview mirror, recognized the telltale signs of "undercover cop car" (the extra side mirrors and dashboard gadgets), suddenly slowed, and frantically signaled their intent to move to the right lane.

At the moment, though, they were stuck behind a left lane loiterer who hadn't yet noticed them. The run-down, rusted sedan was barely driving faster than the semi they were trying to pass.

Morgan was thankful his dad, Charlie, had taken the undercover car option and not the blue and white TRIUMPH COUNTY SHERIFF-emblazoned sedan he knew sat in their driveway. A small gesture on his dad's part, opting for the white cruiser as if it were a combination of a white stallion and an olive branch.

The rusted sedan ahead of them chugged slowly forward. They inched past the neighboring semi, a frustrating, unhurried march.

"It's times like this I wish I could flash the lights, just to speed things up," Charlie said, tilting his head so his neck cracked. He sighed loudly.

Morgan thought back to what he had learned, re-learned, and digested during the rehab program he'd attended. "We can't rush things," his counselor, Salvador, had told him, looking at him from behind his large, clear aviator-framed glasses. "I know you want to go home now, but have you built the foundation you need to live in sobriety?" That conversation had prompted Morgan to commit to another thirty days at the center, funded by a scholarship from Charlie's friends in the Fraternal Order of Police.

"You can't rush things, Dad," Morgan said. He intentionally took a deep breath in, then readjusted the small bun he had managed to grow. He'd come up with the idea of growing his hair out, but just the top half. He'd convinced the local barber on one of his few excursions into town—a distant bit of civilization an hour's drive from the rehab center—to give him a shaved undercut. Morgan had meticulously practiced styling his hair up into a bun, trying to perfect doing it effortlessly.

Knowing a bunch of underpaid police and public servants had donated their own money to keep him in rehab longer, to give him a better shot at life, made his shoulders sag. There was so much pressure. They wanted him to be well, stay sober, and make something of himself. He had vowed to give it his best. "You're not in this alone," he remembered Salvador saying. "Look for your support network, your ride-or-die folks." Morgan chose, in that moment, to tuck away the distressing statistic that folks often relapse three or four times before sobriety is their way of life.

The distressed sedan ahead of them finally pulled ahead of the truck and scooted over to the right lane. Charlie immediately stepped on the accelerator.

"'Bout damn time," Charlie muttered. "Say, I forgot to tell you, and we're getting close enough to home: I brought your phone with me." He moved his arm, lifting the armrest to get at the compartment. He searched around, his eyes on the road ahead of them, before securing the rectangular device. Then he handed it to Morgan. "I charged it up for you, but I never turned it on. We should be close enough to town now that you get a decent signal."

Morgan had nearly forgotten about phones. The last three months had been a no-phone zone, and he had access to social media only through a very public computer they all shared in the main area. He held his phone, once so familiar, the crack on the screen a friendly smile, and powered it on.

He expected it to be overwhelmed with notifications from Instagram, texts, and voicemails from friends, former teachers, and coaches.

Instead, he had four text notifications: one from his dentist's office reminding him of a scheduled appointment, one again from the same office asking him to reschedule his missed appointment. One was from Johnny Tae and had a picture with it. He enlarged the photo to see Johnny Tae, Laela, Sarah, and his old boss at the coffee shop, Gavin. They all smiled as Johnny Tae held up a handmade sign that read: *Get well, Morgan!*

He zoomed in on the picture to see the sign was decorated with coffee mugs, random flowers, and football helmets in Triumph High School's colors, blue and white. One corner had all their signatures: Gavin's loose cursive, Sarah's flowy cursive-print mix, Laela's perfect block writing. He saw Johnny Tae had signed as "City Boy," the nickname Morgan had given the out-of-towner when he first arrived. Morgan smiled and zoomed out, noticing a random hand in the foreground gesturing the "hang loose" sign.

Confused, Morgan read the text:
HEY MAN, JUST WANTED TO SAY WE'RE THINKING OF YOU. HAD MY AUNTIE TAKE THE PIC. THAT'S HER HAND. IDK WHY SHE DIDN'T DO A SELFIE. WHATEVER. WE'RE ROOTING FOR YOU!!!!

The fourth and final text was also from Johnny Tae. It was sent just yesterday.
HEARD YOU'RE COMING BACK SOON! CALL GAVIN FOR OPENINGS ON THE SCHEDULE. WORK WITH ME ON TUESDAY! MISSED YA

He locked his phone, thinking maybe when he unlocked it, more notifications would appear. Nothing.

Salvador's deep baritone voice washed over him again. "You're not in this alone. Find your ride-or-die folks."

Well, Morgan remembered at least two questionable driving situations he had been in with this group last summer, once just with Johnny Tae, the other with him, Sarah, and Laela. His drinking had been the common thread for both incidents, and the stupid choices he'd made as a result.

Morgan winced, knowing as he worked through his program at home, he'd need to both admit the exact nature of his wrongs (Step 5 of the famous 12-Step Program) and make direct amends to the people harmed (Step 9). Laela's face haunted his mind, making his stomach drop. He thought of how his truck … no, how *he* as the driver, not some inanimate truck (he was trying to start taking responsibility for it) had hit her last summer. Even if the incident had been (thankfully!) not serious, he'd never told her. Nor, to his knowledge, had his sole passenger, Johnny Tae.

Suddenly, Charlie's large hand clapped Morgan on the thigh. "I'm glad you're back, son," he said. "It was awfully quiet without you around."

Silence fell, Morgan unsure of how to respond. He imagined how his dad had spent the last few months in an empty house, maybe wandering from room to room or turning on extra lights to feel like someone was there. He smiled sadly, remembering how his mom had plugged an automatic night light in his room a few days after a career-ending football injury derailed his dreams (and Charlie's aspirations) of college ball. She'd told him it was so that Morgan would never feel alone. But then she died that spring, nearly two years ago now, after a fast, brutal battle with cancer. His mom had been his number one cheerleader during his football god era. Before he'd left for rehab, that night light was still in his room, illuminating it in familiar shadows. Like so much of his life, familiar shadows.

Charlie interrupted his reverie, cupping Morgan's shoulder in a squeeze that counted as a hug. "You ready for this?"

Morgan looked up, seeing the county limit sign for Triumph. "One day at a time, right?"

Charlie squeezed Morgan's shoulder again. "That's right, one day at a time." He pulled his hand back to the steering wheel, adding quietly. "I'm so damn proud of you, and I know your mom …" his voice broke, and he coughed. "Well, she'd be proud, too."

"Thanks, Dad," Morgan said. He felt tears well up in his eyes. He didn't ignore them. "So, I was thinking," he started, wiping his eyes, "now that I'm back, can I go back to work? I mean, if Gavin wants me still. I'd like to have something to do."

Charlie chuckled. "If you're up to it, of course!" After a beat, Charlie cleared his throat before asking, "I mean, are you going to be all right? They do serve alcohol there, and I don't want you to …" he trailed off, uncertainly.

Morgan was proud of his dad. Three months ago, the man wouldn't have thought twice, or at least he never would have checked in about it. "Thanks, Dad. That's a good question." He paused before continuing. "I think I'll be okay. I never drank at work to begin with. Buzz Buzz Buzz serves mostly wine, and I don't like that sour fruit taste." He hesitated. "But could you ask me again in a few weeks? Just to make sure?"

Charlie nodded, seriously. "Absolutely. I'm sure Gavin would be happy to have you. It's just been him and that newcomer, Johnny Tae, most of the time anyways. Though the town has quieted down again after the craziness of summer."

The air hung heavy, Charlie realizing what he'd said. "I mean, with the tourists and visitors and whatnot."

It was Morgan's turn to laugh. "No, this summer was crazy. I don't hope to repeat it."

His dad nodded stiffly. "Good." Charlie turned on the signal for the next exit. Morgan realized they were already at the main road to the town center.

Here we go, he thought to himself, surreptitiously looking in one of the side mirrors to check that his hair was the way he wanted it. The once beloved and celebrated football star had returned, wounded in ways his season-ending injury over a year ago couldn't compare. But there was no place left to go except home, with all its familiar shadows. Morgan thought, or maybe even prayed, *Guess I gotta love Triumph.*

Part 1

Hope

Chapter 1

The Best Laid Plans

"We need more singing," Birdie declared around a mouthful of cheddar-rosemary scone. She sat surrounded by folders and papers and highlighters in the corner sofa at Buzz Buzz Buzz, Ara Grace diligently typing on her laptop in a cozy armchair across the table, Nel taking precise notes with her ballpoint pen at her left. The three ministers were planning the first annual Triumph County Christmas Pageant, to be held at the 47th annual Triumph County Carol Sing, traditionally held the second Saturday before Christmas.

"More singing, really?" Nel asked. "The kids will have trouble learning all these songs! I know Victoria could never hold all these lyrics in her head." Victoria was Nel's nearly four-year-old daughter, the loud younger sister to a quiet seven-year-old named Hudson.

"We'll rehearse!" Birdie exclaimed, exasperated. *Am I that out of touch with age-appropriate ability levels now that my own boys are on the cusp of middle school?* "What's a pageant without the songs that make the season?"

"Let's compromise," Ara Grace chimed in. As the newest member of this circle of women pastors and only a first-year pastor at that, she tried to sit back quietly as much as she could, taking in their wisdom. The three were not just colleagues, they'd become friends. Ara Grace felt more confident now, at least here with them. "I think we could have the kids sing one song on their own, and then invite everyone at the town square to sing along with them for the rest?"

"Perfect," Birdie said, contentedly, putting down her stack of papers with finality. "That settles it."

As a rule, Ara Grace didn't *do* children's ministry. She preferred her theology serious. Kids were unpredictable, and telling the Christmas story during Advent, the season of anticipating Jesus' birth, always felt a little like sacrilege; she was a purist that way. Christmas pageants in mid-December were like celebrating your birthday on the first of the month no matter when it fell. Too over-eager and, worst of all, inaccurate. It was still Advent in mid-December! Baby Jesus doesn't come into the picture until December 24th! But she wanted to keep building her friendship with Birdie and Nel, and her congregation seemed excited about a joint children's pageant. *Anything to get young families involved!* Maybe she'd win some points with her church this year and get to experiment more with liturgical accuracy later.

Looking at her peers and now friends, remembering all that they'd gone through together over the last summer, she knew their bond was solid. This ministry thing was all about relational capital, she was finding out. She could tolerate some kid chaos in exchange for that.

Tolerate being the operative word.

* * *

Birdie was working herself into a frenzy about which verses of the hymns to sing, and from whose hymnal, and whether they should distribute sheets to the gathered crowd with just words or with music, too. She was midway through a recounting of the last time she'd heard a child sing the solo verse in *Once in Royal David's City* when she realized she was talking to herself. Nel, usually the one to keep them on track, had her head tipped back against the edge of the couch. Her eyes were closed, as if she was deep in thought, but Birdie looked closer. *Was that drool at the edge of her mouth?* Meanwhile, Ara Grace seemed lost in her own world, brought back only by a notification on her phone.

"Okay, dear ones!" Birdie said cheerfully, but pointedly.

Nel jolted up suddenly. "Oh no, was I …?"

"It's okay," Birdie reassured her. "We can call it a night if we need to. We all get so tired around Advent. We can pick this up another day."

"No, no," Nel insisted. "Let's do what we can. Jacques has the kids right now, and last I heard they're having fun doing the Thanksgiving grocery shopping. I don't want to have to arrange another evening away from home."

"If you're sure?" Birdie said, uncertainly. She noticed Ara Grace put her phone face-up on the table before them, a move reminiscent of her own stepdaughter, Sarah.

* * *

Nel flushed slightly under her tidy cardigan set, hoping the red in the floral pattern would camouflage her embarrassment. Falling asleep in a meeting was *not* her style. Nel was always exhausted this time of year. It had started even before she and Jacques had kids, when she was a brand-new pastor. Her district superintendent had assigned her to a lead minister role at a church in a far-flung Atlanta suburb thanks to her clergy father's meddling, no doubt.

The title was a bit of an exaggeration. Nel did supervise an office administrator, a part-time music director, and a part-time children and youth coordinator, but she was the only pastor on staff. Still, it felt like big shoes to fill, and at age twenty-five, she knew she'd had a lot to prove.

She began her pastorate in August and immediately began planning. She became meticulous—obsessed, really—with making Advent absolutely perfect. From the sanctuary decorations to the after-worship workshops to sermons she was sure would bring the *real* meaning of Christmas to her congregation, Nel went all out. Her first congregation came to expect all of this from her every season, and they expected her to be the one to do it all. The office administrator's full meltdown over an annual cookie exchange that had somehow evolved over her pastoral tenure into a four-hour affair was the last straw for Nel. Honestly, it was one of the reasons she'd requested a new placement.

She had learned her lesson, and since moving to Triumph County, Wyoming, she'd backed off on the Advent intensity. But besides her own perfectionism driving her Advent plans, she had her own kids now. Kids who expected Santa and hot cocoa and cookies and traditions. Kids who needed a magical Christmas. As soon as she turned the calendar to November, packing away the Halloween decorations and hauling out the cornucopias and muted fall-colored table linens, the feeling of dread set in. She slept like a hibernating bear. Or she would have, had Jacques not insisted on taking her to see all the holiday light displays and dazzling art installations. She knew how sweet it was that Jacques wanted to celebrate the holidays in style, creating family memories, but despite her gnawing sense of guilt about not appreciating Jacques enough, it always felt like too much.

Was this her usual pre-Advent hibernation impulse? Or was this something more? Nel made a quick note to set an appointment with her doctor to get her iron levels checked. Looking up, she glanced at her friends. She picked up where Birdie had left off. "I'm sure. I know we're all tired, but can we finish up tonight?"

Ara Grace nodded in agreement. "I like being here when Johnny Tae is working," she said, glancing over Birdie's shoulder to her nephew behind the counter. He was small compared to the giant young man next to him, Morgan—the prodigal son returned. "It's like I get a little peek into his world, and who knows how much longer that will last? Let's keep brainstorming."

The women pored through scripts, choosing one themed after the alphabet.

Lots of small speaking roles, plenty of opportunities for singing, and a clear structure to work from. Perfect. They were just starting to discuss costumes when Ara Grace's phone lit up with another notification. Before she could snatch it off the table, Nel saw the app logo.

"Ara Grace, you're on Bumble?" she exclaimed.

"Why would you know that logo, Nel?" Ara Grace shot back accusingly.

"Just because I'm married doesn't mean I'm completely out of touch!"

Birdie waved her hand in front of them. "Hold on a minute, both of you. What in the world is Bumble?"

A mischievous grin took over Nel's face. "It's a dating app, Birdie. Our girl is on the market!"

Ara Grace rolled her eyes. "Oh please, I'm not a piece of meat. And it's not like I'm getting much interest anyway."

Nel crossed her arms defiantly. "Looks like you just got a match there! Can we take a look? Please?"

Ara Grace relented, angling her phone so Nel could see, too. She had a profile pulled up. Camille, a thirty-one-year-old textile artist living an hour away in Cheyenne. Long, wavy brown hair filled her profile picture. Sweet-looking green eyes. Freckles. Ara Grace was cautiously charmed by the photo.

She was more optimistic about her romantic prospects than she'd been in a while. She'd recently taken "pastor" out of her profile, since the only messages that seemed to prompt were ones from Evangelical men calling her a heathen. *That's Wyoming for you*, she thought. She'd also decided, tentatively, to move her geographic region away from Triumph County and toward the bigger area of Cheyenne.

Ara Grace had been open with her congregation about her sexuality, following the advice of her friend Kai, a seminary friend who'd graduated two years ahead of her. When she'd found out rural Wyoming was what the synod had in mind for her, she'd called Kai in a panic—Kai, her nonbinary friend, dropped in the middle of rural Iowa. "What do I do?" Ara Grace asked her queer clergy role model.

"I know it feels harder now," Kai had warned her, "but it's better to be up-front. You don't want to feel like you have to hide any parts of yourself."

Ara Grace debated telling the search committee she was bisexual, but that wasn't quite true. The attraction she felt didn't belong in any binary, and educating the search committee about gender beyond the binary was something she felt called to do. She'd had to explain the term "pansexual" to more than a few of them, but they had been accepting. This had initially surprised her, breaking down a stereotype she'd held about rural folks. She imagined the search committee had prepared the church members with some conversation. It seemed like they appreciated finally having a settled pastor, and her sexuality was treated not as an open secret or a token of cool liberality but just as another part of who she was: a young pansexual woman of South Korean descent. *Plus, auntie-slash-pseudo-mom to a teenager*, she thought as she caught sight of Jonny Tae loudly cleaning an espresso machine. She was still figuring out who she was, day by day, and she felt the imposter syndrome seeping in again.

How did anyone navigate dating in a small town? Ara Grace was not particularly eager to share with her congregation about that. Her personal life was her business alone, thank you very much. Though once she'd moved her region on the app, she could play around with her profile a little more, knowing the risk of her congregants finding her would be slim. She'd also been able to let go of the fear that she'd match with someone one degree of separation too close to her congregation members.

She glanced up at Nel's face, taking in the picture of her latest match. Nel snatched the phone and was scrolling through Camille's profile. "She's adorable!" Nel exclaimed. Ara Grace hushed her urgently. No one needed to know she was dating, much less matching with adorable textile artists. "Okay, okay," Nel relented. "Textile artist, look at these tapestries in the background of that photo! First Methodist does need some new liturgical art."

Ara Grace sighed impatiently and knowingly. Nel did find a way to keep things focused on her congregation.

"Oh no, Ara Grace, I'm sorry." Nel had gotten to the last sentence of Camille's biography. It read, *Don't come at me with religion, I've been burned before.* She passed the phone to Ara Grace, pointing at the statement.

Damn, thought Ara Grace. *How does anyone date as a pastor?* It occurred to her that, as amazing as they were, these two friends weren't the women to ask.

"It's okay." Ara Grace shook her head as if to clear away the whole situation. "Other fish … you know the saying." She looked back down at her phone and saw a new notification pop up. "Oh, Birdie, it's from your dad."

Birdie leaned closer to read the text over Ara Grace's shoulder.
GUY: ARA GRACE—FOUND A GREAT CAR FOR
JT. CALL WHEN YOU HAVE A MIN

"Birdie," Ara Grace began hesitantly, "how is your dad doing? We bought Johnny Tae a car from him a few weeks ago."

Birdie sighed, biting her lip. She readjusted her curly silver hair, leaning away from Ara Grace. "I'm so sorry," she said. "Dad's not been himself lately. He's been dealing with some memory loss. We're really trying to figure out what's going on."

The "we" was a generous overstatement. Birdie's brother, Paul, spent most days with their father at the auto shop, and he kept insisting that nothing was wrong. Birdie didn't know if Paul believed that, or if he was living in some kind of deep-seated denial of his own making. These lapses— "senior moments," Guy called them—were becoming more frequent. They were starting to scare Birdie. Paul didn't seem to want to have the conversation she knew they needed to have. They needed to do something about their dad.

"Let us know what you need, Birdie," Ara Grace said. "We're here for you."

Birdie squeezed Ara Grace's knee fondly. "I appreciate that, I really do. I think this is one place where I'm going to need to have the hard conversations myself."

Nel and Ara Grace nodded knowingly, each thinking of their own hard conversations they needed to have. Nel's mind went to her husband, Jacques, while Ara Grace thought about Johnny Tae's high school graduation, looming less than six months away. *All in due time.*

Nel coughed and checked her own phone. She tsked and brought the group back together. "Friends," she said, "I do need to get home soon. Jacques just texted me and Victoria's melting down, so he needs another set of hands. Can we set a rehearsal schedule?"

"Sure," Ara Grace said, pulling up her Google Calendar. "Thursdays at five?"

"Sorry, I can't," Nel said. "Jacques and I have couples' counseling then."

"*So* glad you're doing that," Birdie chimed in.

"It's going well," Nel agreed. "How about Wednesdays? Traditional church night!"

Ara Grace felt her body tense at the mention of Wednesdays. "I have our midweek Advent services at seven, but I can do it as long as I can make it to Good Shepherd in time."

"Are you sure you're not spreading yourself too thin, Ara Grace?" Birdie asked gently.

"I'm fine. Totally fine. It's just that they expect this service and I need to make sure it happens."

"Just because they expect it doesn't mean it *needs* to happen," Nel cautioned, remembering her own first call. "You are finite."

"I know!" Ara Grace snapped. Then, softening, she said, "I'm sorry, Nel. That was harsh. I'm just hoping I can make this Advent season something special for Good Shepherd. They've been between pastors for so long. They deserve a pastor who takes them seriously."

Seriously, thought Ara Grace. *I'm nothing if not serious, that's for sure.* She took a deep breath and spent a moment berating herself for being less than kind to Nel, then caught herself. She didn't need to be so self-serious about her friendships too.

"Five on Wednesdays it is!" Birdie proclaimed. "We'll start next week on the twenty-ninth. What if we have it at Good Shepherd then? You guys have a big basement, and then you wouldn't need to worry about getting to the service in bad weather, Ara Grace."

Ara Grace thought for a moment, listing the probable people she'd need to get approval from before nodding. "That'll work, I think."

"Great! I'll get the publicity drawn up," Nel volunteered. She was the best of the bunch at amateur graphic design. Nel stood up to leave and was caught by a wave of vertigo. *That's odd*, she thought. Probably just a little dehydration from the extra cup of coffee. She hurried toward the door, but stopped and called to Ara Grace, "See you Thursday! No need to bring anything!"

Ara Grace smiled and waved. "You're getting a pie whether you like it or not!" she gamely replied.

Thanksgiving was not a holiday in Ara Grace's wheelhouse. She remembered it as a long weekend, a day off work for her parents, nothing more. Appa always got misty and would give small, quiet speeches to the family about how thankful he was for this country. Umma said simply, "We can be thankful, but this is not our holiday."

In seminary, Ara Grace been radicalized by her classmates of color. Thanksgiving was a colonizer's holiday, they'd told her. Why would we be celebrating invasion, pillaging, and stolen land? That was all it took. She had firmly rejected Thanksgiving. She'd never roasted a turkey or created a gratitude paperchain. She had never mixed mashed potatoes, gravy, green bean casserole, and cranberry sauce on her plate to create the distinct flavor that can only be called Thanksgiving dinner.

But when Nel found out Ara Grace didn't have plans for Thanksgiving, she had insisted that she and Johnny Tae come to her house for the holiday. At first, Ara Grace was tempted to decline. She wasn't sure how polite she could be in the face of this holiday she fundamentally disagreed with. It was Johnny Tae who'd convinced her. "You need friends, Auntie," he reminded her. "You make friends by spending time with people." Invitation accepted. She vowed to teach Johnny Tae how to make yuzu pie, a funny syncretism of her Umma's creation. The butter crust balanced the tart custard perfectly.

Ara Grace helped Birdie gather up the scripts and tuck them into her knitted shoulder bag. Then she walked over to the counter where Johnny Tae was pulling an espresso shot, smooth and confident, deep in conversation with Morgan. "See you at home," she mouthed with a wave, registering Morgan's new hair style. *It suits him*, she thought.

Chapter 2

From the Other Side of the Counter

A
t the start of their shift at Buzz Buzz Buzz, Johnny Tae
looked up at Morgan with an unexpected fondness. "Good
to have you back, man," he heard himself say.

"Hey city boy, are you going soft on me?" Morgan asked playfully.
The truth was, he was glad to be back, too.

Morgan thought back to his first morning at Evergreen Recovery
Center. In that medical-issue cot under a scratchy blanket and two
layers of crisp sheets, he had cracked his eyes open and immediately
closed them again. He felt like he'd been thrown in the dryer and
tossed around—sore, disoriented, shaken up. He was beginning to
admit to himself that he wished he hadn't survived the car accident.
Morgan felt like he was trapped under the weighted blanket he
sometimes used to sleep at home, only this one was made of shame
and regret and anger. It wouldn't let him sit up.

A sharp knock had startled him that first morning, and in walked
a short, stocky man in a button-down shirt whose rolled-up sleeves
revealed sharp, colorful designs that Morgan's bleary eyes couldn't
quite make out. "Wake up," the man said, his eyes large behind his
clear aviator glasses. His voice was gentle but firm. "You're going
to start the hard work you've needed to do since your mom died."
Morgan had groaned, then stretched and flopped his legs over the
side of the bed. He sat up gingerly. He wasn't ready to do the work,
but he knew it was time.

Morgan's attention snapped back to the coffee and wine bar just
as Ara Grace burst through the door with Nel and Birdie.

"Oh yeah, they're coming in to plan their joint Christmas pageant thing," Johnny Tae said. "Hi, Auntie, the usual?" He started getting three cups of chamomile tea ready, but Nel stepped up to the register before he filled the cups. "Medium Americano for me today, Johnny Tae. Could you add an extra espresso shot?"

He imagined even middle-aged pastors had the kinds of days that required double caffeine to endure, knowing a bit about that life from the last few months living with his aunt. "Sure thing," he replied.

Morgan pulled espresso shots expertly while Johnny Tae continued the predictable tea orders for Ara Grace and Birdie. They tipped extra, and Morgan and Johnny Tae high-fived. The baristas split their tips evenly after each shift, counting out the cash and springing the drawer open to make change when they needed to. Even though Gavin paid them fairly, the tips were a nice bonus.

"How have things been around here?" Morgan asked. "What have I missed?"

Nothing much. It's been dull without you, Johnny Tae thought, but decided to say, "Me and Laela … it's not gonna happen. I asked her to Homecoming. Rejected."

Morgan half-smiled at Johnny Tae. "Are you sure that's it? Maybe she just didn't want to go to homecoming. High school dances aren't everyone's thing." He thought back to his own forced attendance at senior prom, a night in a too-tight rented tux, one of the cheerleaders he'd hooked up with a few times as his date. He wished he had just gone to the afterparty and avoided the awkward meal and dancing together.

Johnny Tae sighed. "I don't want to be one of those dicks who keeps pushing when a girl's clearly telling me no." He grabbed a rag and started cleaning the latte foamer.

"Right, yeah," Morgan said, "I just think you could try a different setting. Something lower key? I mean, the last big party she went to … you know."

Morgan didn't need to finish the thought. The incident that sent Morgan to rehab had also sent Laela to the hospital. She had stayed for two days compared to his five. The whole thing had been terrifying. Morgan knew about medication interactions, but he'd never thought to ask one of his friends what they were taking before they took one of his pills. He'd learned that lesson that hard way, with Laela's anxiety medication causing a life-threatening reaction. Morgan grabbed the coffee mugs from the dishwasher, placing them back on the rack.

"I hear you, Morgan, but I think I'm done trying to make that happen," Johnny Tae replied. "Got more pressing things on my mind."

"Oh yeah?" Morgan said, curious.

"Graduation is coming up. My dad says he'll help pay for college, take out the loans for me if he needs to, but I know fuck all about what it takes to apply. It's not like I'm getting in anywhere that'll impress him." He leaned against the counter, his back to the entry door.

"I know something about that," Morgan muttered softly. He thought about the drive he and Charlie had taken back into town. He hoped he could stay sober, make his dad proud, but he knew the hope of impressing his dad was long behind him.

"And how the hell am I even supposed to pick one thing to major in? And then work in the same fucking field for the rest of my life?" Johnny Tae shook his head, annoyed. "Anyway, that's my life in a nutshell." There was an awkward pause. Johnny Tae cleared his throat before asking, "So, uh, how are things with you and your dad?" he asked.

"Fine, I think," Morgan replied. "He's stopped bugging me about football. Wants me to stay clean. He's really trying, you know?" Morgan grabbed a towel and started wiping down the counter.

"Yeah," Johnny Tae replied, moving away from Morgan to grab a nearly expired gallon of milk from the fridge. "Yeah, I'm happy for you guys."

Johnny Tae thought of his own father, scarcely more than a checkbook to him. *What I wouldn't give for a dad who tried.* He poured the milk into a steamer cup, distracting himself. "So, what's next? Do you have to keep going to treatment or counseling or what?" He looked up at Morgan quickly. "Sorry, can I ask that?"

"Of course," Morgan said, giving Johnny Tae a playful nudge. "You can ask me about any of it. It'll keep me honest. I'll have virtual appointments with my addiction counselor, Salvador, once a month. He's legit, you'd like him. Helps me a lot with my mindset."

"What about in between?" Johnny Tae asked.

"They encouraged me to go to some meetings, see if I can find a good sober community here. I just tried out the NA group at Birdie's church last night." Morgan hung the towel up on the hook below the register, lowering his voice a bit. "It was fine, but I think I'm more of an AA guy. They had an AA group in rehab, and I liked the higher power stuff. It was more like a community. NA is all about your own individual journey. I feel alone enough as it is. I need to feel like I'm on a path with some fellow travelers."

Morgan thought back to that meeting in the basement of the Christian Church of Triumph. Around a dozen folks, mostly men, sat in metal folding chairs. Morgan knew some of them from growing up, even recognized one of his dad's colleagues on the force. He knew better than to say any of that; anonymous was right in the group's name. The first part of the meeting went about how he expected. They recited the Serenity Prayer: "God, grant me the serenity to accept the things I cannot change, the courage to change the things I can, and the wisdom to know the difference." One of the guys shared his story—they called it a story, not a testimony, Morgan remembered. Less religious that way. They read the twelve steps together—different than the AA twelve steps, Morgan noticed. Subtle changes, but the two were definitely different. Then the facilitator broke them up into groups of three to share about how they were relating to one of the twelve steps; the groups could choose. Morgan found himself in a group with Stan, an older man he recognized as one of his Little League coaches from what felt like a lifetime ago, and Beth, one of the two women in the group. They chose Step 4: "We made a searching and fearless moral inventory of ourselves."

It was the same Step 4 as in his AA group, except the way they talked about it was different. Beth was humorously self-deprecating in her description of attempting to parent with heroin coursing through her bloodstream. He expected her to continue in the same tone, but she took a turn that felt dark to Morgan. "Remembering all that awfulness is the only thing keeping me from using," she said. "The only thing. I was a terrible mom. I did terrible things."

Morgan felt his stomach drop, his insides turn icy. In his AA meeting in rehab, Morgan certainly saw people's shame and heard some pretty harrowing stories, too. But there was a focus on grace, on forgiveness. "Shame runs through our veins like poison," Salvador always said. "It's no good. Let that shit go." He'd thought NA would be a better fit for him because he wasn't that religious. *Maybe I'm a Christian or something after all*, Morgan thought. *I think forgiveness is one of those Jesus things.*

Johnny Tae finished steaming milk for a practice latte, and as he tapped the metal pitcher on the counter and began to carefully pour the milk, he said, "You know, I may not be officially in recovery or anything, but I can still be your sober community." He finished the latte with a flourish: a perfect heart. "But you gotta let me know what there is to do around here besides party."

Morgan smiled. "I know you're a philosophy guy, Johnny Tae. You ever read any Thoreau?"

"Too sentimental for me," Johnny Tae replied. "But yeah, he was the outdoorsy guy, right?"

"'I went to the woods because I wished to live deliberately, to front only the essential facts of life,'" Morgan quoted. "Then there's something about not wanting to die realizing you hadn't lived. Anyway, at Evergreen, they took us on a lot of hikes. It helped. Got me to finally live in the moment. I could take you sometime."

Johnny Tae was about to say something unsavory about cold Wyoming winters when he heard Nel exclaim, "She's adorable!" He glanced over at the corner where the pastors sat, papers strewn everywhere, and held his face in his hands. He knew his Auntie was dating; she had sat him down for a truly painful conversation in which she told him she needed to have an adult life, but he was always going to be her priority. Still, the idea of Ara Grace scrolling a dating app was more than mildly horrifying to him.

"At least *someone's* getting girls around here," Johnny Tae mumbled.

"Oh yeah?"

"Auntie's on one of the old people dating apps. I don't think I was supposed to tell you that, she doesn't want people knowing. Definitely don't tell anyone from her church."

"Hey, that's exciting! My lips are sealed. Seriously, good for her."

"Good for someone. I hope she doesn't bring anyone back to our place. Like, where would they even go?" His mom, Hana, had dropped off Johnny Tae without so much as a call to Ara Grace, so she only had a two-bedroom, one-bathroom apartment, not a place with much privacy. She was locked into a year on her lease, but she promised they'd look for a bigger place if he planned on staying through next year. *Next year,* Johnny Tae thought. *I can hardly imagine next week, but now I need to plan for next year.* The thought terrified him, even as a little shiver of excitement ran up his spine.

It wasn't long before the pastors finished up their planning meeting and headed for the door. Johnny Tae waved goodbye to Ara Grace. Even though he could've walked home after his shift, he loved any excuse to get the car out. *Freedom, thy name is four-wheel drive.*

The robotic frog sentry near the front door croaked amiably and Sarah walked in, followed by Laela, both bundled up in long, warm parkas and sporting knit hats with pom-poms. "Nice hats," Johnny Tae quipped, and he wasn't sure if he was being serious or sarcastic, but before he could dig himself deeper into that hole, Sarah replied, "Thanks! This early in the season, it's nice to get to wear the cute stuff. It's all long underwear and face masks starting in mid-December." At the mention of underwear, Laela blushed and looked at the floor. Johnny Tae could see a tiny smile creeping across her lips.

Sarah continued. "Anyway, we'd like two hot chocolates, please! We're on our way to the grocery store to pick up Thanksgiving groceries for Heather—Birdie—for you know, our family dinner."

"Yeah, you just missed her," Johnny Tae said. "They were here planning that Christmas program thing."

"Two hot chocolates, coming right up!" said Morgan, and he winked at Johnny Tae, which he found terribly embarrassing and kind of sweet.

"Hey, Morgan," Laela called out as Sarah pulled dollar bills from her wallet and handed them, one at a time, to Johnny Tae. "I'm helping out with 'that Christmas program thing,'" she said, quoting Johnny Tae. "It's for kids—anyone, not just church people. Pastor Nel brought me in. They're not sure how many kids will want to do it, but they want to make sure they have enough responsible adults to help with rehearsals. I heard you're looking for ways to stay busy. Want to do it with me?"

"If I count as a responsible adult," Morgan said, smiling, "but yeah, I'm in."

"Awesome," Laela replied, looking at Sarah and Johnny Tae out of the corner of her eye. "These two heard the word 'kids' and refused to let me even finish. I'll text you about rehearsals."

Johnny Tae took the hot chocolates from Morgan and passed them across the counter to Laela and Sarah. "Enjoy capitalist hell tonight, ladies."

"Oh, it's not that bad," Sarah said. "You forget how small this town is. And it's only Tuesday. The crowds really come out on Wednesday."

"Happy Thanksgiving!" Laela added, a little shyly. They turned and left, and Johnny Tae saw them lean toward each other and giggle once the door shut behind them. Girls usually didn't feel this mysterious to him, but Laela was throwing him for a loop.

"Penny for your thoughts?" Morgan leaned his elbows on the counter next to Johnny Tae, and he got a good glimpse of Morgan's hair for the first time, an undercut with a neater bun than he would have expected from Morgan.

"Right now, I'm thinking I have no idea how you managed to grow so much hair while you were gone," he said, honestly yet evasively.

Morgan laughed. "Fresh air and healthy food work wonders. And ditching the booze and drugs, that helps too."

"I used to think man buns were kind of douchey, but yours actually looks cool."

"Aw, city boy, you shouldn't have!"

"Just being honest." He looked up at the clock. "It's nine. Time for me to clock out and get the heck out of here." Johnny Tae was still under eighteen, so his hours were limited by Wyoming child labor laws. Gavin went one step further and wouldn't let any of his high schoolers work past nine on school nights. One more day of school, then a four-day weekend. He almost felt like he could exhale.

"Have a good Thanksgiving, man," Morgan said as Johnny Tae packed his bag and buttoned up his too-thin pea coat.

"You too," Johnny Tae said, holding back a barb about the holiday's colonialist roots. "See you Friday at the tree thing."

Johnny Tae was joining his auntie and, apparently, the rest of Triumph at the all-county Christmas tree lighting on Friday night. Morgan had told him he'd be there. But first, they had to get through Thanksgiving.

Chapter 3

Thanksgiving

"Honey," Nel's voice called out in what she hoped was syrupy sweetness and not exasperated gruffness, "isn't it about time to get the next coat of brine on the turkey?" Jacques had insisted on using some homemade brine he'd read about online. He'd been simmering the concoction since seven that morning, a mixture of apple cider vinegar, dark brown sugar, and rosemary leaves he'd made yesterday for the turkey's initial coat. She lifted the lid to see the dark brown liquid simmering gently. The aroma made her stomach turn, as did the thought of eating turkey meat. *Why does he always have to try new things during the holidays?*

Jacques didn't reply. Victoria was playing nearby and came closer as Nel knelt to place the tray of pumpkin chocolate chip muffins in the oven. Perfection nearly every time, a tried and tested recipe. "Hot!" Victoria said, pointing to the oven.

"Yes, sweetie," Nel smiled. "The oven is hot. We can look with our eyes, but we can't touch with our hands right now." Victoria nodded seriously in agreement.

She stood to see her son, Hudson, building some kind of structure out of his Legos on the coffee table. "Looks good, Hudson!" she said. "Remember that we're going to video chat with Grandma and Grampa Stone soon. Can you move your building to the floor?"

"Ah, Mom," Hudson said. He was still in his pajamas, his hair unbrushed. "Can't we just put the video next to my tower?"

"That sounds like a great compromise," Jacques decreed, sweeping jovially into the kitchen. "Don't you agree, *mi amor*?" He barely glanced at Nel as he moved straight for the brine, turning off the stovetop. He opened the refrigerator and pulled the large roasting pan with the turkey out. He found a ladle in the drawer and started scooping the new brine over the turkey.

Nel bit back a suggestion that a baster would be far more effective. "Sure," she said, compromising. "How long does the turkey have left? Ara Grace and Johnny Tae are coming here after her service, so around twelve thirty or one."

Jacques moved mechanically, ladling the brine. Nel's stomach churned in annoyance. Victoria watching, entranced at her father's rhythmic movements.

Jacques grimaced, some brine splashing onto the table. "It's about fifteen minutes per pound, this is a twelve-pound bird, so about three hours? Is that right?"

"Sounds right," Nel said agreeably. She glanced at the clock. It was nearly ten thirty. She still had to shower, get the kids ready, and finish the mashed potatoes before Ara Grace and Johnny Tae arrived. But at least the main course would be done.

Her phone buzzed on the counter. She picked it up, reading a text from her sister, Vera, on their family thread: READY FOR FAMILY VIDEO CHAT?

Shit, already? She saw her mom's eager response: CAN'T WAIT TO SEE MY GRANDBABIES!

Before calling out to her own kids, "Hudson, Victoria, let's all sit on the couch to talk to Grandma and Grandpa Stone."

She heard Victoria's thudding footsteps behind her as she walked to the fireplace mantle and opened the tablet. "Put it right here, Mommy," Hudson instructed her, pointing to the left of his structure. Nel smiled at her son, tapped the chat icon, and propped it up, facing the couch. She sat down, primly crossing her ankles. She assessed her appearance in the video in those brief seconds before the chat room opened: clearly greasy hair, its bouncy curls flattened after a night of sleep; deep bags under her eyes; some sort of stain on her athletic shirt. She saw Victoria clambering up on the couch behind her on the video screen. Her daughter's nightgown was clearly on backward, its high collar awkwardly hugging the neck. How had Nel not noticed? Victoria must've mixed it up when she went to the bathroom in the morning.

Nel thought back to try to remember how long it had been since Victoria had gone to the bathroom, mentally keeping track of her daughter's potty schedule. They'd been struggling with potty-training, and now that Victoria was over three years old, Nel felt shame. As illogical as she knew it was, she figured their lack of success came down to her own parenting: If Nel just paid better attention, gave more of herself to her daughter's needs, then Victoria would be using the potty. Never mind that Jacques, as their household's primary caretaker, did the same.

"There's the Wyoming bunch!" Vera's cheery voice cooed as the screen changed to the chat room. "And don't you all look cozy!"

Nel gathered her hair to one side before replying. "Ah, well, we are hours behind you out here." She noticed her sister's two kids sitting serenely on either side of her, while her husband, Vance, stood calmly over her shoulder. All four of them looked at the screen, fully engaged.

Hudson quickly shot in front of the tablet. "Grandma and Grandpa, check out the tower I built!" He grabbed the tablet and turned it quickly.

"Whoa there, buddy," Nel's dad, Michael, called out, "You're going to make us motion sick." She noticed her dad was in his clerical collar, having clearly just gotten home from a service.

"Dad, I thought you were retired?" Nel said, as Hudson continued to point to various parts of his tower.

"Oh, you know your father, Nelly," her mom, Marilyn, said. "Michael can't stay away from church for long."

"It's a short-term interim position, only about an hour away," Michael said dismissively.

"We're barely more than an hour away at Vance's parents' place," said Vera, pouting. "But it still feels so far from home!"

Nel tightened her smile. Vera, the "good daughter," living only fifteen minutes from her parents. They all ate dinner together at least once a week. *How charming*, she thought bitterly.

"Yes, well, you know, more churches than there are clergy now, so I have to help where I can," Michael said.

"Speaking of that, Nel, there's a lovely church with a part-time opening here in Atlanta. It'd be so great to have you and the kids closer," Marilyn said.

Hudson spoke before Nel could reply. "Why? I like it out here. We get snow!" He took the tablet to go point the camera out the window.

Nel smiled ruefully as she heard her family's cries. "Hudson," she called after a beat, "come bring the tablet back, please."

He brought it back, setting it roughly on the coffee table. He returned his attention to the building. "Wanna help me, Victoria?" he asked quietly. His sister slid off the couch to join him.

"Well, happy Thanksgiving everyone!" Nel said cheerily. "What do you all have planned?"

She listened as her sister talked about some kind of evening dinner, her parents about a quiet night in, watching a movie. No one asked about her plans. The entire time, Vera and Vance's girls sat demurely on either side of their mother, plaintively staring at the screen. *It's like this is their idea of entertainment,* Nel thought sadly.

"Where's Jacques?" one of her nieces asked. "I haven't seen him yet."

At his name, Jacques called from the kitchen, "I'm here!" he called. "Just getting the turkey in the oven." He came closer so he was in the camera frame. "Nel, I think your muffins are done," he said loudly as he looked her in the eye.

For this alone, Nel could have passionately kissed her husband. "Looks like I've got to go check on those," she said. "Great seeing you all. Happy Thanksgiving!" Directing her attention to Hudson and Victoria, she said, "Come say bye to the family."

"Bye," Hudson said automatically without looking at the screen. Victoria was sorting the single Lego pieces by color, a task she could be completely absorbed by, barely even blinking. Nel flashed the screen so it caught the two of them before saying again, "Gotta go!"

As soon as she pressed the red button, ending the video chat, she sank back into the couch, exhausted. Jacques leaned over to rub her arms, a gesture of comfort. His touch felt forced.

"Family video chat," Nel muttered so only Jacques could hear her, "has got to be one of the signs of the end times."

Jacques laughed. "Why do you let them get to you? They're two planes and an hour drive away."

"Too close," she said, closing her eyes.

Just then, the tower Hudson had been working on crashed to the table, sending pieces everywhere. She waited for the tears, the frustration.

Instead, Hudson shrugged. "I can make another one, right, Mommy?" He looked to her for reassurance.

The constant list of to-dos faded. It no longer mattered if Victoria had her nightgown on backward, if her house needed tidying, if she needed to shower. "Absolutely, honey. How about I help you?"

She sat on the floor next to the coffee table, helping Victoria sort colors and handing Hudson pieces as he asked for them. *This*, she thought, *is all I want*.

* * *

The six attendees trickled out of the sanctuary, stopping briefly to shake Ara Grace's hand before continuing with their Thanksgiving Day. *Six worshipers are better than none!* She tried to give herself a pep talk. But it was hard when one of the worshipers was her sulky nephew, Johnny Tae, who had no choice about attending. *Fine, five worshipers. Five.*

"Wherever two or three are gathered in my name, I am among them," she remembered Jesus' quote from Matthew's gospel. Great that God promises to be present, but Ara Grace had a hard time justifying the amount of energy it took to plan a special service— creating an entire liturgy from scratch, sermon preparation, hymn selections—for just five people. She loved it, but it *was* a lot of work.

Leon, her faithful administrator, wasn't even here. Sylvia, the church organist, had roped her daughter, in town for the holiday, into attending. "We're going out to a Thanksgiving brunch after this," she'd told Ara Grace before service by way of explanation. "Then I don't have to cook, and she doesn't have to clean! Our only job is to eat. After the service, of course." The postlude for the service had been uncharacteristically short, Sylvia's eagerness to get on with her day clear.

The service was something Good Shepherd had "always done," the stalwart traditionalists had told her. And yet none of them, not even Richard Lansington, her most opinionated and outspoken congregant, had attended the service.

She would bring this up to the Council at their meeting. Council was her church's governance board, a group of elected members who made decisions on behalf of the congregation.

As soon as Sylvia and her daughter left, Johnny Tae stood up, pocketing his phone. "Now it's Auntie's old lady, gal pal friend time, right? 'Bout time. I can't be your only social outlet here. You'll bring down my status." His voice dripped with sarcasm.

Ara Grace rolled her eyes. "Because of my 'advanced age' or the whole being a pastor thing?"

"Why not both?"

Ara Grace laughed. "Come on, let's get on to our first, real traditional Thanksgiving meal. Old timey. Americana."

"So, like this town?" he said.

She audibly *tsked* at him. "And yet, you chose to stay here with me. We must all live with our choices, young one." She winked and put her hand on his back. "Let me just put this all away," she gestured to her alb and stole. "I'll grab the pie from the fridge, and we can get going."

Though he had intended to stay just for the summer, Johnny Tae had decided to complete his senior year of high school here in Triumph, living with his aunt. Hana, his mom and Ara Grace's sister, was a serial self-discoverer who'd long ago discovered motherhood wasn't for her. She'd unceremoniously dumped him at Ara Grace's church nearly six months ago now. His father, John James, was a career military man who was stationed in Europe. Though truth be told, after his and Hana's divorce, Johnny Tae had only ever seen his father a handful of times. He preferred to think of his dad as the financial backer of the "Pass Johnny Tae" game. With both biological parents reluctant to actually parent the boy, Ara Grace and her parents, Umma and Appa, had stepped in.

But years later, Ara Grace had gone away to seminary, seemingly abandoning him. Umma, a first-generation immigrant from South Korea, and Appa, American-born of Korean heritage though well into his sixties, couldn't handle the responsibility of raising a teenager in today's world with its apps and ever-changing nature. So, Johnny Tae had been sent to various boarding schools, courtesy of daddy's money.

The problem was Johnny Tae had a penchant for seeing through people's bullshit, and an even bigger skill at creating problems of his own. So, he'd been kicked out of more than a handful of boarding schools in just his high school career. Hence part of his desire to stay in one place for an entire calendar year. The other strong part (that he'd admit only under duress) was his genuine love for his Auntie. And another involved a certain girl he'd befriended over the summer.

Ara Grace was back from the office minutes later, Johnny Tae staring at the church calendar posted on the bulletin board labeled "Announcements."

"Ready?" she asked him.

"Auntie, you're going to have Wednesday services this December? And the kid's program practice on Wednesdays?" She nodded at him. "I don't have to come to those services, do I?"

Ara Grace laughed. "Not unless you get in trouble," she told him. They opened the double doors, stepping out into the brisk cold. "I'm kidding! Even then, you wouldn't have to." She handed him the yuzu pie as she reached into her pockets and pulled out her mittens. "Thank you for being here today."

Johnny Tae held the pie until she was done. His prep for the cold weather was to merely pop up the collar on his black peacoat, which lost all its preppy allure on her punky nephew. "If I hadn't, it would've been really empty in there," he teased.

With their faces turned against the whipping wind, they walked the few blocks to Nel's house. She lived in the parsonage of First United Methodist Church, and her lovely white clapboard house matched the lovely white clapboard church building next to it.

Ara Grace walked up the stoop, pulling out her phone to check the time. "Shit, we're early," she mumbled.

Johnny Tae elbowed her. "Remember," he said, mimicking her voice, "Nel has young, impressionable kids. Watch your language."

"You're right," she said, ringing the doorbell, "watch your language. I picked up all my swearing from you."

Johnny Tae laughed at that. His auntie could swear like a sailor as she explained some theological concept with complete accuracy. "What?" she'd said when Umma had criticized her language use. "The Word became flesh, God became human. A little swearing isn't going to scare God away."

They heard a commotion on the other side of the door, and then Jacques was there. "Ara Grace and Johnny Tae!" he said warmly, gesturing them in.

"I'm sorry we're a little early," Ara Grace started, stepping into their house. She handed Jacques the pie before removing her shoes and setting them neatly next to the lineup of the family's shoes. She looked to Johnny Tae, a clear instruction for him to do the same.

"*No problemo*! Nel is just getting ready. The bird, as you Americans say, is already cooking. The kids should be around here in a minute," Jacques said.

Hudson called out of sight from the nearby living room, "We're already down here, Dad."

Jacques grimaced. "Right, I knew that." He lowered his voice, conspiratorially. "I've been very focused on the turkey, to tell you both the truth. That thing requires constant attention!"

Ara Grace wanted to point out that most young children, like Hudson and Victoria, needed constant attention too, but she chose to let it slide. "I'm sure the dinner will be lovely. It smells delicious."

"*Gracias,*" Jacques said before turning his attention away. "Johnny Tae, how have you been? Staying out of trouble?"

Johnny Tae chose that moment to focus on his jacket button. Last summer, Jacques had helped him, Morgan, Sarah, and Laela to get home safely after a Fourth of July party they'd been at had caused a brush fire. But then shortly after, Johnny Tae had also bumped into Nel, crying and rushing away from Jacques after a nasty married-person fight. Jacques's coldness that night to his wife and his overly genial demeanor with others gave Johnny Tae all the wrong vibes.

Ara Grace answered for him. "Yes, he's doing great! Senior year at the high school, barista at Buzz Buzz Buzz."

Johnny Tae smiled. "Yep, I'm an all-around American kid," he said.

Ara Grace subtly stepped on his foot. "Can I help you find room in the fridge for that pie? It's my Umma's recipe, a yuzu pie." She followed behind Jacques as they talked about their favorite family dishes.

Johnny Tae went to the living room, finding Hudson and Victoria working on some puzzle together. Hudson was coaching his sister:

"You've got to find the edge pieces first, then you put those together before the puzzle's guts get put in."

He plopped down on the couch, pulling his phone out in a smooth motion. He was just starting a text when he heard Nel's voice floating down the stairs.

"Ara Grace! Johnny Tae! So glad you made it! Kids, did you say hi to our guests?" Hudson looked up at Johnny Tae and waved.

He stood up to greet Nel properly, as his auntie would want him to do. She wore a jean skirt that was somehow elegant with a white button-down blouse accented with large gold jewelry. Her hair was pulled up in a tight ponytail. Johnny Tae noticed that she was put together but not in some over-the-top, contoured type way.

Ara Grace met Nel at the bottom of the stairs and wrapped her in a hug. "Thank you for having us," she said.

"Our pleasure," Nel replied. "Did Jacques offer you all something to drink?" She began to list the options.

Johnny Tae chose a can of soda; Ara Grace opted for a beer.

"Johnny Tae," Nel said, handing him his drink, "thanks for coming. Laela said she was heading over to Sarah's with her parents for Thanksgiving."

Laela often babysat for Nel and Jacques, something that started as a punishment and had evolved into his friend's genuine enjoyment. Laela liked working with kids, and though Victoria didn't have a formal diagnosis, Laela had discovered that autism interventions helped the girl. Johnny Tae remembered Laela worrying that perhaps Nel would be embarrassed with such a diagnosis, that it would indicate something was "off." His assessment of Nel so far led him to agree with Laela.

Nel continued, "So I'm sorry, but you'll be our sole teenager. Think you can handle it?"

"He's not a teenager," Jacques interrupted. "He's a young man! A high school senior! *El senor!*" Jacques took a loud sip of his own beer. "He's on the cusp of manhood. He'll help me with this bird."

Johnny Tae looked down, but not before seeing Nel smile tightly. "Of course, I simply meant he's alone in his age bracket at our gathering."

"I'm used to being the only one of my kind," he said, delighting in the awkwardness that hung in the air. *Let them do with that what they want*, he thought. "Could you point me to the bathroom, Nel?" he was looking for an escape from Jacques's intended male bonding. That man was not the type of guy Johnny Tae cared to be with.

Nel pointed him up the stairs. "First door on the right," she said. "You can leave your soda on the counter."

He did so, leaving the chatter behind as he ascended the stairs. He found the bathroom easily. Nel had left a lit apple pie scented candle burning in what he presumed was an effort in home styling.

Johnny Tae pulled out his phone, his real reason for coming upstairs. A few minutes alone. He found the irony in that he, a teen "on the cusp of manhood," was hiding in the bathroom like some parent needing a break from their kids.

He opened the texts, pulling up the recently revived Morgan, Laela, and Sarah thread and typed:

HAPPY COLONIZER DAY. WHO'S HAVING THE MOST FUN?

Definitely not me, he thought as he waited for a reply. None came. He felt that he was nearing the edge of appropriate bathroom use time, so he pocketed his phone, and washed his hands. *Have to keep up appearances.*

He opened the door, and before he even got to the landing, he heard Jacques's voice. "Where's *mi amigo?*"

Hudson perked up. "I'm right here, Dad."

"No, no, I meant, where's Johnny Tae? My chef in training?"

"I can be your helper, Dad," he watched Hudson run to the kitchen, Victoria following dutifully behind.

"Me help! Me help!" she cried.

Nel turned on the couch to look at Jacques, who stared blankly at her. "Jacques, honey, surely there's something they can do."

"Maybe they can help *you*," Jacques said pointedly.

"But I'm just talking with Ara Grace."

"They can help us set the table!" Ara Grace said suddenly, standing up, only to see the dining room table was already set. "Or …"

As the scene below devolved into a petty spat over which parent was to entertain the kids, and his auntie continuing to offer unhelpful suggestions, Johnny Tae felt his phone buzz with a notification. *Yep, they're all definitely having more fun than me.*

Chapter 4

An Extra Helping of Thanksgiving

Sarah didn't even feel her phone buzz with Johnny Tae's text. She was holding one of her brothers, Isaac, piggyback style on her back. They were racing Laela, who had Sarah's other brother, Nathan, on her back, down the hallway. Isaac was screaming in her ear, "Faster, Sarah!" while he twisted to bat his twin brother away.

The four collapsed against the wall, each girl releasing her jockey to the floor. "We won!" Nathan screamed and gave Laela a high five. "She totally beat you, Sarah!"

"No fair!" Isaac cried. "Laela was on cross-country. She runs." He readjusted his glasses. Even though he hadn't been the one running, he was slightly out of breath.

"We'll race again," Laela said. "This time, Sarah and I will be on our knees."

"Like real horses?" Sarah asked, more than a little incredulous. "Come on, Laela. Let's go grab some spinach artichoke dip or whatever Heather has set out."

She refused to call her stepmother Birdie like everyone else did, finding the name too odd to be cool.

The boys protested, but Laela said, "Later. We'll race again later. We need a break. You two can race each other."

That seemed to go over well. "Come on, Nathan," Isaac said. "Bet I can crawl faster than you!"

Someone opened the front door, letting Jack and Ripper back inside. The two dogs tore through the entryway and raced upstairs, their energy parallelling the twins'. There was a squeal of laughter as the dogs and boys started to wrestle.

The two girls moved to the heart of the party in the kitchen and dining room. Laela's parents, Bev and Coltan, sat near the appetizers. Mark, Sarah's dad, sat across from them. Mark grabbed a chip straight off the appetizer plate, then dipped it in the ranch before eating it. "Dad, that's gross," Sarah said, coming into the room. "Grab a plate."

"Where would I be without your manners to guide me?" Mark said. He dramatically leaned across to grab a small, plastic plate. He loaded it with chips and veggies, before using the spoon to scoop a generous portion of ranch and spinach artichoke dip onto the top of it all. "Bev, this dip! Every time I swear I could just eat that and be happy."

Coltan chimed in. "Her dip is why I married her," he said with a wink.

"Eww, Dad," Laela cut in.

Bev laughed. "Now that's not true. When we first got married, my signature dish was microwave nachos."

Coltan looked up, nostalgic. "Ah yes. I remember—stale chips, canned black beans, canned diced tomatoes, ripped up chunks of cheddar cheese, all microwaved at thirty-second intervals to perfection."

The adults laughed heartily. "That was fine eating on our budget! Two kids getting their master's at the same time!" Bev said, smiling.

Laela was infinitely proud of her parents' education, knowing that as Native Americans in modern America, the deck was stacked against them no matter what. If they had lived on a reservation, they'd likely have faced poverty, subpar schools, and poor healthcare. As it was, most Native families lived in urban areas—real cities, unlike Triumph. But often, the way the system was set up meant that they'd live in the same situation of poverty, subpar schools, and poor healthcare, only in a city instead of on some shitty barren land.

On Thanksgiving especially, the injustice of it all stung. Laela thought of the well-intentioned school plays they'd put on in kindergarten of the Christian Pilgrim colonists encountering the Native Americans. It was an original, watered-down "inspired by history" story that even mainstream Hollywood would have approved of. Her classmates had cajoled her to play one of the leads as Squanto (the Anglicized version of his proper name, Tisquantum, she later learned), and she hadn't told her parents. She felt like a traitor either way: betray her family or be forever branded an outsider. The lure of popularity had won out. When Bev and Coltan had come to see the Thanksgiving play, she remembered how stiffly her parents had sat in their chairs.

At the reception afterward, the adults had gathered in clusters, snack plates held between them, while the kids sat at their small tables. As Laela munched on her frosted animal crackers, she remembered Mark clearing his throat loudly, effectively silencing the adult's conversation, before asking the kindergarten teacher, "Say, the kids were cute and all, but that's not the real story, right? The first Thanksgiving."

Even at six years old, she remembered the sudden tense atmosphere in the room. Her teacher stammered something about the spirit of the play meaning to invoke friendship and collegiality, but Mark cut her off. "Seems to me, if you're interested in teaching these kids the meaning of friendship, you'd have stuck to the original. Look how the Pilgrims' 'friendship' worked out for the Patuxets."

Her parents had guffawed loudly, Coltan actually spitting out the juice he'd had in his mouth. They'd left shortly thereafter with Mark, Sarah, and Jen, Sarah's mom, and Bev had explained it all to Sarah and Laela, including that the Patuxets were Tisquantum's tribe. While Mark's comments had loosened her parents' stiffness, Jen had gone quiet. Sarah said that later, in the confines of the car, she'd yelled at Mark for embarrassing her in front of everyone.

But it was this interaction that had solidified Mark, Bev, and Coltan's friendship. And it was that moment of uncomfortable reality that eventually led to the sister-like friendship of Sarah and Laela for so many years.

With that in mind, this Thanksgiving felt a bit like a homecoming. She was glad they had started seeing more of Mark and Birdie again. It felt right, like some kind of reunion of a famous singing group. The pieces falling together, the participants knowing their parts.

They all looked toward the hall when they heard a loud thud, followed by the boys' loud laughter. "Do I even want to know?" Mark asked Sarah.

"Nope," Sarah said. "Ignorance is bliss."

"Boys!" Mark called out. "How about you take a little breather?"

Sarah and Laela took that as their cue to leave, their appetizer plates thoroughly loaded. They passed by the kitchen. Sarah's stepmom, Birdie, was stirring something on the stove while her father, Guy, sat at one of the high-top chairs. "Paul was just telling me ..." he started. Sarah glanced into the kitchen, but saw no sign of Birdie's brother, Paul. He must be watching TV in the family room. Rarely were Paul and Birdie together in the same room for longer than ten minutes, Sarah had noticed.

The girls walked to the entryway, then automatically climbed the stairs. They headed instinctively for Sarah's room. Sarah sat on the edge of her bed. Laela sat on the spinning desk chair. She grabbed a carrot and spun the chair with her feet. "I'd never get any homework done with this," she said. "I'd just spin all the time."

Sarah laughed. "You act like I do my homework in the first place." Sarah wasn't known for her intellectual prowess, or for her academic rigor. Those were Laela's arenas. Sarah was the social butterfly, skilled in conversation and flirtation.

She'd be an excellent salesperson, Laela thought. "It's not like you don't do your homework in study hall," she quipped. "You're not as big of a slacker as you pretend to be."

"Compared to you, Ms. I-Waived-Out-Of-Study-Hall-To-Take-Another-AP, yeah, I am a slacker. And I'm okay with that," she added. "C's get degrees!" she parroted what her own mom, Jen, said each time Sarah's report card was forwarded on to her. Her dad and stepmom felt she was underachieving, a word they loved to say as if they knew Sarah better than she knew herself.

Laela groaned and spun the chair quickly. Her phone fell out of her sweater pocket, hitting the ground. She bent over to pick it up. "Oh, we've missed some texts."

"Yeah?" Sarah said, pulling her own phone out. She read Johnny Tae's message, then Morgan's reply:

HA. WATCHING FOOTBALL WITH MY DAD. KINDA NICE. BUT I GUESS THE TEAM NAME IS KINDA RACIST.

She scanned Johnny Tae's reply:
KINDA IS AN UNDERSTATEMENT. WAY TO PROMOTE AGGRESSIVE SPORTS

MORGAN: AMERICA'S GAME ON AMERICA'S DAY OF THANKS

JOHNNY TAE: BASEBALL IS AMERICA'S GAME

Sarah started typing:
WHO'D WANT TO WATCH THAT? BORING

Laela saw her friend's reply and laughed. "You've always hated baseball."

"And soccer. And basketball. And running, too. No offense to the newest cross-country convert." Sarah tossed her phone aside and bit into some celery. She watched as Laela struggled to come up with a reply, her thumbs writing something before she'd highlight it all and delete it. "You writing a novel over there?"

Laela sighed. "I just don't know what to say."

"Laela, it's not like it's a televised speech. It's friends talking shit, killing time." She watched her friend grimace before putting the phone away without replying. "You okay?"

Her mind flashed back to when Johnny Tae had asked her that question about a month ago.

* * *

School had just let out, and practice for the sectionals cross-country meet was set to start in just fifteen minutes. Laela was struggling getting her drawstring bag puffed full of heavy winter clothes and running shoes out of her locker. She gave a final mighty yank and the bag fell out of the tight space, sending her backwards. Laela nearly lost her balance when Johnny Tae caught her by the elbow.

"Shit, Laela," he'd said, laughing. "You okay?" His brown eyes had been full of concern as he helped her steady herself again.

"I'm fine," she said, laughing in embarrassment. "Should've brought a suitcase for all my practice gear."

She watched him stiffen, a change from the nonchalance she'd come to expect from him. Johnny Tae cleared his throat before saying. "I've been meaning to ask you," he said, "I mean, I wanted to see if you'd want to …"

Her locker neighbor slammed his door suddenly, causing them both to jump. Jonny Tae shook his head for a second before continuing. "Homecoming is next week. Would you want to go with me?"

Yes, her heart instantly answered. *Yes, I'd love to!*

"I'd …" Laela began. But her anxiety kicked in, its dark, familiar relentless voice: *End the night in an ambulance again? Unintentionally mix anxiety meds and booze? Maybe this time the paramedics won't be able to help you. Or maybe this time you get arrested and all your college dreams are gone. Poof. For what? A boy who feels bad for you? He doesn't like you, not really. Who'd like you anyways?* The voice nagged on, the span between his question and her answer increasing.

She started again. "Thanks, but …"

Johnny Tae looked to the floor. "It's fine," he said, quickly. "I just thought … I've never been, seemed like something to do." He adjusted his backpack on his shoulder. "I'll see you around."

She'd watched him walk away. She knew it was the right decision—it *had* to be the right decision—and yet, she *did* want to go with him. She wanted to be normal, like the other people her age. To go to dances and have dates without the constant stream of self-criticism. To be fine.

She was fine, on the surface. On the surface, she was excellent. She was healthy. She was doing great in school, as usual. She'd an awesome first season on the cross-country team. She had a weekly babysitting gig for Pastor Nel on Thursdays that paid her enough that she didn't have to bug her parents for money.

But anytime it came to getting together with people her age, like at a party or other social event, she felt herself shut down. Turtle mode. She'd thrown away the anxiety meds she'd been prescribed over the summer after they mixed badly with whatever she'd been given to drink at that disastrous end-of-summer party. That was her second ambulance exit that summer, the first being a start-of-summer party where she got hit by a truck trying to escape. Lucky for her, the truck was just gaining speed, and its hit only left her badly bruised. Terrible bookends to summer, both started by parties.

Bad things happen when I hang out with people, she told herself. One-on-one, she was fine. But in groups, she felt lost—or, worse, she felt like she was only invited because people felt sorry for her.

* * *

"Earth to Laela?" Sarah interrupted her reverie, snapping her fingers. "You okay?"

"I'm okay," Laela finally answered. "I guess I just feel kinda stupid for this summer. Embarrassed even. It was just so dramatic. So not me."

Sarah nodded. "I'm sorry, Bug," she said, using Laela's old nickname. "I'm definitely glad you're okay. This summer wasn't all bad though, was it?" Positive Sarah, as usual.

"No, you're right," Laela agreed, berating herself. "But … it's just. I don't know, it's all tainted now."

They sat in silence for a moment, their phones buzzing again with what Sarah was sure were Johnny Tae's snarky replies.

"Damn, that boy just won't shut up," Sarah said. "He must be really bored."

"He's over at Pastor Nel's, just him and his aunt with Nel and her family," Laela said matter-of-factly. "I'd be bored, too."

Sarah arched an eyebrow. "You two talking a lot?" Sarah's interest in Johnny Tae was about more than just friendship, but she hadn't wanted to step on her friend's toes. Once Laela had turned him down for Homecoming, Sarah figured that he was fair game. But she had yet to make certain that was the case.

"Mostly just in class. But Pastor Nel told me her Thanksgiving plans when I was watching her kids last week."

"So, you're not into him?" she asked, rushing the question out.

"Sarah!" they both startled as one of the boys yelled. "Laela! Mom says to come down for dinner!"

That was quick, Sarah thought. *Heather must really want to get her brother out.*

* * *

They all crowded around the oval dinner table. Laela sat in between her mom and Sarah. Coltan sat on the other side of her mom, one of the twins beside him. Across from them sat Birdie and Paul, a physical distance created so distinctly between them that not even a fork prong strayed over into the other's table territory. Guy and Mark sat at either head of the table. Nathan and Isaac sat on either side of Mark. Even the dogs took their spots lying beside Mark, one on either side like bookends.

Birdie stood up once everyone gathered around. "Dinner tonight is of course, turkey," this got a whoop from Coltan, "with mashed potatoes, stuffing, and gravy, but it's just turkey breast. We didn't do a whole bird this year, the boys hate turkey."

Isaac or Nathan said, "It *is* gross!"

"So dry," the other chimed in.

Birdie rolled her eyes. "Which is why we have ham stew, too. Sarah led that operation." The group clapped appreciatively before Birdie continued, "Served with cornbread, Brussels sprouts—and yes boys, you do have to eat them!" She cut off any other interruption from the boys.

"And for starters we have a … Mediterranean salad? Cherry tomatoes, goat cheese, and balsamic vinaigrette."

Sarah looked up at Birdie, confused. Guy and Paul were supposed to bring the salad. And didn't salads normally have lettuce?

"The food's all set up in the kitchen, so serve yourself. But before we begin, would anyone like to pray?" Birdie always asked this, and the answer was always the same: an awkward silence. Sarah always thought it was weird of her to ask. She was a pastor, why not just do it? She'd asked Birdie this once. Birdie had said, "I'm a pastor, yes, but when I'm with family, I'm not the family pastor. I'm just me." Sarah had pretended this made sense to her.

When no one volunteered, Birdie prayed: "Dear Lord, thank you for this meal and time together. Thank you for all that you give us. Help us to live in wonder of your bounty, through Jesus' name."

There was a collective, "Amen!" before chaos again ensued. The boys raced each other to the kitchen, one forgetting his plate and having to run back. Sarah and Laela wisely stayed seated. Sarah saw Paul gather his plate and stand, pushing his chair in so that his back was flush to the wall. He stood like this, watching the line form in the kitchen.

Guy, who was also still seated, said apologetically to no one in particular, "I forgot the salad. I knew I was forgetting something when I left. Paul usually helps me remember things like that."

Paul, his plate held against his chest like a shield, placed one hand on Guy's shoulder. "It's all right, Dad. There's plenty of food."

He squeezed his father's shoulder once before returning to his sentry duty.

As the first wave of people came back from the kitchen, Laela and Sarah got up to serve themselves.

"You made ham stew?" Laela asked Sarah, opening the crockpot lid. "Since when do you cook?"

"I've been following some chefs on TikTok," Sarah replied, smelling the honey and roasted peas from the stew waft into the air. "This was one that does alternative Thanksgiving meals. I showed Heather, and she said to go for it."

Sarah shrugged as if it were no big deal. Secretly, she loved cooking—bringing together different ingredients, experimenting with seasonings, trying new ways to cook old favorites. What surprised her more than her natural interest in it was how it had started to be something she did willingly with Birdie.

Laela scooped some of the stew into her bowl, lifting it to her nose. "Mmm!" she cooed. "Sarah, this smells amazing! I'm so impressed!" She elbowed Sarah playfully. "Looks like you've been keeping secrets from me!"

Sarah kept her face down, pretending to struggle grabbing the pathetic pieces of the Mediterranean salad. Now wasn't the time.

* * *

Once nearly everyone had gone through for seconds and thirds, a contented hush fell over the table. Silverware clanked to a stop on their respective plates. "Well, if that wasn't the most delicious Thanksgiving I can remember," Guy said appreciatively.

Birdie frowned, quickly taking a sip of her wine.

"Now begins the fun part. Clean up!" Mark said. "Boys, you help clear the table. Girls, you help me in the kitchen and put the leftovers away."

"We'll help too," Coltan said, making little effort to stand. "We've eaten our fair share."

"Nonsense," Birdie said, standing. "You're guests, and I won't ..."

"Birdie," Bev interrupted, "we're practically family. Please. We've got this."

"Absolutely, let's leave the Nelsons to some family time." Mark said, standing. He used his wife's maiden name, referring to Guy, Paul, and Birdie. Mark turned, avoiding his wife's silent plea.

Birdie slowly sank back down into her chair, her father at the head of the table on her right side. Paul stood, handing the boys his plate, before he too was reprimanded. He chose to sit across from Birdie and Guy, in what had been Laela's seat.

The once contented silence turned awkward as every non-Nelson left. Birdie took another sip of her wine, realizing it was near its end. "Paul, hand me the wine, will you?"

Her brother grabbed the bottle to his right, sniffing its opening before passing it over to her. "I don't know how you drink this," he said, handing it to her like it was poison.

"Beats the dirty water you prefer," she said, referring to his light beer. She gave herself a generous pour before returning the bottle to the table.

"Least this doesn't have pesticides in it," Paul said, taking a swig from his aluminum can.

Guy looked from one of his kids to the other. "Come on now, let a man—or woman—drink what they want. I've always been partial to vodka, myself."

Paul and Birdie looked at him sharply. "No, you haven't, Dad," Birdie said, as Paul simultaneously said, "That's whiskey you're thinking of."

Guy snapped his fingers. "That's right, whiskey," he looked to Paul appreciatively. "The two are nearly the same."

Birdie furrowed her brows. "That's bourbon. Bourbon and whiskey are nearly the same."

Paul glared at her across the table. "All hard liquor is nearly the same," he said, soothingly to Guy.

"Is it now?" Guy asked, tilting his head. "I get confused sometimes, you know."

"Happens to all of us," Paul murmured, draining his beer. "You're fine, Dad. Just another senior moment."

Birdie bit her lip. Their father was certainly *not* fine. Yes, confusion happened with advanced age, but Guy was more than confused.

Birdie tried to think of the word. *Losing it. Slipping. Showing signs of dementia.*

She took a hearty sip of her wine. Today wasn't the day for that conversation. "So, tell me how things are at the shop," she said by way of transition. Car talk would keep them in a safe conversation zone. "What's the latest project you're working on, Paul?" She silently prayed that Bev and Coltan would announce dessert soon so this Nelson family bonding moment would be over.

Paul launched into a story about intake valves and pistons as Guy inserted his own quips about the type of metal they were using to repair which cars. Birdie nodded and pretended to follow along, draining her wine as the conversation continued.

"All right, everyone, dessert!" Bev called out, entering the dining room with a tray of Christmas cookies. Coltan followed behind with a pint of peppermint ice cream and mini bowls.

The less-than-charming Nelson family moment over, Birdie stood to help pass out the scooped ice cream.

"Peppermint ice cream!" Guy said. "That's my favorite!"

Birdie intentionally looked over to Paul, waiting for him to correct him: Moose track fudge swirl was Guy's favorite. It's what they had to have every year on his birthday. But Paul pointedly avoided her eyes.

Maybe Dad's just being polite, Birdie thought hopefully. But even she didn't believe her optimism. Not this time.

Chapter 5

And So This Is Christmas

"Now *this* is how I imagined small-town life!" Ara Grace was practically glowing under the twinkling lights adorning the trees in Triumph's quaint downtown. Within twenty-four hours of Thanksgiving's end, the entire scene had become a Christmas wonderland. Sweet Martha's, the bakery, displayed tiny gingerbread people wearing tiny icing suspenders and intricately piped Christmas sweaters, with a few in Triumph Titans uniforms for good measure. Buzz Buzz Buzz had a sandwich board on the sidewalk out front that read, "Special Peppermint Bark Latte—We Don't Bite!" A smiling dog was drawn underneath. She recognized Johnny Tae's handwriting and wondered how Gavin had convinced him to write such a cheesy joke, giggling as she imagined the conversation. She felt light, almost like she was floating.

"And this is just a preview of what's to come," Birdie replied. "Truly, the next month will be pretty overwhelming for an introvert like me, but it's all good fun."

"When do they light the tree?"

A larger-than-life fir tree—real, not artificial—stood at the intersection of Main Street and Park Avenue, Triumph's two main thoroughfares. Members of Ara Grace's congregation, the Hubbard family, were responsible for this tree and the trees in most Triumph County living rooms. From the wife's side, they had inherited an evergreen farm in addition to the town's only nursery. Though Danielle had left the nursery work to become an accountant, her husband ran the farm's daily operations. This one tree had been growing since before Ara Grace was born, she knew, and that fact alone left her feeling un-cynically awed.

"Right around six," Birdie replied. "You'll be up to speak before the lighting. Once they illuminate that thing, everyone's off to do their shopping. It'll be a nice moment, though. Charlie always emcees."

Ara Grace nodded, and the feeling of lightness was replaced with a low, buzzing anxiety. She swallowed around a lump in her throat. She was completely comfortable preaching every week, so why did this little sales pitch for the new children's pageant feel so hard? Being a pastor to her congregation was starting to feel more comfortable—or at least more worn-in, like a pair of hiking boots that had begun to mold to her feet. Holding the identity of pastor in public still felt awkward, like she hadn't earned it yet. It didn't help that when she'd visited the high school to enroll Johnny Tae, they'd thought she was a student. *What I wouldn't give for some gray hair*, she thought.

Just then, Ara Grace felt a hard shove from behind. She was ready to spin around and give Johnny Tae a piece of her mind, thinking he was the only one who'd dare stage such an attack. But to her surprise, she found Victoria sitting on the ground, legs splayed out as if she'd ricocheted off Ara Grace's back. Several storefronts behind her, Ara Grace could see Nel running, holding Hudson's hand as she dragged him through the crowd to catch up to Victoria. Birdie was already crouched down, speaking softly and soothingly to the preschooler.

"I'm so sorry, y'all," Nel shouted, approaching the group. "She's a runner these days. Not sure how to keep up."

"It's okay," Ara Grace replied, then added, "Is she okay? Are you okay?"

"Oh, we're fine," Nel said. "I only wish I could find Jacques around here. He's over at the bookstore trying to convince Amelia to show his work." She lowered her voice conspiratorially. "Wouldn't be surprised if he's trying to give me a taste of my own medicine," she barely whispered. Jacques was the good parent, the reliable one, the one who was always there. He could handle both kids with no problem. Why couldn't she? She vowed to bring it up in their next couple's counseling session with Sister Eunice.

* * *

In the early fall, Nel and Jacques had followed through on their plan to seek counseling after a tumultuous summer, and they had both been thrilled to find Sister Eunice. She was a Catholic nun, but

the kind who wore crew-neck sweatshirts instead of a habit and who
dropped your blood pressure with a single smile. Jacques had been
raised Catholic, and nuns felt familiar to him. Safe. For Nel's part, she
was charmed by Sister Eunice's gentle questions, no-nonsense advice,
and open curiosity. She felt like Sister Eunice possessed the kind of
soul she wanted to have when she grew up. *When was it exactly*, she
thought, *that a person finally grew up?* She was grateful for telehealth;
Sister Eunice lived in Denver, far away from the prying curiosity of
Triumph folk.

That first session, held via Nel's work laptop because their tablet
was playing *Frozen* and serving as babysitter, Sister Eunice had opened
by asking Nel and Jacques, "What brought you here today? Start from
wherever makes the most sense to you."

Jacques had gone on a romantic ramble about their meet-cute
at Duke Divinity School, the adventures they still hoped to have
together. "But she hardly cares to see me or the kids," he finished.
Nel bristled.

"How about you, Nel?" Sister Eunice asked.

"I, well," she'd listened to Elsa's voice sing for the millionth
time, "Let it go," and thought it was about time she tried it herself.
"Honestly, it feels like I'm being pulled in a million directions right
now and I'm doing the best I can. It really hurts to hear you think I
don't care, Jacques. I do." She forced herself to turn and look at her
husband, sitting to her right. "It's just that there's a lot to manage, a
lot to track, and our family needs me to keep this job." *Can't hold it
back anymore*, Nel thought in time with Elsa's cheery voice.

"It's always 'I' and 'me'," Jacques retorted, "but what about *us*?"

"Just a moment," Sister Eunice interjected. "Let's let Nel finish,
shall we?"

Nel took a deep breath, sipped her peppermint tea, and stared
at the ceiling for a moment. She willed the tears that prickled just
behind her eyes to stay put.

"I don't know what it's like to have a mother who works," she
continued. "My mom supported my dad's career. It was hard on her,
I know that, but she really felt called to motherhood. That was very
much her vocation." She looked to her husband again. "Jacques, I
don't expect that from you, and I know this primary parent thing

isn't your vocation." She didn't yet dare to venture into his lack of consistent employment, saving that for a future session. "But I don't know how to pretend I don't have a job to keep things together at home or be the same kind of partner I was before we had kids. That's just not possible."

"It would help if you tried," Jacques said, sullenly.

"I have an idea," Sister Eunice said. "It's a little unorthodox, but it's the kind of thing I like to have couples try, couples like the two of you, who clearly have a history filled with love and passion, but some of that spark has been lost along the way."

Nel was intrigued.

"For the next week, I want you to act like you're in love. Get a sitter and take each other on a date if you can. Hold hands. Listen deeply to one another. Have a lot of sex." Nel blanched at that one. It felt a little shocking to hear a chaste nun advising others to have sex. "Live as if you are madly in love," Sister Eunice continued, "and see what you discover."

For that next week, Nel did her best to reduce her work commitments so she was home in the evenings, and she vowed to be fully present when she was home. Ara Grace took her hospital on-call shift that week, and she opted out of a meeting about the church's Harvest Dinner—the ladies' fellowship could handle that one on their own. One night they played Uno with the kids, special cards taken out so it was just number-matching, and she was overcome with joy watching Jacques coach Victoria and cheer her on when she matched correctly. The two of them made love tenderly that night, enveloped in a homey kind of contentment. Another night that week Jacques brought her to the steak restaurant, which was Triumph's version of fancy, and they held hands under the table as a jazz combo played sultry tunes. The sex that night was frantic and quick, a bit like when they first met. Nel did her best to put her heart into their little couple's game that week, but she found that in all the pretending, her resentment crept in and settled a little deeper. *Why can't I have a career and a husband who supports it?* she thought. *Why do I have to become an actress to earn that privilege?*

They made it through the week, but Nel wasn't sure it taught her much of anything except that she hated faking it. She wanted to get real with Jacques, to tell each other the truth. For once.

* * *

Back in Triumph's little downtown for the Christmas tree lighting, Nel looked as harried as she felt. "We can help you out," Birdie chimed in, Victoria now in her arms playing with her scarf. "And look, I see a few more helpers over there."

Down the middle of the barricaded street walked Johnny Tae, Morgan, Laela, and Claire. Sarah had a hostessing shift; the restaurant would be busy with everyone downtown. Ara Grace guessed Morgan had invited Claire along to give Laela a familiar friend to connect with, one of her old buddies from the cross-country team. Laela was part of the group, but without Sarah, she tended to get nervous and quiet, Ara Grace had noticed. *That kid's awfully perceptive for nineteen*, she thought. Gavin had given Johnny Tae and Morgan the night off to encourage, as he called it, "good clean fun." Ara Grace was pleased to see the boys were using their night off wholesomely. Johnny Tae looked freezing cold in his New England pea coat; Ara Grace made a mental note to text his dad about Wyoming winter coat funds. She waved in a way that was sure to embarrass Johnny Tae, paused self-consciously for a moment, then waved even bigger. Who cares if she looked like a dorky aunt who loved her nephew? Guilty as charged.

* * *

Johnny Tae looked over at Ara Grace, his goofy aunt, clad in a loud rainbow hat, with a small smile and a nod. He was sort of getting used to having her around, and it's not like his friends didn't know her, too. *This is what it feels like to have real family and real friends*, he thought. Comfortable embarrassment. Could be worse.

This cold, though. He was shivering under three layers of wool, which had been enough for most of what New England threw at him in the winter. It was no match for Wyoming, even in late November. He was starting to almost like this place, but winter might throw him off his game.

Laela and Morgan were deep in conversation about a book she'd finished that afternoon for English class, *David Copperfield*. Johnny Tae was all for reading but he didn't have much patience for what he called "that sentimental shit." Still, their conversation got him thinking. A young kid out on his own in the world, sent off to boarding school, parents MIA. Johnny Tae had to admit he was a little better off than an orphan, but some days he thought he'd prefer it. *If your parents are dead*, he thought wryly, *you can stop hoping for them to show up for you.* In truth, from hearing their conversation, Johnny Tae was considering picking up the book. Even though Charles Dickens was old and long dead, he seemed to understand the pains of growing up without a stable home or reliable parents, trying to make your way in a world that's not designed for you.

Johnny Tae was straining so hard to hear Morgan and Laela's conversation, he nearly forgot about Claire walking alongside him. He was still getting a read on her, even though they shared a few classes. He breathed into his hands to warm them up, thinking of how to start a conversation with her.

"You look freezing," she said, beating him to the punch. "I think my dad has extra jackets. Want to borrow one until you get one of your own?"

"That's okay," Johnny Tae replied. "I'm good."

"Seriously, this is all a lot more fun when you have the right gear!" She gestured around. Johnny Tae noticed everyone was wearing puffy, down jackets with thick hats, gloves, and scarves.

"I'll find something," he said, shoving his thinly gloved hands back in his pockets. He didn't want to be rude, so he added, "Thanks, though, I appreciate it."

"We were just talking about going cross-country skiing next weekend," Claire added. "You'll want something warmer for that."

"Yeah," Morgan added, their conversations threading back together as they weaved in and out of clusters of people on the sidewalk. "We want to show you what a good winter looks like here. A good winter that doesn't revolve around booze. You need a parka, man. You don't have to take an old man's jacket," he glanced at Claire before quickly mumbling, "No offense meant. I've got one you can have. Should fit you well enough."

Morgan was a hulk of a man, barrel chested and wide shouldered. Johnny Tae was sure he'd be swimming in that coat. He felt like a charity case at that moment, but the wind blew lightly again, straight through his wool peacoat, and he was grateful. "Okay, fine," he relented. "But why can't you stay inside like normal people when it's freezing cold?"

"We'd be inside all winter!" Claire protested. "And winter here is long. Like, snow on the ground for five months or more. If we stayed inside when it was cold, we'd go bananas." The others nodded in agreement. "We say there's no bad weather, only bad clothing."

"And it's beautiful," Laela added. Johnny Tae couldn't argue with that. The topography was somehow even more scenic than when he'd first arrived in summer. White-capped mountains, trees glittering with snow, all made more magical he was sure by the soon to be lit Christmas lights.

"We try not to let the winter slow us down," Claire continued. "But for this year's Turkey Trot, I was a lot slower wearing three different layers of pants."

"One of the few times you're slowed down," Laela said, nudging Claire playfully.

They all started sharing about their Thanksgivings after that. Laela wove her way closer to Johnny Tae and asked, "How was Thanksgiving with Pastor Nel and her crew?"

"Totally fine, good food," Johnny Tae replied. "Jacques is trying to play dad with me, I think? It's a little weird. Glad my auntie's making friends, I guess."

"How were the kids?" Laela asked cautiously, but pointedly.

"Oh yeah, you sit for them, right?" Johnny Tae acted as if he just remembered. "They were good. Kids. I don't know. I played Legos with them for a bit, built a tower. Seemed okay."

Laela hesitated before continuing. "I worry about them sometimes. They're both so sweet, but I think Victoria needs more than she's getting." She sighed. "I don't think they want her to have a label, but labels can help when it comes to getting services."

Johnny Tae knew all about labels. "They were doing well yesterday," he said. "I'm not sure about all of that."

Just then, hurricane Victoria slammed into him, chased by Nel, who he swore had just been walking with his auntie across the street. Maybe he'd spoken too soon about things being fine with them.

* * *

Birdie watched the group of teens claim a prime spot near the center of the blocked intersection. Nel was near her, somewhere, no doubt keeping Victoria in her sights and Hudson nearby. Birdie herself was on edge, looking around the crowd until she spotted Paul and Guy, walking slowly but purposefully toward her. Remembering the forgotten salad and countless slips from the night before, she felt her body tense even more. But as soon as Guy saw her, he called to her jovially, "Honey! I can't wait for them to turn this place into Christmas Town. Best night of the year." Her father had called this event the "Christmas Town Transformation" for as long as she could remember.

"Do you remember when Dad almost broke his back falling off the ladder getting the tree decorated?" Paul chimed in as they got nearer.

Birdie smiled. "Oh my gosh, Paul. That was terrifying!" She remembered her mother making Guy swear he'd never volunteer to hang the lights ever again. He was right back up there the next year.

"You two were in what, middle school then?" Guy said fondly. "I just remember thinking, if I survive this, you two would give me absolute grief for it. And you did, sure enough."

A true and clear memory. "That's right, Dad," Birdie said. "We always were giving you grief, weren't we?"

She noticed Ara Grace had slipped away from the group, and Birdie knew this meant the tree lighting ceremony would be starting any moment. She craned her head to find the microphone, amplifier, and music stand that served as a makeshift stage. Just then, she heard a scratchy tapping. "Is this thing on?" It was Morgan, testing the A/V setup with Charlie and Ara Grace close behind him. The crowd winced as the speaker screeched. *Good start*, Birdie thought to herself.

* * *

Co-emceeing the tree lighting ceremony was not at the top of Morgan's to-do list when he had returned just last weekend. But Charlie—his dad and the town sheriff—had invited him to join him this year. It felt like the invite wasn't just to be a football-playing pep rally hype man, but to be a grown-up community member with something to say. He hated public speaking, but he felt like his dad was extending an olive branch and he'd better take it. *Somehow, it's always my responsibility to manage my relationship with my dad,* Morgan thought. *But I know he's trying. I need to try too.*

He thought back to a day in group session, probably about a month into rehab, when they were all doing a journaling activity. "I want you to imagine your future," Salvador had said. "Think about your life five years from now. Imagine yourself sober. Sober and *thriving.* What's your life like?" He paused for a moment. "I don't mean like what job you have or where you're living, but that can be part of it, if you want. The part I want you to focus on is what it *feels* like to be you. What does five-years-sober-you look like? What are the smells that fill your life? The sounds? The emotions? Think about it and then do some writing or drawing. We'll come back together in half an hour."

That day in rehab, Morgan sat and thought and wrote nothing. Five years from now, he was supposed to be a college graduate, debt-free thanks to a sweet football scholarship, criminal justice degree under his belt, crushing it as a new recruit on the force. This was the life his father had planned for him. He'd never given much thought to all those questions Salvador laid out, about what his life would feel like and sound like and smell like. But now, in rehab, it was probably time to think about it all. His football days were long behind him, he now knew, and the DWI charge disqualified him from police service, at least for a while. The bones of his plan were gone. Time to start from scratch.

But instead of journaling, Morgan found himself thinking about his relatively happy childhood. What were the feelings he wanted to repeat? What did he want to be different? When he came up empty, he tried a different angle. *What am I trying to escape when I get blitzed?* he asked himself. Grief, sure. But also, pressure. The pressure to be someone he absolutely was not. These macho-dude expectations. His father's hopes and plans for him. *I want a life where I'm my own person,* he thought. *All I want is to be loved and accepted as my true self, not some fictional version of me.* Now he had to figure out who exactly that true self was.

Back in front of the microphone at the tree-lighting ceremony, Morgan tapped the microphone again. "Testing, testing, one-two-three," he repeated, this time with no feedback squeak. He may have accepted his father's invitation reluctantly, but he was going to do his best to emcee as himself, not his father-approved alter ego. Morgan ran a hand to his small bun, assuring himself. "Good evening, Triumph!" he began. "Happy holidays, one and all." This was already a bit of a departure. The debate had raged for years about whether to focus on religious Christmas, secular Christmas, or a more expansive holiday celebration. Charlie was firmly in the secular Christmas camp, feeling that anyone could celebrate the Christmas spirit. Morgan was more pluralist in his approach.

"I'm Morgan, you likely all know me as either a former Titans footballer or Sheriff Charlie's kid. Whoever I am to you, I want you to take a moment and look at one another," Morgan continued. "I mean, really look. Tonight, we're lighting the Christmas tree, but we're also celebrating the light that dwells within each one of us." He looked over at his father. Charlie's eyes were wide in shock, but there were no tell-tale eyebrow furrows of anger. Morgan, for his part, realized his heart rate was steady; he had no nerves whatsoever. "We gather to share the light tonight," Morgan finished. "Share the love. Without further ado, here's Sheriff Charlie to take us home!"

Charlie clapped Morgan on the back affectionately. "Before we light the tree, we have a few announcements. This *holiday* season," he looked pointedly at Morgan, "we have a number of ways to support our community." Charlie glanced at his paper, clearly reading verbatim. "Greenwood Elementary is hosting a cookie sale every Friday before Christmas. If you don't have the time to bake, let them help you while you let your money help them build a new gym. Our all-county Christmas—erm—holiday craft fair will be set up at the bandshell on Saturdays. Shop local when you're searching for gifts. And before we light the tree, we have one last announcement from Reverend Ara Grace Jung, the new pastor at Good Shepherd Lutheran Church."

Morgan watched Ara Grace curiously. She looked like she was about to pass out. *Didn't she do this public speaking thing for a living?* he thought.

Ara Grace stepped up to the mic, lowering it so it better aligned with her height. Problem was, she lowered it too far, too quick—it settled mid-chest. She fumbled awkwardly for a moment, realigning the mic. Then she began, softly and tentatively. "Hi, Triumph!" He could tell she was trying for peppy and energetic, but with the uncertain waver in her voice, the effect made her seem like a curious teenager trying out a microphone for the first time. "Um, we at First Christian, First Methodist, and Good Shepherd really love kids." A few snickers from the crowd. "We want to get to know yours." Now there was a burst of laughter. "Sorry. Uh, so we're doing something new. We're having a Christmas pageant, rehearsals on Wednesdays and performance at the Carol Sing in a few weeks. Thanks." She moved away from the microphone before remembering. "Oh, and I'm Pastor Ara Grace. From Good Shepherd. Happy holidays." A few weak claps came from the section of the crowd where the pastors and their families stood. Morgan watched Johnny Tae hide his face in his hands. Ara Grace shuffled off quickly and unceremoniously.

* * *

Ara Grace hid back in the anonymity of the crowd. "You did just fine, dear," Birdie said to her. She wasn't crying, but she looked miserable. The rainbow knit hat keeping her head warm, a gift from the search committee when she accepted the call, slouched to the side, giving the effect of deflation.

Birdie knew what it felt like to be new and young. *It takes some time to grow into yourself*, she thought, *especially as a pastor*. She didn't say these words to Ara Grace, fearing they'd be taken as patronizing. But she thought the words in her heart, praying them for her friend all the same.

"That's right, young lady," Guy added, turning to face Ara Grace. "Are you a new student at Triumph High?" Birdie's blood ran cold. Her father knew Ara Grace. He'd sold her Johnny Tae's car just months before.

Birdie watched Ara Grace lean toward Guy, patiently explaining. But a pit settled in her own stomach, embarrassment at her father's gaffe.

Charlie's voice called, "Merry Christmas!" The tree lit up the square in technicolor, and Morgan started "Holly Jolly Christmas" on the sound system. The hope she'd felt reminiscing with her father and brother just minutes before slipped away completely. *No cups of cheer for us this year.*

Chapter 6

Counting Costs

Ara Grace silently counted her congregation's attendance that Sunday after Thanksgiving as they shuffled out of the sanctuary. She made mental notes of who was missing, who she'd need to contact that week, and when those who'd gone out of town got back. While there were lots more than had attended the Thanksgiving service, they were still a little light for a normal Sunday. She hadn't realized how much of shepherding God's people involved literal counting of the sheep.

Johnny Tae had stayed home that morning. They'd agreed that twice a month attendance was a fair expectation, allowing him to sleep in most Sundays or take the morning shift at Buzz Buzz Buzz. On Sundays when Ara Grace had meetings after worship service, he rarely joined her. This was one of those Sundays.

Sylvia played an organ piece as a postlude that included some chime sounds. Ara Grace didn't know the organ could make such distinct sounds. She added to her to-do list that she needed to compliment Sylvia on her postlude choice today— a flavor of Christmas, and rhythmically interesting.

Ara Grace strode to the Fellowship Hall, ready for a cup of coffee before her Council meeting. They'd chosen to meet on a Sunday instead of their normal weeknight since the evening came so much earlier in the winter. Ara Grace didn't mind walking in the dark, but she didn't like the idea of some of her congregants driving in the dark any more than they did. Black ice was a real threat.

She saw Richard Lansington, holding court at the coffee urn. "Grandkids remind me why it's the young that have kids," he said loudly. "I couldn't keep up with them! Jonathan was always wanting to play some truck game with me, and Izzy kept wanting to do my makeup and have a tea party." The group of four around him chuckled good-naturedly. They began adding their own tales of grandkids' energetic hobbies.

"Excuse me," Ara Grace said, getting through to the coffee. "I need a refill."

"Pastor!" Richard said, genuinely surprised to see her. "Good service today."

"Thank you, glad to see everyone back," she said evenly as she positioned her cup.

"How was Thanksgiving? Good attendance? I hope we raised enough in the special offering for the food pantry. They liked the fresh produce our little garden provided last summer," he continued loudly.

Richard had taken it upon himself to start what he called an "urban garden" on the church's back lawn for the community. (Ara Grace had found it humorous that anything in this entire state could count as urban.) It was a lovely project, meaningful and helpful to the community. But it was clearly *his* project. It was not a communal garden. He was the coordinator, the planner, and the recruiter of volunteers. Ara Grace made the mistake of putting an announcement in the bulletin for gardening help without consulting him. He'd promptly chastised her that day in the narthex, his voice rising above the sound of Sylvia's postlude.

"Actually," Ara Grace said, raising the filled cup to her lips, "we didn't have a lot of people for the Thanksgiving service." She blew on the liquid before looking Richard in the eyes. "We had a lot of people insist on its importance, but not a lot of follow-through."

"Holiday chaos," Richard said dismissively.

"We all had Thanksgiving dinner at my cousin's place..." someone from the group holding court before Richard continued. Ara Grace found herself struggling to stay focused on their conversation, her mind forming an argument with Richard.

His son lived about an hour's drive from here, in the town with the warehouse market. Richard easily could have attended service and then gone to his son's. *If the Thanksgiving service was as important as he insisted,* she thought bitterly. Ara Grace knew she wasn't being entirely fair to Richard. He wasn't the only who'd said the Thanksgiving service simply *had* to happen. But the squeaky wheel gets the grease, and Richard made sure his voice and opinions were heard. Always.

She sipped her coffee and nodded as they all continued on about grandkids and the nice family time they'd had. And as Richard again shared a story about his own time with his grandkids, she felt her chest lighten, the bitterness fade. Ara Grace remained frustrated with him, but she discovered she was feeling genuinely happy for good ol' Dick. In his career years, Richard had been some sort of upper-level corporate type who traveled often. He'd missed out on a lot of the day-to-day life with his sons. It seemed like he wasn't willing to repeat his past with his grandkids. *Growth*, Ara Grace thought, *can take time.*

* * *

The various members of Good Shepherd's Council gathered around an oval table in what once served as the congregation's library but had somehow over the years become a general dumping ground. Ara Grace had to gingerly move a fake potted cactus so she could sit at the table with the other five people.

She sat next to Leon, the church administrator and official council secretary ("I can't vote as secretary so it's not a conflict of interest with my job," he had explained at the first Council meeting). On her other side, Tracey, who was a phenomenal nurse at the local hospital, sat with all the treasurer's reports before her, making the copies into neat piles to be handed out.

Danielle Hubbard, who was an accountant and normally served as treasurer for the congregation, was on her first of two years as council president. She sat uncomfortably at the head of the table, the de facto spot for the president.

Rita, one of the congregation's matriarchs, sat across from Tracey. She had her readers on, their colorful beaded tether wrapped around her neck, but she still held the agenda close to her face. She'd been having eye problems since summer. Ara Grace had learned more about corneas from their conversations than she thought was purely necessary. Rita served as the vice-president of the council. The three of them—Tracey, Danielle, and Rita—had traded their positions every few years in a game of hot potato. Rita had served over three decades on the Council.

Rounding out the table was Sylvia, the church organist. Sylvia sat on Council as the head of the worship committee. Unlike Leon, she had never offered a justification for her potential conflict of interest.

"All right everyone," Danielle started, "I have 11:08 on my watch, and I officially call this meeting to order. We have a quorum. Whose turn is it to lead devotionals this meeting?"

Ara Grace glanced down at the agenda, spying Rita's name. "I think it was Rita," she said.

"No, no," Rita quickly replied. "I only do devotionals in June and December."

"But last month we said we weren't going to have a December meeting," Sylvia said, "and you volunteered to lead in November."

"Did I now?" Rita looked thoughtful. "People are saying Council's not doing enough. I don't know if we should take a month off."

Ara Grace quickly cut in, "I'll lead us in a devotional." *It is my job, after all.* She thought for a moment about what had been her main work focus the last few days, and how she could convey its spiritual significance. "Here's what I've been thinking about as we start Advent, the four weeks leading up to Christmas Day. Traditionally, each of the four weeks has a different theme: Hope, Peace, Joy, and Love. Hope for Christ's return and work in our world; Peace knowing God is with us, always; Joy in the unending presence of God; and Love, as demonstrated in God's love for the world." She paused for a moment and then asked, "Which of these four resonate most with you right now?"

There was an awkward silence before Leon, loyal as always, responded, "Joy. I met my baby girl's boyfriend at Thanksgiving, and he's a good man." He laughed to himself and added. "And he's a mortgage loan broker. Boring, steady. He'll be able to take care of her in due time."

Once the ice was broken, the others joined in. Ara Grace admitted to herself the feeling of pride, that this little group of church people who were used to formalities were opening up to her and to one another. She breathed the moment in, deeply. "Please join me in prayer," she concluded.

They continued, fairly uneventfully, through last meeting's minutes, correspondences, and various committee requests, before they got to her monthly pastor's report. Ara Grace was never clear on what exactly she was supposed to say at this time. A justification for her pay? A list of people she'd visited and spoke with confidentially? This time, though, she had a focus: "We had less than anticipated attendance at the Thanksgiving service. Last month, the members of Council were very clear that the service was critical. I'm wondering if that's actually the case."

Silence hung heavy.

Ara Grace continued, "I'm largely worried about the upcoming midweek Advent services. Are they actually important to people, or just a sentimental tradition?"

Rita bristled at that. "Tradition is what has held the faith together for millennia!"

"Yes," Ara Grace conceded, wincing a bit at her own bluntness. *I should've practiced this.* "But I want to make sure we're expending our energy in fruitful, meaningful ministries. I don't want to keep doing things just because they've always been done this way." She pointedly looked at everyone but Rita, seeking their input.

"It's always been done because it's worked!" Rita said. "If these young people would just put their energy into church where it should be…"

"It's no problem to me," Sylvia said, cutting her off before Rita could go on the predictable rant against changing priorities. "A midweek service is never a hassle. I'm used to Wednesday night choir practices as is." She looked at Rita. "For a few weeks, I think a midweek service isn't a big ask of our congregants."

Danielle looked to Leon. "Is making the midweek bulletin time-consuming?" she asked.

"No," Leon said. "It's mostly the same thing every year, with just a change in the readings the pastor chooses."

"If it's no problem to Sylvia and Leon," Rita concluded, "I don't see why we wouldn't have midweek Advent services."

And with that, the matter was settled.

Ara Grace felt disappointed, knowing they hadn't really addressed the issue of tradition versus practicality. But then she remembered the revolving door of pastors this church had had. Things like worship traditions had likely kept this congregation feeling united, organized. *I can't change things too quickly,* she told herself. *It's my first*

Christmas with them. And maybe, just maybe, if she took it seriously, if she poured her heart and soul into those midweek services, they would impact people's hearts. *If I give it my all,* she vowed to herself, *this year, they might remember the true meaning of Advent and not the traditional sacred cows.*

Once Ara Grace vowed to do something, she was like a dog with a bone; nothing could make her drop it.

Council's conversation quickly moved to the new business portion, which had nothing listed in it. "Anyone have anything for us to talk about?" Danielle asked.

"I have a quick one," Leon said. "Whose budget line do the battery-powered candles get charged against?"

Danielle looked down at the latest finance report. "Looks like the worship committee is under budget for the year. Makes sense to pull from that."

Sylvia, the head of the worship committee, agreed. "Yes, we never bought new music this year, and the candles are for worship."

Ara Grace cut in. "Battery-powered candles?"

"For when we sing 'Silent Night' and light the candles," Leon clarified. "Last year, our pews had a lot of wax droppings. Looked like pigeons had gotten in there." He laughed.

"We had to go through with irons connected to extensions cords, ironing wax paper over the candle droppings to clean it up," Danielle added. "It was such a pain."

"And it's not very safe," Tracey added. "Every Christmas Eve, I hold my breath that no one's hair catches on fire."

"That'd beat all," Rita said, shaking her head.

Ara Grace was incredulous. "You want to use battery powered candles on Christmas Eve?" She looked around the table, searching their faces for doubt. Where would the magic glow be? The beauty of one passing the light to another, the physical symbol of how the love of God is shared?

"We decided that, yes," Sylvia said.

"But," Ara Grace interjected. "But, it's a tradition!"

Rita chortled. "Pastor, now who's sounding like an old lady?" she jested, good-naturedly.

Ara Grace shook her head. "I don't know about this. I hear you, Tracey, on the safety issue. And I can appreciate that the wax can get messy, Danielle. But will Christmas Eve really be the same with battery-powered candles?" She heard her own voice drip with sentimentality.

"We did say we'd try it out this year," Danielle said doubtfully.

"Maybe this year," Leon said, "we can offer both. Let the families choose if they'd like the real candles or the pre-lit ones. As a way of transition."

Heads nodded in agreement. Leon had such a natural way of bridging the gaps. Ara Grace tried not to be jealous of his natural social skills, especially when compared to her fledgling, and at times awkward, leadership style.

"You know," Tracey said, looking back down at the financials, "if we only order half as many battery-powered candles this year as we anticipated, we could save a few hundred."

"We could vote, as Council, on sending that saved money to the food pantry," Danielle offered. "Since Thanksgiving service attendance this year was low."

"Oh, I like that!" Leon exclaimed.

Richard will love it, Ara Grace thought. "That is a great idea."

"So, I need a motion …" Danielle continued, the formality of the meeting progressing to include the vote to purchase battery-powered candles and to donate the unused funds to the food pantry.

The meeting concluded. As Ara Grace gathered her things, she found herself smiling. The meeting hadn't gone half-badly. Her Council was thinking outside of the box on some issues, reaching out to the community in meaningful ways on others. *This Advent will keep moving their hearts*, Ara Grace said to herself, *further into Christ and the true meaning of Christmas. Even with some battery-powered candles.*

Chapter 7

One Too Many Kids

Triumph High School loomed over the town like a concrete giant. Built during Wyoming's own small population boom in the 1960s, the Brutalist architectural style was trendy in its time, but it felt to Johnny Tae like a weirdly shaped prison. The original building sat stately and rectangular, with additions sprouting from the sides like wings to accommodate the addition of science labs and a full-size gymnasium. These days, the high school was under-enrolled if anything, but it still bustled during passing periods and at three o'clock sharp when school let out for the day. The school's large, blacktop parking lot had struck Johnny Tae as unusual until Morgan explained to him that people could get a restricted driver's license as early as age fourteen out here. "Too much land and too few adults to get everyone to school," he'd said. "Probably crazy to think about fourteen-year-olds driving themselves to a city kid like you, but it's that or not going, in a lot of cases." The lot filled up early and Johnny Tae usually ended up walking nearly a quarter mile to the one broad entry door of the school each morning. Fine in nice weather, but he was going to need to start bundling up for the morning hike.

This cold Friday morning, Johnny Tae shoved the front door open against a gust of wind, hair frozen into tiny spikes of ice since he'd run out the door before fully drying after his shower. He hurried through the entryway, ignoring the staff's greetings, and scurried past a larger-than-life banner reading "GO TRIUMPH TITANS!" left over from the last game of the football season just before Thanksgiving. He turned down the hallway where his locker stood, a four-inch-wide oasis in a sea of blue metal. He kept some favorite snacks on the top shelf: two packs of Pocky sticks, chocolate and matcha, one big resealable bag of peanut butter M&Ms, and a bag of Cheerios. The bag of cereal was a habit leftover from boarding school, where he often squirreled away cereal from the dining hall to eat later, back in his dorm room. Cereal and school just belonged together, in his mind. Laela and Sarah often stopped by his locker to grab a handful of snacks before heading to class. This morning was no different. As he did his best to stuff Morgan's loaned parka into the slim metal cage, the two girls approached, already rid of their coats and carrying their backpacks and water bottles. "It helps if you fold it up first," Sarah said helpfully. "Parkas like this like to puff back up unless you squish them in an organized fashion." Johnny Tae laughed at that. Squished in an organized fashion. *Only in Wyoming.*

But he tried it, and it worked. "Thanks, Sarah," he said, "You could be a tourism agent for Triumph, you know. Getting people settled into winter here."

He watched Sarah's face tense almost imperceptibly. "Would be fun," she said, "except I'm getting the hell out of here after graduation. Going to move to California with my mom. I'll miss the snow but not the cold."

"You know that already?" Johnny Tae asked incredulously. It felt like everyone had a plan but him.

A ding like an elevator arriving sounded over the school's PA system. The morning announcements started, signaling that it was time to start moving toward their first-period classes. Madison, a member of the school's speech and debate team, was the day's announcer. "Good morning, Triumph Titans!" she began. "Today is Friday, November 29th. The cafeteria menu includes…" Hallway chatter drowned her out, but Johnny Tae heard Laela's quiet voice. "I could never do that," she said.

"Do what?" he asked.

"The announcements," she clarified. "I'd be terrified of everyone hearing my voice all over the entire school." She tightened her backpack strap.

"Not me," said Sarah. "Sounds like fun. I'm not cut out for it though. Don't have that radio voice like Madison. I'm hoping I'm cut out for something they need out in California. That's what junior year is for, right? Figuring all of that out?"

"Shit, you all are so far ahead of me." Johnny Tae exhaled, slamming his locker shut. "I'm a senior and I have no idea what's next." He tried to sound lighthearted, but he knew it was a losing battle.

"You mean you haven't started Dr. Brown's assignment yet?" Sarah teased.

Dr. Brown taught Senior English, and his annual assignment was the stuff of legends. Instead of having his students write a college admissions essay, which had been the traditional senior English assignment for years, Dr. Brown took a different angle. He called it the Personal Values Statement. Students shortened it to "the PV" and giggled at the double entendre. Dr. Brown didn't want them to sell their accomplishments or make a five-year plan—plenty of people would encourage them along that path. Instead, he wanted them to consider what mattered most to them and formulate a set of values they sought to live by. It was meant to be a serious endeavor, but plenty of students brushed it off. Morgan told Johnny Tae he wrote something trite about teamwork and got a B+, so it didn't have to be a whole thing.

Except Johnny Tae was really thinking hard about it. He knew he could bullshit an essay, no problem, but Dr. Brown had gotten under his skin. Johnny Tae's mom, Hana, hadn't given him great examples of how to craft a life you can be proud of, and his dad, Jon James, had been too busy and halfway across the world. His grandparents were hard workers, but they were limited in their career paths due to immigration and education levels. Johnny Tae really wanted to think about how his life could be different.

"I, uh," Johnny Tae replied to Sarah. "I haven't exactly put pen to paper yet." They formed a small triangle, off to the side of the hallway.

"Better get going!" she teased. "What is it— two weeks till the due date, right?" The essay was always due the day before winter break started. At least he'd get a real break after he turned it in.

Johnny Tae felt Laela looking at him. He looked at her, making eye contact. *Don't look away*, he told himself. *It's normal to look someone in the eyes when talking.* Her brown eyes had such depth. He caught his breath. He was still feeling a little shy around her, unsure of where they stood. Or maybe just hopeful that something would happen.

Laela cracked a small smile. "Right now, I'm thinking when I write it next year, I'll say something about education."

Sarah interrupted with a laugh. "This just in: Laela likes school!"

Laela looked at her, her smile broadening. "Not just that. I love kids. Not sure exactly what personal values I'll write about when the time comes, but making life better for kids feels like something, right?"

"Seriously, you two are too much." Johnny Tae heaved a sigh and began walking down the hall, Sarah and Laela joining in step with him. All these interests and passions, so wholesome and earnest. He felt like a big fat zero compared to them. He flushed with shame, thinking about the way he had judged them when he rolled into town from the big city over the summer. He might have trendier clothes, but they were decades more mature.

"Speaking of kids," Laela said conspiratorially, "tonight's the first pageant practice. I'm helping out with the littlest ones and Morgan's going to be helping me. Last chance to join me!"

"Nope," Johnny Tae replied, at the same time as Sarah said, "Hell no!" At least he had that piece of clarity. He did not have the patience or the energy to work with kids. Even if it meant spending more time with Laela.

* * *

That evening, a cold wind whipped around Triumph, but you'd have been fooled by the heat building indoors. "Hey everybody!" Ara Grace called. "Attention! Hello!" Conversation roared around her in the fellowship hall at Good Shepherd. They'd agreed to rehearse on her home turf since she had a service to lead immediately afterward most days, but she was regretting that decision now. It would be impossible to just slip out the door when she was the one holding the keys. Ara Grace took a deep breath. Her first Advent in ministry. She could do this.

She called out one more time, "Let's come together, everybody!" No luck. There were so many more kids than they'd expected, twenty of them among a dozen or so families. It was a younger crew, too. Ara Grace had thought they would get a steady group of elementary school kids, a few younger siblings added in. They'd said ages three and up, but Nel had made the pitch at Victoria's preschool (which was part of Nel's church), and it was clear the parents had listened. The average age of the group appeared to be around four or five. Speaking part assignments were going to be tricky.

Ara Grace felt a hand on her shoulder and breathed a sigh of relief. Morgan. Crowd control. "Clap once if you can hear me!" he shouted. A few claps. "Clap twice if you can hear me!" More than half joined in. "Clap three times if you can hear me!" The whole room was suddenly at attention. Morgan gestured as if to hand a microphone over to Ara Grace. She mouthed *thank you* and made a mental note to catalog this trick for later. Football, much as it pained her to admit, had its benefits, including learning to wrangle loud, rowdy groups.

The pastors had thought it would be a selling point to allow parents to drop their kids off instead of sticking around for rehearsal. "Parents need every extra minute during the holidays," Nel had pointed out.

Birdie had nodded in agreement. "Kid-free minutes are precious when you're trying to play Santa," she added.

Ara Grace had rolled her eyes at that. She had grown up in a house without Santa and lived to tell the tale, no scars to show. Now, seeing the room full of little ones, she understood that Nel and Birdie had been right, the parents did need space and time away. But their little group was ill-prepared for the result of extra preschoolers. *Thank God for Morgan and Laela.*

"Welcome to our first pageant rehearsal," Ara Grace began. "Who knows their ABCs?" A preschool boy with a neat-looking crew cut and a plaid button-down shirt immediately started singing the alphabet, loudly. "Thank you," she said quickly, before the whole room of kids joined in. "We won't sing them all right now, but we will be saying them as part of our pageant. We're telling the Christmas story through the alphabet. How cool is that?" Over twenty pairs of kid eyes looked at her, blankly.

An older girl, Ara Grace guessed maybe third grade, piped up sarcastically, "*So* cool." Oh, great. So they had kids-going-on-tweens here.

Ara Grace took another deep breath. *You've got this*, she repeated to herself like a mantra. The pageant practice had barely started, and she felt like she was losing control of the room. A sermon? Absolutely. A room full of adults ready to tackle a challenging Bible study? She could do that in her sleep. Even a group of teenagers with tough, unanswerable questions felt like a possibility. Ara Grace just wasn't a kid person. This all felt beyond her.

Birdie gracefully stepped in next to her. "We're going to start with some singing," she said cheerfully. "Let's gather up near the piano to get our pitches. Follow our big kid helpers, Morgan and Laela. Nathan, Isaac, stop that," she chastised her own sons, engaged as they were in some sort of staring contest.

The group of kids moved dutifully behind Morgan and Laela to the piano. Birdie nudged Ara Grace and whispered, "Why don't you and Nel do a little planning for this surprise crowd while I keep the kids busy? I know this is a lot more than we planned for." Birdie looked at Ara Grace, creases etching her face with concern. "You okay?"

Ara Grace smiled gratefully. "Yeah," she said. "Thanks."

* * *

Nel sat at a table in the far corner of the fellowship hall with Jessica, one of the young moms from First Methodist. The two women were sorting costumes that each church had brought. Stitched-together rectangles of rough fabric to serve as shepherd robes, three unique blue gowns for Mary, white shirts with cotton balls superglued haphazardly on it as sheep, a mismatched pile of crooks that a couple of the elementary schoolers had already used for a swordfight. The musty smell of the costumes combined with the general funk of the sweaty, wet boots the kids had kicked off as they came in. Nel felt a wave of nausea roll over her.

"And I told him, it's four presents only for the kids this year," Jessica chirped. "Something you want, something you need, something to wear, and something to read. But he wants to get them all this crap that I know I'm going to end up putting together and organizing and throwing away." She sipped from her water bottle. "Oops. Sorry Pastor, didn't mean to nearly cuss."

"You know I don't mind." Nel smiled. It was reassuring to hear that she wasn't the only one struggling with how to navigate the holidays with her spouse. "Jess, how are you handling this smell? It's suffocating me." She tried to sound lighthearted, but she was hoping they could open a window or something.

Jessica lifted her face, looked around, inhaled deeply. "You know, Pastor, I don't smell anything. You must have a super sensitive nose!"

Nel's stomach rolled, and not just from the smell. The realization hit her all at once with a force that nearly knocked her over, even though she was already sitting down. With both of her pregnancies, but especially with Victoria, the first clear symptom (after the carefully sought-after second stripe on the pregnancy tests the day her period was due) she noticed was a heightened sense of smell. It stuck out to her each time because normally, she had a strong stomach for that kind of thing. But both times when she was pregnant, all bets were off. It got to the point where if Jacques had eaten an especially garlicky dinner, she'd sleep in the guest room.

When *had* she last had her period? She couldn't remember. She excused herself to the nearby restroom, apologizing to Jessica and saying she must have overhydrated that afternoon, that she'd be right back. She leaned against the door, more walking through it than opening it, and collapsed onto the tiny wicker loveseat. Thank God for the strange habits of church women's groups, giving her a place to sit that wasn't a toilet seat. She took her phone out of her back pocket and scrolled through her calendar. She tried to remember what was going on a few weeks ago, a month ago. The last time she'd bought tampons was the same trip to Walmart as the trip to buy supplies for Hudson and Victoria's Halloween costumes. Which, as her Walmart app reminded her, was October nineteenth.

A little under six weeks.

Nel was as regular as a clock, thanks especially to a hormonal birth control ring. She thought back. Had she put the ring in after her last period? With all the chaos of that fall, Victoria's challenges with potty training and whatever was going on with her and Jacques. Shit. She had completely forgotten her birth control ring.

She scrolled through her phone calendar again. Sister Eunice's homework assignment of "have more sex" had fallen on what would have been the second and third week of her cycle. Her most fertile.

She felt a wave of vertigo, like the ground was shifting under her. In a way, it was. Nel didn't have time for this today. Or ever. She took a deep breath, filed this problem away for later, and prepared to stroll back out into the melee. She could smell the stench of the onion-scented boots without opening the door. She tried thinking of other possible reasons for her scent sensitivity—dry Wyoming air, perimenopause, stress,

She was nearly bowled over by a panicking Ara Grace, who pushed open the bathroom door. "What are we going to do?" Ara Grace asked in a frenzy. "It's too many kids."

Too many kids, Nel thought. *You got that right.* She took a deep breath and composed herself the way she always did for church. She smiled with the same energy she'd used when entering a patient's room during her clinical pastoral education internship at a hospital in Durham. Neutral, nonthreatening, and positive, even when something truly terrifying could be waiting on the other side. "Let's look at the script," she said serenely. Ara Grace softened.

They returned to the group, and it was as if Nel's calm had spread like a fast-moving virus; the room's energy shifted. Nel looked over to see the group of kids listening to Birdie, completely rapt. They began to sing. "Jesus our brother, strong and good!" Off-key and shouty, but absolutely joyful.

Nel and Ara Grace decided they would divide the kids into speaking roles and nonspeaking roles for the twenty tiny actors and actresses, allowing them to choose for themselves. Then, Ara Grace would take the older ones to practice the script, and Nel would take the ones too little for a speaking role and fit them for costumes. Morgan and Laela, happily leading exaggerated hand motions with Birdie, would divide up. Morgan with Ara Grace, Laela with Nel. They had a plan. Nel was good with a plan.

* * *

Laela looked over at Morgan, all goofy grins and cheesy dance moves. This was so much fun; she couldn't believe Johnny Tae and Sarah would want to miss out. It was chaos, sure, but chaos with a bunch of tiny humans who adored you unconditionally and nonjudgmentally. For her part, Laela was chasing down the littlest ones who didn't quite have the attention span to sit still in rehearsal. She used the best tool in her babysitting toolkit—calm-down time. When one of the preschoolers tried to run away, Laela gently scooped him up and set him in her lap. She took deep breaths and did a few stretches, and the little one mirrored her actions without realizing that's what he was doing. Soon, he was regulated and ready to join in the singing again. Helping the kids process their emotions and bring their minds and bodies back into the space felt like magic to Laela. She absolutely loved it.

Nel came in to announce to the group that after they practiced "Mary Had a Baby," they'd be dividing up into speaking roles and nonspeaking roles. "If you can read," Nel explained, "and you like talking in front of big groups, a speaking role is right for you." *Uh-oh*, Laela thought. They were about to be inundated by preschoolers wanting big parts without the actual reading skills to pull it off. She took a deep breath and got into her best creative babysitter headspace.

Nearby, Victoria was wailing. "But I wanted to read the letter V! V for Victoria!" Laela knelt down, took Victoria's hands in hers, and said, "Sweet girl, I'm sorry, you're not able to read the script yet. But what if you and your brother did V and H together? If he did the reading while you held the letter? Hudson," she looked at Hudson, who had rushed to his younger sister's side protectively once her tears started, "what do you think, buddy?"

Hudson grinned. Laela knew how much it meant to him to play the big brother role. They'd avoided another meltdown. Laela made eye contact with Nel across the room, and saw her eyes were filled with tears that Laela knew she'd never let spill over.

As parts were shuffled, fought over, and reshuffled, Laela and Nel joined back up with Jessica to find costumes in the right size and style. A pair of four-year-old twins made their way over to the costume table, giggling with glee. "We're going to be Mary and Joseph!" the sister declared. "That's wonderful," Nel replied. She found a blue pillowcase with head and armholes cut out and a rope for cinching. Laela brought over a green pillowcase and shepherd's crook. The two of them dressed the pair. Nel handed them a baby doll wrapped in a white scrap of cloth.

"Jesus," the brother cooed, grabbing the doll and hugging it close. His sister snatched it out of her hands, saying, "*My* baby."

Laela looked at Nel, who stepped in gracefully. "You can take turns, sweethearts. That baby is going to need a lot from both of you."

Chapter 8

Sunday of Hope

The organ trilled. Her congregants stood to sing the familiar words of the Gospel Acclamation as Ara Grace stepped into the pulpit. She took a breath, calming herself. She still had some nerves each time she preached. Her mentor had said if they ever went away, she probably wasn't preaching the Gospel anymore. She wasn't sure about that. Surely, at some point it must become familiar, but this Sunday, she felt more anticipation than usual.

Today's sermon was different from what she'd preached here yet. Instead of a close reading of the text, in which she went through the significance of what happened and why it mattered, she was venturing out into pop culture. Well, sort of. Americana culture, she corrected herself. Perhaps her Thanksgiving with Nel's family had swayed her, or it was life in this small town.

She read the Gospel, a teaching from Jesus as told by Mark about the end times. When the congregation sat back down, she found herself looking in the back corner where Johnny Tae sat.

"The end of the world," she began dramatically, "is now." That ought to catch their attention. A few looked at her curiously.

"Ever since the birth of Christ, we've been in the beginning of the end. It's like we're reading the long-anticipated final book in a series, and now, this moment, is part of that last book. We are waiting for the final moment when everything is finally made right."

She looked down to her notes to make sure she had the wording she'd carefully crafted exactly right. "A universal restoration of all that God has ever created. A universal restoration initiated by Christ."

She felt the congregation was following the sermon in a way they hadn't before. Their faces were engaged, they sat forward in their pews with their bulletins idly in their laps. Pastor Ara Grace went on to explain how the ending of all pain and sin, the universal restoration is a reason to hope.

"And 'Hope,'" Ara Grace said, "'is the thing with feathers / that perches in the soul.'" She continued, quoting the entirety of Emily Dickinson's poem. She looked up, having memorized the final lines, "Yet, never, in extremity / it asked a thing of me." She let the words hang in the air.

"Hope," she concluded, "gives without expectation."

The day's hymn, the communion liturgy, the final hymns all seemed to blur together. On this, the first Sunday of Advent, Ara Grace felt confident. She strode out of the sanctuary as Sylvia played the postlude. Uncharacteristically for her, she placed herself at the sanctuary doors, eager to hear their reactions in a receiving type of line.

The first few folks who came out shook her hand, thanking her for a "nice" service. Another few people said hi to her as they left. She noticed most of her regulars were heading directly for coffee hour, as usual. After waiting for a few more minutes, she followed the crowd, the aroma of coffee and the sound of chatter increasing.

Johnny Tae had staked out his chair closest to the donuts, his black coffee before him. Richard sat next to him with his own creamy coffee concoction in his hand. The two had a strange, budding friendship forming.

"Pastor," Tracey said, catching her at the coffee carafe, "that was a fun sermon you gave this morning!"

"Thank you," Ara Grace said humbly. "It was fun to write."

"Do you remember, Tracey," Rita started, standing beside Ara Grace to add some sugar in her coffee, "when that retired pastor who did pulpit supply for a year used the same poem?"

"That's right!" Tracey said. "I couldn't remember if it was him or the summer intern we had."

"No," Rita frowned. "She used T. S. Eliot a few times."

Tracey nodded as Ara Grace's heart sank.

"But Pastor," Tracey said, placing her hand on her arm, "We've never had someone use it for Advent!"

Somehow, the sentiment fell short. Ara Grace smiled. "Great literature is timeless," she said, "and is always teaching us." *I sound like a wannabe sage.* She shook her head. *Next week, I'll do something completely new. For their sake.*

* * *

At First Methodist, Nel sat attentively in her seat on the chancel, just behind the pulpit. She was grateful not to be on full display; she was wondering now whether she was coming down with something. Her sensitivity to smell had stopped, so her pregnancy fears had waned. She dismissed that brief terror at the pageant rehearsal as misplaced fear of more than anticipated kids.

Still, she just couldn't shake this feeling of exhaustion. Her eyes drooped every few minutes, and she sipped water from a discretely hidden glass as she willed her eyelids to stay open, just for one more hour.

Her face was only visible to a few congregants on the far-left side of the sanctuary, but she could see around the pulpit to sneak a peek at the pray-ground, an area with coloring books and crayons and quiet toys and noise-canceling headphones. It had been Laela's idea; Nel had enlisted her to help Jacques with Victoria during worship over the summer for a few Sundays so he could "actually worship one of these days." Laela had discovered a blog post about pray-grounds and making worship spaces sensory-friendly. Nel had given her a budget, from their personal family account, and told her to run with it. Laela had created a gorgeous, inviting space that Victoria couldn't wait to enjoy. Nel paid Laela for the Sundays she'd been promised a babysitting gig, plus extra for her creative genius, and then told her she'd worked herself out of a job: Victoria no longer threw screaming tantrums when Jacques stopped her from running circles around the sanctuary. Her daughter, with her rat's nest of untamable curly hair, donned a pair of hot-pink noise-canceling headphones during the entire service, and spent most of the time in the pray-ground, at the child-sized table, coloring intently, actually seeming to pay attention. The pray-ground had been a game-changer.

The organ prelude concluded and Nel stood confidently, taking a deep breath. "This is the day that the Lord has made," she began, "let us rejoice and be glad in it! Welcome to First United Methodist Church of Triumph on this first Sunday of Advent. You are welcome here. Not just the put-together version of you. Your complexity, your messiness, your longings, your foibles—we invite the full you into this space to encounter God and one another in community. In Psalm 62, we read, 'For God alone my soul waits in silence, for my hope is from God. God alone is my rock and my salvation, my fortress; I shall not be shaken. On God rests my deliverance and my honor; my mighty rock, my refuge is in God.' Friends, let us find hope, deliverance, and refuge together."

Nel surveyed the sanctuary. She saw the group of twenty-somethings who had recently begun attending together, seated behind Karen and Shirley, two women in their nineties whose husbands both had died in the past year. The two recent widows were weathering this difficult season thanks to one another's friendship; even though they'd both attended First UMC for decades, it took their husbands' deaths to really spark a friendship. The pair had even switched pews to sit together. Nel noticed Pamela, the leader of the women's circle, sneaking in the back a few minutes late. Nel knew she had been bustling around the Fellowship Hall preparing the snacks for coffee hour. In the pew just behind the pray-ground, Jacques sat serenely, Hudson on his right, flipping through a hymnal, Victoria snuggled up on his left in her now-signature hot pink headphones, silicone pop toy in hand. Everything that was important to her was laid out in one place. Maybe she, too, would find a way through this season after all.

*　*　*

Birdie looked out at her congregation, feeling the affection that always welled up in her when she began the communion liturgy. Something about the ritual always made her choke up, no matter how many hundreds of times she experienced it. Birdie's spiritual sensibilities could have found a home in lots of different denominations, but the Disciples of Christ, where she had grown up, was the only one of those that celebrated weekly communion. The warmth and fellowship of gathering around a table felt earthy and a little mystical to Birdie. The symbolism of Christ giving himself to us so that we might give ourselves to one another was the root of her hope for humanity and the planet. And in her congregation, the elders—lay leaders who shared officiating responsibilities at the table—wrote their own prayers. It was a fantastic opportunity for real-stakes theological teaching for adults. To Birdie, it all felt like such a treat.

Gertie was assisting today. Her permed, snow-white hair formed a halo around the top of her head, mouth held in a soft, serene smile. She wore her signature pink, knit Afghan. Gertie had grown up Catholic and had considered joining an order of women religious. The structure, order, and purpose had attracted her need for clarity. Instead, she met her husband, Harold, a charmer with a penchant for controlling the people around him and an enthusiasm for a good whiskey. Harold and Gertie had four children, each as different as the four directions of the wind. Their only collective goal was to escape their father's iron fist. Now grown, the children lived in far-flung cities across the world: San Francisco, Austin, Berlin. Their eldest, Audrey, had settled in Seattle, so at least one lived relatively nearby.

Harold had died of a heart attack some twenty years ago, the week after they moved their youngest, Solomon, into his dorm room at the University of Wyoming. Solomon was terrified that the stairs and his moving boxes had done his father in, and had told his mother this over a moment of weakness. "No, Solly," Gertie had reassured him, speaking what had been a hard truth to conceal for the first time. "Your father's been stressing his heart with his temper and his drink ever since I first met him. This isn't your fault, and don't you forget it."

In the twenty years since Harold's death, Gertie had come to life. Birdie had come to think of Gertie as a sort of Christian mutt— eclectic in her denominational affiliations. She left the Catholic Church of her youth and explored all Triumph had to offer in terms of religious life. She found familiarity and warmth at St. Thomas Episcopal Church, whose daily eucharist services she'd attended for years. Wednesday evenings during high holy times were spent at Good Shepherd Lutheran, where Ara Grace's many predecessors led midweek services. Gertie joined the women's group at First United Methodist, Nel's current church, and still considered herself a member of that Methodist ministry. She'd landed at First Christian right around when Birdie returned. Gertie loved having the leadership of a female pastor. The first time she was invited to serve as an elder and stand at the communion table, she felt like she was being given the best gift she could ever ask for.

That Sunday, Birdie knew what prayer Gertie would say to bless their shared meal. Unable to shake her high liturgical roots, Gertie used the same prayer over the bread and the cup each time she officiated. It was based on the Rite II service in the Book of Common Prayer, which she knew well from her Episcopal days. She had the prayer well and truly memorized. Dementia had begun to impact her daily functioning; her pies, which used to win awards, were now tainted by sugar-salt mix ups and she sometimes showed up for worship on the wrong day of the week. But she had not forgotten her prayer, the one her friends at First Christian had come to expect on the Sundays they saw her at the table.

"Holy and gracious God," Gertie began. "In your infinite love you made us for yourself, and, when we had fallen into sin and become subject to evil and death, you, in your mercy, sent Jesus Christ, your only and eternal Son, to share our human nature, to live and die as one of us, to reconcile us to you, the Father and Mother of all."

Gertie continued, nearly ninety full seconds of memorized prayer. She hadn't missed a single word. Her voice didn't falter for a moment. If her memory was a bit like her hair—slightly mussed and windblown, a little worse for wear—this prayer was like her fingernails, which she had professionally lacquered once a week. Beautiful. Perfect. Complete.

Birdie exhaled the breath she hadn't realized she was holding. Gertie was worse off most days than her father, but here she was, still leading worship and serving the church. There was life with dementia. A rich, fulfilling, meaningful life. Even a spiritual one. As Birdie served Gertie the elements first before sending her out to serve the congregation, she looked her in the eye and said, "Bread of life, cup of blessing."

Gertie smiled, eyes shiny with tears that her dignity would not allow to fall. "Amen, Pastor. Amen."

Part 2

Peace

Chapter 9

Chaos of the Highest Order

Birdie pulled her red pickup into the church parking lot and sighed deeply. It had already been a long morning, but her dashboard clock read only 9:02. The twins had decided today was the day to test out Mark's cans of shaving cream, and they'd filled the sink to the brim before abandoning their science experiment. Sarah had worked a late shift the night before—*too late for a girl her age*, Birdie thought—and had no patience for a clogged sink when she needed to get ready for school. The screaming had been ear-splitting. The arguments had been never-ending. The mess had been … Well, that would be cleaned up later today.

After she took the keys out of the ignition, Birdie tried her best to channel her non-anxious presence. She closed her eyes, breathed in, and let the air out slowly through pursed lips. She prayed the Serenity Prayer: *God, grant me the serenity to accept the things I cannot change, the courage to change the things I can, and the wisdom to know the difference.* Reinhold Niebuhr wasn't her favorite theologian, but she could always go for some good recovery wisdom. *God, if you could make me even-tempered today, that would be nice too*, she added spontaneously. Just as she reached for the handle on her car door, she felt her cell phone vibrate. It was a text from Greg, the church musician.

GREG: YOU AREN'T ASKING PEOPLE FOR MONEY, ARE YOU? GERTIE CALLED SAYING YOU'D TEXTED HER ABOUT SOME EMERGENCY.

Greg was about Birdie's age, which is to say, young enough to have heard of text phishing. Birdie had first encountered it happening to pastors the past summer from Ara Grace, whose young female colleagues across the country had commiserated in their online group when, one by one, it started happening to them. Someone would get their hands on the church directory and start texting members, pretending to be the pastor, spinning a yarn about a crisis, and eventually asking them to send money or gift card information to some online account. Birdie knew she was lucky to have avoided this so far; so many of her members were not tech-savvy enough to navigate something like this. *Even-tempered*, Birdie reminded herself as she quickly typed a text message back.

BIRDIE: DEFINITELY A SPOOF, NOT THE REAL ME. COULD YOU SEND ME THE EXACT WORDING OF THE TEXT WHEN YOU GET A CHANCE? DID YOU RECEIVE THE SAME ONE?

GREG: SPOOKY TIMING, JUST DID. HERE IT IS

GREG: HELLO, IT'S PASTOR HEATHER, I NEED TO SPEAK WITH YOU URGENTLY ABOUT A SENSITIVE CHURCH MATTER—

GREG: THEY GAVE THEMSELVES AWAY INSTANTLY WITH THE "PASTOR HEATHER" THING

Birdie smiled wryly. A small piece of good news, and one of the benefits of going by a nickname.

BIRDIE: THANKS. WHY DON'T YOU CALL GERTIE AND MAKE SURE SHE DOESN'T SEND HER LIFE SAVINGS AWAY? I'LL GET MARTHA TO SEND AN E-BLAST. MUCH APPRECIATED, GREG

GREG: YOU GOT IT

Accept the things I cannot change, Birdie repeated, almost like chanting a mantra. *Accept the things I cannot change.* She stepped down out of her truck, placing her phone in her back pocket. She walked into the building, leading with her trademark calm exterior, trying to coax the calm inward.

There was no calm inside First Christian Church of Triumph. Martha, the long-faithful office administrator, grabbed Birdie as if she were a life preserver and Martha was drowning. Birdie had barely entered the office suite.

"Pastor!" Martha gasped, holding onto Birdie's arm. "I don't know what we'll do ..."

Birdie smiled, thankful for Greg's forewarning text. "It's okay, I already heard from Greg." Just then a glaring mechanic clunk sounded behind her. Birdie turned to see multiple lights flashing on the church's one printer.

"Greg already knows?" Martha nearly gasped. "Is it because it's Wi-Fi connected? All this new technology, I can't keep up."

Birdie felt the buzz of her phone against her backside. She still had her coat on, her work bag slung over her shoulder, and her purse in her hands. She looked around for somewhere to place the items.

"It just happened so fast, I didn't know what to do," Martha continued. "I tried restarting the computer," she explained. Birdie felt her phone buzz for a second time.

She dropped her bag on the main desk, and set her purse haphazardly on it. Martha was still talking as she grabbed her phone, checking the screen.

A text from Jane, and another one from Larry. She heard a thunk, and vaguely saw her purse fall to the floor, its contents spilling onto the floor.

Martha clicked her tongue, horrified, as Birdie opened her messages.

JANE: LOOKS LIKE YOU'RE BEING SCAMMED. UNLESS YOU GO BY PASTOR HEATHER NOW?

LARRY: HEY WHAT'S THE SENSITIVE MATTER? SOMEONE DIE OR GET ARRESTED? IN WORK MEETING, CALL YOU IN A FEW

This scammer works fast.

"Pastor," Martha chided Birdie out of her reverie. "You shouldn't leave your purse on the floor! My mother always said it means you'll have no money!"

Before Birdie could even reply to Martha, Jane, or Larry, her phone started to ring. Gertie's name flashed on the screen.

Birdie slid the "accept" button, "Gertie?" she said as a hello.

"Good morning, Pastor, I'm sorry to bother, especially when you're having an urgent matter …"

"No, Gertie …" her phone buzzed with another text.

"But I just spoke with Greg, and he said something about you being spooked? I wanted to talk with you about why?"

Martha was at Birdie's feet, gathering the spilled contents of the purse. She picked up a superhero action figure—Isaac's, Birdie recognized—and was getting ready to grab what looked like some used tissues.

"No, you don't have to do that!" Birdie said to Martha.

But Gertie replied in her ear. "Pastor, if you're spooked, I thought maybe I could help. With Harold sometimes…"

Martha had looked up at Birdie for a second before clasping her hand over the tissue. She crawled to pick up Birdie's wallet.

Birdie sighed. Martha's helpful stubbornness knew no bounds. She fell on her knees, shaking her head at Martha, grasping at the other detritus that had fallen out.

"No, no, Gertie, that's very sweet of you," Birdie said, "but I'm not spooked, I got spoofed." She tried to emphasize the "k" and the "f" sounds in the words. "Someone is pretending to be me."

"That's the urgent matter?" Gertie asked.

Birdie sat back on her heels, pressing her hand into her eyes. Her phone buzzed again, indicating a text. Please let it be from someone she'd already talked to.

"Gertie, no. That text wasn't from me," she said. Martha had grabbed Birdie's purse and held it open before her, bidding Birdie to drop her items. Birdie obliged, and continued. "Did you reply to that text?"

"Yes, and then you said to send money to a website or give you the codes to gift cards, that you were with a woman whose husband was deployed overseas and her kids were sick and they needed help with rent." *For the love of God*, Birdie thought, *this scam is pulling all the heart strings*. "But I couldn't get the website to work."

Thank God, Birdie thought sincerely. She saw Martha move toward the printer.

"Greg called me and said you were spooked"—*clearly, she didn't get the difference I was trying to enunciate*, Birdie thought. "I figured maybe the wife was threatening you."

Her phone buzzed for a third time. Birdie's shoulders slouched. She moved her feet out from under her, now sitting on her bottom on the office floor. The compassion Gertie had for others, her willingness to assist Birdie even in this fictitious scene, sucked all the anger out of her.

"Gertie, the person texting you isn't me," Birdie closed her eyes, leaning her head back against the desk. She spoke slowly and clearly, hoping the beeps Martha was making the printer emit didn't distract Gertie. "Someone—a scammer, a hacker, a bad actor—got our church directory and phone numbers. They are pretending to be me to get people to send money."

The phone line was silent for a moment. Then another. "Gertie?" she asked. "You there?"

"So, then the woman with the sick kid," Gertie said, "she's all right?"

Birdie audibly sighed, envisioning Gertie absorbing the information under her trademark Afghan sweater. "There is no woman. It's all made up."

"But why?" Gertie asked.

Because people will do anything for quick money. Because this person doesn't think anything of manipulating kind-hearted people out of their savings. Because so much of the world is hurting. "I don't know, Gertie," she answered truthfully. "But it's not true. Do not send any money or gift card codes." Her voice was stern. "I will never ask you for money over the phone or in a text."

She opened her eyes in time to see Martha squatting behind the printer. Birdie shut her eyes again quickly.

"I'm sorry, Gertie," Birdie focused again on their conversation. "It's all a scam."

"But you're okay, Pastor?" Gertie's voice was soft, dripping with concern.

Birdie smiled. "Yes, I'm all right." Her phone buzzed for a fourth time. *All right enough,* she mentally amended. "I'll see you Sunday, okay Gertie?"

"Yes, sure thing. See you then." Gertie hung up the phone before Birdie could end the call. Her screen showed four new texts, three from her congregants.

The lights in the bay overhead once blinked once before going out. She heard Martha mutter, "Now that beats all…" before she crawled out guiltily from behind the printer. The office was illuminated by windows to the outside and the remaining light in the hallway.

"I think I blew a fuse," Martha said by way of explanation. "I was trying to restart the printer this time instead of the computer."

Birdie leaned her head back against the desk again, searching for her inner calm. Her phone illuminated with a fifth text notification. She closed her eyes against it all, starting her prayer over. *God, grant me the serenity…*

* * *

"Thanks so much for coming in."

Nel and Jacques sat side-by-side in tiny plastic chairs, across an equally tiny table from Emily, First Methodist's preschool director. Emily gave them a polite but warm smile. Nel felt like she wanted to crawl out of her skin.

"Yes, well, short commute!" Nel quipped. Her office was just down the hall from the preschool wing. She looked over at Jacques and saw irritation flash across his face. *So we handle stress differently*, Nel thought defensively. *Let me have one stupid joke. A mom joke. That's a thing, right?* She reached toward him, laying her hand on top of his. He took her hand in his, wordlessly, without looking at her.

"I want you to know how much we love Victoria here," Emily continued. "She's creative and spirited and fun. We adore having her in our classroom."

There's a "but" coming, Nel thought. Emily had called this off-schedule conference— "during Advent, I know, I'm sorry Pastor Nel"—and wouldn't take no for an answer. Something was going on with Victoria at preschool. Something that couldn't wait until after Christmas or the new year. Nel had to simmer her deep instinct to defend her daughter at all costs.

"If this is about the potty training, I'm happy to come and change Victoria's pull-ups if she has accidents," Nel jumped in. "We're working really hard on it. She's just taking a bit to catch on."

"This isn't about the potty training," Emily said reassuringly. "We know Victoria is working hard on that skill, and we're able to support her in it. Though I may take you up on the changing offer. Sometimes, we can't spare a teacher to do it immediately when she needs it."

"Okay," Nel replied. "Done. Then what's the problem?"

"I'm curious what Victoria is like at home. What have you two noticed about her behavior and her moods?" Emily's face remained neutral, the same polite smile fixed on her lips but not touching her eyes.

"She's a delight," Nel said quickly. "Lots of energy, but isn't that every three-year-old? She and Hudson love to play together. They make a dynamic duo."

"Slow down a minute," Jacques interjected. "Nel, I'm sorry, *mi amor*, but you hardly see Victoria on a normal evening. Yes, of course she's a delight to us. She's our daughter and we love her."

Another "but" coming, and this time from my own husband, Nel thought bitterly.

"But she is also an enigma to me," Jacques continued. "She doesn't often want to play like Hudson did at her age. And her feelings are bigger. More expressive. My impression is that it's just the difference between boys and girls," he glanced at Nel meaningfully, "but I want to know what Emily thinks."

Okay, I'll give you that, Nel conceded in her head.

"We've noticed tantrums as well," Emily replied. "Victoria is very particular. In our experience, she's far more particular than our average student. We try to keep the kids on a routine, but things happen, as you know. If we have to stray from the plan for the day, we have a really hard time reorienting Victoria and calming the tantrum that always comes."

"Creature of habit, just like her mama," Nel said. Jacques shot her another angry look.

"What do you do when she has tantrums at home?" Emily asked.

"We have a calm-down space for her. Bean bag chairs and a breathing ball and all that." Nel had gotten the idea from Laela, who had seen it on an Instagram influencer's feed.

"And does it work?"

"Not generally," Jacques jumped in, before Nel could minimize again. "It is a challenge, no matter what we try to put in place."

The discomfort Nel was already feeling ratcheted up to the next level. This was their *child*. How could Jacques possibly be siding with

Emily over her, believing somehow that there was something wrong with Victoria, something that they couldn't handle themselves? They were Victoria's parents, after all—the ones who knew their child better than anyone. Surely, they knew what they were doing. Or ... at least better than some sterile education setting. Before she knew what was happening, tears pricked at the corner of her eyes. She resolutely refused to let them spill over. Nel was not a crier.

Emily pulled out a pamphlet with one hand and placed a hand over her heart empathetically. "Listen, I have a resource I want to share with you. It's called Early Intervention. Since Victoria is still three, she qualifies. It's a birth-to-three program. Call this number and let them know you want an evaluation. They'll come to your home, or here to preschool if you'd prefer, and get a sense of where Victoria is in her development. If there's anything that needs support, they provide it for free. She can get an aide here in our preschool classroom, or services at home to address the challenges you've been having. It's been a life-changer for so many of our students over the years."

Nel looked at the glossy pamphlet, primary-colored blocks stacked in a cheesy little logo advertising the Early Intervention program. Underneath it, she saw the logo for Early Childhood Special Education. *Special education? Seriously? That's what she's suggesting?* Nel closed her eyes, pretended she was in a yoga class, and breathed big, long belly breaths.

"Many of our families have an initial evaluation, learn a few tricks, and then discover their child doesn't qualify for services," Emily added. "But just in case there is something that could help Victoria out, I really recommend going for an initial evaluation. It's completely free to families and it all happens at home."

"Thank you, Emily," Jacques said, sounding sincere. Nel glanced over at him. He looked concerned, but peaceful. Resolute. Nel knew he would say he would call about the evaluation, schedule a time soon. Pretend to be reliable. And he'll have misplaced the pamphlet before Christmas rolled around, the call never made. But here, in front of Emily, Jacques would say the right things. Nel no longer believed his charm.

Nel felt like a failure. There was something wrong with her daughter that she hadn't wanted to see for more than a year, and that even now, she couldn't face. A sense of overwhelm filled her body. Another insurmountable challenge for her to face. She felt like she was drowning, literally flailing through water trying to breathe. She thought about the next family FaceTime, about her sister's perfect children, her mother's pitying looks. *Maybe I don't have to tell them about this at all*, she thought fleetingly.

"See you in an hour at pickup!" she chirped. "Jacques, honey, I've got to run. Talk later?" She rushed back to her office before Jacques could corner her for a conversation, leaving him to walk home alone.

* * *

Books were strewn across Ara Grace's office. She had used the small professional expense budget her congregation afforded her to buy a bunch of Advent resources, and now none of them felt right. She had hoped the Wednesday evening services could be a place to play with new ideas and fresh possibilities, but she feared the attendance would be lower than at the pitifully-attended Thanksgiving service. *Christmas has taken over Advent, even here*, she thought bitterly. She gathered the books into a pile, paging through the one on top, a small pamphlet published by a very cool group of young Lutheran pastors. The pamphlet offered liturgy "for busy pastors who want to see the church transform." They clearly imagined a much more competent pastor than Ara Grace. She was not nearly cool, competent, or trusted enough to pull off these edgy liturgies. She was the fresh young city pastor out in the country, and she couldn't even bring "city culture" to them without feeling like a fraud.

She set the pamphlet down, stood up, and stretched, her button-down shirt untucking from her Dockers to expose a thin strip of skin. She quickly shoved her shirt back in and ran her hand through her hair. This called for a field trip.

The sanctuary was dim, the only light coming from the weak, late-afternoon sun peeking through the stained glass, mixed with the garish glow of the multicolored lights from the church Christmas tree. Rainbow-colored shadows danced around the pews. Ara Grace still felt uninspired, but now she was uninspired in a beautiful space, at least. She sat down in the third pew from the front, left side—always her favorite spot at her seminary church home—closed her eyes and breathed deeply, wishing the artificial Christmas tree at the front of the sanctuary was real. Her members who owned the town nursery, the Hubbards—whose evergreens graced nearly every home in Triumph each Christmas—had tried for years to donate a live tree. But "some people" feared it would be a fire hazard and risk their church insurance, when in reality they feared the sap would stain the sanctuary's red carpet. Ara Grace wished she knew who these faceless people were so she could try to convince them otherwise, even if it wasn't really appropriate to have a Christmas tree during Advent. *What I wouldn't give to smell a little bit of evergreen right now.*

Ara Grace stood and walked to the back of the sanctuary, peeking in the storage closet. *Chairs!* The stacks of plastic chairs were usually reserved for Christmas Eve and Easter Sunday, rare overflow days when the pews would burst with members, former members, family members, and all kinds of people hoping to celebrate together. Today, in this season, she would use the chairs for another purpose. *Sort of the opposite purpose.* She hauled the chairs two at a time, dragging them up onto the chancel near the altar. She imagined an intimate circle sitting up on the chancel together, sharing communion sort of like a dinner church. *Jesus only had twelve disciples, right?* She thought. *Wherever two or three are gathered ...*

On her third round of gathering chairs, she found some resistance in the chair in her right hand. She pulled hard, then harder. The Christmas tree suddenly went dark, and Ara Grace heard a terrible jingle. The tree was tipping and would hit the ground in a moment. She reflexively reached out an arm, dropping the chair with a weak clatter and catching the tree just in time. It was a good thing the chrismons had been crocheted by a long-deceased member back in the 1980s. No glass to shatter and break, just yellowed, once-white Christian symbols to collect and hang again.

Ara Grace set the tree upright. She gingerly patted its prickly, plastic branches, then strung the cord back to the outlet, plugging it in. Nothing happened. She tried again. The tree remained stubbornly dark. *Shit. Now I've really gone and done it.* The sudden, violent unplugging must have shaken a cord loose. Or maybe she'd blown an entire fuse. She had no clue where to even check for a fuse box in the building.

Ara Grace felt heat spread throughout her body, adrenaline rushing through her veins. "It's a golden calf!" she shouted to no one in particular. Maybe to God. All the idols in this damn church. The carpet and pews were too precious for real wax and real trees, but their personal Wednesday evenings were too precious to spend even half an hour worshiping God in a new, meaningful way.

Huffing, she settled the chairs—eight of them now, probably more than they'd need—into a semicircle. She lay down on the lacquered wood floor of the chancel, staring up at the dusty ceiling fans. She took her phone from her back pocket, unlocked it, and started a new message, typing Leon's name into the "To" field. She stopped, her fingers hovering over the screen. Would anyone even notice if the tree wasn't lit? She turned her head left and right, took in the setting sun through the stained glass, and breathed deeply, locking her phone without drafting the message.

Back in seminary, their pastoral care professor had taught them a body scan meditation. "Good for folks experiencing chronic pain," Dr. Young had said, "or anxiety. Or for anyone, in those tough moments." Ara Grace started at her toes, focusing all her attention on how they felt, tensing them tightly, then relaxing. She moved through her legs, trunk, arms, and shoulders. When she got to her face, she could feel the clench of her teeth, the tightness behind her eyes. She scrunched her face up like a discarded piece of paper, crumpling herself completely. Then, finally, sweet release.

Chapter 10

The More, the Merrier

When the third new parent came by, begging whichever pastor was closest to the door of Good Shepherd Lutheran's basement to let their children take part in the program too, Laela knew the pageant practice that afternoon was going to be rough. Ara Grace was currently cornered by a mom whose three boys she recognized from her own neighborhood. Laela would have bet money that Ara Grace would hold the line; surely, Johnny Tae's aunt would be sensible, even if Pastors Nel and Birdie were pushovers. She watched in horror as Ara Grace smiled and nodded. "Of course!" she heard her say to the mom, spreading her arms out in welcome. "The more kids, the merrier! Just fill out this emergency form."

More kids? They were easily at thirty kids, and it was still a few minutes before the actual rehearsal start time. How many kids did Triumph have? There was *one* elementary school. Laela looked around, seeing Pastor Nel and Jessica, one of the moms, pulling out costumes again for the kids to try on. Birdie was near the upright piano, arranging music, with a few of the older kids helping her. Morgan was leading most of the rambunctious crew in a game of Ships Across the Ocean. She smiled, seeing Victoria in her bright pink headphones in the crowd.

Laela took this opportunity to beg for last-minute reinforcements. She pulled up the group chat with Sarah, Johnny Tae, and Morgan, knowing Morgan's phone was on silent. Her thumbs flew across her screen.

LAELA: HEY WE'RE SWAMPED HERE. KIDS
MULTIPLIED. PLEASE HELP?

She looked up in time to greet a returning family signing in, their
two kids running to join in Morgan's game. A reply already swished
across her screen.

SARAH: IF I DIDN'T GET TO HAVE THE FUN OF
MAKING THE KIDS, I'M NOT WATCHING THEM.
END OF STORY

Laela rolled her eyes. Sarah could be so vulgar sometimes.
Though they were friends, she wasn't sure if the two of them would
have reignited their childhood friendship if they'd lived somewhere
with more people. She was getting ready to type something about
how Sarah helped out with Nathan and Isaac all the time, when yet
another new family arrived at the door. Laela put her phone away,
smiled at the parents who each held the hand of a kid wriggling to
get free, and asked, "Can I help you?"

At this point, she figured she wouldn't waste any of the pastors'
time getting one of them over. They'd all said yes.

"We heard about what great fun the pageant practice is from our
friends, the Ulveins," said the mom. Laela discreetly looked down
at her list to figure out which kids were the Ulveins. "And we were
really hoping we could get our kids in."

"It's not too late, is it?" the dad asked. He had one of those
Bluetooth earbuds in and kept his sunglasses on, even though the
sun was already behind the mountains. "I mean, you've only had one
practice so far." He released his grip on his kid, who ran toward the
group with Morgan.

"No, it's not too late. The more kids," Laela held out her arm as
she echoed Ara Grace from earlier, "the merrier."

* * *

Practice was supposed to have started five minutes ago, but
Morgan saw another family checking in their kid at the door. Ara
Grace and Laela were positioned there, making sure kids were signed
in. He saw Ara Grace tell Laela something and gesture toward
Morgan and most of the kids.

Guessing that this was the signal to get the kids to start, he bellowed, "All colors!" sending the remaining non-stationary "seaweed" kids running across the small room. As predicted, all the kids were tagged. Laughter erupted from the group. "Okay, okay, if you're seaweed, I need you to sit down!" Every kid sat down, their socked feet either scrunched under them, sitting crisscross style, or out in front of them, toes still dancing from the fun. "So that's what smells in here … all the seaweed!" Morgan joked.

He saw Birdie and the older kids coming toward him. "Great, now I need you all to listen to Pastor Birdie while she tells us what we're doing next." The group dutifully turned their faces toward Birdie, who met him at the front.

Morgan walked discreetly away, or as discreetly as he could, being the largest person in the room. He met up with Laela near the end of the group.

"Thirty-seven kids at last count," Laela muttered to him. "Isn't that an entire football team?"

Morgan laughed softly. "Triumph was no-cut, so … depends."

Laela shook her head. "I texted Sarah and Johnny Tae for help."

At that, Morgan snorted, crossing his arms. "What'd they say?"

"Last I looked, only Sarah replied." Laela blushed thinking of the text. "You'll see it when you look at your phone."

"I think Johnny Tae is on tonight with Gavin," Morgan said. "But even if he weren't, I don't really see this," he gestured with one hand to the sea of kids before them, "as his crowd. He's more intellectual." *Like you*, he thought. Although Laela seemed to genuinely enjoy working with the kids, much to his surprise.

Laela nodded. "Beggars can't be choosers, right? Besides," she started as if she was reading his mind, "I didn't realize how much I liked working with kids until I had to this summer. Intellect is great, but you gotta do something with it eventually."

Just like brawn, he thought, unconsciously flexing his biceps. The longer time passed, the more he realized the part he missed most about regular football practices was the camaraderie built while honing one's physique. The endless hours in the weight room, pushing each other to lift more, squat more, do more … the time spent between sprint drills, gasping for air with others nearby … charging the sleds, pushing against them while teammates cheered you on.

Morgan still worked out at the local rec center. But without teammates working toward a shared goal, weight lifting had lost a lot of its allure.

He surveyed the room before him, the nearly forty preschool and elementary-aged kids seated, the three pastors, that mom—Jessica, he thought was her name—sorting costumes, Laela at his left, himself … this was his current team.

He smiled. *Not bad.* "Well," he said, clapping Laela on the shoulder like he'd done with his old teammates. She stumbled forward, her foot squeaking on the tiled floor to catch her balance. "Looks like it's just you, me, the pastors, and that one mom. Up against this mighty sea of kids."

He saw Laela scan the crowd for a minute. "That's a six-to-one ratio," she said. "We'd each be in charge of six kids."

At that moment, Birdie started assigning kids to spots around the room. "Fourth- and fifth-graders, you're going to be with me, by the piano. Where are my second- and third-graders?" At least five kids' hands shot up. "Great, you're going to go with Pastor Ara Grace over by the …" Birdie looked to see where Ara Grace was standing.

"Bathroom!" Ara Grace called out, helpfully.

Birdie tilted her head a bit, then echoed, "Bathroom. Right. But wait, not yet!" The first graders, a group of about seven, were assigned to Pastor Nel for their first costume fitting.

"Kindergarteners, you're going to go with Morgan," Morgan whooped enthusiastically at his name, "and you'll meet right here."

"The rest of you, go to Ms. Laela by the flag. Everyone got it? Ready, set, WADDLE!" Birdie called. She waddled like a penguin over to the piano, but the kids ran in all directions.

Laela counted at least eight preschoolers moving towards her, Victoria and her bright pink headphones one among a sea of wriggling toddler-like bodies. She grabbed Morgan's arm as he walked away. "I may have been wrong about that ratio."

Morgan threw his head back and laughed heartily. "Intellect isn't everything, remember?" He turned to look at his current teammate one last time. "You got this," he gave her a thumbs up and dramatically waddled to his group of kindergarteners, quacking.

Laela didn't have the heart to tell him penguins don't quack.

***

Ara Grace called her second- and third-graders toward her. "Quickly now! Sprint like a … lion!" she called over the tumult. She was learning some tricks and tips from this pageant experience. *Like how Birdie is consistently late in starting practice.* She glanced down impatiently at her watch. Practice was supposed to be ninety minutes, but they were just getting started fifteen minutes in. Her midweek service was just a flight of stairs away, she reminded herself. No need to panic just yet.

"Come on, little lions!" Ara Grace goaded. "Let's get together and …"

"Cheetahs are faster than lions," the kid nearest her stated. "Why can't we be cheetahs?"

Ara Grace turned her attention to a boy she remembered from the previous week as being difficult, but she couldn't remember his name for the life of her.

"Um, you're right, buddy," she said. "But lions have cool manes."

"Not all of them," he retorted. "Only the boy lions."

"That's not true," one of the girls said. "Girl lions grow manes sometimes. I saw it at the zoo." The girl had blonde hair and a snaggle tooth. Ara Grace instinctively looked towards Laela for confirmation on that science fact before realizing her group might as well be in a separate room from Laela's. *How did they have so many kids for this pageant?* she wondered to herself, a mixture of giddy excitement at the unexpected interest and a fair amount of panic at having to lead her own group of kids now.

"All right, fine," the boy said. "But if we're going to be fast, we need to be cheetahs. Not lions."

"Right," Ara Grace said, "well …"

"Why are we even talking about cheetahs and lions?" a third kid from the group piped up. Ara Grace wasn't sure which one spoke. "Aren't we supposed to be barnyard animals?"

She looked at her clipboard, trying to remember what roles this age group was assigned. "Actually, you all are shepherds."

The boy huffed loudly. "That's got to be the most boring job."

"Not true," the girl who channeled Laela's know-it-all attitude said, "the most boring job is …"

Certainly not this one, Ara Grace thought ruefully. "Thank you, but all our roles are important as we tell the story of Jesus' birth!" she chirped with forced enthusiasm. "Now, we have some new friends, so let's go around and say our names, okay?"

"Oh!" It was the voice of the third kid. Ara Grace turned to see a girl in jeans and a green and white baseball jersey with TRIUMPH written across the chest. "And then let's say what our favorite food is that starts with the same first letter of our name!" she said.

"Sure," Ara Grace said. "Everyone circle up, and let's see, do you want to start?" She looked to the third kid who'd suggested it, who nodded.

"My name is Bridget, and my favorite food is," Bridget fidgeted with the hem of her baseball jersey before answering, "Banana bread! With chocolate chips!" Bridget turned to the boy to her right. "Your turn."

"Her name is Bridget and she likes banana bread, my name is …"

"Banana bread with chocolate chips!" Bridget corrected.

"That's okay," Ara Grace cut in, "you don't need to say her name, too. Just your own."

The boy looked up at her, one eyebrow cocked. "But how are we supposed to learn each other's names then?" The circle nodded in consensus.

Because that will take at least twice as long, Ara Grace thought to herself. "All right, go ahead."

His name was Jon, and he liked Jell-O. Next to him was Jade, who also liked Jell-O, but she had to come up with something else, so she liked jalapenos. Then the group got into a lively debate on if that counted, since jalapenos made a "h" sound and not a hard "j" sound.

Ara Grace silently prayed for patience.

* * *

The older kids resumed their spots by the piano, arguing over which songs the little kids should sing and which ones they should sing. Birdie's two sons were partial to "Little Drummer Boy," while the rest of the group felt that was clearly a baby song.

Birdie's phone buzzed in her back pocket. She pulled it out to see her dad's name on the screen. He hardly ever called her; she always had to call him. "Hi, Dad," she said, turning from the bickering group. "What's going on?"

"Are you okay, Birdie?" Guy's voice was full of concern. "Where are you?"

She sighed, struggling to concentrate over the noise of all the kids. "I'm at Good Shepherd, Ara Grace's church. It's Christmas pageant practice and …"

"How was the hospital?" her dad cut her off.

"What?" Birdie was sure she misheard him.

"The hospital, you texted me yesterday to say you were at the hospital and needed help."

The scam! Birdie hadn't thought to tell her own father about the spoofed number, the hacker asking for money.

"No, Dad, that wasn't me."

"I know, you were with that Marine's wife."

"No, Dad, see …"

"I don't need to know the details," he continued. "I just want to make sure you got the money I sent."

Birdie's stomach dropped. *Not her dad.*

"How much did you send?"

"What you asked for. $200." Birdie closed her eyes, the argument behind her fading. Her dad was a mechanic. He'd worked his entire life. He was good at fixing cars, but not at making ends meet.

"Dad, I …"

"I just want to know that Marine's family got all they needed," he said. "The church came through for them, right?"

Birdie's mind quickly turned. Should she tell her dad he got scammed out of $200? Should she lie to keep him comfortable?

"I'll talk with you about this later," she said, opting for the easiest way out. "I need to get back to the kids and practice."

"I won't keep you," he said, jovially. "I just thank God that woman found you and our church. With all the people out there who'd love to take advantage of this poor family for their own good …"

As his voice trailed off, Birdie felt her heart shatter. "I'll talk with you later, Dad, okay? I love you. Don't send any more money, even if I ask for it." She hung up before he could question her.

She walked back to her group, now figuring out if "Angels We Have Heard on High" was too difficult for the first graders, who were the angels, to sing. "It's not a baby song," Isaac was saying, "but it's not super hard. Not like something we can handle."

Birdie didn't know what she could handle anymore.

* * *

Nel ignored her headache as she had the kids line up from tallest to shortest. "This will help us find the best costume for you," she explained. She was surprised to see her own son, Hudson, was the tallest. When had he grown so tall? She saw the hem of his pants hit just at the top of his sneakers. She rubbed the growing headache, thinking of how she needed to get him new pants before Christmas. *And update the grandparents on his new size, assuming they haven't already shipped the packages out.*

The shortest, a boy she remembered from Hudson's class at school, stepped forward. "Mrs. Pastor?" he said.

"Pastor Nel," Jessica corrected him, handing him the smallest set of angel wings they had.

"Mrs. Pastor Nel?" the boy said again. "My tummy hurts."

Nel looked at him critically. His face was flushed and his skin pale. He had been playing roughly with the other kids and Morgan at the start of practice. "Do you need some water?" He nodded.

"Here, let's go to the water fountain. Mrs. Nicholson? Can you handle this for a minute?" Jessica was already on to the second shortest, giving the girl a harp and halo.

Nel and the boy walked across the room, nearing Ara Grace's group. They were in a circle introducing themselves by name and a food, it sounded like. Nel smiled approvingly at Ara Grace.

"There you go, sweetheart," Nel said, pointing to the water fountain between the bathrooms. "Drink up."

"My name is Pastor Ara Grace," she heard her friend say, before a chorus of kids shot her down. "You have to say *all* our names!" one girl cried.

"And all our foods!" a boy yelled out. "Don't forget Walter likes Waffles Soggy, not Soggy Waffles 'cause …"

Nel's stomach turned at the thought of soggy waffles. Too much sweetness, and that texture. She felt her tongue get thick and dry.

She'd grab a swig from her water bottle near the costumes when they got back.

Her boy stopped drinking, wiped his face on his sleeve, then turned around and came back toward Nel.

"Better now?" she asked, placing her hand on his shoulder.

"Not really," the boy said, then clutched his stomach. "My tummy really hurts." He started coughing.

Nel gently patted his back, thinking he had swallowed some water wrong. Then the boy gave a mighty heave, doubling over.

Nel quickly learned his snack before practice had been purple grapes and what looked like pretzels.

The boy heaved a second time, spewing more acidic bile and food remnants. Nel kept her hand on his back, but turned her head and shut her eyes. "It's okay, sweetheart," she said, summoning up her maternal compassion. Her own stomach churned. Her mouth felt like cotton.

"Sick!" One of the kids from Ara Grace's group yelled. Nel opened her eyes to see Ara Grace herding her kids away from Nel and the boy.

The boy chose that moment to stand up straight. He looked at Nel. "Mrs. Pastor?" his voice was high and wobbly, on the verge of tears. "I don't feel so good." He held out a hand to her to hold.

Nel forced herself to look in the boys' eyes, and not at the luminescent bile on his outstretched hand. "It's okay, sweetie," she said again, stroking his shoulder. "We'll call your parents and ..."

The boy suddenly bent over, a third wave spewing from his mouth. He grabbed Nel's wrist as he barfed, splattering bile. Bits of partially digested food landed on Nel's boots and pants. His hand was sticky against her wrist.

Nel belched silently, tasting the bile rising in her own mouth. *Oh no*, she thought. The boy went for a fourth heave when she broke away, running toward the nearby women's restroom.

She vomited into the trash can, making it just in time.

* * *

Later that night, after her sanitizing shower, after the kids had gone to bed, and after Jacques had criticized her for having to see a congregant that evening, that whatever was happening could surely wait until her work hours tomorrow, Nel locked herself in the gas station bathroom stall.

She'd driven twenty minutes out of town, past four other gas stations, just so she could be sure (or at least, more sure) that she wouldn't be recognized.

She ripped open the box of the single pregnancy test. The easy-read kind she had used for when hoping and waiting for Hudson and then Victoria. The kind with the lines: one line for negative, two for positive.

Back then she'd thought of that second line as an equalizer. Once it appeared, once it was undeniably there, she and Jacques would see eye to eye. They'd work together to raise the baby they had both wanted. Back then, she'd prayed and hoped and wished for that second line. She'd imagined the tiny, impossibly adorable socks, miniature bow ties, and ruffled headbands she often saw at department stores. Her computer hid a secret spreadsheet detailing each parenting book she intended to read and when. *Ina May's Guide to Childbirth* as soon as she got a positive test, *Bringing Up Bébé* in her second trimester, *Dr. Spock's Baby and Child Care* when she got closer to delivery. There was a whole tab devoted to potty-training books (that weren't working for Victoria) and another filled with books about how to teach children to read. Nel had been filled with hope about what this next stage would bring for her and Jacques. Two lines equal a family.

Now, her prayer was reversed. Just one line, a subtraction sign. Nothing to add, nothing to equalize.

Her hands shook as she unwrapped the test, removing the stopper at the end. She squatted over the toilet, not willing to sit on its questionably clean rim.

She began to pee. From habit and memory, she maneuvered the test to get a clean sample without even looking. Keeping the test face down, she finished, then capped the end of the test so she could set it down on the toilet paper holder.

She pulled up her pants and flushed. *This is going to be nothing*, she told herself, willing it to be true. *Just perimenopause or stress.*

She put her coat back on and slung her purse across her shoulders. The entire time, the test lay flat on the toilet paper holder. Face down. Knowing, but not sharing.

Nel inhaled deeply, closing her eyes. The scent of urine and bleach filled her nostrils, making her head spin.

She turned the test over.

Chapter 11

Heart to Hearts

Ara Grace pressed against the church's door just as a gust of wind whooshed from behind. The door flew out of her grasp, banging against the usher's stand inside. *Shit, shit, shit!* she thought as the wind howled around her.

She scurried inside and quickly pushed the door shut. Her eyes were momentarily useless as they searched for light. The weak winter sunlight streaked in from the distant stained-glass windows in the sanctuary. A large, pyramidal blob stood draped in shadow—the broken pre-lit Christmas tree.

Ara Grace sighed heavily. Her work backpack felt heavy on her shoulder, cutting through her thick, puffy parka. Her scarf suddenly felt too tight around her neck, her hat too constricting. She dropped her bag with another loud clunk and ripped off the scarf and hat.

She was stuffing them in her backpack when Leon approached her from the office hallway. "Pastor!" he said, smiling. "I was wondering if you'd decided to work from home today."

It was closer to lunch than morning. "No, no," Ara Grace tried to justify her tardiness, "I just figured with all the evening work on Wednesdays …"

"Pastor," Leon interrupted her, stepping closer to her, "I didn't mean that to sound like I was judging you! I know you put the work in, and you have every right to work at home." His deep brown eyes met hers, and she felt the truth in his words. Sometimes, she felt like she was under the microscope, her every action judged and debated. She was grateful to Leon for the reassurance.

"Thank you," she said, unzipping her coat and leaning to pick up her bag.

"Leave that there," he said, gesturing to her bag. "I want to show you something."

Ara Grace loved Leon. He was a kind, caring person, and a dutiful and hardworking administrator. But she just wanted to read some commentaries on the upcoming texts for Sunday, get in some deep rabbit hole with Origen or another Ancient Church great, and come back up for air when she had the right, pure theology—the correct interpretation to pass on to her congregation.

Leon sensed her hesitation. "It won't take long, come on." He turned, fully trusting she would follow.

She shrugged out of her coat and walked in his wake. As he opened the doors to the sanctuary, Ara Grace started thinking through potential problems: The organ needed repair, again; the oil in the candles had run out; the paraments that draped the altar and pulpit were stained.

Leon walked straight to the artificial Christmas tree. Ara Grace stopped abruptly, still at least ten feet from the tree. Leon made a show of plugging in the Christmas tree. No results. "Weird, right? Do you know what happened?"

Ara Grace nodded, her voice even. "Yeah, yesterday, I was pulling up chairs for midweek, and a chair leg got stuck on the power cord …" She trailed off, but Leon looked at her, waiting for her conclusion. "And it must've wrecked it." After a beat, she added, "I'm sorry."

Leon tilted his head. "Why didn't you tell me?"

Ara Grace shrugged, embarrassed. "I didn't want to bother you."

"Pastor," Leon said, "we text each other irrelevant memes on a daily basis." This was true. She'd learned he had an affinity for cat, dog, and llama jokes, which she also loved, even if she didn't have a pet of her own. "Were you going to fix it, or just leave it dark for Sunday?"

She felt a bit like a kid in the principal's office. "Honestly, I don't know."

Once at home, she'd toyed with the idea of buying new lights, draping the tree in them, and using an extension cord to keep the tree lit so no one would know. Then she'd settled more toward playing ignorant at worship, should anyone even notice its outage. She'd chalk it up to an indication that the congregation didn't need more distractions this Advent season.

"Do you really think anyone would have noticed on Sunday?" She voiced the question at the heart of it for her. "The plastic tree is up, the chrismons are up, the star that Sylvia bought ten years ago at a garage sale is up. The tree is traditional, just like it's always been. Would the lights even be noticed?"

Leon smiled, and took a step away from her, moving toward the tree. "So, is that what this is about? Traditions?"

Ara Grace thought for a moment, then nodded once. "Stupid traditions, yeah. Golden calves. The ones that take away the meaning of the season."

"Ah yes," Leon demurred. "And the meaning of the season is?"

"God loved everything so much that God became a part of it, joined in Creation and specifically with the human reality," she instantly replied.

Leon nodded, thoughtful. "Human reality? Like traditions that bring comfort and joy to people?"

"Leon, you know what I mean," Ara Grace said dismissively. "The stuff that doesn't even have a theological reason behind it. The stuff of convenience." *Like the stupid pre-lit candles they insist on.*

"And yet God, the Great Creator, became a part of Creation, as illogical as that is, huh?" Leon said. He turned his back on her, walking to the wall. Ara Grace was glad he didn't see her face flush.

Leon knelt on one knee, looking at the outlet. He pressed something. From Ara Grace's angle it looked like he stuck his finger in the outlet. Then he again plugged the tree's cord in.

Lights instantly shone on the tree, shining through the crocheted chrismons. Even Ara Grace had to admit it was beautiful.

Leon stood up slowly. "It's a GFCI outlet, you just tripped the switch." He walked back to her, then stood by her side to admire the plastic, dilapidated tree.

"Pastor," he finally said, "let Advent and Christmas be what it is, as it is, to the people here. It might not be as broken as you think."

* * *

Birdie felt uncharacteristically nervous as she scrolled through her phone looking for Nel's number. She'd already ordered them both drinks; she couldn't back out now. Her phone had been thankfully quieter since the texting scam of earlier in the week. The benign coffee shop music played in the background, just audible above Gavin's drink prep. Birdie selected Nel's name, smiled at the tongue-in-cheek subgroup title CLERGY CHICKS, and pressed "call."

The phone rang twice before Nel answered. "Hey Birdie," she said cheerily.

"Hi Nel," Birdie began. "Are you at work?"

"Yeah, I'm just in my office, what's going on?" Nel sounded concerned.

"Oh nothing, I just was at Buzz Buzz Buzz getting a latte. And well, I hit my tenth cup so I got a free one, and I got you one, too."

"Birdie, that's so sweet, but ... Nel's voice trailed off.

"I'll be at your office in about five minutes," Birdie continued over Nel's protestations.

Gavin brought the two drinks on the counter, steam rising from the cups. He bent down to grab the whipped cream container and shook it loudly before hissing out giant swirls onto each cup. Some of the whipped cream splashed back onto his rectangular glasses.

Nel was sputtering some excuse. Birdie placed the phone on her shoulder to grab the two drinks, but Gavin caught her eye and shook his head. He brought out a four-drink carrying case and placed the drinks in opposite corners, then removed the gray glasses and wiped them on his purple apron.

"See you soon, Nel!" Birdie said, ignoring Nel's feeble protests and hanging up before the other woman could refuse her further. She reached out to grab the tray, but Gavin pulled it slightly away, placing his glasses back on his face.

"Did I just catch you lying?" he asked, a smile on his lips.

Birdie looked confused. "What? No, I *am* on my way over to Nel's."

"Right, but since when do you keep track of your drink cards?" Gavin's smile grew wider. "I know you have at least four different ones floating around in your purse."

She felt the heat rise in her cheeks. "Oh, that," she said dismissively, looking down. Birdie always struggled to remember where she placed the drink punch cards whenever she ordered, and besides, she got enough out of the coffee and wine house without needing any freebies. She inhaled, then met Gavin's eyes. "You know how Nel is, she'd never accept it if I bought it for her out of the blue." *And I need an excuse to talk with her.*

Gavin moved behind the pastry display, opening it from his end. "I can't go turning a pastor into a liar," he said, using the tongs to select a blueberry muffin and a craisin muffin. He placed them in separate pastry bags, then stuffed each in the remaining open drink spots on the carrier. "So here. Your loyal customer treats."

Birdie was about to argue, but Gavin put his hands up. "Nel needs this, Birdie," he said in a lower voice so the other customers wouldn't hear. "She's not been herself lately."

Birdie nodded. "Thank you, Gavin," she said, in gratitude both for the drinks and pastries and for his concern for their friend.

She turned, tray of goodies in hand. "Give her my love, Good Reverend Birdie!" he called out. Birdie turned around to see him wink widely at her, just as the robotic frog sentry at the door ribbitted her departure.

* * *

Nel glanced around her office, trying to find something out of place for her to organize before Birdie's drop-in. Her anxious energy needed to be channeled into something, anything, to keep her mind off the thousands of fears running through her head.

She settled on rearranging some of the Bible commentaries on her bookshelf. They were organized in biblical order, so the thick commentary on the Twelve Minor Old Testament Prophets wedged right before a slimmer commentary on the Gospel According to Matthew. Her fingers trailed along the spines, trying to find one out of place. The hefty book explaining each of Jesus' parables caught her eye. It was positioned between a slim volume on Revelation and a generic Bible dictionary. It should be closer to the Gospels, since all of Jesus' parables were in the Gospels. She pulled the book off the bookshelf, thumbing through its pages.

She'd lost herself reading about Matthew's version of the Parable of the Sower when Birdie knocked on her open door.

"Hi Nel," she said, carrying an entire tray of drinks and pastry bags.

Nel set the still opened book down and rushed over to her. "Birdie," Nel said, "let me help you with that."

Birdie handed her the tray, then rubbed her hands together. The cold seemed to follow her in, its fingers reaching out from the shadows of her down parka jacket. "One of those is a peppermint mocha, and the other one is a regular mocha." She unzipped her coat and hung it on the coat rack next to the door, carefully closing it behind her. "You can pick which one you want, but I'm taking the craisin muffin." Birdie settled herself into one of the two corner chairs and looked up expectantly to Nel.

Nel stood above her friend, the tray balanced in her hands. "Um …" she started, looking awkwardly at the tray, avoiding Birdie's eyes.

"Just set it down in the middle, we'll figure out which one's which." Birdie motioned to the coffee table between the two chairs. She looked around the room. "Nice office, Nel! I've never been in here."

Nel set the tray down and folded herself into the empty chair nearby. She crossed her legs, angling them away from Birdie and back toward her dark walnut desk. She grabbed the nearest latte, opening its lid and sniffing. "Peppermint," she said definitively. "You want it?"

Birdie waved her off and grabbed the other latte. "No, this is the one I wanted anyways." She took a sip, then reached for the nearest pastry bag. "Here's yours. Blueberry."

Nel took the outstretched offering. Her stomach turned at the thought of the soft blueberry muffin speckled with walnuts. Mixed textures. She kept the bag closed, placing it in her lap. Nel blew on the still opened latte.

"Not a blueberry fan?" Birdie asked. "You can have the craisin if you really want it."

Nel shook her head. "No, I'm not really hungry right now."

Birdie frowned, then inhaled loudly. "Okay, I'll get to the point. Nel," she started, "What's going on?"

"What do you mean?" Nel asked, holding both hands around her latte. "I'm fine."

"Are you though?" Birdie looked pointedly at her. "You've been … off." She sipped her latte, adding. "You seem more tired than I've ever seen. And did you puke yesterday after the youngest Ulvein barfed? You ran into the bathroom and were there for quite a while."

Nel was silent, debating whether to refute the evidence or come clean. Birdie picked up her latte without breaking eye contact. "I overheard Hudson telling Jessica you puked the other day, too."

Nel looked away, embarrassed to have been tattled on by her own son. "My stomach has been weak recently." She tried to smile, but Birdie pressed on. "Are your kids okay? Are you feeling all right? Really, Nel. I'm worried about you."

You and me both. Nel sighed, heavily. "I've got a lot going on." The issues with Jacques. The next, never-ending uphill battle she was now going to face with Victoria having "Special Education" stuck to her educational career. The town's Christmas program. Her upcoming Christmas sermon. The pregnancy test. She shook her head, unwilling to go there herself.

In the silence, Birdie opened the other pastry bag, tearing off a piece of the craisin muffin. "Want to talk about it?" she finally asked.

Nel knew Birdie was genuinely offering. If she declined, Birdie wouldn't push, and if she accepted, Birdie wouldn't gossip. She felt tears sting the corners of her eyes. "I don't … I don't even know where to begin."

Birdie placed her hand on Nel's shoulder. Nel could pick up the faint, sweet smell of craisin on her hand. "Whatever's heaviest."

Nel shook her head. "Look, I am not ready to go there," she said. "I appreciate it, Birdie. But that's something I need to figure out on my own." *Without Jacques knowing.* Remembering him, Nel ventured, "Have you ever done couple's counseling?"

Birdie nodded. "When we first were getting married, and then again when the boys were about three." She smiled, ripping off another piece of the craisin muffin. "They always say it's the terrible twos, but for us, it was the terrible threes. That's when Isaac wasn't able to do all the things that Nathan could, and part of that had to do with his vision. We had to drive over an hour one way to get to the pediatric optometrist."

Birdie seemed momentarily lost in thought.

"Jen made her 'trip' out to California permanent around then, leaving Sarah with us full-time, but she wouldn't pay any child support.

So, we had some legal issues to contend with. And Sarah, she was about ten but she was already sixteen in her mind. Strong-willed, one hundred percent girl, just like now."

Birdie laughed a bit before continuing. "Between just keeping up with the appointments, the attorneys, the clothes, the childcare, blending three kids into one family, and our jobs, Mark and I didn't have time for each other. Except to fight."

She ate some more of her muffin, chewing thoughtfully. "Mark didn't want to do marriage counseling the second time around. By the time he was in couple's therapy with Jen, they were already done. He worried it was a sign that *we* were already done. But I promised that wasn't the case, and because we had done a bit before we got married, we were both able to admit that how our marriage was at that time wasn't how we had imagined it to be."

Nel was thankful she had, at that moment, reached for her latte so that she wasn't looking Birdie in the eyes. What her friend was saying was so much part of what she was feeling. When she married Jacques, their plans of a wedding, family life, and marital bliss consisted of one adventure after another. He'd wanted to travel the world, a permanent nomad. She'd thought the idea of overseas mission work was what God had in plan for her future ministry. They both agreed to have their kids in the States, not wanting to experiment with prenatal care in other countries (on her part) and not wanting their kids to potentially be denied American citizenship (on his part).

But now, Nel wanted the permanence of a home. She wanted her kids to have a place they could come back to, a town that they'd hate and stretch against its confines until discovering the wider world to be a macrocosm of their hometown.

Nel wanted someone to share the monotonous routines of daily life and find adventure in them. Jacques wanted to escape from the everyday routine. He wanted newness, craved the turmoil of inconsistency, the chaos of uncertainty.

She had changed, breaking their agreement. *But who didn't grow up and take on the responsibilities of adulthood?* she thought bitterly.

Realizing Birdie had gone quiet, Nel returned her focus to her friend. "Thank you, I think that's a bit of what we're facing," she said. "Jacques and me. Life in a small town wasn't in our fifteen-year plan when we got married." She laughed, hoping Birdie couldn't hear the bite of sorrow it held. "But the problem is," Nel looked up, meeting Birdie's rich, caramel brown eyes, "I don't want the life we had planned. I want the life we have now. Or at least, the life I have now."

Birdie nodded, silent for a moment. "And Jacques doesn't, I presume?"

Nel looked away, shaking her head.

"I imagine you feel a bit like a traitor," she ventured. "Wanting what was supposed to be temporary, changing the script on the Calomino-Stone Life Plan."

Familiar tears pricked again at the corners of Nel's eyes. Birdie was *good* at this. Closing them, she said, "And that makes me the bad guy." A single drop escaped, falling down her cheek.

"Does it, though?" Birdie's question caught Nel off guard, and she glanced sharply up at Birdie. "Are we supposed to be the same person we were ten years ago? Ten days ago? Heck, ten minutes ago?" She frowned dramatically. "Because Jesus was born as a full-fledged adult, right? His first words were the Lord's Prayer."

Nel laughed despite herself. "No, they'd be the Sermon on the Mount, if you go by Matthew's account."

"Ah, but according to St. Luke, what about teenage Jesus saying he simply *had* to be in His Father's house? Chronologically, that'd be his first words, right?" Birdie playfully offered.

They both giggled, the mood notably lighter. Despite the brevity and mildly irreverent joking, Birdie's point was made: Change is part of the human condition. The truth of it made Nel feel slightly less like a traitor, and more like a normal, flawed human.

"It's called growth, Nel," Birdie said. "You can't grow into who God made you to be without change."

The two women sat and chewed silently: Birdie on her muffin, Nel on the potential mind shift before her."

"Thank you, Birdie," Nel said. "I needed this." She lifted the latte to her lips, draining it, hoping her friend understood her deeper meaning.

"And I needed this," Birdie said, pointing to the space in between them. She laughed at Nel's concern. "I know what you meant, don't worry." She crumpled up the empty muffin bag, moving to stand.

"You know, I'm happy to talk with you, anytime. You're not a chore, you're a friend."

They both stood, and Birdie hugged Nel tightly. "Thanks, Birdie. Same to you."

She helped Birdie grab her coat and walked her to the office door, saying good-bye. She returned to her dark desk with its familiar, worn pleather chair and noticed she'd left the commentary on the parables lying open. Nel picked it up, ready to shut it, when her eyes fell on Jesus' words, "If you have ears, hear!"

I'm listening, she vowed silently. *I'm not a bad guy.* She left the book open on her desk, relegating it to the corner by her desk phone, to serve as a visual reminder to keep listening.

Chapter 12

Breaking Dads

B irdie had set aside the day intentionally for hard conversations. As she walked from Nel's church to her parked truck, the wind whipping her curls against her face, she began to mentally prepare herself for the next one. She spotted her red pickup just up ahead, angled tightly between two other pickups. One was a large, silver oversized truck with extra wide wheels that sat outside the wheel wells. As she neared, she saw a pair of balls, dangling from a net, from the truck's trailer hitch. Truck balls. *If Isaac or Nathan were to ever drive home with something like that…* but Birdie wasn't sure how to complete the thought. In her mind, her boys were too young to reek of heavy, heated testosterone. What would the next five or ten years bring? She shook her head, vowing to deal only with what the current day had in store for her.

The big silver truck wasn't familiar to her. As she squeezed herself between her comparatively mini-pickup truck and the massive, well-endowed behemoth vehicle, she half-expected to see flames emblazoned along the other truck's side. She was disappointed, until she saw the rear passenger window had an etched American flag with, "IN GOD I TRUST. ALL OTHERS PAY CASH."

She unlocked her truck, easing herself into her cab, before closing the door promptly behind her. She'd anticipated wind, but the other truck's massive form must have been blocking the ever-present wind; the result was that she'd slammed her truck door. To any onlooker, she appeared angry.

Birdie's cab echoed in silence. She closed her eyes, breathing in the cold, the solitude, the tranquility. A prayer from Clement of

Rome came to her mind, and she mentally recited what she could remember: *Almighty God, reveal to us what we do not know, perfect us in what is lacking, strengthen us in what we know, and keep us faultless in your service.* She liked the petition's succinct nature, and its focus on knowing and not knowing. She was thankful for the time with Nel, and placed aside any lingering curiosity about what her friend was facing. Birdie focused her intentions on the paradox of knowing we do not know as she prepared for her next conversation partner … with her dad.

* * *

"Morgan, you home?" Charlie's question sounded like a play on the old, early family sitcom, where the patriarch arrives home after a hard day at the office, triumphantly hollering, "Honey, I'm home!" Morgan wasn't sure if his dad intended the joke.

"Hi, Dad," Morgan replied. "No work today, and at the gym, I did a short weight circuit."

Charlie shrugged out of his large, thick coat, hanging it on the same hook he'd used for decades. He looked at Morgan, sprawled out on the couch in sweats, phone in one hand, TV remote in the other. Charlie sniffed the air dramatically. "Either you barely worked out, or you showered."

Morgan responded with an eye roll. "C'mon Dad, I'm not that disgusting."

"Anymore," Charlie amended, throwing himself down on the couch nearby. "Remember when you'd have your two-a-day practices in the summer? You'd come home after a couple hard hours in the morning, throw yourself on the couch without even changing. And you'd pass out. Like a light switch." He snapped his fingers to make his point. "It was a smell that could wake the dead."

Morgan laughed. "Yeah, I was too lazy to change out of the shirts for afternoon practice."

"You weren't lazy, you were smart. By then, your mom was making you do your own laundry. Less changing meant less laundry."

At that, they both laughed. "God, I was a biohazard."

Charlie leaned over, untying his shoes. "Your mom swore you'd get jock itch one day."

"She was right, I did!"

Charlie looked at Morgan, wiggling his foot out of one shoe. "You never told me."

Morgan shrugged. "It was easy enough to figure out that's what I had, and easy enough to fix on my own."

The other shoe was off, and Morgan saw his dad stare intently, wiggling his toes. "I wonder how many other things you felt like you had to fix on your own," he barely heard Charlie mutter. His dad got up to put his shoes near the garage door, under his coat hook. Same spot as always.

"How was work?" Morgan asked, changing the subject.

"Great," Charlie said. "We solved all the cold cases, the new recruits love their beats, and we're fully funded for the upcoming year." As Triumph's elected chief of police, Morgan knew these three areas were his main worries. These large, insurmountable tasks that he felt he had to solve on his own. Maybe Morgan and his dad weren't so different from each other.

Charlie shook his head, returning to the couch. "No, it's really not that bad. Though I did have to remind a new recruit that it's not the badge that makes the man, but the man that makes the badge. I sent him home early after I overheard him bragging in the kitchen about meeting his quota for speeding tickets."

Morgan looked sharply at his dad. "I thought you guys don't have ticket quotas?"

Charlie nodded. "Exactly, son. We don't. So, when I came in and heard him talking about that to another young recruit, I told him," Charlie dropped the casual cadence, and put on what Morgan knew as his "officer voice." "If you think that being part of *my* force means printing out speeding tickets, you can go home now." Each word was clipped and pointed. He pulled his feet up on the couch, sprawling out a bit and watching the commercial on TV.

"What'd he say to that?" Morgan found that he genuinely wanted to know. Did the new recruit challenge his dad, going toe-to-toe?

"Oh, he back-pedaled real quick," his dad returned to a normal tone. "He said that he was just doing his job as a traffic cop, and that each speeder meant both less traffic reports and more money for Triumph." Charlie ran a hand over his face. "I asked him where his copy of the Triumph Municipal Charter was. 'At home, sir.' Then you'd best go back home and read the section on Municipalities, Income, and Criminality. Come to my office, first thing tomorrow, for your quiz." Charlie had ended back with his officer voice.

At that, Morgan stared at his dad. "Are you really going to give him a quiz? Like a pen and paper test?"

"God no, Morgan. That's just more work for me." Charlie adjusted a pillow. "I'm going to have him explain to me how the police department is funded, and where the revenue from criminal activity goes."

Morgan knew the answer to that: Taxes funded the department. Whatever money was made from traffic stops went to the judicial branch. He nodded appreciatively. "That's really smart, Dad."

Charlie looked over to his son, eyebrow raised. "You think so?"

"Yeah," Morgan coughed, suddenly uncomfortable. "I do." *You didn't just rip into him about being wrong*, he thought, remembering some of their previous fights when the officer voice became the dad voice. Law and order intertwined with love and discipline.

A beat passed, and a college basketball game resumed. They watched the players pass the ball, shoot for hoops, miss, then try again in the other direction. The squeaking shoes cut through the crowd's cheers and the announcers' explanations.

"Can I tell you something?" Charlie asked, tentatively.

Morgan looked out of the corner of his eyes, seeing that his dad's face was square to the television. Whatever he was going to say, they were going to talk to each other through the TV.

He heard Salvador's voice in his mind: "People can change, but you gotta keep giving them positives, hope that they're doing it right. When you see your dad is trying to really talk to you ..."

Meet him partway. "Sure," Morgan replied, squaring his face equally to the basketball game.

"I hate basketball."

Morgan sighed, and threw the remote at him. "Then you pick what to watch." He was satisfied that it had hit his dad on his left arm with a *thwack*.

"Ow! Okay," Charlie sat up, grabbing the remote. He turned the guide on, scrolled through the channel options, and picked a rerun of *The Golden Girls*.

"Seriously, Dad?" Morgan asked. "You trying to be funny?"

"No, it's funny. Promise." The show was on commercial break, so Morgan moved to get up.

"I can change it, I can change it," Charlie said quickly. "I thought maybe you'd want to watch something fun with me." The last two words nearly trailed off into silence. "We can watch what you want."

Morgan sat with his feet on the ground, looking at his dad. *Meet him partway.* He inhaled and ran his hands through his hair. "How about we find something we both want to watch?"

Charlie sat up, too, swinging his socked feet to the floor. "Or ... what if we do a round of Mario Kart?" he tossed the remote back to Morgan, who heard the timidity in his dad's voice.

"All that talk about speeding make you want to race?" he asked.

Charlie shrugged. "I remember you liked to play it." That was true, but well over five years ago. Before Mom got sick. Before alcohol and pills found their way under his skin and levitated him into a false, tentative peace.

Morgan had fallen out of touch with video games when they turned into first-player war scenarios. It felt too realistic. He missed the playful graphics and lightheartedness of kid video games, the overly large cartoon eyes and digital bodies that didn't bleed, hearts that didn't break.

Salvador's face came into his mind. *Meet him partway ...* "All right, you're on. But when we get to Rainbow Road, I want an over-under bet on how many times you fall off." He stood up, walking toward the cabinet with the controllers.

Charlie stood up too, stretching. "You get that sorted, and I'll go warm up a frozen lasagna." As he walked past Morgan, he clapped him on the back. "I'm glad you're here. I missed you."

Morgan had to strain to hear that last sentence. His dad had already taken a step away, and the laugh track of *The Golden Girls* had sounded at that moment.

"I missed you too, Dad." Morgan softly replied, meaning it. He hadn't meant for Charlie to hear it, but given that his dad froze mid-stride in order to nod definitively, matter settled, he knew Charlie had made out his words. And Morgan found that he was glad they'd both been heard, even if it meant the other had to work a bit harder to discover.

* * *

Birdie pulled past the familiar mechanic shop, its sign "Car Guy's"illuminated in the early dusk. Her mom had come up with that name, a pun on Guy's generic name. Her dad had leased this space for as long as she could remember. Though rundown—the blinds in the window were constantly askew and the concrete on the front stoop was cracked—Guy took pride in the space. He had two plastic evergreens placed on either side of the main entrance for the season.

She pulled into the back parking lot, stopping her truck a space away from her father's. No other cars were parked there. Birdie was thankful for the privacy.

Stepping out of her cab, she shuffled across the ice patches, head down against the ever-present wind, making it to the back door. Pulling it open, warm air from the interior wafted heavily toward her. The strong combined scent of oil, grease, and gasoline filled her nostrils. She inhaled deeply, one of the scents of her childhood.

Birdie had spent countless hours and days here as a kid, growing up not too far from this shop in a two-bedroom house her dad still lived in. She would help her dad with the records and books after school and in the summers. She learned more than she remembered about car engines and carburetors. Most days, she'd come straight here after school with her brother Paul. They'd do their homework in the front office, waiting for Guy to be done for the day so they could walk home together.

Whenever and wherever she smelled the tinny, sweet smell of gasoline, she was instantly back in this shop.

She caught sight of her dad over by the familiar, once-green lathe machine. He had some metal axel rod in hand and was positioning in the machine's pincers. "Hi, Dad!" she called loudly, walking toward him.

Guy turned around, his safety goggles amplifying the surprise in his eyes. "Birdie!" he exclaimed. "What're you doing here?"

Birdie placed a hand on the large machine's exterior and then instantly regretted it. Her palm was covered in a grimy dust of metallic shavings and grease particles. "Here," Guy said, handing her a stained red towel from his back pocket.

"You'd think I'd know by now, huh?" She wiped her hand on it. Some of the visual mess was gone, but still felt the residual gunk clinging to her palm.

"I got to clean it, I know," Guy said apologetically as he pulled off his safety goggles and set them right where she had placed her hand. Birdie didn't know if he was talking about the lathe machine or the towel. "So, what brings you in?"

"I told you yesterday when we talked, I'd stop by," Birdie said. "Remember?"

Guy squinted, racking his brain. "Did you now?"

She waved him off. "It's no matter, Dad. I just wanted to talk to you."

"Then let's go to the office. You want tea? I can turn the kettle on." Guy stiffly got off his stool and walked toward the front of the shop. He deftly zigzagged past cabinets of tools, a car chassis that had been on stilts since she'd started dating Mark nearly fifteen years ago, and a new pile of plastic bucket car seats stacked one on the other. They were still wrapped in plastic.

Birdie pointed to them. "What are these?"

Guy looked dismissively at them. "Oh, I'm doing some custom work for a fella. He wants removable bucket seats in his truck bed so that when he goes hunting, he can sit out back. I ordered a couple of options so he can figure out which one he wants."

"He doesn't have a deer blind?" Birdie didn't think sitting in a truck bed was going to make for successful hunting.

Her dad shrugged, speaking over his shoulder. "Beats me. I just handle the cars."

They entered the office area, which was differentiated from the shop section by a plain white wall, threadbare carpet, and halogen lights instead of industrial bucket lamps. Her dad grabbed one of the stackable chairs lined up against the wall and motioned for her to sit in the wheeled office chair behind the desk. "So, what can I do you for, Birdie?"

She slid into the chair, the cushioning on its seat long ago depleted. "I wanted to see how you were doing."

Guy laughed. "You could've called, no need for you to stop by! I know you're busy."

Birdie shifted uncomfortably. "Dad, I always have time for you." She took a deep breath, drinking in the stabilizing aroma of the shop. "How have you been feeling?"

"Fine," he said. "My knees hurt, of course—stupid cold weather—but I've been good. I need to see the doctor soon to get my blood pressure meds renewed. They always call me when I got a month left on my meds."

Birdie's mind flashed to a new worry—her dad's ability to follow through on his medication instructions.

"Anyways," her dad said. "What were we talking about?" He looked around the office, muttering to himself. His eyebrows knit in frustration.

"Dad, I wanted to talk with you ..."

"About that family!" Guy said, proud of himself.

Birdie's eyebrows knit in frustration this time, a nearly perfect mirror of her father's just seconds before.

"I know, I know, pastor confidentiality," he winked at her. "But can you at last tell me how they're doing? Did they get the money I sent?"

The scam. "Oh, Dad, no actually," her eyes danced over the gray, stained carpet. She inhaled deeply before meeting Guy's equally tired gray eyes. "Dad, there was no family."

Guy sat back in his chair. "What do you mean, Birdie?" He rubbed his hands on his legs, processing. "Did you make it up? If you and Mark need money, I'm still happy to help you all out, Birdie."

She felt the rift in her heart dig deeper, her father's bleeding-heart compassion shredding her. This man was willing to help still, despite his meager income.

"No, Dad," Birdie said calmly. She placed her hands on the dusty office table that lay between them. "It wasn't me. At all. It was a scam."

She watched him digest the information, practically hearing the cogs of his brain click, click, clunk with comprehension.

"A scam?" He repeated. "I heard about folks doing that. I just never thought ... they'd impersonate a pastor?"

Birdie nodded. "It's pretty common, I guess. They go after churches all the time." She swallowed the question that burbled in her throat: *Dad, couldn't you tell it wasn't me? Why would I send a text to you as 'Pastor Heather'?*

As he rubbed his hands on his legs again, she watched, transfixed. This man had been her superhero. Physically imposing but soft as a teddy bear, over the years she'd watched her father shrink in stature. His hunched-over stance now cut inches from his once great height. The large, barrel-chested frame she remembered never being able to wrap her arms fully around had depleted. His shirt now hung loose. "My little Bird," he'd call her as a child, throwing her up into the air so she could fly, catching her after a fall that felt like feet. Where was her invincible father now?

"Dad," Birdie began gently, "I'm getting worried about you. Your memory isn't what it used to be."

Guy's gray eyes locked on hers. "Because I fell for one scam? Aren't these guys professionals? Birdie," he said, his tone placating her, "it's how they make their money."

She shook her head. "It's not just that. You're forgetting other things, like that I was even going to come by to talk to you. Or …"

Guy stood up suddenly, his eyes turning to steel. "Birdie, come on now. Paul's not concerned and I see him all the time. Never once has he said anything about this."

Birdie's legs shot up under her too, standing to meet her dad's gaze. Their eyes were level to one another, her father's former height no longer an advantage. "Paul's ignoring the problem like he always does!" she spat.

"Don't you go picking on your brother now," her dad said, wagging his finger at her like she was a child again. "He's done more for this country …"

Birdie turned her head, using the opportunity to push back in the office chair she'd just vacated. She was not going to get anywhere like this. Her nostrils inhaled the sweet gasoline smell again. "Look, Dad," she said softly. "I'm worried about you. Doesn't that count for anything?"

Just then, the rumble of what sounded like a semi-truck roared, approaching the little shop. Guy looked up at the clock. "Sounds like Tino's truck," he said to himself. "Though he's early." He moved toward the front window to look out.

"Who's Tino?" Birdie asked, trying to remember all the names of the random people her father had helping him around the shop: Gill the painter, Randy the mechanic, Danny the welder.

"The hunter," her dad said without turning around. Tino parked and killed the engine, a sudden quiet flooding the air.

"He thinks he's going to hunt in *that*?" Birdie said, joining her dad at the window at the oversized silver pickup truck, its passenger window emblazoned with an etched American flag. Birdie started laughing at the incredulity. Tino was Truck Balls.

She watched as her dad stepped outside to meet the man, a rather imposing figure with his police uniform strapped tightly to his frame. Together they walked into the office, talking.

"Sorry I'm early," Tino was saying. "My shift, um … it ended earlier than I thought, so I figured I'd come check out those bucket seats on my way home."

"It's no problem," Guy said, walking through the door Tino held open for him. "I was just chatting here with my daughter. Birdie," Guy looked up at his daughter and gestured toward the man behind him. "This is Tino, one of Triumph's newest police recruits."

"Pleasure to meet you, ma'am," Tino said, bowing his head at her.

"You as well," she said, stifling another laugh. Up close, Tino looked barely old enough to drive. His clean-shaven face was likely the result of his age, not his grooming. He kept his aviator sunglasses on, even though it was dusk and they were inside. She half-expected him to have a toothpick or cigarette hanging out of the corner of his mouth, like he was trying to fit some stereotype of an officer he had in his head.

"Well, Dad," she said, turning her focus to Guy. "I guess I'd better be off."

Guy took a step toward her, enfolding her in a bear hug. "Thanks for stopping by, kid," he said loudly. "I'll think about what you said, Birdie," he muttered into her hair. "Promise."

Guy led Tino to the back, Birdie following in their wake to get to the back door. Her dad had remembered Tino's name and that he was coming by today. He seemed to be handling the car shop. Maybe she was overreacting.

Near the back door, where her dad hung his coat and dropped his stuff on a shelf he'd built out of an old arm rest, she saw an orange bottle of pills. She glanced over her shoulder. Guy and Tino were looking at the bucket seats, their backs to her. She snatched at the

118   For the Love of Triumph

bottle, its full contents shaking as she read the label: Vasotec. Blood pressure meds, a brand-new bottle. Dispense date just three days prior.

"I need to see the doctor to get my blood pressure meds renewed," her dad's voice echoed in her mind. Birdie placed the full bottle back on the shelf, wincing that the residual dust and gunk from earlier had left a mark on the once immaculate white label. She wondered if her dad would even notice.

Chapter 13

Solid Values

"**G**ood afternoon, class!" Dr. Brown's voice cut through the nervous chatter in his first-period senior English class. Such was the respect the group had for him that they all hushed their conversations.

"As you know, we're a week away from winter break, which means a week from the due date for your personal values statement. Today, the plan is to pair up and share what you have so far."

Johnny Tae internally groaned, trying not to let the sound escape. He'd known this day was coming, but he figured he'd get some inspiration over the course of the week. Nothing. Absolutely fucking nothing. Johnny Tae appeared self-assured, but he was coming around to how little he really knew about himself. He knew he hated his parents, that much was a given. But what did he value? His value couldn't be "hatred of parents." As Dr. Brown's assignment rubric asked, what got him up in the morning? What kept him up at night? What made his heart break? What made his heart sing? It all felt far too big to put into words. He knew what he didn't like, what he didn't want, what he didn't believe. He had a much harder time laying claim to what he stood for.

Dr. Brown was youngish, probably a little older than Ara Grace, Johnny Tae thought. He knew his teacher had some wild story about road tripping out West and stopping in Triumph when his car ran out of gas, but he didn't know the details. He did know that Dr. Brown treated them like people with thoughts and ideas of their own. He also knew that, as much as he appreciated the intrinsic respect Dr.

Brown had for them, it made it that much harder to have not started this assignment at all. On some level, he felt like he was letting this decent teacher down.

Dr. Brown wasn't one to let the class choose their own partners and bullshit each other about what they had (or, more likely, hadn't) written. He assigned partners, and he paired Johnny Tae with Pete Thompson.

Pete was a quiet farm kid, and Johnny Tae hadn't gotten to know him at all during his months so far in Triumph. He was straight-edge, not the type to show up at big bonfires or parties. Laela, Sarah, and Morgan had to have a thousand stories about Pete, their lives all entangled like the vegetable vines in his Umma's garden. Johnny Tae was sure Pete would have his assignment finished already. To his surprise, as they found two nearby desks and arranged themselves to face one another, Johnny Tae noticed that Pete had a piece of paper with just a few bullet points scribbled down. He heaved a sigh of relief.

"Hey man, I'm Johnny Tae," he offered. "New kid. I don't think we've really met."

"Pete. Nice to meet you. It's hard not to notice you around."

Johnny Tae felt an accusation of racism rising in his throat like bile, but he swallowed it down.

"Looks like you actually got started on yours," he said, motioning to the paper.

"Yeah, it just felt pretty simple to me. Not much more than this." Pete held up the paper so Johnny Tae could read it. The bullet points read:

FAITH—JESUS IS KING

FAMILY—LOYAL TO THE END

FELLOWSHIP—SHARE LIFE WITH CHURCH AND FRIENDS

It was so unbelievably, incredibly basic, Johnny Tae could hardly stand it. He rolled his eyes, then hoped Pete didn't see him as he turned the paper back around. He felt a pang of jealousy at Pete's straightforwardness. If only life were that simple for him.

"Hey, great you have it figured out." Johnny Tae tried to sound enthusiastic, but his sarcasm dripped through. "What are you doing after graduation?"

Pete cracked a small smile that pinched one of his ruddy, weather-worn cheeks. "Got a gig on an oil rig with my cousin. They start you at 60K. You're gone a lot, but it's worth it." Pete droned on about what his cousin did, being outside, living in formerly abandoned motels, a group of guys, like some fraternity without all the school crap.

Johnny Tae tried to picture himself on an oil rig in some part of this godforsaken state *more* remote than Triumph County. Nope. The money sounded good, but the lifestyle seemed terrible. Another "no" to add to his list.

"Good for you, man," Johnny Tae managed.

"What about you?" Pete asked curiously.

"Literally no idea," Johnny Tae said, just as Dr. Brown called the class back together to debrief. *One week to go.*

* * *

Buzz Buzz Buzz was quieter than usual that Friday evening. The weather report was calling for freezing rain—ice. Snow, folks in Triumph could handle. Chains on their tires and they were good to go. Ice was another story. The winding mountain roads turned hazardous. Johnny Tae had walked the few blocks to work, not trusting himself with his car under that forecast. He carried a pair of rubber spikes that he could stretch over the soles of his boots for the walk home if he needed to. His auntie had made sure Johnny Tae's dad sent money for proper winter gear when she realized recently what winter would really be like here, after more than two weeks of him wearing Morgan's old winter coat. His dad had come through right quick with the cash.

Morgan was running the register while Johnny Tae made drinks, but mostly they were talking. A few folks came in to grab pastries to-go before the storm hit, and Ara Grace was tucked into a faraway corner sofa, a glass of white wine next to her. He figured she was working on her sermon and prayed she wasn't answering thirst messages from online dates. Judging from the look of concentration on her face, he was pretty certain she was working. *Big Friday night plans*, he thought. The shop was empty besides her. After an hour of small talk with the random customers and Morgan as time allowed, Johnny Tae couldn't hold it in any longer.

"Morgan, you gotta help me with the PV," he pleaded. "I have nothing. I actually have no idea what I want my life to look like. All I can think about is what I *don't* want."

He was equal parts relieved and infuriated when he saw a smile break across Morgan's face.

"City boy," Morgan said. "None of us really know what we want. That's why Dr. Brown didn't ask you to write about where you want to be in five years or ten years or whatever. He's smarter than that. He's asking you about your *values*. That was the big focus in rehab—values." He cleaned the keys on the register, clearing off some whipped cream before teasing Johnny Tae, "You're getting all the benefits of rehab with zero cost!"

Johnny Tae shook his head, annoyed at the Morgan guru shit. *Just tell me what to do, man!* "Cool if I take five?" he asked, needing to clear his head.

Morgan nodded, gesturing to the empty cafe. "You can take more than five if you need to."

Johnny Tae untied the apron around his waist, hanging it carefully on a hook next to the espresso machine. He walked through the cafe to the restrooms in back, nodding to his auntie along the way. Once he was inside the nearer of the two single-occupancy rooms, he drafted a text message to Sarah and Laela.

JOHNNY TAE: JUNIORS, YOU TWO SEEM TO HAVE YOUR LIVES TOGETHER. WANT TO HELP ME WITH THE PV? MORGAN'S IN HIS GURU ERA HE'S NO HELP. SOS

* * *

Sarah and Laela sat cross-legged on the floor of Sarah's room, phones in hand. "Oh, Johnny Tae," Sarah sighed. "Did that just come through for you too?"

"Sure did," Laela replied. "He's elbows-deep in an existential crisis, what do you expect?"

"It just doesn't have to be such a big thing," Sarah countered. "It's one assignment. His aunt literally preaches about values every week for a living. He could copy something she says one Sunday."

"I don't know, I kind of like that he's taking it seriously. Making his own way."

Sarah smiled, a twinkle in her eye warning Laela some good-natured teasing was coming. "Oh, you like it, huh?" Sarah's voice was instantly suggestive.

"Come on, Sarah, you know what I mean."

"Think he'll go to Mistletoe Madness?"

"I'm not sure and I don't really care."

"Really? *Really?* Sounds like your Homecoming fiasco all over again."

Laela's stomach clenched. "Drop it, Sarah."

"Okay." Sarah looked up from her phone. "But are you going to go to Mistletoe? Because I was just scrolling through beauty TikTok and there are a ton of looks on here that I think you'd like. Festive but subtle, you know?"

Laela nodded suspiciously. "I really don't know if I want to go."

"You don't have to," Sarah reassured her. "I get it."

Laela's shoulders relaxed. Having a friend who maybe understood her anxiety made the world feel manageable.

"Let me try one of these looks on you, though," Sarah said, showing Laela her phone. "No pressure to go, no pressure to actually wear the look either if you go. I just thought it would be fun to try. My mom's flying me out to Cali over spring break and I want to impress her with my skills. See if she thinks I can hack it at aesthetician school."

Laela noted Sarah's pace speeding up, and she felt for her friend, wanting to please her mom. She was grateful in that moment that the pressure for her was internal. Laela wasn't interested in impressing anyone, not really. She thought back to the hike she'd taken with Johnny Tae last summer where he'd wound up covered in mud. *That* look had worked for her ...

"You know what? I'd love it," Laela replied to Sarah's offer. She settled in for the latest TikTok holiday makeup trend, leaning back against the foot of Sarah's bed.

* * *

When Johnny Tae hadn't heard back from Laela or Sarah in the five minutes he'd requested from Morgan, he sighed, ran a hand through his hair, and pumped himself up to go back to the front. He decided to crack open the back door to the cafe to give himself a little jolt of cold air, trying to get the energy to make it through his shift, his life.

The instant he cracked the door, it flew open with a bang. Already, icy gusts were coating the trees in a layer of white on one side. Johnny Tae could barely see across the alley. He thought back to summer, the lightning storms that soaked everything in their path and brought wild, sparking spiderwebs to the sky. The incredible lightning storm of his own arrival to Triumph. The lightning storm that had brewed between him and Laela. Now, with the temperature well below freezing, those sparks had turned to tiny frigid projectiles, hell-bent on beating him down.

The lightning storms of summer were exciting, no doubt, but they had been terrifying, too. Getting a little wet and muddy, though, was nothing compared to this ice storm. Johnny Tae felt beat down. Beat down by school, by the weight of the future, by what he wanted or maybe didn't want from Laela. He closed his eyes and thought, *What if I changed my temperature? Maybe I don't need to be such a goddamn ice storm.*

"Close the door, dude!"

Morgan's shout and the bitter scent of espresso grounds broke Johnny Tae from his reverie. In just a couple of seconds, a layer of ice probably a quarter-inch thick had formed on the inside of the door, still flapping around outside. Johnny Tae heard Morgan say something about keeping the door on its hinges and heating costs and frostbite. Morgan had a big cafe trash bag in one hand while carefully balancing the canister of used espresso grounds in the other. "It's really picking up out there. I think it's time to call it a night." Johnny Tae couldn't have agreed more.

* * *

Three hours later, Laela was trying to fall asleep, but her face was feeling kind of strange. She liked the look Sarah had chosen for her, silver eyeliner swoops and a nice primer with some shimmer, plus a bold red lipstick to pull the look together. Sarah had sculpted her eyebrows with some lightly sparkly brown pencil. Laela wasn't used to wearing makeup … ever. She had admired herself in the mirror, smiling at this sophisticated version of herself. She even toyed with the word "pretty" to describe how she was feeling. Maybe the dance wouldn't be so bad after all. Sarah had gushed over her face, taking plenty of photos to send to her mom.

Later, when Laela had washed the makeup off before bed, her skin had felt a little raw, kind of sensitive, like she'd just gone skiing on a cold day. But now, awake in the dark room, a powerful itching was creeping up her cheeks and around her eyes.

She and Sarah lay together in Sarah's queen-size bed. Laela listened to Sarah's slow, deep breathing as she debated what to do. She crept out of bed, careful not to disturb Sarah, and found the bathroom through the dark hallway with her phone's feeble flashlight.

When she managed to find the light switch and flip it on, she immediately recoiled in horror. Her eyelids were swollen nearly shut, her cheeks looked as shiny and red as fresh apples, and her neck was starting to get in on the action. She was definitely, seriously allergic to *something*.

She rummaged through the medicine cabinet behind the mirror and then through the drawers under the sink, looking for something to help. She slathered herself in calamine lotion, found in the twins' drawer, prone as they were to summertime bug bites. The calamine was cool and smelled familiar, like mosquito bites when she was a little girl. In Sarah's drawer, she found some chewable Benadryl. *Better take a few of these, too*, she thought. She looked up drug reactions on her phone, careful not to make that mistake again, and then sat on the bathroom floor, leaning her face against the cool ceramic of the bathtub. *Definitely not going to any dance looking like this.*

* * *

"Laela, wake up!" Sarah's voice jolted Laela awake from her curled-up position on the bathmat. One of the dogs stuck its cold wet nose right in her face. Sarah shooed it away before kneeling near her. "We've been looking all over for you! I was so panicked when I woke up and you weren't in the bed."

Laela sat up and blinked her eyes, noting they had their full range of motion. She pushed herself up off the floor and looked in the mirror. A little red and blotchy, but no worse for wear.

"I'm sorry," Laela started. "The makeup. I think ..."

"You look awful," Sarah interjected. She picked up the half-empty calamine lotion bottle Laela had left on its side, her eyes taking in the nearby Benadryl bottle. "Laela, what the hell? Are you okay?"

"I think I had an allergic reaction." She touched her face gingerly.

"Oh my God." Sarah took out the makeup bottles she'd used last night and looked on the back. "Hyaluronic acid," she announced, pronouncing the word carefully. "It's what was in the shimmer primer. Most people have no trouble with it, but some people are extra sensitive. Oh shit, Laela, I'm so sorry."

"No harm done," Laela said, then corrected herself. "I mean, nothing a little Benadryl couldn't fix." She tried to sit with the tightening feeling in her chest, tried to count how many blue things she could see in the bathroom, tried to take a few deep breaths and count backward from ten. All her usual anxiety management strategies.

But Sarah wasn't fooled. "Listen, Laela, we don't have to try TikTok makeup trends ever again if you don't want to," she said, putting her hand on Laela's shoulder. "We don't have to go to the dance. It's really okay."

Laela pressed her hands to her face, trying to curb the itch that still lingered under the surface. "I think I'm allergic to being a teenage girl."

"And I think I'm a terrible aesthetician," Sarah replied.

The two girls dissolved into giggles, their failures fading in the shared humor. They hurried downstairs, hoping Birdie had left them some breakfast.

Chapter 14

Sunday of Peace

"Oh my, it looks especially beautiful this year," Sylvia sighed, gazing at the tree with one hand to her cheek as she sat on the organist's bench.

Ara Grace glanced at her but stayed silent, focusing her attention on finding the right preface and words of institution for communion based on the week's readings and the liturgical setting. The oversized red book rested on a special golden stand. Colored ribbons according to the liturgical season marked spots—although, much to her chagrin, the colored ribbons were not in their proper places.

"Don't you think so?" Sylvia continued.

Green, the color for Ordinary Time, marked the place for Christ the King Sunday, which itself ought to be white. But the one white ribbon the makers of the altar book had allotted was suitably marking Easter. She didn't have time to dwell on why they couldn't have included more than multiple ribbons when the liturgical calendar switched colors so frequently.

"Pastor?" Sylvia asked, louder this time.

Ara Grace looked up, feigning ignorance. "I'm sorry, what were you saying?"

"The tree. It looks simply magnificent!"

Ara Grace glanced at it. The branches skewed in unnaturally straight lines, the lights beamed a steady, dull white. "Isn't this how it looks every year?" she asked, cautiously. "I mean, I don't see a difference from last week at least." She couldn't see any lingering damage from its fall earlier in the week.

Sylvia frowned. "I suppose it does," she conceded. "Maybe that's why it's so beautiful. It's the same."

Ara Grace thought she could see honest-to-goodness tears well up in the organist's eyes. She closed her own eyes, biting back her annoyance with the season.

"Hey Sylvia," she said, walking towards the organ, "I want us to try doing something different this week." She saw Sylvia's eyes glance frantically to the music before her. "Not musically, but in the service. When we pass the peace, I'm going to ask that people do so silently."

Sylvia waited a beat before asking, "Do you want me to play background music during that time?"

"No," Ara Grace said. *That would defeat the point of being silent.* "I want people to acknowledge each other with God's peace, but not to talk to each other. It's been getting a little out of hand, the amount of time people take to talk to one another during the service. They can do that at coffee hour afterwards."

"Pastor, I think a lot of people look forward to that moment in the service," Sylvia shifted on the bench. "I'm not so sure."

Ara Grace silently bit down her retort: *People can talk before or after the service. The service, not even an entire hour, is meant to worship God, not each other.* "We're going to try it. Just this week."

Sylvia avoided Ara Grace's eyes. "I don't know about trying new things during Advent ..."

"Silence goes with the theme for the week: Peace." She tried to keep the pleading tone out of her voice, evoking confidence and assurance.

"All right, Pastor," Sylvia said, turning her attention to the music in front of her again. "Thank you for letting me know."

Later, in the service, after the sermon, the Apostles' Creed, the prayers of intercession, Ara Grace announced to the group gathered for worship, "As we move now to share God's peace with one another, I ask that we do so silently. Let us dwell on the peace of God by withholding our voices, trusting our actions to speak to one another."

She moved to the front of the altar to head toward the congregation. Before she made it to the first pew, her congregants were already mingling about, shaking hands.

Talking. Softer than normal, but talking.

Richard made his way up to her, talking in a stage whisper, "Peace, Pastor. Hey, neat idea. The quiet makes you really appreciate the Christmas decorations!"

Ara Grace remained silent. She shook his hand with a controlled smile, sighing heavily in her inmost being.

* * *

Nel hadn't been able to eat that morning. She'd tried to pretend it was due to the time crunch, the rush of getting the kids ready while Jacques was at an overnight shift at the firehouse. Getting two kids and herself ready for morning worship was no small task and took a fair amount of bribing and cajoling.

And yet, truthfully, she hardly noticed Jacques's absence that morning. Even if he had been there, he'd have been another person for her to be responsible for, another chess piece for her to move on the board of her life. She'd have to bribe and cajole him (more subtly, of course) to help get the kids ready, reminding him for the umpteenth time that it was not appropriate for the kids to wear their pajamas to church.

The guilt crept in. Deep down, Nel knew this was related to the low-grade anxiety that had plagued her most of her life. The need to perform. The need to justify her existence up against her perfect sister. Sometimes it all just felt like too much, and even though it wasn't fair to pin it on Jacques, it was what she was left with.

She'd gotten the kids fed, dressed, and cleaned up, running a comb through each child's curly hair and making sure they at least swiped each tooth with a toothbrush. That morning, Hudson chose to wear his favorite sports jersey, Messi's Argentina jersey in blue and white vertical stripes. Victoria insisted on wearing a Valentine's dress with pumpkin leggings, and weirdly, the red, black, and orange combo seemed appropriately festive. Nel wore her typical black slacks and black clergy collar shirt with a smart suit jacket. Even though she wore a robe every Sunday, which covered her body in its entirety, the look made her feel complete. Whole. Enough.

This morning, Nel's stomach hadn't been able to settle. She felt gas bubbles creep up her throat. Even the plain toast she'd made had smelled too burnt for her to eat.

"Comfort, O comfort my people," the sermon scripture for that day from Isaiah echoed in her mind. *You're going to need to comfort me, Lord, before I can comfort your people …*

As she walked with her kids the few paces to church (all of them wrapped up snug in their thickest winter coats), she felt a warmness rest on her shoulders, as if someone had placed an arm around her neck, bringing her in for a walking hug. The sensation felt peaceful, calming. She looked down and smiled, thankful for the quick answer to prayer.

The inner warmth of that moment stayed with her as her congregation began to come alive for Sunday worship. Members serving that week as ushers, setup volunteers, readers, and greeters arrived, all lumbering versions of their usual selves under massive coats. They smiled as they studiously removed each outer layer of protection against the cold, becoming recognizable once more to Nel and one another. The church's heater hummed softly in the background.

Ten minutes before service began, the coat racks already teemed with puffy jackets stuffed fuller with various scarves, hats, and face masks, boots lined up below. Hudson and a few other kids were playing tag through the coats. A bemused Sunday school teacher looked on while catching up with Jessica.

All these people, Nel thought, *here despite the bitter cold and chaos of life, all to worship God together*. She felt further warmed.

She made sure Hudson and Victoria were both connected with Rachel, the red-haired yoga instructor who'd eagerly agreed to be their adult this week, and the service started.

Looking out from her presider's chair, Nel saw the congregation, this one entity composed of individuals, most of whom she knew by name and at least part of their story, rise to sing. A great swell rose within her as they swelled like a wave.

When she stepped into the pulpit, her eyes were cloudy with tears. She spoke the reading from Isaiah 40 more from memory than from the text printed before her:

Comfort, O comfort my people,

says your God.

Speak tenderly to Jerusalem,

and cry to her

that she has served her term,

that her penalty is paid...

He will feed his flock like a shepherd;

he will gather the lambs in his arms

and carry them in his bosom

and gently lead the mother sheep.

"What brings us comfort?" Nel began. "The certainty of life? The hug of a good friend?" This isn't how her sermon, typed out before her in large font on plain white paper, was set to start, but she felt the stirring within her.

"Maybe a better question is to ask what brings us discomfort. What is it that causes us angst and anxiety?" She surveyed her congregation, remembering their stories. "The hardships of life, the struggles of mortgage payments, the death of a loved one, an unwelcome present reality ..." she trailed off, realizing she'd hit a nerve within herself.

"These all," Nel continued, "are real. These all are valid. And these all matter to God. But Isaiah tells us today that we are comforted. Our angst is welcomed and healed by God."

She continued with the rest of her planned sermon, all except the paragraph about how God leads the mother sheep. That one, she felt, was still too personal.

* * *

"Come, O long-expected Jesus," Birdie sang, clearly and with feeling. This was one of her favorite Advent hymns, as long as they sang it to her favorite hymn tune, Hyfrydol, a traditional Welsh hymn. This one was often sung to a tune called Stuttgart, which felt far less expansive and lyrical. Birdie appreciated the Chalice Hymnal's replacement of the antiquated-sounding "thou" in the title line with the more personal "O." She laughed to herself about her worship preferences and particularities, sounding like Ara Grace. Birdie was not orthodox in her theology or her aesthetic, but she had opinions.

Just like her congregants. "From our sins and fears release us; Christ in whom our rest shall be," she continued. *I could use some rest*, she thought. She had been up all night worrying about her dad.

Birdie let her mind wander for a moment as the hymn progressed. She found herself reflecting on yesterday, when she was startled by a loud pounding as she worked on her sermon in her office—a bad habit, she knew, to leave things to the last minute, but it had been that kind of week. The noise sounded like it was coming from outside, but she had a hard time figuring out which door in the L-shaped building. Her heart pounded in her chest, hoping it was just Greg needing to sneak in to spruce up the Advent decorations, or maybe Martha dashing in for something from her own office after forgetting her key. She tried not to think of other possibilities.

After trying the main door off the office suite and finding it empty, she realized the sanctuary doors were rattling. *Someone really wants to get in here.* Birdie considered calling Mark, taking out her phone for a moment, then slipping it back into her pocket. She'd peek out and see who was there.

She cracked open the door and found her father. Guy was outside in the cold sleet with windblown hair and the start of a crack on his right index-finger knuckle, no doubt from the heavy pounding he'd been doing.

"Dad!" she cried. "Get in here, we need to get you warmed up!"

"Where is everyone?" Guy asked, looking dazed. "I figured I was late."

"Late? For what?"

"Church! Worship! The Lord's Day!" Guy shouted back. "Or did you forget?"

Birdie's heart sank. "Dad, it's Saturday."

Back in worship that Sunday, Birdie looked out into the congregation, finding Guy's flannel shirt and silver hair. Paul was sitting reluctantly beside him. Birdie had given him a quick call to make sure he could give their father a ride for the correct day, but the two hadn't had the talk she knew was coming. *Dad can't take care of himself anymore*, Birdie thought. *We both know it. So who's gonna call it?*

She took a deep breath and looked down at her hymnal, finding that they were already at the final line. "By your all-sufficient merit, raise us to your glorious throne," Birdie finished with the congregation.

Raise me up, Jesus, she prayed.

Part 3

Joy

Chapter 15

Secrets Unfolding

A ra Grace raced down the back stairwell at Good Shepherd, careful to sidestep the creaky, maybe-rotten part of the third step from the bottom. Her evening worship service had run long. She was sure she'd missed the after-pageant cleanup, but she still hoped to catch Nel and Birdie before they left. She desperately needed a venting session. The third midweek Advent service had gone fine, but no one seemed particularly charmed by her candle lighting prayer liturgy. And there were only three people in attendance, so who was she really charming? She needed the wizened voices of those who'd traveled and led their congregations through Advent.

She turned sharply out of the stairwell, then nearly tripped as she came to a stop. She'd forgotten what a mess the kids had created. Posters sporting giant, colorful capital letters still littered the floor. Shepherd's crooks hung from a coat rack. A baby doll lolled, half-on, half-off a folding chair. Jessica had taken the costumes home, thank God, but it still looked like a tornado had torn through the place.

Laela and Morgan were splayed out on the floor, looking like they'd been battered by the whipping Wyoming wind, too. Upon seeing Ara Grace, Laela jumped up and dusted off her overalls. "Pastor! Sorry! We were just working up the energy to get this mess cleaned up."

"It's totally okay, Laela," Ara Grace said reassuringly. "You two can head on home. It's getting late. Let the clergy handle this one." It was true, plus Ara Grace felt like she could speak more freely with the teens out for the night.

Morgan and Laela quickly grabbed their coats and headed out, both waving and mumbling goodbye as they climbed up the stairs. Ara Grace thought she heard Laela mention the library. Seeing her book-stuffed backpack, she considered all that these teens were carrying on their young backs.

Ara Grace spotted Birdie, shuffling her sheet music back in order in her binder over at the piano. Nel was collapsed in an uncomfortable chair, leaning on the card table before her. She looked easily as tired as the teens. Her shoulders slumped with the weight of the world.

Ara Grace headed for her friend, thoughts of her own complaints sliding away with each step she took toward Nel.

* * *

Nel had sunk into the chair for just a moment, yawning and stretching her arms over her head. The pageant team had done a run-through with props at that night's rehearsal. An early shepherd's crook sword fight had led to a strict prop code of conduct (1. No Violence. 2. No Props in Mouths. 3. Violators Get Props Taken Away.). Laela's creation, of course. "Three commandments are a lot easier to remember than 10!" she'd chirped cheerfully. Nel envied her energy. She was about ready for a nap, or a *very* early bedtime, but she knew she'd better help clean up. Jacques had picked up the kids after practice, and she'd just seen Ara Grace send Laela and Morgan home, insisting they'd helped enough. It was just the three of them: Nel, Ara Grace, and Birdie.

Nel stretched her arms across the table, where the letter F stared back at her. "F is for family ..." she remembered one of the older boys saying as he narrated the chaos that evening. *F is for family? More like F is for failure.* Nel stared across the room grimly as she considered her many shortcomings as a mother, wife, and pastor. Just an average Wednesday night for this mother of young children. *You can have it all*, she remembered hearing, *just not all at once.*

Birdie and Ara Grace suddenly appeared on either side of her, unbidden harbingers of peace. "Nel, you know we love you," Birdie said. "Why don't you head home and get some rest?"

And somehow, it was this small kindness that broke her. When was the last time anyone had offered Nel some rest? Her carefully crafted veneer crumbled all at once, weakened by the many cracks it had suffered over time.

Wet, hot tears streamed down her face. She hiccupped a sob so loud it surprised her. She barely registered Birdie's arms around her, but the smell of patchouli calmed her. She tried to breathe it in.

"Okay, out with it," Ara Grace commanded, sitting at the table, once Nel had regained a sense of calm. She'd handed Nel a wad of toilet paper hastily grabbed from the bathroom.

Birdie offered soothingly from the chair beside her, "I know this is more than just a little marital conflict. We promise we can help, and we promise we'll keep it confidential." She shot Ara Grace a conspiratorial smile. "We are pastors, after all."

Nel weighed her options. Jacques absolutely could not know … not yet. She wasn't ready for that conversation while their whole shared life felt so tender and fragile. She feared what he would likely say. Her family doctor here in Triumph was a member of Birdie's church and had a husband on the volunteer fire squad. She knew doctors were bound by confidentiality laws, but she also knew people talked in this small town. She didn't have her own therapist; it felt disingenuous, triangulating even, to tell Sister Eunice without sharing it with Jacques. But Birdie and Ara Grace? These women were consummate professionals. More importantly, they were her *friends*. If there was anyone to tell, it was them.

"I'm pregnant," Nel blurted out before she could second-guess her decision.

* * *

Laela and Morgan watched Ms. Davis, the librarian, start to turn off the lights around the Triumph County Library. They'd been surprised and grateful to be cut loose early by Ara Grace after a truly delightful, fully exhausting pageant rehearsal. The quiet of the library soothed them, a stark contrast to the cacophonous roar of the kids in the last three hours. Morgan had just sat in a nearby chair, scrolling through his phone in the silence, while Laela had worked on some homework.

Laela walked with a new confidence in her step. She felt surer than ever that she wanted to be a teacher. Watching these kids blossom made *her* blossom.

She thought of Victoria at rehearsal that night, holding her letter V sign proudly. Hudson had the speaking role of the two of them, but Laela had an idea to give Victoria a way to shine.

Just before they went on their pretend stage, Laela whispered to Nel's two kids, "Why don't you say the first part together? V is for vulnerable? Can you say that, Victoria?"

Hudson counted them off. "1, 2, 3 …"

"V is for vulnerable!" Victoria giggled as she pronounced it more like "vubble," but the sentiment was there. Given that Victoria had melted down at more than one rehearsal at this point and spent most of the time running in circles around the room or counting the yellowing ceiling tiles, Laela was so proud to see this ham side of her. She wanted to spend her life helping kids become more fully themselves.

"You know, Laela," Morgan said as he gathered up Laela's piles of books, "you could go to Mistletoe Madness on Saturday. I can handle the kids, especially since so many parents signed up to help."

Laela froze. She was hoping no one would notice the little coincidence, Mistletoe Madness and the Christmas pageant falling on the same night. She paused for a moment, weighing what to say next. What she *could* say … it all seemed very "vubble," to quote Victoria.

She then remembered Morgan's rehab stint had been very public, whether he liked it or not. She envied his bravery, although maybe, upon reflection, it came with having a public figure for a dad, this expectation that parts of your life are fodder for town gossip.

"Honestly?" She took a deep breath, ready to try to match his bravery. "I have social anxiety. Dances really aren't my scene. Backstage at the Christmas pageant is my happy place."

She held her breath for a moment and waited for Morgan to respond. His eyes were filled with such kindness, such tenderness toward her, she almost wanted to cry. "No shit?" Morgan said, finally. "You're so *together* all the time. And with the kids …"

"It's more of a peer thing," Laela clarified quickly, her face flushing as words spilled out. "It's why I want to work with kids. I love them because they don't hide anything. There's no subtext to try to decode with them, no stupid games to play. Looking like you've got it together all the time is like a game. Kids don't have to play it yet, not really."

"I get it," Morgan replied, offering a gentle smile. "In rehab we talked a lot about how everyone wears masks, like self-protection, you know? It's nice when we can take our masks off. Be our true selves. I'm grateful we can do that with each other."

Laela had to smile at that. Rehab wisdom wasn't getting old yet. "Me too."

"Time to call it quits, you two," Ms. Davis said. "Or at least do your 'business' elsewhere."

Laela swore the woman winked at her. She felt her cheeks blush at the suggestion.

* * *

Morgan sat in the oversize bean bag chair in his room at home later that night, turning their conversation over and over in his mind. Laela's confession bucked the trends of most people he'd hung out with, but her openness felt refreshing. He'd spent so long trying to fit into someone else's idea of who he should be. Skipping a high school dance would never have crossed his mind. The realness of his time at Evergreen felt alive in their conversation. They were getting to know each other's real selves, not the false selves everyone else expected to see.

He remembered a conversation with Salvador back at Evergreen. He'd been busy in the art therapy room, trying to calm his thoughts with an intricate coloring sheet, flowers twisting and turning around each other in a swooping, repeated pattern. Morgan had never tried art much growing up; he had this idea that art was girly, and that's the last thing his dad wanted him to be, though he didn't remember his dad ever saying as much. The flowers on the page twisted and turned pleasantly under the smooth, glittery paint pens Morgan wielded. The next thing he knew, he had colored his nails a vibrant, sparkly purple.

"Hey, looks nice!" Salvador remarked over his shoulder.

Morgan knew it was supposed to be encouraging, but he couldn't help but feel caught. He stood up quickly, grabbing at his chair to keep it from falling behind him. As he rushed to leave the art room, Salvador laid a gentle hand on his shoulder.

"Morgan," Salvador said gently. "There's nothing wrong with expressing yourself."

That's what you think, Morgan thought.

Now, sitting in his room, Morgan imagined sitting with Laela, painting their nails together with real nail polish, telling her about his true self. He thought he might finally have some words to describe the unwoven, untangled feeling he'd felt at Evergreen. The last few weeks he'd pored over Reddit, finding recovery and gender-creative subreddits, learning there were others who were like him, who gave words to what he felt. His sober, broken, patched-up, sensitive self. His curious and questioning self.

First, though, Morgan still had to confess to Laela about last summer.

Work the program, Salvador's words came back to him. *Make amends.*

Before Morgan could be honest about his identity, he needed to be honest about his past.

* * *

Ara Grace stared blankly at Nel. Birdie's strong, sure arms enveloped her in a hug. "Oh, Nel. How are you doing with it?"

Nel pulled away and wiped a stray tear from her cheek. "Clearly incredibly well," she said wryly.

Birdie laughed good-naturedly as Ara Grace continued to look on, unsure of what to do here. Her most put-together friend was sobbing and she had no idea how to interpret her reaction. Was supermom Nel really upset about the prospect of another baby? Ara Grace knew Victoria was a handful, but Nel always seemed so calm and controlled about it.

"Seriously though," Nel continued, "I don't want another baby. Is it awful to say that out loud?" Her voice broke with fresh tears. "It's true, though. And I can't help feeling awful for that."

Unbidden, the faces of her friends who struggled with infertility flashed before her. She knew each of them would cry tears of joy to be in her situation. Yet here she was, nearly sobbing in despair.

She inhaled before continuing. "We only ever wanted two kids." She began to list off reasons, and the floodgates opened. Secrets spilled out. "Our family is completely at capacity, financially and otherwise. Victoria might need early intervention. Jacques and I are not in a good place at all." She took a shaky breath. "A third kid is the last thing we need right now."

Ara Grace understood then, and before her brain could catch up to her voice, she blurted out, "Abortion is illegal in Wyoming now."

"Don't you think I know that?" Nel snapped.

Ara Grace flushed. Birdie, one hand still on Nel's shoulder, gave Ara Grace a gentle pat on her arm.

"I'm sorry, Ara Grace," Nel said. "That was harsh. But yes, that's a big part of why I'm getting so emotional. I don't really have options."

"But you do!" Ara Grace replied quickly again. "I'm part of this group, Seminarians for Reproductive Choice. They're connected to this amazing group that helps pregnant women get the abortions they need. They do everything—appointments to childcare to transportation to paying for the procedure. I could get you connected."

Nel sighed. "Thanks. I'm not quite sure I'm ready yet, but it's good to know it's available. You're a good pastor."

She was already putting herself back together, Ara Grace noticed, becoming the perfect Nel they were used to seeing.

"I know you don't need to hear this," Birdie interjected, "but once you get to your age, pregnancy isn't something to take lightly. I had a hard time with the boys. It was worth it for me, but I don't blame anyone for not wanting to go through what we went through. We'll support you whatever you choose, Nel."

Birdie's wisdom won again. Ara Grace remembered that Birdie had told them once about complications with the twins during her pregnancy.

"I just … I really don't know about my bishop, and especially my DS."

"They never have to know," Birdie replied sensibly.

"It's all just too much right now," Nel said before taking a deep breath. "Thank you," she said with her trademark composure. "I … I do appreciate you both."

She reached for both of their hands then and gave them a tight squeeze. The moment was quick, hurried.

After Nel and Birdie had left, once they'd deemed the church basement acceptable and Ara Grace had ushered them out ahead of her, she returned to the basement.

Ara Grace turned it over and over in her mind as she scrubbed tables for the third time, trying to get costume glitter out of the tiny grooves in the Formica tabletops. What did it mean to be a pastor with secrets? With parts of yourself that you'd never want to share? What did it mean to find joy in this work when so much of it was about keeping yourself out of it?

The small flecks of costume glitter remained stubbornly in the grooves of the table. Something no one could get out, no matter how hard they tried.

Chapter 16

Future Plans

OUTOFWYSARAH: YOU GOING TO MISTLETOE MADNESS?

Sarah surreptitiously typed, balancing her phone in the crook of her elbow, hoping Birdie wouldn't notice. She was supposed to be helping her stepmom make dinner. It was an activity they did weekly together, and Sarah almost looked forward to their time mixing pungent herbs and spices, cubing vegetables, and ad-libbing on recipes found online.

But tonight, Birdie had chosen to make some family recipe her own mother used to make. With the traditional recipes, no variation was allowed.

Sarah swore that on those nights, Birdie would look at the picture of her mother in a knit, red sweater, hair wild about her as it hung in their kitchen, almost willing the long-dead woman to appear.

Her phone illuminated with a reply. Glancing up, she saw Birdie basting the roast chicken with full concentration.

OKJTAE: IVE SEEN THE POSTERS BUT WHAT THE HELL IS IT? SOME KIND OF CHRISTMAS BOMB CAMPAIGN WITH OVERLY EAGER ELVES?

Sarah smiled. She'd never realized how folks could, if they were persistently pessimistic like Johnny Tae, interpret "mistletoe" to be a weapon instead of the generic holiday plant hung hopefully overhead. She had some thoughts on how to conveniently find herself with Johnny Tae beneath one of those plants, an "Oops, how did this happen?" moment filled with the nearly unbearable tension of "will-we-won't-we?"

OUTOFWYSARAH: SCHOOL'S WINTER DANCE!!!
EVERYONE DRESSES UP LIKE ELVES OR SANTA.
LET'S GET PEPPERMINT SCHNAPPS BEFORE AT
EVAN'S

Dear Evan Matthews, a year behind her in school, threw the *best* parties, with or without his parents' say so. It was after a party at his place last summer that Laela and Morgan had both ended up at the hospital, but Mr. and Mrs. Matthews were still lenient with Evan. Sarah wasn't sure if that was cool or gross of them.

But Mistletoe Madness was the same night as the Christmas Pageant. Sarah reasoned that Laela and Morgan wouldn't care or even know if they were off at Evan's, since those two would be supervising the pageant like some lame parents. It's not like she was going to get blasted anyways. Just something to push her, to ensure that once she and Johnny Tae both got under that mistletoe, she'd have the liquid courage to lean in.

Another text notification came in on her phone. One from "Mom," spelled with a purple sparkly heart for an O. Jen had done that herself the last time they'd been together, nearly three years ago now. Recently, Sarah's mom had promised to fly her out to California for a few nights this winter break, maybe even for New Year's Eve. She'd said she was looking at the best fares and flight times, that she'd get back to her soon. But even Sarah knew that her mom said a lot of things. Sarah was about to switch over to that conversation when Birdie's voice called out to her.

"Sarah, can you get started on the salad?"

She pocketed her phone. "Sure," she said, thinking of rebuttals to all of Johnny Tae's potential reasons to decline an evening out. Together.

Her mother's text remained unread.

* * *

Johnny Tae reread Sarah's message. Peppermint schnapps, she'd said. He was sure there'd be more than just peppermint schnapps, and tried to think if he'd pick that over a beer or a joint. Would he even have to choose? From his last experience at the Matthews' mansion, opulence and abundance were their guiding family principles.

His face must've been scrunched in thought because Ara Grace asked from her armchair, "All right, what is it?"

He placed his phone face down next to him on the couch. They were in what amounted to the living room although, in typical Ara Grace fashion, there were mismatched shelves and furniture pieces, things she'd accumulated over the years and refused to let go of. One of her more charming features, he figured, given that he too counted as something she'd accumulated and kept.

"Oh, nothing," he shrugged. "Just a school thing."

Ara Grace nodded. "That senior essay still?" She placed her own phone down on her stomach, watching him.

He'd mentioned the assignment to her about two weeks ago when she asked about end-of-semester projects. "That's part of it," he said, sighing heavily.

"I'm impressed that you're taking it so seriously, Johnny Tae," she said. "I figured you'd pull it out of your ass at the last minute."

He could feign offense, but his auntie knew his style. "Still a possibility," he admitted.

The television flashed, moving directly to the next episode of the true crime drama series they were streaming. A narrator's deep voice dramatically intoned, "In small-town America, where everyone is known, a murder so vicious as to confound the federal investigators brought in from the big city …"

Ara Grace *tsked* audibly, looking for the remote. "I hate the small-town ones. They make it out to seem like small-town life is perfect and charming and most of all, peaceful."

Johnny Tae pointed to the floor where the remote lay. "Triumph is peaceful as hell. Nothing happens here."

She looked up at him skeptically, remote in hand. "Really, Johnny Tae? Nothing? I seem to remember this summer certainly being *something*. And it's not just you, or your friends. I'm certain life happens in every small town, and where life happens, shit happens."

He looked at her, cracking a knowing smile. "Shit, Auntie, are you being defensive over Triumph?"

She paused the show and looked at him. "Of course I am! It's our home, Johnny Tae." She paused herself a moment, too, before amending, "Or at least it is for now."

"Wait, are you thinking of leaving?" he asked. "I thought you said first pastor jobs are three years?"

"No, I'm not leaving!" she said quickly. "First calls, not jobs, Johnny Tae, usually last three to five years. But some people leave earlier, some stay longer." Ara Grace sighed, looking thoughtful. She flipped through the options on the TV screen, her mind clearly elsewhere.

"Huh," she said after a moment. "I think I needed that reminder. I've been really pushing to make everything better now, but it's just my first year."

"First few months," Johnny Tae added.

"Right, yes," she conceded. "So, I'm staying here for a while at least, but …"

Hearing the shift in Ara Grace's tone, Johnny Tae reached for his phone, ready to tune her out and tell Sarah, sure, what the hell? A night out would be fun, it'd been a while.

"Oh no, sir," she said sharply. "We're talking about it: what are you doing after graduation?"

Why don't you tell me? he thought, desperate for an answer he could scoff at and chafe against.

* * *

Sarah found a bag of craisins in the cabinet leftover from Thanksgiving. "Mind if I use these?" she asked Birdie.

"We're not using them for anything else, go ahead."

"But I can use them tonight? On the salad?" Sarah clarified.

Birdie looked at her, oven mitt raised in mid-air. "Yes, of course! It sounds delicious."

"You sure?"

"Yes," Birdie said with emphasis before asking more softly, "now why do you keep asking?"

Sarah brought the bag back to where she had already chopped the greens. "It's just that when we're having a traditional recipe," she ventured, "you don't like to try anything new."

She felt Birdie's eyes on her, but she kept her attention on sprinkling the craisins near evenly in the bowl.

"I'm sorry, Sarah," Birdie said. "I do get pretty set with my mom's old recipes, don't I?"

Sarah shrugged as Birdie chuckled good-naturedly. "I get it," Sarah said, "you don't want to offend your mom."

She looked up in time to see Birdie frown slightly. "I doubt she'd mind, but for me, I want these meals to be how I remember her making them. Because I want to share a bit of who my mom is, or was, with my family," Birdie said.

She peeled the oven mitt off her hand, laying it on the counter beside Sarah's unofficial station. "It's nothing personal, Sarah. I think you're a great cook and very creative," she said, her hand resting Sarah awkwardly on her back.

Sarah shifted slightly away from Birdie's touch. "Okay," she said nonchalantly.

Birdie scooped up the oven mitt and moved back to her side of the kitchen. "Do you want to make some kind of vinaigrette for the salad? We've still got about ten minutes before the chicken's done. Pull up something from TikTok—you always have good luck with that."

Sarah laughed loudly at that. "Heather, remember what happened to Laela's face? *That* was from TikTok."

Birdie's hand covered her mouth. "Is that why her face was all puffy that morning? I thought maybe she'd been crying. I didn't want to ask."

"No, I think she's allergic to the hyaluronic acid in the foundation. She let me do a practice round of makeup for Mistletoe Madness."

"Are you all going to that? I thought it was the same night as the children's Christmas pageant?"

"It is," Sarah confirmed. "I think Laela's not going anymore after I messed up her makeup. She's using that pageant as an excuse to not go." She opened a cupboard to grab red wine vinaigrette and olive oil. "She's been weird about going out recently."

"Poor girl," Birdie mumbled.

Sarah tensed. "It's not my fault! I didn't know she was allergic to the foundation. If she ever wore makeup, maybe she'd know!"

Birdie looked carefully at Sarah. "Of course it wasn't your fault. I meant 'poor girl' because of all that she went through last summer."

Instantly, Sarah deflated and felt the heavy weight of guilt in her stomach. Laela hadn't been much for parties or even gatherings prior to last summer, and then with Johnny Tae moving to town, the three of them started hanging out together. And it had felt good, right even, to have Laela back as her best friend.

But Sarah knew she was the "bad influence" in Laela's life. If she hadn't been so chill about drinking and pills, if they hadn't already gotten into trouble earlier that summer … She shook her head, remembering standing by Laela's hospital bedside not once, but twice in that short season.

"I'd still like it if you'd try to make it to the pageant," Birdie said. "You can stop by before or after the dance. I think the boys would like it, having you there. Especially since you'll be gone for part of Christmas break. Your brothers adore you."

Half-brothers, Sarah corrected in her head.

"Are your break plans sorted? Do you know the dates yet?"

Sarah remembered the unread text from her mom. She pulled out her phone, seeing another two had come through in the brief silence, both from her sparkly-hearted MOM. She pulled up the conversation, glancing quickly to see if there were any dates or plane information. She saw instead her mom's message:

I'M SORRY

… followed by some excuse she'd read later, then two more brief ones:

U MAD?

And

ILL MAIL UR XMAS PRESENT.

"She's working on it," Sarah said, instantly protective. The lie came easily. As she pocketed her phone, she wondered if her mother had the same easy ways about lying. Sarah whisked together the herbs, oil, and vinegar loudly, trying to get Birdie to change the subject.

The woman knew, thank God. "Sounds good. I'm going to pull the chicken out. When you're done, want to get everyone for dinner?"

Sarah stopped whisking, poured the dressing into a smaller, but better-looking ceramic bowl, sprinkled some pepper over the top, and left the kitchen, grateful for the conversation to be over.

She grabbed her phone to tell Johnny Tae maybe they shouldn't go, the guilt of Laela's summer experiences still weighing on her, when she saw his response and her stomach leapt.

OKJTAE: COUNT ME IN

* * *

Johnny Tae shifted uncomfortably on the futon. He knew it well—it had been his bed for most of the summer before it was decided he'd stay for the school year. The day the decision had been made and cleared with both his far-flung parents, Ara Grace had bought him a twin mattress. "Time for you to be a real boy!" she'd teased, hauling it up the stairs as a surprise. They'd crammed it into what she'd intended to be her office before Johnny Tae arrived. The bed still had no frame, and it was a bit small for him, but it was infinitely better than the paper-thin mattress of the futon.

He tried to pretend his current discomfort was from the futon-turned-back-to-couch and not from Ara Grace's line of questioning.

"I'm not trying to push you," his auntie said. "But if you want to go to college next year, we really need to start visiting campuses. And you should've already applied to a few by now."

"I know, I know," Johnny Tae said.

"Look, you don't have to go to college!" Ara Grace quickly said. "You can go to a trade school, or take a gap year and travel around, or …?"

"Auntie?" Johnny Tae said, cutting her off. "Just stop. Please."

"But have you thought about it? Your future? What you're going to do?"

"Yes!" he nearly bellowed, startling them both. "Of course I have! And I have no fucking clue, okay? I don't know!"

He was nearly panting, catching his breath, in the silence that followed.

"Look, every year, I get shipped to some new school. Including this one," he said quieter now, avoiding Ara Grace's eyes. "Something planned *for* me. I don't know what I want to do, but I want it to be *my* decision. It is my decision, my future."

Ara Grace nodded. "I hear you. But Johnny Tae?" She waited for him to look at her. "Remember what I said. I'll always have a place for you." She'd first told him that on the night he thought he was headed to jail, another destination chosen for him.

When he was silent, she said it again. "You hear me? Or do I need to text it to you for you to respond?"

He rolled his eyes at her but took it as permission to grab his phone. "Yes, Auntie."

"I mean it," she said, the familiar intensity in her voice soothing to Johnny Tae.

"I know you do," he said.

Ara Grace turned the show back on, selecting an episode set in New York City.

While the narrator introduced this crime, a "macabre who-done-it that kept authorities guessing until its shocking conclusion," Johnny Tae quickly wrote Sarah a response.

Count me in.

He'd been doing the good, responsible thing for a while now. And he knew Morgan, out of high school, wasn't interested in going to some high school party. He wouldn't be risking Morgan's sobriety if Morgan wasn't going to be there anyway.

Or so he reasoned with himself.

But a night of being a kid, a teenager, and forgetting all the pressure and shit of what's next, what's next, what's next … that was a decision he felt ready to make.

* * *

Sarah placed the ceramic vinaigrette bowl next to the salad, the first place in the family buffet line. The chicken was already cut and plated on a large oval tray. She was just about ready to call for the rest of the family when Birdie asked her, "Now what sauce do you think could go well with this?"

She was standing opposite Sarah, on the other side of the counter, her face buried in the opened refrigerator door.

"With the salad? I already made the vinaigrette," Sarah said. Unless that was too much of a departure from the traditional, and now her stepmother had changed her mind, like mothers must be prone to do. Sarah felt her annoyance bubble.

"No," Birdie said. "For the chicken."

This *was* a change, a departure from the original. "But you made a gravy," Sarah pointed out.

"Right, but there's no reason why I can't offer something else in addition to it." Birdie turned to look at Sarah, shrugging slightly. "Like you said, just because my mom made it one way doesn't mean we can't give it a little update. A glam-up, as they say."

Glow up, Sarah corrected in her mind. She smiled, realizing the effort Birdie was making. "You sure?"

"Of course I am," Birdie said. "Now tell me what else would go with it." She began listing the spices she'd used, as if Sarah hadn't noticed during their evening together.

Sarah walked around the counter to stand beside Birdie. "Honestly, grab the Italian dressing."

Birdie turned to her, aghast. "A salad dressing? On meat?"

Sarah laughed. "It's good, I swear! Think of what sandwich shops put on sandwiches—it's all just salad dressings."

"Go figure," Birdie said softly, grabbing the bottle from the fridge. She let the door close behind her as she turned to place the salad dressing next to the chicken platter. "Maybe I'll have you meal plan for the family before you head out to visit your mom."

Sarah winced, her disappointment in her mom (no purple heart for an O) growing.

"Heather," Sarah began before stopping. She didn't want her stepmom to turn into a pastor and try to comfort her. Or to be petty and count this as one more strike against her husband's ex. Sarah's eyes rested on the buffet arrangement ready for the rest of the family: her dad and the twins, who'd eagerly show up not only to this one meal but to anything Sarah asked them to.

"Yes, Sarah?" Birdie said, reminding Sarah to continue.

"My mom bailed. Canceled on me." She rushed the words out, then grabbed the vinaigrette bowl. She whisked it with a fork, unnecessarily busying herself.

"Ah dammit," Birdie sighed. "I'm so sorry, Sarah." She reached out with one hand, squeezing Sarah's arm. She left her hand there.

"It's fine," Sarah instantly said. She had a strange wish that Birdie would hug her.

But she pulled her hand back. "If it's about the cost of a plane ticket, I'm sure we could help out a bit," Birdie said. "I mean, not the whole thing, but part of it, surely."

She shut her eyes, still feeling where Birdie had reached out to her. She thought of the offer, wanting desperately to say yes. It'd be so good to see her mom and even better to get out of the frozen tundra for a few days. *We could help,* Birdie had said.

And it was that, her use of "we," that made Sarah shake her head no, firmly. "We" didn't mean just Birdie. It meant her dad, Mark. It included Isaac and Nathan.

And it meant her, too.

She knew her dad's cattle ranching business wasn't lucrative. That was the family's main income. Despite Birdie's dedication to her work, Sarah knew the woman hadn't had a raise in years. It had nothing to do with her skills and everything to do with lack of church funds.

Sarah couldn't ask her family to cough up hundreds just to fly her away on a golden vacation to see her mom. Not when her own mother wasn't doing a thing to make it happen. *Not even swiping one of her many credit cards,* she thought.

"No, thanks, Heather," Sarah said, returning to the moment. "Maybe later, this spring or summer." The lie came across easily. She avoided meeting Birdie's gaze.

"Of course," she said, easily. "Whenever you want, dear."

Birdie took a step in her direction, and wrapped Sarah in a one-armed hug. Sarah felt Birdie's head tilt toward hers, an additional gesture of compassion.

Without thinking, Sarah turned quickly, wrapping herself in a full hug from Birdie.

This family, Sarah was beginning to understand, was what she wanted.

Chapter 17

Frosty Conversations

Nel saw Laela walk through the doorway and she groaned with guilt. She hadn't gotten around to cleaning up Victoria's glitter-glue disaster and regretted giving her children unfettered access to the arts and crafts cabinet, even when it made pastoral phone calls much easier. Legos covered the floor like a spiky, threatening carpet. Hudson was jumping from couch to couch, taking his Paw Patrol figurines on what sounded like epic rescue adventures but looked like utter mayhem.

"Sorry!" Nel called from the kitchen, where she was working on plates of frozen chicken nuggets and sweet potato fries for the kids. "Haven't had a chance to tame the wild beasts yet today!"

"Don't worry, Pastor Nel," Laela said, and Nel appreciated her genuine smile. "Wild beasts are my specialty!"

The kids rushed over to her, and she hugged them both. Hudson bounded back to the couches as Laela walked toward Nel in the kitchen, Victoria in her wake. She turned to Victoria with a conspiratorial air and said, "Hey girlfriend, do you think you could find all the yellow Legos and get them into our magic box before it's time for your mom and dad to go?"

Victoria smiled up at Laela, hands covered in glitter glue, and nodded. "Let's get those hands cleaned up first, though."

"She hates wash…" Nel started, but Laela already had Victoria's hands under the faucet, scrubbing them with lemon-scented hand soap while they sang the ABCs together, twice through to get their full twenty seconds in. Nel never felt more like a failure as a mother than when she saw Laela in action. *Wild beasts are definitely her specialty*, Nel thought.

Jacques bounded down the stairs, sweeping up Hudson and tickling him until he was nearly crying with laughter.

"Can I play dispatch, buddy? Call the emergencies?"

Hudson loved this idea. Nel was so bad at pretend play. She wasn't creative enough, and then she was bored, and then she felt guilty for feeling bored, so she tried to be more creative, and then she felt dejected at how little creativity she seemed to have. A vicious cycle. Jacques thrived on these little moments of connection, stepping into the kids' stories and playing make-believe. Nel wished she had it in her.

"Should I keep the kids out of the bedroom again for this one?" Laela asked.

Nel had been open with Laela about these babysitting nights being cover for therapy; she trusted Laela and felt like even if the teen were to tell anyone, it would project an air of proactiveness and health to be seeking marriage counseling. Plus, with all that Laela herself had gone through last summer, Nel thought her honesty about therapy could encourage Laela to seek help.

But this night would be different. She was thinking she might talk about the pregnancy, and that was a secret that absolutely could not get out. Nel didn't want to place that burden of secrecy, or temptation of hot gossip, on Laela. She waited for Jacques to make his way over to the women in the kitchen, masterfully extracting himself from the joyfully chaotic playroom.

"Actually, I thought we'd take this one from the car," Nel said, smiling knowingly at Jacques. "Maybe we can run out for a quick drink after, then come back to relieve you. If that will work?"

"Sure, of course," Laela replied. "The kids will be in bed anyway, so it's all the same to me. Go have fun."

"Oh, we certainly will!" Jacques replied, placing a kiss squarely, insistently on Nel's forehead. Nel breathed a sigh of relief. Neither Laela nor Jacques had suspected the real reason for the change of venue.

* * *

"Pastor, can we talk?" Danielle asked tentatively, peeking her head into Ara Grace's office.

Ara Grace snuck a glance at the clock. She was supposed to be at the hospital for a shift soon, but she had some time.

"Of course!" She tried to ignore the cold fear that spread over her. Despite serving as Council president, Danielle hardly ever stopped by the church during the week, busy as she was with her own job.

Danielle sat down, still wrapped snug in her puffy winter jacket. "I wanted to talk to you about Christmas. Advent. The season."

"Yes, we are in Advent, Christmas won't be here for another couple of weeks!" Ara Grace tried to quip lightheartedly.

"That's just the thing." Danielle avoided her eyes. "Some people have been complaining. They feel like you're being so legalistic about all this Advent business."

Ara Grace paused, unsure of how to respond. Her heart thudded in her ears. "I'm just doing what I learned in seminary." She hated the lame excuse, and quickly changed course. "Could you give me some examples?"

Danielle unzipped her jacket, readying herself to stay a while. Ara Grace winced.

"Well, we love to sing Christmas carols here. And there's confusion as to why you'd keep the congregation from doing what they love."

Ara Grace read right through Danielle's words, thinking of a conversation she'd had with Sylvia recently over her trying to include Christmas hymns during Advent. Were people talking about her? Behind her back?

"I'm thankful—*we're* thankful for your leadership and presence," Danielle corrected herself. "I think to be sure that your tenure here is long and fruitful, I'd like you to consider a few ... suggestions."

Her heart pounding, Ara Grace nodded for Danielle to go on. She hoped she conveyed grace and not terror.

"Look, a little change is okay. Good for us, even," Danielle continued. "But I want you to understand that this church means a lot to us. To our people. We know you have a lot to teach us, but, well ... we've been here since before you came, and we'll be here after you leave. People would really like it if you'd move just a little more slowly."

Ara Grace suddenly felt the hot sting of tears behind her eyes and blinked them back. Her face flushed. *We were here before you arrived, and we'll be here after you leave? From Danielle, her council president, of all people?*

"Sweetheart, let us keep some of our traditions," Danielle soothed. "And we'll be happy to let you try some of your new ideas on us, all in due time. A give and take."

Ara Grace took a deep breath. What was she supposed to say to all of this? And *sweetheart?*

"Worship planning brings me such joy," Ara Grace began, a quaver in her voice. "I want to take Good Shepherd on a journey. We don't wait or anticipate much anymore when we can get next-day shipping and instant streaming movies. I was hoping to offer a different," she bit back the words *theologically accurate*, "perspective. Can't we be patient about the traditions? Let them come when it's time?"

"But you see, that's not how it is here," Danielle replied. "We do wait out here in Triumph. A snowstorm comes and we have to wait until the county brings out the plows, which can be days. You know that the internet isn't very fast here unless you want to pay more. A lot of us don't even have it in our homes, especially far out from town. Our traditions help us to prepare our hearts for Christmas."

She inhaled, keeping her composure. "So, you'd like it if we … if I … backed off?"

Danielle bit her cheek, thinking. "In a way, yes, I guess. It's just been a lot, too soon and too fast. Like last week, we already have a lot of silence in our lives. A lot of waiting. We want joy. That's what Christmas is about. For us, at least."

Ara Grace looked down. She had never felt so out of sync with a community before. They have enough silence and waiting? Really? She thought of her friends, the congregants she knew whose lives were so busy with purchasing gifts, seeing friends, attending Christmas parties that they had no time to possibly help at another church thing. At least, so they told her. She felt a pang of doubt, followed by a sharp spark of anger.

"I see you don't need the Advent journey," she said. She saw Danielle stiffen. "Or at least not as I've come to understand it. I'll have

Sylvia plan out the hymns for the last two Sundays as she normally would. Before …" *I came and screwed everything up.*

"Thank you, Pastor." Danielle said, standing up. "Please know that we do really appreciate you and what you're trying to do. It's just … the holidays, Christmas especially, they have that sentimental value, you know?"

As Danielle left, Ara Grace felt deflated, unaware of the tension she'd been holding. She wasn't ready to reflect on how she might have pushed too hard, too soon in her pastoral leadership with the people of Good Shepherd. But she wondered if her congregation was the only one hanging on to sacred cows this Advent season.

* * *

"*Mi amor,*" Jacques said flatly, his voice muffled by his winter clothing, "we don't need to turn on the car. We have our jackets."

Nel glared at Jacques as she shivered in the passenger seat of their car, hand frozen on the keys in the ignition. "I'm cold," she said monotonously, and turned the key. The engine purred to life.

Jacques leaned over and shut the car off. "We're going to boil the planet if we keep idling our cars forever," he argued.

Nel scoffed, mad at his insensitivity to her discomfort and his apparently newfound morals. "Okay, Mr. Environmentalist, I don't want to boil the planet either, but I don't want to freeze myself." She cringed at the thought of entering a counseling session already in the middle a fight and ventured, "Can we turn it on for ten minutes to get it warmed up?"

Jacques conceded, giving a silent nod and looking out his window. She turned the car back on and cranked the heat, enveloped by the sudden swoosh of heat.

Nel tapped her phone clumsily with the gloves that were promised to be touch-screen friendly but seemed to only work about a third of the time. With a quiet grunt of frustration, she pulled off her right glove and got connected to the telehealth portal, where Sister Eunice was already waiting for them, a cup of tea in her hand.

"Well, don't you two look cozy!" she said with a serene smile. Nel had a pom-pom hat shoved over her hair, a pashmina wrapped around her neck and shoulders like a blanket, and a parka that could have fit two of her inside. Jacques looked like a picture from an L.L. Bean catalog, sleek beanie, neck gaiter, and slim puffer jacket insulating him against the cold. Nel seethed at the gall he had to look good in this weather.

"Cozy is one word for it!" Nel replied through gritted teeth. She propped the phone on the dashboard. Jacques, ever the charmer, asked Sister Eunice how the weather was in Denver. Nel could not have possibly cared less. Sister Eunice sensed the tension through the airwaves and deftly brought them to their true purpose for being here.

"So, how has the experiment been going? Practicing falling in love again? I've been eager to hear from the two of you."

"It's Advent now," Nel sighed, "it's hard."

"I know it's Advent and you're busy," Jacques said, "but I feel so much distance from you. We haven't had a good conversation in months, haven't had sex in weeks."

"Oh, is that what this is about?" Nel interjected sharply. "Because if that's the issue?"

"Now did I say that?" Jacques looked pointedly at her. "I was just saying I feel a distance between us. That is one such example of the distance."

Sister Eunice watched serenely from her warm office and Nel wanted to scream. Instead, she clenched her teeth, waiting for the woman to intervene. "Jacques, I'm hearing that you feel Nel is pulling away. Nel, I sense some anxiety coming from you, perhaps even some anger. Could we explore that a bit this evening?"

Nel turned it over in her head, the idea of telling Sister Eunice about the pregnancy. Telling Jacques too. But who would that serve? Certainly not her. She was already so unsure about the future of this clump of cells, this potential life, this precursor to a whole new *child*. Not Jacques, who would get attached and make this even harder than it already was. And Sister Eunice? Nel knew she didn't need to protect her, but it still didn't seem quite fair to force her to arbitrate this argument, even if it was her job.

"It feels like I'm being pulled in too many directions all at once," Nel said carefully, slowly. "I don't have anything left for Jacques after pouring myself out for my congregation and the kids."

"Oh, it's *my* congregation but *the* kids?" Jacques asked, bitter.

"Jacques, you know what I mean."

"Do I? How do 'the kids' exhaust *you*? I'm the one taking care of them all day! They're just *the* kids to you, but they are my everything."

"Are they? Then what are you doing to help them?" Nel's anger flared, but she knew this wasn't the road to go down. Jacques did everything to help them. She stopped herself before continuing more calmly. "How can't you see that they're my everything too? I don't express it the same way as you, but I love them just as much."

"You say that, *mi amor*. You say that."

The conversation devolved from there as they traded the usual barbs. Nel worked too much, Jacques didn't work enough. Jacques was selfish, wanting only to please himself. Nel was overly worried about pleasing others. In their fighting, Jacques had forgotten to turn off the car and Nel had neglected to turn down the heat. They both began to sweat under their winter coats.

After exhausting their arsenal, neither agreeing to a compromise, a cold silence fell over them. They could hear the wind whipping against the car and feel it gently buffeting the sedan side to side.

Sister Eunice glanced between them. Still looking serene, she challenged them. "I hear the issues. We're rehashing the same patterns over and over again. I want to help the two of you see a way out of this cycle. I wonder … are you finding any joy in your marriage?"

Both Nel and Jacques were silent. Nel hoped Jacques might swoop in to save the day with one of his beautiful soliloquies, but he was not her rescuer today. She couldn't think of a single damned thing that gave her joy right now in the whole entire world, let alone in her marriage.

"This might be a place to focus until our next session," Sister Eunice continued. "Search for joy with each other. Within each other. Within your shared life. See what you find. Point it out to each other when you notice it. They don't have to be perfect moments. Just try to notice when there's joy."

Nel was blindsided by a vivid image of her children, rehearsing for the pageant, Hudson so sweetly helping Victoria and making sure she felt included. Her throat felt raw, and her head hurt just behind her eyes. *Joy*, she thought. *We can find joy.*

* * *

Ara Grace wasn't sure she'd ever been so happy to hear her sister's voice. "Hana!" she exclaimed, uncharacteristically bubbly in her attempt to fight through the dark cloud hanging over her. She sat in her office, alone now in the church after Danielle's unexpected visit. She needed some time to think. In the meantime, if she couldn't make Advent and Christmas happen just right for Good Shepherd, she could make it good for Johnny Tae. But first, she needed some buy-in.

She'd called her sister, forgetting until the phone started to ring that it might be a strange time to call. She tried to quickly reason that her sister was a time zone behind her. At least, assuming Hana was still in San Francisco.

"Sister, hey," Hana's voice said smoothly, "is something wrong with Johnny Tae? You never call me."

"Everything's fine, I promise."

Ara Grace tried to remember the last time they'd talked on the phone, or even exchanged more than just a GIF. She knew without looking that there were more bubbles from her side of the conversation in their text thread than her sister's, more unanswered and unlaughed-at memes begging for Hana's attention.

"Things are really picking up at church," she said. "I'm trying to get organized for the holidays to make sure I have time to get it all done. What are you thinking about for Johnny Tae for Christmas? What's J.J. thinking?"

Jon James, Johnny Tae's mostly absent father, used to go by the moniker J.J., though Ara Grace wasn't sure that was the case anymore. She tapped the knuckle of her right index finger on the edge of her desktop computer keyboard, the only physical manifestation of the anxiety she was feeling.

"This is what you called about?" Hana asked. "A smart watch. Did you want to chip in for it? I've still got to order it. Maybe I could just send you the money and you could buy it? Pick out one he'd like?"

Ara Grace leaned against her forehead against her hand. "How about you fly out here to see him? I think the best gift you could give him this year is *you*. Being here, spending some time together. Do you think you could swing it?" After a beat of silence, Ara Grace added. "Maybe after the New Year? MLK weekend even?"

Silence. *She can't just leave this one read,* Ara Grace thought.

"Yeah, I'm just not sure. I've got this empowerment retreat that goes until the twenty-third, and by then it's like, what's the point, you know?"

The point is your kid, Ara Grace thought bitterly, *the one who needs some reassurance that you love him.*

"I hear you. I just … he's still your kid. Your son." She waited for Hana to respond with an excuse. Hearing nothing, she continued. "I love having him here, and he's building a good life for himself. Don't you want to see that? I'm so proud of how far he's come since the summer. What if he wants to stay? How are you going to keep being his mom if you never visit?"

"Jeez, lay on the guilt," Hana monotoned. "I'm shocked he has any interest in staying in that shithole town."

"Oh, come on," Ara Grace felt herself get defensive at the moniker.

"I mean, I get why he likes being with you. You're stable. You get him."

Why is it always my job to be the stable one? Ara Grace asked the universe, or maybe God. She could feel Hana trying to conclude the conversation. Lay on the "you're so good, I don't know what we'd do without you" bit and then disappear to live her latest life.

"You're still his mom," she said. "I love him so much, but he needs his mom. His *empowered* mom." She added the emphasis trying to sway her sister.

"I'll see what I can do, okay?" Hana conceded. "I'll call you soon."

And with that, Hana hung up. Ara Grace sighed. She might not be able to produce Hana for Johnny Tae's Christmas surprise, but she was still going to find a way to bring some joy into their holidays, damn it! At least she could do it for someone.

Chapter 18

Winter Wonderland

With perfectly spaced twinkle lights, red and white striped ribbons wrapped around the light poles, and evergreen garlands—real ones! —draped from the multicolored awnings in the town square, Ara Grace felt like she was walking around the set of a Christmas romcom. There was even some gentle snow slipping out of the early night sky, dusting everything in a light powdered sugar.

But instead of a hot date and swirling butterflies in her stomach for company on this picturesque evening, she was walking the town square with Birdie and her dad, Guy. *Sums up my current dating life,* she thought wryly, thinking of her dismal online dating prospects. She gave a little shudder thinking about her latest conversation with a man two hours away:

WHEN WE MEET, CAN YOU WEAR YOUR CLERGY COLLAR? IT TURNS ME ON.

She'd left that message unanswered and promptly blocked him. Her call wasn't some kink or fetish; this was her life. Anyone who didn't understand or respect that wasn't worth her time.

Unsurprisingly, few dating prospects were popping up for a queer pastor. Either her willingness to date anyone regardless of gender identity was a red flag ("Why can't you just pick one?" the drunk question of a first and only date echoed in her mind) or her career sent people running. She had laughed out loud just the other night at a message, shocking Johnny Tae out of his homework funk.

"What's so funny?" he'd asked.

She'd turned her phone to him so he could see the latest message from a woman three hours away. *I, too, am ordained through weddings. com and think we'd have a lot in common.* He hadn't found the humor in her years of schooling and internships and training being equated to a one-time, online fee. "That's sad," he'd said instead. *How right he is*, she thought to herself.

Ara Grace decided to block out thoughts of dating on this magical Christmas night. "When the time is right, it will happen," Appa had told her years ago. "You can't hurry love, you just have to wait," he'd sung offkey, quoting The Supremes. She smiled, thinking of her dad.

She was able to feel Birdie's anxiety over Guy as they meandered. Whenever Guy took a turn, Birdie would reach out a mittened hand as if to correct him, bring back to the path she had in her mind. Guy, in his oversized, pleather jacket, didn't notice.

But Guy was in a rare mood tonight, reminiscing accurately (as far as Ara Grace could tell) on previous Christmas Walks the town had held.

"The Unitarians were the ones who really knew how to make this a party," Guy said, walking toward the colorful booth tent of the Triumph Unitarians. Kwanzaa, Christmas, and Hanukkah lights hung from the tent's beams; Tibetan prayer flags were draped along the edge of the table. Small cups with steaming red liquid lined up for the taking. Guy examined the offerings before grabbing one on the left side. "Before they offered mulled wine, I snuck a flask of whiskey in my jacket. Viv would have another in her purse. That's how we got to be so popular," he said, elbowing Birdie. "We kept the rest of the parents sane as they chased their little hellions."

Birdie rolled her eyes. "My parents, the bootleggers." She grabbed one of the mulled wines herself, sipping gingerly. "Want to split this with me?" she asked Ara Grace.

"Sure," she said, though the cup itself was barely more than a shot glass. Birdie asked for a second empty cup, and deftly poured the drink evenly in two. Ara Grace took the offered cup, blew on its steaming surface, and took a sip. She was pleasantly surprised by the tannic taste of red wine, orange, and bourbon. "I see why you wanted to share this!" she sputtered.

Guy and Birdie laughed. "It's good, innit?" Guy winked, taking another swig of his.

Birdie lowered her voice, "Town secret: The ones on the left of the table are mixed with bourbon. They go the fastest ... and last the longest."

"Remember the year Mark learned that lesson?" Guy said. They were walking along the sidewalk, past store windows decorated in fake snow. "The year he helped with the set up—that Martha woman recruited him to set up the tents and tables because the park district fellas all got hit with the flu. Remember?"

Birdie stopped walking and looked at her dad. "Yes, you're right, Dad."

"He'd been sipping mulled wine all afternoon, and by the time the thing really started, he was ... well, all I'll say is he was in the Christmas spirit." He laughed. "Mark's a big boy, you know. Takes a lot to knock him like that," he explained unnecessarily to Ara Grace.

They were standing in front of a small boutique shop, its window display decorated with an old-timey living room scene. A stereotypically straight, white family of five (a mom, a dad, and three young children) gathered around a Christmas tree, perfect boxed presents wrapped in ribbons. Guy examined the setup, frowning. "Birdie girl, why do people get so soppy at Christmas time, do you think?"

"Come on, Dad, you're saying this isn't what you remember of our family Christmases?" Birdie said jokingly, gesturing to the scene's dog and cat curled up with one another by the fireplace.

"Certainly isn't my memory of family Christmases," Ara Grace murmured. Often one or both of her parents were working the evening shift, which made any kind of family meal impossible. The day was usually spent in a long church service, followed by a quick gift exchange (one gift for each person, until Johnny Tae was born and then thoroughly spoiled with an assortment of toys and clothes). Umma or Appa would leave for work at either the twenty-four-hour drug store (Umma's job) or the overnight courier service (Appa's second job, after his main job as a bank teller), leaving Hana and Ara Grace to find some Christmas spectacular or movie marathon on TV. *Certainly not window-worthy.* In the reflection from the shop window, Ara Grace's knit rainbow hat was all that showed of her.

She turned and walked away. Maybe that was why she wanted this Advent and her first Christmas as a pastor to be right. So many Christmases had been disappointing in her youth. Never mind the absence of a jolly, white-bearded Santa, she would've loved to sit in her own parent's lap and honestly tell them what she wanted for Christmas. Time with them when they weren't tired or getting ready for another shift at work.

"How do you feel about hot cocoa?" Guy asked from over her shoulder. He motioned towards a dark blue tent. Silver tinsel in the shape of a cross adorned the side that faced them. "This is the best one. Did you ever get their recipe, Birdie?"

"It's just the off-brand cocoa from the grocery store, Dad. Only difference is they double the amount."

Guy frowned. "That can't be right. Ara Grace, you come taste it and tell me if it doesn't taste different to you." He walked around to the front of the tent.

Birdie waited the few steps for Ara Grace to catch up. "Trust me, there's nothing else in there." Her eyebrows knit together in concern. "You alright, honey?"

Ara Grace nodded. "Yeah, Christmas is just …" she couldn't finish the sentence.

Birdie placed a hand on Ara Grace's arm. "It can be a lot, all at once," she said softly. "But it doesn't need to be perfect. It never is. Isn't that what grace is about?" Birdie nudged Ara Grace playfully.

"I'm the Lutheran here," Ara Grace retorted. "I think I know grace."

"Yes, yes. Your denomination has the exclusive trademark on grace," Birdie laughed. "So, give it a shot."

"Only if you will with Guy," Ara Grace ventured. They were near the front of the tent. "He seems to be having a good night?"

Birdie squeezed Ara Grace's arm. "That's all I can hope for anymore, I think. But I'll give that whole grace thing a chance with him, too."

"Sounds like a deal," Ara Grace said, smiling.

* * *

The normal Wyoming wind was muted that evening since the tents placed in the town square blocked the avenues it could travel. The suspension of movement in the air gave Nel a feeling of unexpected peace. She imagined looking down on the scene, a perfect Christmas scene with light snowflakes, soft lighting, and her own family of four bundled in their matching red hats and scarves. A smart-looking family with a mom, dad, daughter, and son, all walking together, clearly members of an ordered set. She closed her eyes, trying to seal this moment, searching it for joy. *This is good.*

Jacques's hat was askew, thanks to Victoria sitting atop his shoulders. Their daughter's mittened hands kept readjusting his hat to signal which way she wanted Jacques to turn. Jacques obeyed even the slightest change, acting a fool to her wild laughter. "Daddy, no!" she squealed when Jacques turned nearly in a full circle. "Too far!"

Hudson joined in on the fun, poking Jacques in the side. Jacques gave an exaggerated squeal and leaned over, acting like Victoria was going to fall off. She screamed in joy as Hudson sidestepped to Jacques's other side, poking him again and darting out of reach and Jacques lumbered over in mock pain.

Nel watched as they all giggled and smiled. She wondered to herself how Jacques could be so lost in the moment as to not care about the sideways looks some Christmas Walk goers directed at the loud scene before she too abandoned herself to the moment. As Hudson ran past her, she grabbed him in a bear hug. "Gotcha!" she said, lugging him up against her.

He was big, heavier than she remembered. His hazel eyes, so like her own, seemed to dance in the glow of the Christmas lighting. He pretended to struggle against her hold. "Mommy!" he cried out.

Nel lifted him a bit higher as Jacques came closer. "Not so fierce now, are you?" he teased, jostling Hudson's hat. Suddenly Jacques grabbed them both, squeezing them in a bear hug. "My family," he said. They were squished together, one mass of humanity awkwardly united.

Victoria's feet kicked out as she jostled in joy, a kick grazing Nel's forehead. She winced.

Seeing this, Jacques stepped back. "All right, my girl, time for you to use your walking feet," he said, lowering himself to the ground.

Nel also gently placed Hudson on the ground and watched as he reached up to help his sister climb off their dad's shoulders. Once she was on the ground, he held her hand protectively. Hudson was in full big brother mode. So good, so pure. Nel's face hurt from smiling. She willed her brain to remember this feeling.

"C'mon, Victoria," Hudson said, pulling her along. "Let's go look at the windows!"

Jacques and Nel fell into step behind them, their focus both on the kids ahead.

After a few paces, husband and wife were nearly touching. Nel could feel the heat coming off Jacques's body. "Thank you for getting the kids ready," she said, leaning in closer toward him.

"You did have them the last few Wednesdays for practice." He shook his head and reached one hand up to readjust his hat. "No, I'm sorry. We're a team, right?"

As his hand came back to his side, Nel snaked her arm through his. "I'd like that," she said.

* * *

Birdie and Ara Grace rounded the corner and faced the tent. Guy already had hot cocoa in both hands. "Now you tell me there isn't something special about this!" he said, thrusting one cup toward Ara Grace.

She passed the cup she held in her left hand, the one with mulled wine, to Birdie to hold for safekeeping, then took the cup Guy proffered. It was the same dark blue as the tent, with shiny cross stickers placed on it. Across the back of the tent, a homemade sign read, WISE MEN STILL SEEK HIM.

Ara Grace took a sip, making eye contact with the woman behind the counter. It was someone she didn't recognize, a middle-aged woman with sour, pursed lips. Her eyes were fixed on Ara Grace's rainbow hat.

Ara Grace turned her back on the woman, her stomach hot. "Birdie?" she asked, raising her eyes up to her hat in a silent gesture.

"Ah, right." Birdie said and coughed loudly, awkwardly. "We should go get ready for the children's pageant. Come on, Dad."

Guy silently swiped a third cup of cocoa, oblivious to the silent conversations happening around him.

"Let me guess … grace?" Ara Grace mused to her friend as they walked away.

Birdie shook her head. "I'll have to follow your lead down that avenue. I'm still learning."

Her honest admission was as pure as the delicate snow. Ara Grace gave Birdie's hip a little nudge. "You know, a wise pastor friend of mine would say, 'Aren't we all?' to that."

"Huh. What makes this pastor friend of yours so wise?"

"Her advanced age," Ara Grace deadpanned, taking a sip of the hot chocolate.

Birdie gave her a hip check back.

"Watch it!" Ara Grace warned. "You might need a hip replacement if you keep doing that."

Both women laughed loudly. The evening felt good, right. Maybe this was what Christmas was supposed to feel like, being with those you love.

Chapter 19

Mistletoe Madness

Johnny Tae looked around the party, disappointed by how familiar it all was. Even if it was his first time in Evan's basement instead of the posh outdoor party scene of last summer and even if it was his first winter here, his first (and last) Mistletoe Madness, it was like all the other parties he had been to. Same Chads and Channings trying to out-alpha one another. Same choice between an overly fruity, sweet drink or a weak beer. Same story, different town.

He spotted Sarah, her ubiquitous red cup in hand, talking easily with a guy. He looked closer, noticing the guy's face was angled downward just a bit too far, taking in Sarah's chest. *Subtle, Jake.* Johnny Tae startled that he knew who the kid was, and downed his own drink to try to forget that he knew more: Jake Franklin was a junior, a server at the fancy restaurant up in town, and a notorious class clown.

His cup now empty, he walked lazily back to where Evan was acting as surrogate bartender. "Barkeep!" he called, jokingly. "Another!"

Evan was quick to play along, throwing a towel over his shoulder. "Ah, what'll it be, my good man? Beer? Schnapps with pop? We've a fine selection tonight."

"Something strong," Johnny Tae said. "You got any shooters?"

"Do I have any shooters?" Evan asked sarcastically. He pulled open a drawer, revealing a mix of mini bottles filled with vodka, whiskey, and various colored liquids. He pulled out an amber colored whiskey bottle. "This is a personal favorite."

Johnny Tae scrutinized the label, recognizing it as a wannabe bougie brand. "I'll take it."

"I can't let you drink alone," Evan said, grabbing a second for himself. He unscrewed both bottles, handing one to Johnny Tae. "To Christmas?"

He lifted his own little bottle in a gesture of cheers. "To breaking traditions."

"Traditions!" Evan yelled, clearly mishearing.

Johnny Tae threw his head back, downing the bitter drink in one swig. Evan had done the same. "Thanks, man," Johnny Tae said, placing the empty bottle on the counter. He grabbed a water bottle nearby to help even out the drinks. He was driving this evening and didn't need to be foolish about it.

"Oh shit, you doing shots, Matthews?" someone—thankfully someone Johnny Tae did not recognize beyond the vague first name Mateo—said. "Count me in!"

As a crowd gathered around the bar, Johnny Tae took the moment to excuse himself. He found one of those sac chairs—bean bags for the new millennia—unoccupied in a dim corner and sat down in it. He'd misjudged the middle; something like an armrest bulged up on his right. He took a sip out of his water bottle before reaching for his phone, opening Instagram.

The first story that popped up was Laela's. She had posted a selfie with herself and some cherubic looking preschoolers, costumes over their bulky winter coats. "Little snow angels," she'd captioned it. Johnny Tae saw the glow in her face, her cheeks reddened from the cold or the excitement. He pressed the heart icon and stared at the screen some more, wishing she were here … or maybe that he was there.

Just then, Sarah sat unceremoniously down on the armchair bulge. "There you are!" she exclaimed. Her red sequin skirt had slid up, revealing more of her white leggings than she likely intended. Her knees rested against Johnny Tae's midsection.

Johnny Tae locked his phone and slipped it back in his pocket. He held up the water bottle. "Taking a water break," he said by way of explanation.

The sound of people chanting, "Shots! Shots! Shots!" erupted.

He winced. "I'm afraid I was the one who started the shots with Evan," he said conspiratorially.

Sarah laughed. "He'd have found someone else if it hadn't been you." She took a sip of her own drink. "He loves shots, but they get him in trouble. Fast."

"Don't they do that to everyone?"

"Morgan can take down a handful, no problem." Sarah said, then corrected herself, "I mean, he used to. It was quite the party trick."

At the mention of Morgan, Johnny Tae chugged a bit more of his water. "The guy's so big, I could see it." *I'm glad he doesn't anymore.*

As if sensing his thought, Sarah said, "It's probably a good thing he stopped. His liver would've been shot by the time he was thirty." She stretched out her leg, curling one ankle. "Pre-parties are fun and all, but I'd love to actually go to the dance."

Not one for cheesy, canned pop music, Johnny Tae didn't respond. They had almost another hour before the pre-party group was set to head to the dance. Frankly, he was content if they never went to the dance and stayed in Evan's basement, drinking all night. At least the Spotify playlist of Christmas music threw on something original every now and again.

Sarah drew back her outstretched leg and readjusted, so the bulged-up armrest sank a bit. Their shoulders touched, and they were leaning toward each other.

Johnny Tae angled himself so he could look her in the face. She had on shimmery eye shadow and delicately placed sequins at the corners of her eyes. Her straw-colored hair, which normally hung loose around her shoulders, was tied up in two complicated buns at the top of her head. She'd even placed glitter down her hair part. Her lips were candy cane red and shone with gloss.

He tried to imagine what Jake and other guys thought when they looked at her. Sarah was cute, undeniably. But with all the extra sparkle and colors she had on, it didn't add anything to Johnny Tae's impression of her.

Realizing he'd been silent a while, he coughed and said, "So, what do you want for Christmas?" wincing as he realized how cheesy the question came across.

* * *

This was it; Sarah could feel it. The electricity between them was magnetic, a practical rainbow of colors. This was something she could control: the way a guy looked at her with desire in his eyes. She might not be able to get her own mother to give a damn, but she knew what it took to get a guy's full attention.

She glanced around. She didn't spy a nearby mistletoe, and it wasn't late enough in the night for her to claim drunkenness if it went south, but he wouldn't reject her. Surely.

Not from the way he'd been looking at her, studying her, drinking her in since she'd sat down. Being so close to him, she could smell him, not reeking of Axe, Irish Spring, or some other overly scented male musk, but a subtle almost woodsy scent of pine and something else, something clean she couldn't quite name.

"So, what do you want for Christmas?" he'd asked, then instantly blushed.

This is good, Sarah thought. *He's nervous, too.* She purposefully looked him square in the eye, a smile playing on her lips. "Oh, so you're Santa now?"

He rolled his eyes and shrugged. "Can't do anything to make your wish come true, but sure. I'll be the Big Guy in the red suit." He'd subtly moved back from her. Sarah figured he was taking her in, looking for a better angle. She lifted her chest so his eyes could better see the cleavage line she'd carefully contoured with makeup.

"I think you could, actually," she said, her voice low. "I want a little fun."

When he smiled in response, Sarah closed her eyes. She leaned in, her lips landing firmly on his, still stretched in a smile. There was a moment's hesitation before he kissed back. His hand reached up her back. The two of them didn't pull apart.

Sarah tasted whiskey and finality. As they continued, she put her finger on the other scent: Hand soap, of all things.

*   *   *

At first, Johnny Tae was taken aback. Her plastic lip gloss smeared over his lips, leaving them sticky. But she'd said she wanted fun, and Johnny Tae was no stranger to a random party hookup. It had been a minute, though, and he tried to respond appropriately. He put a hand on her back, not quite pulling her in, but holding her in a type of hug.

What the hell? he figured, pulling her closer.

She smelled of hairspray and tasted overly sweet, like peppermint schnapps.

* * *

The group had caravanned, a string of pickup trucks and SUVs steadily, slowly driving down the mountain to the high school. Sarah had called shotgun in Johnny Tae's car, and any inkling she'd had about trying to make it a romantic moment died when Evan insisted on riding with them. "I gotta see the new car, man!" he'd said. When Sarah had asked how he'd get back home, Evan had dismissed her. "There's always a way." She almost envied his confidence. Or was it naivete? The whole ride down the mountain, Evan had quizzed Johnny Tae about the truck, specs like engine size, mileage, and space capacity. Sarah had toned him out, scrolling through her phone in boredom.

They were now all reconvening in the parking lot, a group of about twenty. Someone passed around a flask again. Sarah waited until Johnny Tae had taken a swig before putting her lips on it. The cheap vodka raced down her throat. She felt the anticipation, the excitement. It'd been a while since she'd had a night like this. She was just buzzed enough to not feel the punishing cold. She grabbed Johnny Tae's arm to adjust her high heel, her chest pushing out to keep her balance. She noticed more than a few guys in the group watching her. She smiled broadly. She *did* look good tonight.

"Shit, who's got gum?" Evan asked.

Mateo quickly handed him a tin-foiled strip. "I've got more if you need it."

Evan unwrapped it and quickly chomped on it. His face soured. "Not peppermint?"

Mateo shook his head. "Sorry man, all I had was bubblegum. Classic." He smiled broadly and nodded.

"Dammit. Give me some more." Sarah watched as Evan took another four sticks from Mateo's grasp and quickly chewed them. He stored the wad of gum on the side of his cheek.

Sarah chortled. "You look like a damned chipmunk," she said to Evan. The group laughed along with her.

He smiled, good-naturedly. "Yeah, well, everyone sober up. Gotta go through the teacher gauntlet."

"The what?" Johnny Tae asked.

"The teacher gauntlet," Evan repeated. "They stand in a line at the entrance, and you have to shake their hands."

"They pretend it's to see you outside of school hours," Sarah elaborated. "But really, it's to catch you if you're drunk."

"Um …" Johnny Tae started.

Sarah waved him off. "They never check that closely. And you seem fine to me." She leaned coquettishly against him. *Let him take that in all the ways I mean it*, she thought.

The flask was pocketed, hidden under a garish Christmas sweater, and the group headed toward the door.

Fast paced music spilled out of open doors into the brightly lit lobby. Four teachers stood just outside the gym doors. The blonde wooden basketball court floor shone with neon lights behind them.

The first part of the group shook the teachers' hands and made small talk. Sarah and Johnny Tae queued up behind Evan. Sarah smiled at each teacher, carefully looking each of them in the eyes.

"Dr. Brown, my man!" Evan said loudly as he came up to the fourth and final teacher.

"Mr. Matthews, my student," Dr. Brown replied. He grabbed Evan's outstretched hand. "And how are you this evening?"

Sarah saw as Evan made to pull his hand back, but Dr. Brown held on. The motion threw Evan off a bit. "Good, man. Real good." Evan said, smiling still. He'd shoved the wad of gum off to the side of his cheek again.

"I'm glad to hear that," he said. "What's that you've got in your mouth?" Dr. Brown gestured with his other hand to Evan's cheek.

"Ah, just some gum," he said, placing a hand over it.

Sarah saw Dr. Brown's eyes narrow. "I see."

"My orthodontist used to prescribe gum for me to chew so that my bite would be right," Evan prattled on.

Suddenly, Sarah felt the room was too bright, the music too loud. A sense of foreboding fell over her, dampening her spirits.

"Is that so? How about you show me the evidence of your orthodonture then. Smile big." Dr. Brown leaned close.

She knew this trick. He was trying to get close enough to smell alcohol on Evan's breath. Panicking, she gave Evan a little shove with her hip.

The wad of gum fell out of his mouth, dropping to the floor in a wet plop.

"Oh no," she said, pulling Evan down to the ground with her and away from Dr. Brown's nose. He seemed confused. "You dropped your gum." She was chuckling despite herself.

Evan caught on. "Oh no," he echoed. He picked up the wad with his hands. "I better go throw this away." He moved to the trash can behind the teachers.

"Best go to the bathroom," Dr. Brown said. "And wash your hands."

The bathrooms were in the opposite direction.

"Oh, um …"

"Absolutely," Johnny Tae said quickly. "C'mon, Evan." He pulled Evan with him, toward the front doors. Sarah followed closely.

"That was too close," Johnny Tae hissed.

Sarah laughed loudly. "That was fun," she said. "Evan, your face …"

"No," Johnny Tae said. "Not fun. Not worth it."

Sarah rolled her eyes as Evan joined in the laughter. "It's fine, man. I'll throw this away, rinse my mouth, and go back."

Johnny Tae shook his head. "I'm not going back."

"You wuss," Evan said. "What're you going to do instead?"

"I don't know, but I'm not getting caught."

"Man, whatever," Evan said, shrugging him off. Johnny Tae turned and walked outside.

Sarah followed him. "Wait for me!" She called after him. She knew she looked good, and while she'd wanted to dance with Johnny Tae, she was happy to fool around in his car.

The wind was cold, breath-takingly so. She caught up to Johnny Tae. "Wait, your car's this way," she said, pulling his arm.

He looked at her, confused. "I'm not going to my car."

"But I left something there," she said. She was frustrated at how dense he was being. "Help me out."

He sighed, and they quickly got to the car. He unlocked the door and Sarah got in, quickly.

Johnny Tae stood outside, looking around and shivering. "Come help me," she said. She could see his dramatic eye roll.

He begrudgingly opened the door, throwing himself in the driver's seat. "What'd you forget?" he said, closing the door behind him.

She leaned forward, kissing him again. She felt his hesitation. Sarah reached out a hand, cupping his face.

Still, he pulled away. He looked down, his eye catching something in the backseat. "What ...?" he asked, leaning in that direction.

He pulled a small water bottle out from under the passenger seat. It was one of those milk carton-like water bottles, not even half a regular plastic size. It was filled with an amber liquid. Uncapping it, he sniffed it. "Whiskey," he said. "Evan brought an open bottle in my car?"

Sarah could sense his rising panic. "It's fine," she said, grabbing it. "More fun for us!" She took a large swig of it, her face souring. "Shit, that's strong." she coughed.

She handed it to Johnny Tae to finish. He hesitated. "If it's empty, no one can say it had anything in it." He was pissed, but the logic made sense. He took it from her and took one long pull. Sarah finished the rest in silence.

Sarah repositioned herself, squaring her shoulders to face him. He was looking away, out the windshield in front of him. "We should go home." He said. "I should get you home." He shook his head, though it was starting to spin. "I can drive you home."

Sarah pouted. "I wasn't done yet."

"With what?" he asked.

She reached her hand out, stroking his neck. "Having fun," she said in what she hoped was a sexy voice.

He turned to her. His eyes were unsteady, pupils large. She leaned in a bit but stopped herself. She wasn't going to do all the work.

He leaned forward, then stopped. His lips inches from hers. She could feel his hot breath. "Sarah, I ..."

She arched an eyebrow. "Yes?" she asked softly.

"I'm just ... this isn't serious, right?"

She shook her head. "Just fun." It almost felt true when Sarah said it aloud, like it was just another hookup.

He kissed her quickly. The two fell back into each other.

When Sarah's lips landed noisily again on Johnny Tae's neck, he flinched. His elbow hit the car's horn, its blast startling them both.

They sat in silence for a brief moment, catching their breath. "Now that *was* fun," Sarah said, satisfied. She reached out for his hand, but he was angled away, grabbing for the door.

Chapter 20

Quite the Performance

Nel stood off to the side of the metal bandshell's stage as parents with smartphones jostled one another for the best position to take videos of their kids. She scanned the crowd for Jacques and found him leaning against a light pole. Evergreen garland and Christmas lights snaked around the pole. With his dark mop of hair and the knot of the red scarf peeking out of his cracked black jacket, he looked like a movie star. He was handsome, and Nel loved seeing him when he wasn't aware she was watching. It felt so intimate and usually made her stomach drop with butterflies.

Tonight though, her stomach was strangely still. His chin jutted out, and to someone just glancing at him, it would look as if his attention were directed toward the stage and the kids. She studied the sharp angle of his jaw, carefully shaved to keep the scruff she secretly adored at bay. Jacques's attention was focused off to the side of the bandshell. Nel sighed. The frozen reservoir lay behind them, and she gathered her husband's attention was captured not by the kids, the Christmas atmosphere, or the result of hours of hard work, but by the natural barren winter landscape just beyond the town's lights.

"D is for Dancing," the girl named Jade said loudly into the microphone. "For when Jesus was born, the angels danced in celebration."

Victoria's preschool group of tiny, crooked-haloed angels danced on cue, limbs flailing, eyes glued on Laela as she did the motions they mirrored. The crowd chuckled. Nel could hear parents' hearts melt with the cuteness. Her own chest warmed seeing Victoria with her peers, part of the group. Her own precious angel.

The preschoolers stopped dancing and crouched. The next kid from Ara Grace's group, Walter, stepped up to the microphone. "E is for Em-man-well," he said rapidly, mispronouncing the name. "One of Jesus' nicknames." Nel looked over at Ara Grace, expecting to see her shake her head in frustration. She knew how often her friend had gone over the pronunciation with Walter in practice.

But Ara Grace was equally enraptured with the kids on the stage, the smile genuine and wide on her face. Ara Grace gave Walter a thumbs up as he rejoined his group, then pointed at Birdie who was in the makeshift orchestra pit below the stage. *A Christmas miracle.*

Birdie cued up the song from her phone, and the opening notes of "O Come, O Come Emmanuel" rang out. Together, the preschoolers and lower elementary-aged kids sang the first verse. Morgan, crouching next to Birdie so his large frame didn't block any parents' view, held a large poster and pointed to the words as they sang.

Nel heard her son's voice ring out over the others. His voice was loud and confident. Though she wasn't very musical, even she could tell her son sang on tune. Her heart warmed further, seeing how seriously he took this moment.

She clamped her eyes shut, wanting the seal the moment in her memory. Her two kids, perfect in their own ways … the entire Christmas atmosphere so charmingly quaint, the pageant being so well-received. The warmth in her chest spread. It was all so flawless. She allowed herself to be swept up in the moment. *This, just as it is.*

Nel's mind flashed back to Christmastime as a little girl. They'd gather around the Advent wreath in their own home, her dad's strong baritone voice singing out this very hymn as she took turns with her younger sister lighting each week's candles. Nel would try to light them all, but her mother's hand would stop her. "No more, no less," she'd say. "We can't rush things." As more candles were lit each week, her father's commitments increased as Christmas got closer. As their family's finances decreased the ability to buy gifts for everyone in their circles, Nel's mom would also say, "God doesn't give us more than we can handle. No sir. No more, no less."

Eyes still closed, Nel's hand unconsciously rose to her stomach. *No,* she thought, *this, just as it is, is good. No more, no less.*

She looked out at Jacques again. Despite the scene before him, his entire focus was still squarely on the frozen landscape behind the stage.

* * *

Morgan squatted on the ground behind the bandshell stage. His football kneel stance felt right. He was exhausted, even though he hadn't been the one to perform. He looked around, waiting for someone to give something akin to Coach's famous post-game speeches.

A mob of kids ran up to him, Laela's smiling face floating above them. The little ones threw themselves on his large frame, using him like a playground set. He laughed as he gently pulled them off, much to the kids' squealing delight.

"Morgan!" Birdie's son, Nathan, yelled excitedly, following the smaller kids. "Morgan! What do you think? How'd we do?"

The entire wiggling mass of little kids stopped and looked at Morgan, expectantly.

Flustered, Morgan cleared his throat. "Uh, you guys," he started, "I mean, you all were *awesome!*" The kids smiled at that. "You really nailed it!"

Basking in his praise, the kids began to chatter all at once. Isaac, Birdie's other son, stood at a distance from the group. He pushed his glasses up his nose and looked at Laela.

"What did you think, Ms. Laela?" Morgan prompted, standing up.

"I am just so proud of you!" Her smile provided more warmth to the group than the standing heaters. "All of you," she said, pulling Isaac in for a side hug.

The kids rushed to their next target—Ara Grace, who yelped as they enveloped her in a mob hug—and Morgan was left with Laela and Isaac.

Isaac looked down at the ground. "Do you think anyone noticed I messed up my line?" he asked.

"Ah, don't sweat it, buddy," Morgan said, clapping him on the back. It was rougher than he anticipated, and Isaac nearly lost his balance. Morgan winced.

Laela frowned. "Isaac, I'm sure it seemed like a big, huge mistake to you," she said comfortingly, "but I promise, to everyone else, it wasn't noticeable." Isaac looked down, skepticism etched on his face. Laela crouched to speak into his ear, low enough that Morgan could just barely make out her words: "You are your own harshest critic, bud."

It was a line Salvador had said to Morgan back in rehab. His mind instantly went back to the exposed brick of Salvador's office. The papers strewn about. The decor of his kids' artwork littering the lone bookshelf, the books themselves leaning precariously against each other. Morgan had memorized the disarray in an attempt to avoid Salvador's eyes. "Why are you beating yourself up still, Morgan?"

He'd focused on one book's spine—*The Wounded Healer,* he remembered it for the weird title—when he'd finally, after multiple sessions, whispered the truth to Salvador, "I was drunk. I drove my truck … and I hit someone."

Now that someone, crouched low whispering into the ear of Isaac, was a friend. And he still hadn't fessed up.

Morgan's hands clenched, and he bounced one fist off his thick thigh in anger. He sought to wound himself. Despite Salvador's brusque response to his confession ("Shit, Morgan. I see why that's been weighing on you," he'd said, eyes wide through his clear aviator glasses), Morgan still gnawed on the guilt like a dog with a long-loved bone. He didn't deserve Laela's forgiveness. Equally, he feared her discovering that it was him who'd hit her with his truck at that early summer party, the first one Johnny Tae had gone to with him. Morgan feared telling her that he was the coward who jumped out of the car, saw she was going to live, and hopped his drunk ass immediately back in and drove away.

He was further ashamed remembering the high he'd felt having gotten away with it.

Laela looked at Morgan then, concern spreading across her face. "Right, Morgan?" she asked. "It's hard to be nice to yourself, isn't it?"

Morgan nodded. He was afraid to speak for fear his voice might crack and the truth would spill out.

* * *

Laela grabbed for another off-white robe, working her way through the pile of discarded costumes with Morgan. Jessica had made a trip back to Ara Grace's church with the pastor, dropping off the first load of costumes. Morgan and Laela had wanted to finish sorting the costumes into the blue plastic totes before the two women came back. Efficiency was key. Everyone was cold and exhausted after the performance

It was later in the evening, almost time for the Christmas Walk to shut down. The kids had gone around to the various booths with parts of their costumes still attached. Laela and Morgan kept trying to chase the pageant kids around the event until Nel had gotten back up onto the bandshell stage in between a song to announce the kids needed to return their costumes. Then a deluge of halos, shepherds' staffs, gloves, and hats had shown up behind the bandshell. N*ext year, we'll get all the costumes right after.* Laela surprised herself with the thought, so Pastor Nel-like in its perfectionism.

Morgan had gone quiet shortly after the performance. Laela presumed he was just tired. She longed for curling up under one of her mother's knit blankets, sitting on the couch watching some mindless documentary. Soon, she told herself.

"Here," Morgan said, handing her another golden pipe-cleaner bedazzled headband. "You've got the bag for these."

"Now that is *cute!*" Sarah's loud voice made both Morgan and Laela turn suddenly. "Bug, you totally should wear that!"

Laela noticed Sarah stumble a bit in red plastic heels. Her friend's pale face had almost comical pink orbs on both her cheeks. Sarah's long coat wasn't buttoned or zipped. *I want a girl in a short skirt and a long jacket.* The lyrics to the old song came into Laela's mind.

It was then that she noticed Johnny Tae trailing Sarah. He wore a black beanie, his hands dug deep in the pockets of his coat, hugging himself. He'd popped the collar up against the wind. He looked ridiculous, and yet Laela's heart still skipped a beat.

"Hey," he said quietly.

"Oh my god, Laela, you guys totally missed it! You know how Evan Matthews always has the pre-dance parties?" Sarah continued, her words a fast slur. "Well, Morgan, *you* know about those. Anyway, so we were there and ..."

"Sarah, you look cold. Let's go to Buzz Buzz Buzz and warm you up," Laela cut in, glancing at Morgan. Surely Sarah had her wits about her enough not to regale her in front of Morgan about a drunken party. She narrowed her eyes at Sarah, a warning.

It was then that Laela noticed Sarah's shimmer red lip gloss was smeared.

"Oh, I'm fine," Sarah said, waving a hand. "Besides, I've got Johnny Tae here to keep me warm." She reached one arm out behind her toward Johnny Tae, trying to grab him. Sarah's hand grasped the sharp angle of his elbow, and she pulled him close.

Johnny Tae stumbled into Sarah. The collar on his coat fell, revealing his neck.

Laela saw a purple mark smeared in gloss. A hickey. Her heart dropped.

Her eyes flew from Johnny Tae to Sarah, who prattled on. Of course. Of course he'd moved on. Who wouldn't? She was Sarah. Beautiful, carefree, good-time Sarah. The fun girl. The social one. The cool one.

And Laela? She was anything but. Volunteering with kids on a Saturday night, longing to be home watching a documentary.

Loser.

"... and then Dr. Brown asked Evan Matthews to smile so he could see the 'evidence of orthodontia,' whatever the hell that means," Sarah continued, clutching Johnny Tae.

"It means braces," Morgan said. He moved as if to block Laela from their view.

"Right, so Evan grins, and Dr. Brown gets way up in his face. And Evan," Sarah started laughing. "Evan's gum wad just fell out." Sarah evidently thought this was a great punch line. "Can you imagine? This big wad of gum just plopping to the ground? Right at Dr. Brown's feet! Dr. Brown was all suspicious, but before he could get closer or anything, we left. Not getting busted tonight!"

"Yeah," Johnny Tae finally said. "So we figured we'd see what you guys were doing." He spoke carefully, measured syllables, his face intent with concentration. "See if you, uh, wanted to do something. Together."

Laela glared at Johnny Tae. "Your back-up plan."

"No," he said quickly, "that's not ..."

"Oh c'mon, Laela," Sarah said. "Don't be such a wet blanket. Let's do something!" Her enthusiasm felt intrusive. It wasn't contagious this time.

The hollow bang of an empty plastic bin broke the tension. "Sarah, Johnny Tae!" Ara Grace suddenly appeared next to the offending bin. "You made it! But you're about an hour too late. Show's over, I'm afraid."

"We're just cleaning up," Morgan said, pointedly next to Laela. "I'm sure you two wouldn't want to help out with that."

"But what about after? You're basically done," Sarah said, dropping Johnny Tae's arm to gesture at the pile. Sarah lost her balance and stumbled forward, catching herself just barely. She wobbled unsteadily.

Ara Grace moved toward Sarah, hands out to catch her "Whoa there," she said. She looked at her critically. Laela could see the moment Ara Grace understood what was happening: the woman's eyes hardened into a glare. Laela felt her own stomach drop, as if she were the one in trouble. Ara Grace's voice was surprisingly stern for her young age. "I think you've already had your fun tonight." She cast a second withering look at Johnny Tae. "And I don't think you're the only one."

"Oh, Ara Grace, don't …" Sarah said.

"Go sit on the stairs, Sarah," Ara Grace spoke sternly but calmly, throwing one hand toward the bandshell. "You too, Johnny Tae. Sarah, I'll drive you home when we're done here."

"No, Auntie, I can," a slight hiccup escaped his lips. "I have my car," Johnny Tae said, holding his keys up.

In a flash, Morgan snatched the outstretched key, surprising them all. "You're in no condition."

Ara Grace sighed sharply. Laela heard her mutter something under her breath that she presumed was Korean. "Give them to me, Morgan." Ara Grace's words were sharp. "I think I'll be driving your car for a while, Johnny Tae."

He swore and stomped his foot. "Auntie, you can't do that!"

"Watch me." Ara Grace's words were colder than the air around them.

"Pastor," Morgan said, "We can clean this up. I'm sure we can store it with Gavin in the back until you can get it."

Ara Grace looked around. The Christmas Walk crowd was sparse, the festive tents were packing up. Sarah hugged her jacket tightly around herself and shivered slightly, a movement Ara Grace noticed. Finally, she nodded. "Tell Gavin I'll get it right after church tomorrow," she said. "Let's go, you two. Thanks, Morgan and Laela."

Johnny Tae subtly popped his coat collar up again. Laela guessed it was to prevent his aunt from seeing the rude, purple hickey.

But perhaps she already had. As they walked away, Laela noticed Ara Grace's short figure posted in between the two like a sentinel.

Chapter 21

Sunday of Joy

Nel congratulated herself on her choice to hire Earl Fate's bluegrass trio for that Sunday morning's special music. The mayor was always a draw, of course, but he also played the banjo like nobody's business. His daughter, Sarah Beth, happened to play fiddle and was able to keep up with it, despite two kids running her ragged. Nel had no idea how she did it, keeping up a career and a hobby and kids roughly the same age as hers, but she was grateful for some more kid chaos in the sanctuary that morning. The trio was rounded out by Becky, Earl's wife and Sarah Beth's mother, who had a strong, deep singing voice that Nel was sure came from, at least partially, the diaphragmatic strength needed to wrangle thirty middle schoolers in a classroom. Her English classes were legendary.

The Fates smoothly transitioned from prelude music that had everyone clapping and—well, you couldn't exactly call it dancing, but it was *something* like that—in their seats, to singing their opening hymn. With Earl's chords strumming pleasantly in the background, Sarah Beth played the melody of Marty Haugen's "My Soul Proclaims," and then Becky motioned for the congregation to stand and sing. "My soul proclaims your greatness, O God, and my spirit rejoices in you."

As Becky began the solo verse, Nel found that she had subconsciously placed her left hand over her belly. She imagined Mary, young and afraid, growing life just like her. She knew it wasn't fair, but a pang of guilt overtook her. *If she could go through with it, how could I be considering ending it?* Late last night, she'd called Ara Grace's chapter of Seminarians for Reproductive Choice, and they'd taken over the details of getting her appointment made and the logistics worked out. "We'll see you on Wednesday at ten a.m.," the chipper voice had said in her ear, and she had no idea whether she felt relieved or terrified, or ready just to run the other way. The choice was made. "My spirit rejoices in you," Nel sang as she and her congregation joined in for the chorus.

* * *

Johnny Tae tried to muffle his groan as the organ barreled on to yet another verse. The minor notes clawed his ears. He was reminded of the cold, stern voice of his auntie that morning. "You do not have a choice," she'd said, bursting into his room as he lay curled in his bed. The bed she'd surprised him with just months before. "You lost that privilege. Get dressed."

He'd obeyed without hesitation. He'd been fitfully dreaming of Laela's brown eyes, so full of hurt and anger when she saw his neck. He put his hand over the hickey, looking around the piles of clothes for a scarf. He'd found instead a dirty purple apron from Buzz Buzz Buzz. Morgan's sunken frame, disappointment reeking from his friend like some bad cologne, came unbidden into his mind, too. He deserved to be punished this time, he agreed.

Back in the church, the air thin and cold, his stomach was hot with regret. He burrowed himself further into his hoodie, trying to curl in on himself. Why try? The logo on his hoodie, a prep school he'd been kicked out of some three years prior, folded into his chest. Another mistake.

Johnny Tae curled his feet under the pew. His foot nearly hit the coffee tumbler Ara Grace had handed him that morning, her eyes avoiding his face, her body tense. "Here," she'd said. "Plain coffee. There's some ibuprofen if you need it in the bathroom." The same coffee tumbler she told him he could bring into the sanctuary space, just be careful to not spill it.

And of course, just now he'd nearly messed up that brief gift, that privilege. He'd nearly messed that up, too. He closed his eyes against the angry tears that pooled.

* * *

Ara Grace tried to focus on Leon's soothing voice reverberating in the sanctuary. Her admin, her coworker—her *friend*, she caught herself realizing—served as the lector that morning. He read the Old Testament portion, a longer reading today from Isaiah. She tried to reposition her spirit toward joy and grace, willing herself to get over the boiling white anger that steamed within her chest.

She didn't know who to be more upset with—Johnny Tae, for so spectacularly messing up, or Hana, for so blatantly not giving a damn about her own son?

Sure, Johnny Tae deserved some extra understanding, an extra dose of grace for having Hana as a mother.

And where was his dad in all this? Colonel or Lieutenant Colonel J.J., or Jon James West? Ara Grace's anger seared toward the man she'd seen fewer than ten times, first when Hana's body swelled large with pregnancy—so large her gaudy new wedding ring didn't fit on her finger—and a handful of times when Johnny Tae was a baby. She couldn't pick him out of a crowd if her life depended on it.

Her heart fell, realizing the same was true for Johnny Tae.

Two adults who really should've known better, either used a condom that night when they'd first met or set aside their individual problems for the sake of their child. That child they were abandoning again this Christmas.

But hadn't she, Ara Grace, provided her nephew with stability these last few months? *Because a few months can make up for a lifetime,* her own bitter voice said in her head. She should have stepped in sooner, gone part-time through seminary for his sake. That would've been the Christian thing to do, right?

Her eyes found Johnny Tae, still seated, in the back of the sanctuary. *Ungrateful.* The thought came unbidden into her mind, her anger rising again. He was responsible for his choices, even if it pained her to see the results.

She focused her attention on the bulletin in her hand. Leon's voice led them in a reading of the Psalm 126, a song of restoration.

Gracious God, she prayed silently, *help me.* She thought of Jesus' righteous anger, of his overturning tables when the temple—the one place God's presence was guaranteed to dwell—had been turned into a money-making scheme. An ancient version of Disney World. Her own anger quelled, giving way to her true feeling—dismay. A wave of sadness washed over her. Despair at her sister's inability to parent. Sorrow over Johnny Tae's choices last night. Sadness that the world was so harsh and cruel. Grief over Nel's situation, one that wasn't far off from what Hana had faced all those years before. The choice she knew her sister had made the second time it happened, when Johnny Tae was learning to walk and J.J. had been back in the States on leave. She felt grief pulsate within her. Leon's baritone boomed the start of the Psalm's final line. "Those who go out weeping," he prompted. The congregation's voices merged into one, "Shall come home with shouts of joy."

* * *

In Good Shepherd's fellowship hall, the faithful stragglers gathered their things to leave. Richard sat next to a mute Johnny Tae, both drinking coffee in silence. Richard drank from a "#1 Grandpa" mug he'd brought from home, Johnny Tae from the tumbler his aunt had filled for him that morning.

Johnny Tae couldn't say he liked Richard in particular, but he gave the man credit: Whenever Johnny Tae darkened the doors of Good Shepherd, Richard sought him out. The man had been a steady presence. He had quickly stopped pressing the teen for conversations and, unlike other older people, he never tried to fill the silence between the two by regaling Johnny Tae with stories of his long-ago youth. He always asked Johnny Tae about school, and if he caught Johnny Tae scrolling through TikTok, he'd ask to see the latest "funnies," as he'd call them. That bit did annoy him, which was why Johnny Tae sat at the round table, his phone hidden in his hoodie pocket.

His knee bounced up and down. Nerves, anger, or the results of being over-caffeinated, he wasn't sure.

Richard tipped the remaining sip of coffee from his mug, then clapped the table. "Well, it seems to be time for me to start heading out." He stood, then carefully pushed his chair in. "Long commute, you know." He winked, another annoyance, at Johnny Tae. They both knew he lived just a few houses from the church. "I better warm up the car," he joked, slapping his thighs. Richard strolled past him and gave his shoulder a tight squeeze. The move reminded him of something his Uppa would do.

"Johnny Tae?" his aunt's voice rang out, a question. From the tenor of it, he couldn't discern the degree of anger she was carrying. "I just have one more thing to grab from my office. Meet me in the narthex."

He turned his head, and found Ara Grace by the light switches. She flicked them off without waiting for a response.

Still mad, he concluded. He stood, moving through the darkened church halls toward the entryway. Noticing a light peeking out from under the bathroom door, he tapped on the door. With no response, he cracked it open. Johnny Tae scanned the floor for feet hanging out of stalls. No one was in there. He turned the light off himself. Everyone else had left, leaving his aunt again as the last to close up.

"Thank you." Ara Grace's voice startled him. He turned, seeing her holding his jacket out to him. "I don't know what I'd do without you. You're the only one who helps me close," she said. Her voice didn't have the tight syllables, the telltale anger. It was drawn out, defeated.

He shrugged, reaching for his coat. "Thanks for getting my coat," he said.

"Johnny Tae?"

"Yeah, Auntie?" he maneuvered himself into the jacket, holding on to the coffee tumbler.

She murmured something, her voice rising in a question. He leaned in closer to hear as she repeated herself. "Shall we go home?"

Home. Her eyes locked on his face. Johnny Tae knew his aunt had chosen the word intentionally. He lowered his eyebrows, trying to keep his face neutral.

"I'm still allowed?"

Ara Grace didn't laugh at his poor attempt at a joke. "Look, you made a huge mess of things yesterday. That's on you," she said flatly. "And it's on you to fix it. But you've still got your keys."

He readied himself to argue, but Ara Grace pointed to his coat pocket. Reaching in, he felt the familiar curves of his key chain. He pulled it out, noticing it was lighter than normal, but his focus was on the new addition. A cartoonishly cute bear about an inch tall hung on the end of it. Squinting in the shadowed hallway, Johnny Tae laughed. The bear had "D.A.R.E." handwritten across its brown chest.

"I keep the car keys for at least a month," Ara Grace said. "And you … 'just say no to drugs.' Or something. I don't know. Judging from your general attitude, I'm guessing that you're beating yourself up." She walked ahead of him. "Don't turn that into a dirty joke."

His auntie, so awkward and yet so stubborn. He followed her, feeling slightly lighter than he had all morning. Only slightly.

"Wait, Auntie, don't we need to go pick up the bins from Gavin's?"

"I forgot!" She stopped, turning to him. "See? What would I do without you?"

* * *

Birdie stood before her congregation, a weary but contented smile gracing her face. She'd left the rest of her brood at home, letting Isaac and Nathan bask in the glory of their pageant performance and leaving Mark to deal with the fallout from Sarah's wild night. There would be time for those conversations later. Today, Birdie had the great privilege of reading one of her favorite scripture passages in the entire Bible.

"A reading from the Gospel of Luke," she began. "The words of Mary, from chapter 1, verses 46b through 55. With some gender-inclusive language those of you who know me are familiar with:

My soul magnifies the Lord,

and my spirit rejoices in God my Savior,

for God has looked with favor on the lowliness of her servant. Surely, from now on all generations will call me blessed;

for the Mighty One has done great things for me, and holy is God's name.

God's mercy is for those who fear her from generation to generation.

God has shown strength with her arm; God has scattered the proud in the thoughts of their hearts.

God has brought down the powerful from their thrones, and lifted up the lowly;

God has filled the hungry with good things, and sent the rich away empty.

God has helped his servant Israel, in remembrance of her mercy,

according to the promise God made to our ancestors, to Abraham and to his descendants forever.

Birdie usually stuck to gender-neutral God language, but she delighted in challenging her congregation a bit with the divine female. She used it sparingly, and only when she felt it was theologically called for. Mary's song to God? Absolutely the time to spend some theological capital.

"Think of Mary, the teenage mother," Birdie began. "If I had found myself pregnant and unmarried at fourteen in the world, especially the one she was living in, I would have been terrified. Beyond terrified," she clarified. "I'd be plotting my escape route. This was not a condition any young girl would want to find herself in."

She paused for a moment before continuing.

"Pregnancy is one of the most amazing things the human body goes through, and growing a whole new life is undoubtedly a gift. But it is also physically taxing, emotionally draining, and in a lot of ways, just plain confusing. It is an incredible thing to offer one's body for such work. And Mary faces this possibility, not with terror, though she may feel it, but with joy. She *chooses*," Birdie emphasizes the word, hoping those listening for the traditional third Sunday in Advent theme would get her meaning without flat-out saying it, "to make this sacrifice because she believes it will change the world. She knows this child growing within her is God, and not just a God of power, but a God who will hold power to account. A God who will turn things upside-down for all of us. A God of full bellies and fuller souls, of mercy and promise forever.

"Each one of us is faced with a choice." Birdie breathed in slowly. She saw Paul propping her father up as he dozed, periodically letting out a loud snort. Guy wore a bright blue button-down, its collar folded over in his slumber. "A theologian many centuries ago, Meister Eckhardt, wrote, 'We are all meant to be mothers of God. What good is it to me if this eternal birth of the divine Son takes place unceasingly, but does not take place within myself? And, what good is it to me if Mary is full of grace if I am not also full of grace? What good is it to me for the Creator to give birth to his Son if I do not also give birth to him in my time and my culture? This, then, is the fullness of time: When the Son of Man is begotten in us.'"

She let the words hang heavy, the words of Meister Eckhardt (or Mr. Eckhardt, as Mark jokingly called him) billowing like clouds over the congregation. "What are we mothering? What are we midwifing into existence? What are we waiting for, in this season?"

Birdie thought about her own answers, about her reticence to mother her own father, and how much he needed the grace of her decisiveness. She needed to midwife a new family dynamic into being. It was the only way to restore the joy at the center of their family's history, the joy that had been missing for so long. What was she waiting for?

As if in reply, she caught sight of her father twitching himself awake on her brother's shoulder. At that moment, Paul's gaze was focused entirely on Guy. Birdie noticed a blue hue from their father's shirt reflected in her brother's face. Maybe Paul was willing to carry a new dynamic into fruition with her.

Part 4

Love

Chapter 22

Values

Nel's phone vibrated against her thigh as she sat on the couch, Victoria draped over her lap and Hudson snuggled against her side. She took the kids on Sunday afternoons, most of the time. She tried to give Jacques a little time to himself after a morning of wrangling their two bundles of energy solo. This Sunday, though, she was feeling more than a little resentful. She had led her congregation through a stirring bluegrass service that morning. Her sermon was a fiery take on the Old Testament text for the day, Isaiah's proclamation that God "has sent me to bring good news to the oppressed, to bind up the brokenhearted, to proclaim liberty to the captives, and release to the prisoners." She knew she could not preach on Mary's song this year with what she was going through, but she could certainly channel her spirit as she listed all they were waiting for this Advent. Good news. Liberty. Release. In the vague, theological terms of her sermon, it had all felt so powerful. Now, she just felt drained. Trapped. Like that freedom was nothing she'd ever be able to access herself.

She picked up her phone and saw that the vibration was an appointment reminder for Wednesday in Fort Collins. Good news. Liberty. Release. Nel realized she hadn't told Jacques about the trip. He was out in the garage painting, and she and the kids were so cozy. She decided to text him, an easy half-truth she'd planned.

NEL: HEY, GOT A MTG IN FT COLLINS WEDS A.M. WINTER BREAK FOR BOTH KIDS. CAN YOU TAKE THEM?

Nel wasn't expecting a response anytime soon. When Jacques was in his studio, he was serious about eschewing distractions. She settled back into the couch and turned to the next page of *Olive, the Other Reindeer*, a Christmas book the kids could agree on. Nel herself thought it was pretty sweet. She had barely started her next sentence when she felt her phone buzz again.

JACQUES: SERIOUSLY? WHAT'S IN FT COLLINS?

Nel could hear her heart pounding in her ears. She tried to ground herself with the weight of her kids, reminding her that she was present, she was safe, and it was all going to be okay. Bile rose in her throat. He was really going to make this harder for her? Nel decided she'd read a few more pages before texting back. Less than a page later, another buzz.

JACQUES: IT'S ALWAYS ME PICKING UP AFTER YOUR BULLSHIT

A tightness gripped her throat. Nel pressed kisses to her children's heads and gave them each a squeeze. "I'll be right back, my loves," she managed.

In the kitchen, she turned her back to them, closed her eyes as tightly as she could, and tried to breathe. Turning around, she leaned on the counter, staring at her phone's lock screen. A photo from that summer, Hudson blowing bubbles while Victoria laughed hysterically, trying to catch them. Nel could see Hudson sounding out the words, continuing the book with Victoria, playing the role of big brother so perfectly. She opened her texts.

NEL: SORRY. DS NEEDS TO MEET WITH ME ABOUT SOME URGENT STUFF. I WANT TO STAY EMPLOYED.

Lying through her teeth. Classy. But she had no idea what else she was supposed to do here.

JACQUES: OF COURSE (EYE ROLL EMOJI) ISN'T YOUR DS IN DENVER?

Texting was not the way to do this, Nel knew, but it was what they had right now.

NEL: WE'RE MEETING IN THE MIDDLE.

SHORTER DRIVE. THIS CONVERSATION IS
OVER. THANK YOU FOR TAKING WEDNESDAY
MORNING WITH THE KIDS.

Then, after thinking for a moment, she added:
NEL: IT'S WINTER BREAK, MAYBE LAELA CAN
BABYSIT?

Almost immediately, Jacques replied:
JACQUES: I'M INSULTED THAT YOU THINK I
CAN'T HANDLE MY OWN KIDS.

Nel began to type, "That's not" and then stopped. She didn't
have the energy to have this fight again. She was tired. Her body
ached. Her head pounded. Her heart still raced. She set her phone
on the counter face-down and walked back to the couch, snuggling
in between her kids for the last few pages of their book.

* * *

Johnny Tae lay across the couch in the living room he shared with
Ara Grace, grateful his auntie had gone out "to get a few festive things
for Christmas—and *no*, that does not mean booze." He'd been directed
not to leave the apartment, that he was well and truly grounded and
she would figure out what to do with him next.

He was well and truly exhausted. Not just exhausted, but ashamed
and a little frustrated, too. It was a relief to have escaped any real
trouble last night, but he still had Sarah and Laela to contend with.
He looked at his phone, toggling between his messages and Instagram.
In his message inbox, he could see the first few words of a message
that he didn't have the heart to open yet:
SARAH: HEY JT, LAST NIGHT WAS GR…

Last night was great? Johnny Tae wasn't sure a drunken, sloppy
kiss counted as great, and he didn't want to know what else was inside
that message. He left it alone.

On Instagram, Sarah's story featured a picture of herself in front
of her mirror at home, playing with different makeup looks, starting
about an hour before they'd hung out the night before. Classic
GRWM, the social media abbreviation for "Get Ready with Me,"
content. Then, a video clip of the pregame—careful not to show any

alcohol, of course, but it looked as rowdy as it had felt. And then, to his horror, a picture of the two of them, Sarah kissing his cheek. She had added a little dancing glitter heart above their heads.

Johnny Tae's stomach dropped, then seemed to fill with lead. He'd had fun with Sarah last night. Of course he had. He would not, however, have described the experience with dancing glitter hearts. He braced himself, then toggled back to his message app, opening the text from Sarah.

SARAH: HEY JT, LAST NIGHT WAS GREAT. SORRY I GOT A LITTLE SLOPPIER THAN I MEANT TO. COULD WE TRY FOR A SOBER REDO?

No. That was the first word that came to Johnny Tae's head, and it became the only word he wanted to type. No. It had been a mistake. He wasn't interested in Sarah as anything more than a friend—a *good* friend, one he could count on, but just a friend. He quickly typed a message.

JOHNNY TAE: I HAD A GOOD TIME BUT IT WAS JUST FOR FUN. YOU'RE A GOOD FRIEND. LET'S KEEP IT THAT WAY.

Before he could think, he sent the text, then tossed his phone onto the floor and closed his eyes.

* * *

Sarah's head pounded, but she continued her makeup tutorial video, determined to try to make this work. She had been chugging water since her hangover had woken her up at six that morning, and she was waiting for the ibuprofen to kick in. She was working on her "Morning After a Wild Night" tutorial. Her phone was propped up between two of her textbooks on her desk. *I've gotta get myself a tripod one of these days.* She smoothed two small smears of CC cream over her cheeks, noting for her viewers that it helped with "that morning-after redness." She was trying to think of practical tutorials, and what teenage girl didn't need help looking normal after a night of partying?

Mary Chapin Carpenter's Christmas album started playing from downstairs, the folksy chords of "Come Darkness, Come Light" filtering up through the vents. *Heather's home. Great.* Sarah wasn't excited for the tongue-lashing she was sure she had coming after last night. Though her stepmom had seemed pretty distracted. Maybe she'd leave Sarah's dad to handle things alone. Either way, the music was making it next to impossible to record, so she took her phone off its precarious perch and opened her notifications. She had texted Johnny Tae earlier that morning, trying to seem noncommittal, but she really was into him. He seemed into her last night, too. No response yet. She stared at the screen, willing Johnny Tae to text her back, and as if her mind had some kind of magic powers, she felt a vibration, and he did.

As she read the words, she started to panic. *Good friends? Let's keep it that way?* Such a cheesy letdown. Sarah felt like her chest was full of the spiced eggnog her stepmom loved to make on Christmas day, after all the services were done. Warm, spicy, sharp. Sarah didn't like that eggnog. It was too heavy, too spicy, too much.

Too much.

She felt stupid, suddenly. She thought of Laela, her friend's vague words about Johnny Tae. What was she thinking?

Sarah took out her phone and, with no joy, texted Laela.

SARAH: CAN WE TALK BUG? I THINK I MESSED UP.

She hit the send button. Looking in the mirror, she saw the weight of a fatigue she had no business taking on at her age. *Time for the shimmer eyeshadow*, she thought glumly as she turned her camera back on and started recording again.

* * *

Johnny Tae's eyes shot open suddenly, and he sat up, running his hands frantically through his hair. *The PV. Oh shit.* He had been thinking about the personal values statement, of course he had, but the fact that it was due *tomorrow* just hit him like a ton of bricks. He needed to put pen to paper, as it were. Or maybe, actual pen to actual paper.

"Auntie!" he called out, before remembering Ara Grace was shopping. He felt like it would've been disrespectful to enter her space, but he felt no such honor for the stacking cubes in the living room. He opened one and immediately closed it. It looked like it was full of church bulletins. Johnny Tae had no idea why his auntie would keep paper bulletins stuffed in a living room drawer, but he didn't question the ways of weird pastors. The next cube was more his speed—yellow legal pads and basic black ballpoint pens. He figured Ara Grace wouldn't mind if he took one of each. He sprawled out on the floor, taking a throw pillow to rest under his chest. He propped himself up on his left elbow and began to write.

"What do I value? As a kid in America, I grew up learning to value my material possessions. Honestly, my dad wasn't in my life very much growing up and the only thing he did was send me expensive toys he knew my mom couldn't afford. It didn't take very long for me to figure out how empty that was. We can collect all the gaming systems and fancy clothes we want, and sure, it might be fun for a while, but it won't make us happy."

Some good anti-capitalist stuff at the top never hurt anyone, Johnny Tae thought. Then he thought of his mom.

"It's hard to know what my mom values. She's usually trying to get away from me, and I honestly don't blame her. I've given her a lot to want to run away from. But it's shitty"—he crossed out shitty and corrected it— "hard, not knowing much about what your mom cares about. Especially when she doesn't seem to care much about me."

Too honest? Johnny Tae didn't care. He was on a roll now.

"Last summer, my mom dropped me off in Triumph to be with my aunt. My aunt who's barely older than me. I honestly don't know what she was thinking. But it was the best thing that could have happened to me. Ara Grace is weird, but she has a heart. She made me realize how important family really is to me. So that's my first value. Family. People you can really count on, especially when things are tough. People who love you no matter what, and who teach you how to love other people no matter what. Family has never been something I really felt like I had until now."

He thought about all he'd put Ara Grace through these past six months. He was embarrassed to realize his eyes were welling up, thinking about how, even after all that, she was out right now doing what she could to make his Christmas special. He didn't deserve her.

"My second value is grace. One thing I've learned from going to church with my aunt is that none of us gets what we deserve because none of this is about what we deserve. It's about the humanity and dignity of all of us. It's about screwing up, learning from our mistakes, apologizing, and forgiving each other. I don't know if I believe in God, but I know I believe in grace."

He thought about screwing up, and his mind drifted to Laela. *Shit.* He had some apologizing to do, and he hoped there would be some forgiveness waiting for him.

"I always thought it was most important to be the smartest guy in the room, or the most jaded. The one who knew things. But here in Triumph, I met people who are so smart they could run circles around you and yet, they're kind. They're honest. They care. So, my third value is kindness. It actually matters. I've never been around people as kind as the people here, and it's changed me."

Now he sounded like a total sap. He vowed to never let any of his friends read this. Definitely not his auntie. It felt good to bare his soul a little bit, as long as it was just for Dr. Brown.

"I always thought I wanted to go far away for college. Maybe Europe. I was always trying to escape from my life. I lived that way here for a while, too. I don't know what I want to do next, but I know I'm seeing the value in putting down roots somewhere. Really finding my people. My last value is roots. And right now, those roots are growing well here in Triumph. I want to see what I can do with a good set of roots."

Not a masterpiece, but good enough. Johnny Tae debated typing it up, but he couldn't quite bear to read it again. Instead, he ripped off the four sheets it had taken to get his thoughts down, wrote his name at the top of the first page, scrounged around in the storage cubes for a paper clip, and fastened the pile together.

Just then, Ara Grace burst through the door, arms filled with plastic bags. "Hide your eyes!" she shouted. "Surprises in here!"

Johnny Tae smiled good-naturedly and retreated to his room, tucking his paper into his backpack. He thought for a moment, then took the papers out. He wanted to keep the handwritten copy for himself. He liked this version of himself and wanted to remember it.

He quickly typed up the paper and submitted it online. Now, he could relax.

Chapter 23

Clear Winter Air

Laela's phone buzzed with a notification. The winter sun was shining into her face. She had been up for hours. Her homework was done for the weekend. The work had kept her from thinking of the tears she wanted to cry. Anger, frustration, regret, hurt. The feelings fought for attention in her head. Now she was working ahead in chemistry, balancing reactions meant for later this week. How much H_2O was given off from this reaction? Or how much carbon was released from this one? "The carbon atom doesn't like to be left alone," she remembered her teacher saying. "It always needs a pair."

Her phone buzzed again. Sighing, she turned it over, half expecting to see Sarah's name, or in a small corner of her heart, hoping to see Johnny Tae had messaged her.

She had basically rejected Johnny Tae this fall. So why was she surprised when he'd moved on? And why was she surprised when it was Sarah—her beautiful, carefree, fun-time, blonde-haired friend—who he'd picked?

But it was a text. Two texts, actually, from Morgan. She opened her phone, reading the first one. It was just an image of two pairs of elliptical-shaped plastic planks.

MORGAN: DO U HAVE PLANS TODAY? WANT TO SNOWSHOE?

Laela thought for a moment. She had nothing else to do, and the sun was bright. The weather station on her desk said it was already 27 degrees outside, warm for this time of year.

She didn't think Morgan was angling for a romance. She'd heard through the small-town gossip about his various hook-ups over the years. He had been the star of the football team, the sheriff's son, decently good-looking. And the quick death of his mother had made him more attractive to the girls in her school, the sorrow for some weird reason drawing them to him. But he'd quickly turned his sorrow into heavy drinking. The further brokenness had made most of her female classmates want to cure him, to fix him themselves. *Nothing like a savior complex*, she thought.

Laela realized she'd never had that feeling for him, neither to fix him nor to be romantically involved with him. Their age difference—Morgan had been three years ahead of her in school—plus distinct interests made it so they never really ran in each other's circles.

But having done the Christmas program together, Laela had gotten to know him. And to her surprise, she liked him. His budding man-bun had made his large, square physique less intimidating. And his playfulness with the kids had been fun to watch. She reflected for a moment on the warmth she felt toward him. Was it romantic?

Her phone buzzed again.

MORGAN: IM LEAVING IN 15 LMK

Whatever she felt toward him and about the whole Johnny Tae and Sarah situation, she wasn't going to solve it by balancing inert chemical equations. She wasn't sure, and she bit her lip as she typed back.

LAELA: SURE. PICK ME UP ON YOUR WAY?
MORGAN: K

His reply was quick. She hurried to get her winter gear on.

* * *

Morgan walked up to Laela's front door, bedecked with a festive green wreath. Laela's dad opened the door before he could ring. "Hi, Mr. Wayland," Morgan said, waving with a pair of purple snowshoes. He stood on the mat, the words WELCOME HOME under his feet.

"Morgan!" her dad greeted him warmly. "Just Coltan, come now."

Morgan stepped inside and pulled his ear muff off. He looked around. A Christmas tree stood cozily in the corner of the front room. There were nested bookshelves built into the walls. Books of various widths and heights filled each shelf. One shelf, high and out of reach of grasping hands, had various science decor: a glass beaker filled with gray pebbles, an anatomical sketch of a trout, a collection of flowered seeds. *Books and science*, Morgan thought, *very Laela.*

"The show was great last night," Coltan said.

It took Morgan a moment to realize he was talking to him. "Yeah, the kids did really great."

"Laela told me she convinced you to help out with it," Coltan continued. "Lucky you, huh?" He laughed at his own joke.

Morgan shrugged. "I needed something to do. Gotta keep busy!" He swung his arms and clapped his hands together, as if showing that he needed to do something right then.

Coltan nodded, thoughtful. "It's good to be with people. Helps me out, too, when things get too loud in here." He tapped his temple. "And I guess there's nothing like little kids to keep you busy. And they're certainly loud enough."

Laela came into the room then. "Morning, Morgan! I'm almost ready."

"No rush," Morgan said.

"I was just telling him how great the show was last night," Coltan said. "I don't know how you two did it. All those kids! And how'd you memorize all those words to the songs?"

Laela perched on the edge of the couch shimmying her foot into a boot. "That's nothing compared to what we have to know for school," she said.

"True," her dad replied. "So, where are you two going to go this morning?"

"I figured we could go by the reservoir?" Morgan said, looking to Coltan. "Are the trails there decent, Mr. ... I mean, Coltan?" He knew Laela's dad worked there, though in what capacity, he wasn't sure.

"They're not groomed, but the trails are used often enough. You ought to be fine," Coltan said.

"That works for me," Laela said, standing with her coat. "Bye, Dad!"

Coltan handed Laela her hat as she kissed his cheek. "Now young man," he directed his attention to Morgan. "You need to have her back by dark," he said jokingly.

Morgan paused, uncertain.

"Dad!" Laela hissed. "Stop it!" She ushered Morgan out ahead of her. He barely had time to wave goodbye to Coltan.

* * *

Laela hoped her dad wasn't watching them through the windows, taking notes to share with her mom when she got back from her errands. "I couldn't tell if it was a date," she imagined her dad saying to her exasperated mom. "He came to the door to get her, what do you think that means?" She smiled even as she rolled her eyes, knowing her parents wanted good things for her. Good, normal things, like friends and dates.

Laela tried the door of the old sedan, but found it locked.

"Oh, sorry," Morgan said. "Let me get that for you." He made a motion as if to open the door himself, then stopped. He pressed the unlock button on his keys.

Laela opened the door and quickly climbed in. The inside upholstery was worn thin.

Morgan lowered himself into the car, the purple snowshoes awkwardly falling into Laela's lap. "Brought these for you," he said. "But yeah, you should probably wait till we're at the trail to put them on."

"Cool," Laela said, faking ease. "New car?"

Morgan started the engine. "Sort of," he said. "I totaled my truck, and this is all we had left."

"Right," Laela said. She winced, thinking about the accident that had finally sent Morgan to rehab and all that happened that night.

"You know, that old one wasn't even my truck," he said. "It was my mom's. This was always meant to be my car. I just used hers after she died." He paused for a moment. "Though I wasn't great with it."

Lovely conversation, she thought. *Really romantic.* "Oh," she said instead. Was it just her, or was Morgan tense?

They drove without speaking, the drone of a pop station providing background noise. They arrived at the trailhead a few minutes later. Both of them fell out of the car, Morgan carrying four walking sticks.

"So, it's been a while since I've snowshoed," Laela said, taking two of the sticks from him.

"My mom always said if you could walk, you can snowshoe," he said, bending down to pull the straps around his boots. "But I can't do it without the walking sticks."

"Probably a good idea," she said, stepping into her walking shoes. "Sometimes my hip bothers me on uneven terrain."

"Always?" Morgan asked.

"No, just since last summer. When I got hit," she said, the end of the sentence softer.

Morgan's cheeks reddened.

Laela cleared her throat. "Well, shall we?"

Morgan followed her, the two of them moving in silence.

Laela led the way along the trail, knowing it from her cross-country runs. It hugged the banks of the reservoir. Though the sun was bright and the glistening icicles on the trees dripped occasional drops onto the snow below, Triumph was still firmly in winter's grasp. Trucks were parked out in the middle of the frozen lake, the ice so thick it could easily hold the two-ton weight, while their drivers sat nearby in portable fishing sheds. The lure of ice fishing was foreign to Laela, though she supposed it gave sitting in the cold a purpose.

They trudged on. Both of them became winded quickly from the weight of their snow shoes and winter gear, leaving little opportunity to talk.

After cresting a good-sized bluff, Morgan called from behind her, "I need a break. My quads are killing me." He found a downed tree and sat on it, motioning for Laela to sit beside him.

Laela shook her head, standing. She rested on her poles, then unzipped her jacket a bit. The cold wind, normally so biting, refreshed her warm body.

"Shit, you're a good workout buddy," he said, reaching into a deep pocket of his snow pants. He pulled out a thin, insulated water bottle. He held the bottle up in mock toast to her. "I don't know how you're still standing."

Laela's eyes were focused on the trail ahead of them. "It's easier for me to just keep going, you know? Sometimes I just press on, forgetting that I could even stop."

Morgan nodded. "I get that. You get lost in it." He chuckled a bit, shaking his head. "You almost sound like me about drinking."

She thought a minute before she said, "At least I'm only hurting myself."

Morgan was silent at that.

* * *

He needed to tell her. Morgan knew that was one of the reasons he wanted to even go snowshoeing today. Step 4 was "making a searching and fearless moral inventory." He was working his program. This was part of it.

"I'm sorry," Laela said. "I didn't mean it to bring up your rehab, I know it could sound like…"

"No," he cut in. "You're absolutely right. I was hurting myself."

"At least when you totaled your truck, you didn't have anyone else with you," Laela said.

He shrugged, as if to say he was always alone. Laela continued. "I don't know if anyone told you, but your dad, he was really sad while you were gone. Johnny Tae said he'd come into Buzz Buzz Buzz after his shifts and just stare at the cashier's spot, like he thought you'd pop up from the backroom. Just for hours some nights. Gavin would sit with him sometimes."

Morgan paused for a minute, imaging it. His dad spent his free time at Buzz Buzz Buzz while he was in rehab? This was news to him. He mulled over this gentler image of his dad, one who sat in coffee shops for hours without purpose.

* * *

Stupid, Laela thought. *Stupid, stupid.* Was talking about what happened while someone was at rehab triggering? Was talking about his dad triggering? He'd been talking about his mom, or at least mentioning her so casually this morning, Laela had assumed it was fine to talk about his dad, too.

Laela tried to cover the silence, speaking quickly. "Your dad wasn't the only one. We all missed you."

"Did you?" Morgan looked up at Laela, holding her with his eyes. His thick eyebrows arched with the question, concern etched on his face. She couldn't tell if he meant *you* as in her, Sarah, and Johnny Tae, or just her.

"Of course," she said.

"Laela, I've got to tell you something."

Her stomach dropped. She wasn't ready for this.

* * *

Morgan took off his gloves, nervously wiping the sweat on his snow pants. "Listen, you know last summer." His eyes met hers, and he read the anxiety on her face. "I messed up. Bad."

She nodded along, wide-eyed.

"Not just when I crashed the truck after Evan's party. Before that, too." He looked away from her. "When you got hit. That ... that was me." Guilt clenched thickly in his stomach.

She was silent. Morgan snatched a glance at her, unable to read her face. He said it again, "That was my truck. I was driving. I was drunk, and I didn't want to get caught, and I saw you get up and you looked like you were fine. Johnny Tae made sure of that. And, well, I'm so, so sorry."

"Morgan," Laela said, "I knew it was you."

Morgan started. "You did?"

"Of course," Laela said. "Don't you know everybody's car in this town?" She gave a small laugh.

"Why didn't you say anything?" Morgan asked.

She let out a long breath. "Lots of reasons. For one, I didn't want you to get in trouble," she said.

"But we weren't even friends then, not really," Morgan said.

"Yeah, but I still didn't want that for you. You'd just been through so much already." She broke his gaze. "For another, I didn't think people would believe me. You're the sheriff's son. Couldn't I have been mistaken? Couldn't another truck have hit me? I didn't want all that interrogation."

"I'm so sorry," Morgan said again.

"Honestly though?" Laela said. "I just wanted it to be over. I wasn't even that hurt, I shouldn't have even gone that night. I figured if I didn't say anything, it would ... disappear. And it did. Sort of."

Morgan waited a moment, the discomfort in his midsection releasing. She'd known. All along, she'd known. This massive weight, this guilt he'd been carrying like some kind of Sisyphus, rolling it over and over in his mind ... it had been for nothing.

Suddenly, a thought came to him. "You kept going until it was all right," he said.

Laela smiled. "That's one way to look at it."

"Listen, Laela, again, I am so sorry. I shouldn't have been driving that night. I shouldn't have driven away. And I should have told you a while ago."

"Why? I already knew. I just told you."

Morgan stood up. "Because I wasn't being honest with you. I don't want to be that guy." He thought for a moment, before going on. "I don't want to be that person, only looking out for myself and my own ass. And I sure as shit don't want to be the one who's running from the people he's hurt. Physically or emotionally. I'm sorry. I want to do better."

Laela smiled. "Morgan, you are better. Already! Yeah, what you did was crappy. And not owning it up to it wasn't cool. But you're not that person anymore." She put her hand out to him, then pulled it back. "I couldn't have done that Christmas program without you. The kids loved you. And you've been so …" she paused as she sought the right word, "*deliberate* about staying clean and doing what you need to. I only wish Johnny Tae and Sarah had been as good about it, too."

Morgan watched Laela's face fall, her eyes darting to the snow beneath her feet. Her hand dropped, and she took a step back.

"What's wrong?" Morgan asked. She made a motion to shake her head no, but Morgan said, "You don't have to press on alone, you know."

Laela spoke softly. "It's just… I can't believe what they did."

"Drinking?"

"That, and …"

Morgan nodded once. "You saw the hickey."

"Who didn't?" her voice was bitter. "I know Sarah is fun and pretty, and who wouldn't want to, but …"

"Are you into Johnny Tae?"

Laela met his eyes but didn't speak.

"Wait a second, you shot him down for Homecoming. You said no, right?"

"Listen, Morgan, I've enjoyed getting to know you better," Laela said gently. It seemed like she was trying to tell him something difficult. "You're fun and …"

"Wait, Laela, I'm not into you." He said bluntly.

She gave a little gasp of, "Oh!"

"I mean, we're friends, right? I'm good with that. I'm not looking for anything else from you." Morgan wondered at having a "define the relationship" moment after waiting to confess the guilt he'd been holding on to for months.

"Oh good," Laela said, visibly relaxing. "I didn't know if you thought this hike was a sort of date …"

"No!" he said, then clarified quickly. "I'd been feeling so guilty about not telling you about hitting you, and I felt like you've been such a good friend that it wasn't right. I wasn't being honest. So no, not a date.

"Not that you're not date-able," he added quickly. "Just not my type." He reddened. "And I'm not really in a place to date right now anyway."

It felt right to end on that truth.

Laela sat down on the log Morgan had risen from before. "Well, now that we've cleared *that* up," she said, laughing. "You hit me; I knew that. You were not hitting *on* me, I did *not* know that."

He laughed, too. "Can I sit down next to you?"

"Of course. And pass me the water, I left mine in the car."

* * *

Now that things were clear between them, Laela found herself smiling. They sat in comfortable silence with the tension out of the space between them. They watched the unchanging, frozen scene before them.

"There's still one question you didn't answer," Morgan said as he screwed the lid on the now empty water bottle. "Are you into Johnny Tae?"

She turned her thoughts inward, figuring out her own truth on the matter. Finally, she sighed. "Yes."

"Since when?"

"Probably late in the summer?"

He turned to look at her. "Then why'd you tell him no for Homecoming!"

"I didn't tell him no," Laela said. "I didn't say much of anything. I was having a panic attack at the idea of going to a dance with everyone. But it wasn't because I didn't like him."

"Well, shit," Morgan said, smiling. He pulled his still bare hands up to his face, and breathed into them. "That is classic! You've got to tell him."

"What? No!"

"Yes! He thinks you're not into him."

"But," Laela began before looking out at the trail. "Then why'd he and Sarah …"

"Because he's trying to move on!" Morgan said loudly, articulating every word. "I thought guys were the dense ones, seriously."

"Doesn't matter," Laela said bitterly. "I can't compete with Sarah."

"Do you think Sarah likes him?" Morgan asked.

Laela shrugged. "She's never seriously dated anyone. Could be she's really into him, could be she's bored."

"Maybe," Morgan began gently, "you could ask her who she's into? And while you're at it, ask Johnny Tae, too?"

"We should probably talk with them," she said. "In general. What they did last night wasn't cool."

"Agreed, it was shitty. But," he said, clapping her on the back, "you're still avoiding confessing your truth to Johnny Tae."

Morgan wasn't wrong. But it didn't make Laela feel any more confident.

He started pulling on his gloves again. "Let's go back. Maybe we can get lunch or something. I'm starving." He stood up.

"Ok," she said. "But just as friends, right?" She grinned at him.

"Friends." Morgan agreed, holding out his hand. She clasped it.

* * *

Later that evening, Laela rested comfortably in her family's front room. Sure enough, she had come home to her parents eagerly waiting for her. They had been conveniently lounging in the front room instead of busying themselves elsewhere. Before Laela had even gotten her shoes off, her mom had blurted, "Were you on a date?"

Laela told them about snowshoeing and lunch afterwards, and she made abundantly clear to them that it was *not* a date. "We're friends, and I really like having an older friend," she had told them. Her dad had made a joke about how he was glad because he wasn't sure if his small physique could intimidate Morgan into "gentlemanly behavior." That got Laela and her mom started about stereotypes in dating, and soon the whole family was involved in a deep discussion about gender norms. *A typical family afternoon.*

Now that night had fallen, the front room was lit only by the Christmas tree. For once, Laela wasn't buried in a book, homework, or some other project. She sat, focusing on various ornaments.

Her first Christmas ornament, a gaudy pink bejeweled thing from her dad's mom, Zoe. She'd been so excited for a girl to finally be part of the family, having had three sons of her own, that she'd picked the most outrageously "girlie" item she could find. Laela smiled sadly, remembering how her grandma had bought her stereotypical girl clothing—all frills, tulle, and above all, pink—until she was old enough to talk. It had been at Christmas, when she was three years old and opened a gift from Zoe. It was another puffy pink skirt. Laela had said, "But I don't like pink!"

Her mom had rushed to cover the faux pas, correcting that she didn't like pink today, but tomorrow she surely would. Except her grandmother had waved Bev off, and laughed loudly. "Then tell me, Laela, what you like and I'll buy it for you!" After that, all her clothes from Zoe had been rich purples and vibrant yellows.

All she'd had to do was say what she liked. Her grandmother was more than happy to provide.

Morgan, currently in his guru era, might be right. *Speak your truth.*

She mulled over what that would look like. Would she tell Sarah to quit being so flippant with people's hearts? She imagined Sarah dismissing her as a wet blanket, again. Could Laela admit to her fun-loving friend that she wasn't sure what role she wanted alcohol to play, how she worried she'd use it as a crutch for her anxiety? Handling her feelings about Sarah felt more comfortable than talking to Johnny Tae.

The different colored lights danced on the tree, throwing shades of color on her family's collection of beautiful ornaments. Benign brown ornaments—one made of clay, another a mini drum—shone with an unnatural, plastic hue.

Wasn't pretending everything's fine just as unnatural?

She picked up her phone, readying herself to message Sarah. But her friend had beaten her to it. A text from Sarah sat on her home screen:

CAN WE TALK? BUG I THINK I MESSED UP

Laela opened the message, ready to speak her truth.

Chapter 24

The Body Knows

Nel felt the sharp, sudden tightness in her lower back that Sunday night as she lay next to the empty space Jacques used to inhabit. She wracked her memory, trying to remember if he was at the fire department for a shift or if they'd traded verbal volleys in their last disagreement that he'd internalized.

The throbbing continued, both in her back and in her mind. Sighing, she gave in. She shuffled to the bathroom, rubbing her lower back. The hallway lights were still on, and she realized Jacques was downstairs in their kitchen or living room. She tried to practice what Sister Eunice had counseled them on, assuming the best of the other person. *Maybe he's wrapping Christmas presents*, she tried to think, drowning out the snide voice in her head: *More like ordering last-minute Christmas gifts*. Nel vowed to investigate after the bathroom.

Without turning on the lights, she pulled her thick flannel pajama pants down and squatted on the cold toilet. She grabbed the wadded-up toilet paper, stood up, and stopped cold. There was a wet, liquid mess. Had she missed the toilet? Had Victoria tried to go to the bathroom in the middle of the night?

She felt sticky warmth between her legs. It was her. She was the culprit. She waddled over to the lights, her pajama pants still on the floor between her legs. She leaned one hand against the bathroom sink and flipped the switch, looking down. Then she let out a yelp. Rich, dark red blood showed in her pants. The basin of the toilet had the same red.

Nel's mind flashed to the day she got her first period. She'd been at a friend's house for a sleepover, a congregant of her father's church, and she'd woken up early to find her pajamas wet with menstrual blood. Nel had been scared to wake her friend, but the girl's mom—what was her name? Mrs. Giri? —had been awake. Noticing Nel had been in the family's one bathroom for a long while, she knocked gently on the door. "Nel, honey? Everything alright?"

Nel hadn't answered, a mix of embarrassment and excitement at reaching this moment in her life in such an undesired, messy way. Mrs. Giri had said softly through the door, "Bottom left drawer has some pads, if that's what's going on."

Minutes later, Nel emerged from the bathroom. Mrs. Giri was standing outside. Nel looked down. "I'm sorry, Mrs. Giri."

"Why, girl?" She placed a hand on Nel's shoulder. "Your body is just doing what it's meant to."

"But I made a mess. And I should've known …" Nel said, trying to think of the last few days and what symptoms she'd had.

Mrs. Giri had stopped her, grabbing her hands. "Please don't worry. Was it your period?" Nel nodded. "Not your first time?" Nel nodded again. "Oh, Penelope, congratulations!" Mrs. Giri wrapped her up in a hug. "What a big moment for you!"

Looking around at her bathroom now, so far from that warm Atlanta one all those years ago, Nel realized the last statement of Mrs. Giri was still true: This was a big moment for her. She suspected her body was miscarrying. The unwanted pregnancy had ended itself.

Why, then, did she feel a twinge of sadness?

She stepped out of her soiled pajama pants, then delicately cleaned herself up. Bare from the waist down, she walked to the bedroom and quickly grabbed replacement underwear and pajamas, slid her phone off the nightstand, and found a long-forgotten pad from the linen closet before re-entering the bathroom.

She alternated between sitting down on the toilet and standing up to walk around the bathroom in discomfort. She was sweating. She Googled symptoms of miscarriage, affirming her suspicion. Nel tried to distract herself with plans. She noted the signs that required medical intervention, and she vowed to get another pregnancy test tomorrow to confirm that her body had stopped producing the telltale pregnancy hormone.

After some time, she squatted back on the toilet. She had an overwhelming urge to push. Nel recalled Hudson's birth, how beautifully uncomplicated it had been. The simplicity of her body knowing what to do, the needlessness of all those birthing classes. As she listened to her body and pushed, she also remembered the opposite birth experience she'd had with Victoria: an emergency C-section after a few sharp contractions. She vividly remembered bright lights above her head, her body shaking from the anesthesia and hormone rush at the birth, her inability to even hold her screaming baby as the doctor stitched her back up.

At that moment, Nel felt her body pass the pregnancy. She shook slightly. Resting her face in her hands, she was surprised to find she'd been crying. *It is done.*

She lost track of how many times she'd flushed the toilet. She'd already used an entire roll of toilet paper. Jacques had to suspect something was going on.

Yet unlike all those years ago, there was no sweet knock on the bathroom door. Nel opened the door, half hoping he'd be standing in the hallway or his silhouette would be coming up the stairs. She was caught between wanting to be found and fearing being discovered.

Only the empty hall hugged her in its dark, thick carpet, waiting to hold her cold, bare feet.

Nel closed the bathroom again and looked at herself in the mirror. Did she look like she was miscarrying? What would that even look like? She pinched her cheeks to try to add some color and adjusted her hair before stopping herself. She was acting either like a schoolgirl about to get in trouble or as if she were prepping for a big date. She washed her hands under the faucet, resolutely not looking in the mirror, and turned off the light.

Jacques was already in bed. He must have walked by the bathroom without her hearing him. *And without him checking on me.*

She delicately crawled into her side of the bed. She knew he was awake—she didn't hear his rhythmic breathing.

"Everything all right?" he asked, not rolling over to greet her.

"I think so," Nel replied. Though she wasn't sure Jacques would agree.

Chapter 25

The Start of Something New

In the dark of the early winter morning, Birdie shoveled the steps leading up to her house. Jack and Ripper took turns chasing each other in the snow. They ran in the tracks left by Mark's truck. Her husband had started the tedious job of plowing the snow clear from their long, snaking driveway. His truck's tail lights were distant red beacons moving slowly and steadily away from the house. The old, dented plow had been a staple on his truck since mid-October, ready for times just as these.

Typically, the kids would have been roused out of their beds to help out. All hands on deck on the ranch. But this week, the last before Christmas and a two-week break, involved more tests and project due dates for the three kids. Plus, Sarah's bad mood after she and Mark had it out over her recent partying (*which was, no doubt, a side effect of Jen's cancellation on her, the poor girl*, Birdie admitted to herself) could only be solved by sleep. Or so she prayed. Birdie and Mark had decided to do most of the morning chores themselves. A small mercy for everyone would be to let the kids sleep.

Birdie wasn't sure how effective their plan had been. Ripper barked in excitement. His yip reverberated off the barn and garage door, echoing back to the house. She tried to keep the scrape of the shovel quiet. Its metal lip gritted against the stairs' wooden planks anyway. *It's the thought that counts*, she comforted herself.

When the steps were done, she began working her way to the barn. The horses needed hay and fresh water. A physical chore. It wasn't too frigid that day, another brief mercy deep in the winter, so she readied their blankets. When each horse was draped in its thick woolen jacket, looking sharp and festive, she led them out to the corral. The sky was kissed lightly pink. Dawn was well on its way to full-blown morning.

When Birdie glanced at her watch, she panicked. She had a little more than half an hour to get the kids up, dressed, and in the car for school. No shower for her this morning. She silently prayed Martha wasn't going to be at the church, for the other woman's sake more than her own.

She walked quickly into the house, whistling for the dogs. When they didn't come, Birdie panicked further. She whistled again, sharply. "Boys!" she called. Her voice echoed back. She did *not* have time for this.

She stomped on the deck to clear her boots of snow. She heard Ripper's bark from inside. Relieved, she mentally thanked Mark for bringing the dogs in.

Opening the door, her voice rang out again, "Kids! Get up! We've gotta get going!" Jack and Ripper ran to her, their tails whipping happily.

She was surprised to see Sarah, fully dressed, coming down the stairs. "Nathan and Isaac are just brushing their teeth."

On cue, Nathan yelled out, "Almost ready, Mom!"

Sarah grabbed her coat from the rack. She made a face. "Heather, I'm sorry, but you smell like the horses." Birdie looked down, ready to blame her boots. Sarah pulled the white scarf from her coat's sleeve. "How about I drive the boys this morning?"

Birdie grabbed the coat rack for balance. The kids were not only up, but ready for school? Sarah was offering to drive the boys?

As if by explanation, Sarah said, "Ripper's barking woke us all up. I told Nathan and Isaac if they didn't get ready, you and Dad would cancel Christmas. They got ready pretty quick with that." She shrugged herself into her coat.

"Sarah, I ..." Birdie fumbled over her words. "Thank you."

Nathan and Isaac scrambled down the stairs, boots already on. "I'll go start the truck. Be there before I leave," Sarah said to the boys.

In a flurry of limbs, the boys got into their coats, grabbed their backpacks, and left. The silence that followed in their wake was deafening.

Birdie took off her coat and boots. She walked numbly in her socks to the kitchen, expecting to find a mess of breakfast. But their empty cereal bowls were stacked almost neatly in the sink.

Mark was seated at the table. "Christmas miracle, am I right?" he asked, a spoon of oatmeal hovering in midair.

"I'm having a hard time coming to grips with it," Birdie admitted. "Are our kids actually grown?"

Mark chuckled, finishing his oatmeal. He stood up to walk to her. "I think if you say it out loud, the magic breaks." He leaned forward to kiss her cheek, then winced. "Birdie my dear, can I interest you in a shower?"

"Only if you join me," she said. Together, they went up the stairs in their quiet, empty house, giddy as school kids.

* * *

Her good mood surrounded her as she finalized the Christmas bulletin in the office that morning, circling the usual mistakes without a trace of annoyance. Her very soul thanked God. She remembered the prayer of the fourteenth-century mystic anchoress, Julian of Norwich. "All shall be well, and all shall be well, and all manner of things shall be well." The prayer was her reality. *Or being manifested*, she thought, smiling at Sarah's TikTok influencers' theories of the world.

The kids were becoming more independent. She thought of them last Christmas: a sulky Sarah disappointed again that Mark wouldn't let her hole up in her room to open her newest makeup kit, the boys ripping open their gifts of cartoon-based video games. This year, they had both asked for first-player, realistic animation games.

She remembered her father had started to show signs of forgetfulness then. He'd asked when they were going to open presents, despite wearing the new sweater vest she and Paul had given him just that morning. She'd dismissed it as sundowners or the result of eggnog on an empty stomach. Her mood dropped a bit, realizing it had been one of the earlier signs.

Birdie's phone rang. From the tone, a jazzy, generic tune, she knew it was her brother. She picked up papers at random, searching for the phone. Finding it, she slid the green rectangle to answer. "Hey, Paul."

"Birdie?" It was her father's voice that responded.

"Dad?"

"Yeah, hey Birdie, it's Dad. Listen, did I leave my phone at your house?"

Birdie thought of the last time her dad had been at the house, over four weeks ago for Thanksgiving. "At Thanksgiving?"

"Yeah."

"Dad, that was weeks ago."

"No, it wasn't."

Birdie sighed, unwilling to contradict him. "I'll look around, Dad. Hey, is Paul near you?"

She heard the shuffle of the phone. "Birdie?" Paul's voice.

"Paul, he hasn't been to my house in weeks." Her voice was flat.

"I know, I think it's at the shop ..."

"He thinks Thanksgiving just happened."

"Yeah, the days are so short now, they all blend together. You know how it is."

No, she did not know how it was. Her life in this season was benchmarked by Sundays and services, each date tattooed onto her memory.

"What are you doing today, Paul?"

"I was going to help Dad out at the shop, I'm off today so ..."

"Great, let's get lunch."

"Ok, I'll ask Dad."

"No, just you and me. We need to talk, Paul."

All shall be well, Birdie comforted herself.

* * *

Paul had agreed to meet her at Buzz Buzz Buzz. He'd tried to weasel out of it, saying he wasn't hungry, he didn't really have the money to get lunch. But Birdie had persisted—how often had that been the case for her? —and got him to agree to coffee.

She was standing at the register, studying their seasonal menu that she knew by heart, when the robotic frog with a little Santa hat adorning his bumpy head ribbited.

"Hey Birdie!" Paul said warmly as the door closed behind him. "I walked over from the shop. Found dad's phone. He'd put it in a tool drawer, must've accidentally put it there when cleaning up yesterday. Typical Guy." It had been their joke about their dad's quirks— typical Guy, as in, "he's so normal, it had to be something every generic guy did."

Birdie smiled, more forced than she was ready to admit. "Yeah, I think it's becoming a bit more atypical Guy, Paul."

Gavin's voice cut through the beady stare Paul threw in her direction. "A brother–sister coffee date! I love it! What'll it be today?"

They both ordered—chai tea for Birdie, black coffee for Paul— and Birdie instinctively walked toward the couch in the corner. The Clergy Corner, Gavin had started to call it. It certainly did feel like she was about to have a pastoral conversation. The gray line between the compassion her job required of her blurred with her familial fealty.

"Paul," she said as soon as he sat down in the chair Ara Grace normally occupied, "I'm worried about Dad."

He had the grace to take a sip of his coffee instead of reply.

"I know we've talked about this before. But he's more and more forgetful. Not just because of the phone," she said, predicting that he'd be ready to dismiss that. "Other things, too."

Paul placed his coffee down on the table between them, then met her eyes straight on. "I know. I am, too."

Birdie tried to hide her shock.

"The other day, I caught him taking another dose of his cholesterol meds. He thought he hadn't taken them, despite the calendar we have hung up and the day-of-the-week pill container." Paul's face dropped. "I've been having him cross off the day every morning so he knows what day and date it is."

Birdie's heart dropped, but she found herself impressed with her brother's intervention. "That was a good idea you had," she said soothingly.

Paul nodded. "It worked for a little bit. I'm worried that he's going to accidentally overdose."

"Me too," Birdie said.

"And he's not catching the notes I leave for him anymore …"

Birdie tilted her head in confusion. Paul caught the look and explained. "I started leaving notes for him when I go to work. I put them on the bathroom mirror so he'd see them. I came home once and he was worried I'd moved out."

She placed her hand on his arm, a pastoral reaction that seemed unsisterly. "Paul, why didn't you tell me any of this?"

He yanked his arm away. "Because you'd say we have to put him in a home. That I can't take care of him. Like with Mozza."

Birdie had to reach back into the far recesses of her brain to recall the reference Paul had made. Mozza, short for Mozzarella, was a mouse Paul and Birdie had rescued at their dad's shop one winter. Paul had found him in an old-fashioned mouse trap, the little gray mouse's leg almost severed. He'd brought the mouse to Birdie, pleading with her to save it. Birdie, as the responsible older sister, had acted as triage—get a cardboard box, make a nest out of a handful of shredded paper, place the mouse in it, unhinge the trap, and set out some water. They'd created a little recuperation station for the critter. It was almost cozy.

Paul had come up with the name Mozzarella, because mice eat cheese, as every elementary-aged kid knows, and it had stuck. Mozza survived over the weekend, and most miraculously, their parents never knew. Guy wasn't one to hang around the shop's office, and their mom, Viv, had been determined to clean up the storage room for the umpteenth time. When Birdie had to stay after school for some reason and couldn't help care for Mozza with Paul, she'd told him to change the water and leave cheese out again. Paul had eaten the entirety of his cheese stick at lunch that day, and not wanting to leave the mouse hungry, he'd left Mozza some cheese puffed curls. Mozza was dead the next day, right next to the cheese puffs.

Birdie shook her head. "Paul, Mozza was never going to make it. We found him in a trap, the poor thing had no foot, we fed him processed cheese and water."

Paul waved her off. "It was my fault."

Birdie tried to hide her exasperation. They were talking about a mouse, dead some forty years. This had nothing to do with their dad. She tried to redirect. "Paul, Dad is not a mouse."

"No, but you think a nursing home is that much better than a box with shredded paper?"

"Yes!" she replied quickly. "With trained staff, and facilities built for people in his condition ..."

"His condition?" Paul interrupted. "We don't have a medical diagnosis. This is all just our best guess as to what's happening."

Birdie nodded. They hadn't yet let the primary care doctor in on what was going on. But that was at Paul's insistence. "Paul, I think it's safe to say he's got dementia. Maybe even Alzheimer's. We could get a diagnosis within the week."

She saw her brother's face crack. Decades ago, when they were kids, she had been able to read his expressions. Now, she wasn't sure if he was about to cry, lash out, or admit defeat. How had they grown to be strangers to each other?

"Do you think it's what she'd want?" Paul asked, his voice low and his face downcast. "Mom?"

Birdie leaned back, cradling her chai. They'd never been a family to talk about end-of-life plans or worst-case scenarios. Until her mother's final week, Viv and Guy had been quiet about her medical prognosis.

She thought of her parents' marriage. By today's standards, it would have seemed unequal, with Guy running a car shop that provided the family's income and Viv expected to support the business, regardless. But they'd had a deep respect for each other: Guy never belittled Viv, even in front of his often-misogynistic car clients, and Viv did *not* demurely accept whatever her husband said as Gospel Truth.

"I do," Birdie finally said. "I think she'd want him to be safe." She thought of her mom's attention to each of her kids, her support for them. How she wrote letters by hand each week to Paul while he was enlisted. How she worked to include vegetarian options in their family meals when Birdie declared that eating meat was amoral. "What's more, Paul, she'd want us to be happy."

He looked her in the eyes, and she could read his question instinctively. *What even is happy?* She thought of all her brother had sacrificed these last few years, living with their dad, running his car shop. Did Paul even like to work on cars, living in his childhood home? She'd assumed he was just too lazy to do much else—she inwardly cringed at the realization. What if Paul wanted to date, but he didn't want to bring women back to his childhood room with his memory-impaired dad? She thought briefly of Ara Grace's predicament.

Birdie nudged him with her foot. "I'm serious, Paul. You've done so much already, given up so much of your life to help him stay home." She set down her chai for emphasis. "I'm sorry I never told you thank you before now, but thanks. For caring for Dad, for living with him all this time." She felt tears well in her eyes. "For all the things I didn't see." Her voice cracked. "I should've noticed."

Paul met her eyes. "Ah, don't do that," he said, placing his own coffee down. "You're going to get me," he sniffled loudly before looking up at the ceiling, eyes bulging.

Birdie laughed. "What's the matter? Real men don't cry?"

Paul chuckled. "No," he said, still not looking at her, "I just don't want my sister to think she made me cry." He looked at her, then kicked her gently with his foot. "Big sisters get all high and mighty over stuff like that." He grabbed his coffee from the table, and held it up in a toast to her. "So, Big Bird, what's next?"

She rolled her eyes at the nickname. "Really? All these years, and you still think it's acceptable to call a woman 'big'?"

Paul smiled. "Doesn't count when she's your sister." He shrugged broadly. "I don't make the rules, lady."

Birdie ignored him before continuing. "We should probably start visiting some places. With Dad. It's important he knows what's going to happen …"

"I can get him in with the doc for the diagnosis," Paul said.

And there, brother and sister, seated together in the Clergy Corner, sketched out the next steps for moving their father into a care facility.

A New Year's resolution both could agree to.

Chapter 26

Due Date

It was officially PV Day, and Johnny Tae's hands trembled slightly as he entered the school. Even though he'd already submitted his paper online, he clutched a printed version in one hand, his other hand shoved in his pocket, protecting against the cold wind. *Where even are my good gloves?* he wondered, then startled a bit at realizing he had more than one pair of gloves already. He wasn't sure if he was shaking from the cold or the nerves. It felt impossibly vulnerable to put himself out there like this. But it was just Dr. Brown. He was sure it would be safe in his hands. He was looking forward to the symbolic moment of handing Dr. Brown the paper he already had in his inbox.

The writing had felt like a pretty big deal, saying he wanted to stay in Triumph. He still wasn't sure he wanted to shout it from the rooftops or anything, but it felt significant. He thought Laela and Sarah should know, eventually, but that all still felt like a hot mess. He couldn't ask either of them to have a serious conversation right now without it being misinterpreted. So here he was, left turning in his PV to Mr. Brown, keeper of his inner workings. For now.

* * *

Laela watched Sarah pull into the school parking lot. Laela had been early, after asking her dad to drop her off on his way in to work. There was a windowsill in one of the school's hallways she liked to hang out in before the school day started. It was up on the top floor, overlooking the parking lot, but it also had a great view of the hillside leading into town. She felt like she'd never get sick of the mountains. Here on her perch, Laela could watch her classmates arrive, and she could also see the sleepy comings and goings of her community waking up for the day.

Laela saw that Sarah, for her part, actually looked pretty perky. She had driven the minivan, which means she had taken twin duty that morning. Laela smiled. Sarah may have messed up this weekend, but she was still trying with her family. That was a positive sign.

In all their years of friendship, Laela was used to forgiving Sarah. She thought about the "Best Friends Forever" necklaces they'd had as little kids, two sides of a heart fitting together like puzzle pieces. Sarah's impulsivity was a perfect fit for Laela's caution. Sarah's loud, outgoing personality balanced Laela's quiet, introspective one. It meant that Laela had done a lot of work not being a doormat, and she had a lot of practice owning her truth and offering forgiveness. Sarah went out hard, Laela reined her in. That had always been their dynamic.

Johnny Tae was different, though. The two of them didn't have that comfort level. Laela was still nervous around him, her anxiety overpowering any rational thought. She was mad at him, but she understood, too. She had gotten pulled into it all herself over the summer. Laela knew from her years of friendship with Sarah that they'd have to talk about what happened, and that she also probably couldn't avoid her feelings of betrayal forever. She just wasn't quite ready for all of that yet. She didn't know what she wanted it to look like.

She put away the book she'd been using to settle her nerves— *Love Medicine* by Louise Erdrich, a member of the Turtle Mountain Ojibwe whose writing was honest and painful and real. Laela found it comforting to read a Native woman's words about the trials and tribulations of life in community. This life isn't easy, no matter what angle you're coming at it from. Family, whether blood or chosen, is messy. Laela held onto that comfort as she descended the stairs, hoping to catch Sarah as she came in the entryway.

As it turned out, Johnny Tae was already waiting there. Laela's stomach dropped. She felt the beginnings of a panic attack rising in her chest. She took a couple of deep, shuddering breaths, then grounded herself by identifying five things she could see: the old-timey speaker where the announcements played each morning, a posted flyer about free meals available for students during winter break, a lime-green pair of sneakers on a freshman girl just ahead, a gray spot of slush on the ground. That was four. The fifth was Johnny Tae's hat. Knit and cozy, it looked like it was probably keeping his head warm. Johnny Tae looked as nervous as Laela felt.

"Hey," she said shyly. "What's that?"

Johnny Tae was quick to fold his paper in half. "Oh, the PV is due today."

"No way! Any big epiphanies?" Laela was trying her best to be playful, lighthearted like Sarah would be, but her heart continued to race. The anger and hurt weren't gone.

Johnny Tae's face seemed to soften. She watched a crease between his eyebrows melt away. "I wouldn't say I had an epiphany, but it didn't totally suck. For once."

"High praise," Laela replied, smiling. She saw Sarah come through the doors and try to brush by them, but Johnny Tae stopped her.

"Sarah!" he called out. "Happy Monday!"

Laela saw Johnny Tae doing the exact same thing she was: trying to act normal. She knew they'd all need to hash this out eventually, but for now, this worked. Sarah didn't look happy to see them together, exactly, but she waved and shouted, "Happy PV Day, Johnny Tae!" Laela's shoulders relaxed. Maybe they could get through all of this after all.

"I'd better get to class," she said to Johnny Tae. "See you later."

"Have a good day, Laela," Johnny Tae said, a little softer, less playful, more intentional. *That's enough for now*, Laela thought.

* * *

Dr. Brown didn't need to silence the class at all that morning. The nervous energy in the room was palpable. Papers rustled, but Johnny Tae didn't hear a single voice. Apparently, he wasn't the only one thinking big thoughts over the past weekend. Dr. Brown took them through a lecture on expository writing, reminding them that even if they didn't want to be authors when they grew up, they needed to know how to write so people could understand their work. It was clear that no one was really tracking. They sat with their papers on their desks, waiting.

"If you submitted your personal values statement online, thank you. But I know a lot of you are in it for the tradition. The pageantry. The magic. So, if you brought a hard copy, you can bring it up to me now."

Johnny Tae had to hand it to Dr. Brown. He knew how to make kids take things seriously. Johnny Tae had probably seen half the kids in this class at the dance, drunk off their asses, dancing like no one was watching when literally everyone was. And now, they were solemnly walking forward, papers in hand, looking for anything like they were about to present a gift to the king.

Dr. Brown looked Johnny Tae in the eye as he handed his paper in. For once, Johnny Tae met his gaze. He felt proud of his work this time. Like he finally cared enough about something to put some real effort into it. It was cheesy, but it was *his*. Dr. Brown smiled, seeing Johnny Tae standing tall. "Thank you, sir," he said to Johnny Tae. "See you Sunday."

Johnny Tae stopped short. "What do you mean?"

"I'm a member at Good Shepherd. I don't make it there very often, but Christmas Eve is one of those days I don't like to miss. I assume you'll be there, given your aunt's role."

He couldn't believe it. This damned paper was going to follow him even over winter break.

"Yeah, I'll be there."

"Good. Looking forward to it. Have a nice break, Johnny Tae."

"Thanks. You too, man. I mean, Dr. Brown."

"Thank you. Lots of grading to do, but we'll make it."

Johnny Tae left the classroom feeling a million times lighter. Now he needed to find Laela. He wanted to apologize.

Chapter 27

Hard Truths

The sun rose on Wednesday morning in a haze of deep red. Clouds trapped the almost maroon color. As Nel went about making her coffee, she wasn't sure the sky wasn't displaying a sunset, that it had gotten its colors and time all mixed up. Or maybe she was projecting her feelings of confusion onto the very sky itself.

She thought of the old rhyme, *Red sky at morning, sailors take warning.* Being in a landlocked state, she wasn't sure there were many sailors who heeded the warning from the Wyoming sunrise. She hardly did herself.

Under the red haze, she walked Victoria over to the church's preschool while Jacques took Hudson to school. Nel was supposed to be driving to Colorado today, down to Fort Collins, to end her pregnancy. But that pregnancy had ended itself three days ago. The two at-home pregnancy tests (different brands to be sure) she'd taken since that evening had been negative. Her cramps had subsided, and besides continued bleeding, it was almost like the whole thing had never happened. Almost.

She'd already told the church office and preschool staff that she wasn't going to be in that day, so she had the day to herself. She couldn't go in and lie to them. Plus, she didn't quite feel up to a day of pre-Christmas work: She felt like the opposite of Christmas joy.

She forced herself to return to her deserted house. Nel would text Jacques that the bishop had canceled. At this point, lying to him felt normal.

The emptiness of the day stared back at her, dauntingly. She just wanted to hide, to be alone. If she were on the second floor, eyes peeping into the parsonage would be less likely to see her. So, she decided to hole up in her bedroom. She prepared for her hideaway by filling up her water bottle, grabbing a box of crackers, and purposefully leaving her phone in the kitchen. There'd be no chance now that someone would have "one quick question" for her.

As a distraction, she grabbed a *National Geographic* from the kitchen counter. Jacques subscribed, and he'd gotten into the habit of leaving them piled up. Nel felt as if her lax attitude to the clutter was representative: She couldn't change the man, but she tried to accept what he had to offer.

She couldn't help feeling as if it still wasn't enough. Not anymore.

* * *

"Nel? Why are you here?" Jacques' voice cut through her stupor. The crackers she'd grabbed were very dry, and the steady *crunch crunch crunch* she'd made chewing them was loud. She hadn't heard Jacques enter the house, or walk up the steps to their room.

She looked up, feeling instantly guilty. Her mind raced to remember if she'd ever actually texted her husband ... and her stomach dropped when she realized she hadn't.

Jacques stood in their bedroom doorway, a hand on his hip.

"I, ... um ..." she took a sip of her water, buying time and clearing her mouth. "My meeting was canceled." Then she remembered Jacques was supposed to be out doing errands today while the kids were in school. "Don't you have things to do?" she asked, pointedly.

"Your meeting with the bishop?" Jacques asked, incredulously, neatly avoiding her jab. "Don't they plan those things weeks in advance?"

"Something came up," she said. Evasive, but true.

"For her or for you?"

It felt like they were dueling. Her heart pounded faster. She didn't know if she wanted to fight like this. Not anymore. Admitting that meant she stood on the precipice of something big and unclear, but she felt certain that standing on the imaginary edge wasn't for her. Her mind scrambled for something to say, a decision to make. *Should I ... ?*

"For me, Jacques," she admitted.

"What happened now?" His voice held no compassion. "Doesn't seem like a church emergency if you're in bed, eating."

Nel set the crackers aside and looked at him. "It was never going to happen."

"What's that mean? You made a big deal," he held his arms wide in emphasis, "of being sure I remembered to pick up the kids …"

"No, there was never a meeting." She'd jumped off that imaginary edge.

Jacques looked at her in stony silence. She could see him trying to piece together what was happening. "You just wanted a day alone?" He surmised. "And you didn't think I could give you that? That I couldn't handle the kids for one full day?"

Nel felt tears well up in her eyes. She willed them back. "No, that's not it." Her voice was quiet.

"Then what *is* it, Nel? Huh?" He shook his head, clearly frustrated. "Because you've been acting weird as hell these last few weeks."

So, he *had* noticed. "Then why didn't you say anything?" she asked, her voice heavy with malice. *Old habits die hard.* "Sure as shit didn't feel like you cared."

He threw his hands out again. "You think I don't care? We're in counseling, like *you* wanted! I was getting the kids today, like *you* wanted. Everything you've wanted, I've done. And not even a thank you, not once!"

He raised his hand in the air. "And you just … you just make shit up! You *lie* to me. You say, 'Try harder, Jacques,'" he mimicked her quite well, even in the heat of this moment. "'Do more.' 'No, not like that.' And then, you're here at home, sitting in bed, telling me *I'm* the one who doesn't care!"

"I'm in the middle of a miscarriage, Jacques." In her mind's eye, the branch she could've grabbed to stop the fall slipped just out of reach. "Okay? I was pregnant, and today was my appointment to get an abortion."

Jacques took a step away from her. "What? With who?"

It took Nel a moment to realize what he was suggesting, and her anger at his insinuation raged. "With you, you asshole!" She threw the covers off her angrily to stand up, to match him as an equal. "You really think I was sleeping around? That I got knocked up from someone else? How *dare* you."

"Then why not tell me? If it wasn't someone else, why lie about it?" His eyes were hard. Nel had never seen him this angry.

"Think for just one damn moment: When would I have time to sleep with someone? Huh? Between work and the kids and you, I have no time for anything or anyone else! Not even myself!"

Jacques ground his teeth, staring at the floor. Rage pulsated his body. "Why didn't you tell me then? It was *our* decision to make."

"No, Jacques," Nel said, stepping toward him and the door. "It was mine."

"Oh, because you get whatever you want again, is that it?"

Nel stopped as if Jacques had reached out a hand to touch her. He registered her pause, smirked at her, and continued. "That's it, isn't it? You didn't want a third kid. It'd mess up your plans and your life."

She wasn't the only one who'd stepped off that imaginary ledge.

"Where do I fit in your plans, Nel? Am I just the babysitter to your kids? The chef you come home to?"

Maybe there had been a time when Jacques would've phrased the question differently, using "we" instead of "I." But Nel was no longer sure there was ever a "we" between them—just two separate people trying to live life together. No "relationship baby" they shared, as Sister Eunice talked about. Just two people, more often at odds with one another than standing shoulder to shoulder taking on life together.

Jacques continued, "Because the more *you* do, the more you get what you want, I don't count or matter. I'm not important to you anymore." He cursed in Spanish, his voice breaking, and turned around.

Nel inhaled, then asked, "Where am I in your plans?"

He glanced at her over his shoulder, his voice icy. "I didn't think I was allowed to have plans. Yours were all that mattered."

A hot tear fell, then the cascade started. She closed her eyes, slumping onto the bed. She clasped her hands together, her right hand finding the familiar weight of her wedding ring. It was a long drop down over that edge, and she still wasn't sure if she'd reached the bottom.

Would he count it against her if she said the word first? Did it even matter at this point? Without opening her eyes, the tears still streaming, she asked him quietly, "What is it that you want, Jacques?"

She felt him turn, moving closer to her. He sat on the bed beside her, their shoulders not touching, their legs not brushing.

"It wasn't supposed to be this way," he said, his voice heavy with emotion. Whether he meant their marriage, their life together, or this conversation, Nel wasn't sure. "We tried, Nelly. We tried." He sighed heavily.

Nel said the words then: "It's over." She opened her eyes, tears still streaming.

Beside her, Jacques nodded. She noticed his own tears falling. "I think it's been over for a while."

"We're overdone," Nel joked, meekly.

Jacques didn't laugh at the pun. "In some ways, yes."

He wiped his face with his shirt sleeve, a gesture so vulnerable and innocent, she felt as though she was intruding. This man, her husband. This man, a stranger.

Nel wanted one last kiss, one last moment to remember how they were, to remind themselves that they hadn't been a mistake. Maybe, just maybe, *this* moment was the mistake.

But Jacques stood up.

Nel felt the finality. What's more, she felt the resolute assuredness that this was the right decision.

She let out a breath she didn't know she'd been holding.

Chapter 28

The Eve of Everything

Waking up on Christmas Eve before her alarm with just the barest hint of a sunrise, Nel found herself alone in bed, wrapped tightly in her comforter. This shouldn't have bothered her. She and Jacques had hardly shared the bed over the last few weeks.

But to wake up alone on Christmas Eve morning, on the cusp of the magical sense of anything-can-happen and Christmas miracles still exist, was finality. *My marriage is over.*

Nel wondered in the darkness at her choice of words, the possessive "my" in place of the shared, equal "our." Thinking back, she couldn't recall a time when the two of them had shared the marriage. Even in the pre-kid days, their lives had been a sharing of chores and scheduling dates in accommodation of Nel's work schedule. Jacques's accusations weren't wrong. She knew she worked more hours than were strictly necessary, but not out of a need to feel validated or beloved. The work, this life as a pastor, was who she was to her very core. There was no clear line between where Nel ended and Pastor Nel began. Was that bad? She wasn't sure.

She rolled herself to a seated position and turned on her nightlight. She inched her toes into her slippers, stood, and searched for her warm terry-cloth robe. She'd bought it for herself last Christmas, and handed it to Jacques to wrap. He'd taken this to mean he was done shopping for her. Besides a school-made gift from Hudson, this robe was all she had to open at last year's family Christmas.

She found the robe in the laundry pile. It was splayed on top of the heap haphazardly, bulky jeans and sweaters rising to make it look as though it were the shell of a former beast. She snatched it quickly and wrapped herself in its husk.

Nel couldn't shoulder all the blame for a singular-focused marriage. Jacques had been a willing participant. Her stable income allowed him to pursue his Bohemian dreams of an itinerant living. He was the nearly-starving artist. Without the wife's support, he would be a fully starving artist.

The kids were still sleeping, their bedroom doors shut to her in the hallway. It was a small mercy. She padded quietly down the stairs.

Jacques surprised her by being up, a pot of coffee already brewing in the kitchen. Most of the evidence of his couch-bed slumber had been hidden from view, save for his special orthotic pillow still lying on the couch.

"Morning," she said meekly to him.

"Merry almost Christmas," he replied. "Any sign of the kids?"

"Still sleeping," Nel said. She grabbed two coffee mugs as she waited for the coffee to finish brewing. "Can we figure out today?"

Jacques sharply laughed. "We're only ten minutes into the day, so sure, why not plan it all out?"

Nel chose to ignore the edge in his voice. "I was hoping the kids could come to the family service, at five."

Jacques nodded. "Makes sense. Their friends will be there."

"Right," Nel agreed. "Should I ..." she hesitated. "Should I see if Jessica's family's going to that service and have the kids tag along with them?"

"No, that's not ... you don't have to."

"I wasn't sure if you'd be going." Nel watched the coffee drip slowly into the pot, its work painstakingly slow.

"Of course I'm going. It's Christmas Eve." Jacques grabbed one of the empty mugs she'd set out, then snatched the coffee pot. He poured its contents into his cup. The carafe had just a splash of coffee left. The machine sputtered as it resumed its interrupted brew.

"All right, thank you." Nel focused her attention on the coffee.

"Nel, you don't need to thank me," Jacques said, bringing his cup up to his lips. "The kids love the Christmas Eve service. I want to be there with them."

She nodded, understanding. They were silent for a while; the only sound was the steady rumble and drip of the coffee machine.

Jacques cleared his throat. "While we're talking about our, uh, 'plans,'" his voice was a whisper, "could we agree to not tell the kids? For a while? I don't want to ruin Christmas for them."

"Absolutely," Nel agreed. "They don't need to know. Not yet."

"I reached out to Dean, remember him?" Dean was an old friend of Jacques's who was a videographer for a respected nature show. Nel nodded. Dean had been a small man whose demure personality fit his near-invisible role behind a camera. "He said he could get me in on a migratory birds special they're filming."

The coffee machine beeped, letting them know the coffee was ready. Nel reached for the carafe. "That sounds like a good fit. When?"

"It starts in ten days. Down in Panama," Jacques said into his cup.

Nel's hand was steady as she poured her own coffee. "I take it this will be a multi-week gig?" She saw him nod. "So, I'll be on my own with the kids."

"Right," he said. "Perhaps we could use it as a kind of … trial?"

Nel was fairly certain no test-drive of separation was necessary. "You're suggesting we tell the kids after you get back?"

Jacques sighed. "Or at least it would give us time to think through the logistics."

Nel raised an eyebrow, waiting for him to continue.

"I can't afford a place on my own," he finally said. "I need a job."

Which is what I've been trying to get you to do for the last few years. Nel swallowed her words by taking a sip of coffee.

"Just let me get a job. Let me get on my feet. Then we can tell the kids."

Their marriage may have been unbalanced. That was undoubtedly a contributing factor to its demise. But Nel thought that perhaps if they started this coparenting business on equal footing …

"A few weeks, right?" Nel asked. He nodded. "Deal."

She lifted her coffee mug to toast.

Jacques clinked his mug against hers. "Deal."

* * *

Later that day, at First United Methodist's five p.m., family-friendly Christmas Eve service, Nel snuck glances at the congregation during the opening hymn. She saw families clustered together in the pews, parents acting as bookends to packs of kids, grandparents smiling at shenanigans they'd never have allowed their own children to indulge in.

She found some faces she recognized from previous big church holidays, names she'd forgotten but would ask for again today when shaking hands. Then she nearly startled, seeing Charlie and Morgan. They stood in the back of the church, Morgan's hulking frame looking like an oddly placed door. She saw him wave to a kid, one of the pageant kiddos from the massive Ulvein family, seated in a pew a few rows ahead of him. The kid waved back wildly. Charlie leaned close to Morgan, whispering something. Nel noted he had to nearly stand on tiptoes.

Morgan bent closer to Charlie, listening intently. He smiled and stepped out into the aisle. Charlie stepped ahead of his son, and together, they reached the pew with the kid. Nel watched as the Ulveins shuffled together to make room for the two men to sit beside them. *One family joining another.*

Her eyes settled over the crowd on her own family. Jacques stood in the front row, Hudson and Victoria on either side of him. The kids were dressed up, not in the outfits Nel had carefully laid out with matching accents of red and green, but in appropriate nicer attire. Victoria held her father's hand, swaying to the tune of the song. Hudson grasped the hymnal, his eyes focused on the words.

This was their last Christmas together, all together as a family. The realization struck her in the pit of her stomach. Would Jacques get the kids at Christmas in the future, since it was a work day for her? Could she and Jacques co-celebrate the holidays, or would the kids get two separate holidays? *How is any of this going to work?*

Her mind raced; her cheeks felt warm. She feared she might start to cry. The opening hymn was nearing its conclusion, "O Come, All Ye Faithful." She stopped singing to catch her breath and clear her mind. She needed to focus on the task at hand.

She glanced up and her eyes landed on the Ulvein's pew. One of the older Ulvein children had maneuvered her way to stand between Morgan and Charlie, looking pleased with herself. She was clearly avoiding her mother's gesture to return. The two youngest Ulveins were starting to act out for their parent's attention, and Mr. Ulvein threw Charlie a questioning look. Charlie nodded, smiling down at the girl beside him protectively, as Mr. Ulvein picked up the youngest to comfort. Meanwhile, the Ulvein kid who'd been ecstatic to see Morgan stood on the pew's seat to be eye level with his pageant leader. From what Nel could tell, he was showing Morgan the bulletin, as if explaining to him how the service progressed.

The faithful gathered. God's family grows, each year finding one another again.

Nel's sadness remained, but it no longer threatened to overwhelm her. Instead, something like hope arose. The unknown of future Christmases, the details of what was to come … all that could wait.

For now, it was enough to be together, this Christmas, with her family and her congregation.

* * *

Ara Grace was surprised by how much paper was strewn between the pews after her church's family Christmas Eve service. It was as if the bulletins had been used as confetti, thrown into the air to celebrate the Savior's birth.

"Reminds me of the last day of the semester," Dr. Brown remarked, looking around where he stood. "You'd not believe how much of a mess kids leave behind."

Holding up her current handful, Ara Grace said, "I'm starting to get the picture."

Dr. Brown walked the pews on the other side of the church, returning the hymnals to their racks and picking up crud.

They met at the back of the church. "At least there were no wax spills at this service," he said, reaching for the pile of paper Ara Grace had. "But I do miss the smell of extinguished candles." He breathed deeply for emphasis.

Ara Grace thought back to the chaos of the service. "It probably was safer," she conceded. "Thank you for helping clean up." She wasn't sure if Dr. Brown was technically a member of her church, or if he had chosen this service to attend as his Christmas duty. She knew at one point he'd been on the church's membership roster.

"Of course," he said. "Do you have a minute? I know you have another service."

"Sure," she said. There was an awkward pause. "Is here okay? Or do you want to meet in my office?"

Dr. Brown laughed. "Sorry, wherever is fine. This is fine." He leaned against a pew, placing the papers they'd collected next to him. "I just wanted to talk to you about Johnny Tae."

Ara Grace's stomach dropped. "What'd he do now?" she asked, automatically. Then she corrected herself. "I mean, I know he was struggling with writing that paper for your class. We talked about it. I can be sure he finishes it."

Dr. Brown shook his head. "No, he's a fine young man. Really, a good guy. He turned his paper in … on time," he added for emphasis. "I was wondering if you'd read it."

"No," she said, her insides still uneasy. "What did he say?"

"Well, that he's found his home. Here, in Triumph." Dr. Brown said. "With you."

Ara Grace didn't speak, not trusting herself.

"I was quite surprised, too," Dr. Brown admitted. "But then again, teenagers often hide their real feelings behind indifference. I just wanted you to know in case he conveniently forgets to tell you." He pushed himself off the pew. "Teenagers can be forgetful like that too, sometimes."

* * *

After a light Christmas supper with Paul and Guy, Birdie's whole family had caravanned to Triumph's city outskirts to Christian Church of Triumph. Sarah had volunteered to drive not only the boys, but also Paul and Guy. Birdie and Mark were blissfully alone, together, in the cab of her truck.

"Darling, you're doing the right thing," Mark said as she signaled to turn. Birdie knew he wasn't talking about her driving. "They're both going to be all right."

"You know what Paul told me tonight?" Birdie said.

"Oh, Birdie girl, don't go paying no mind to …"

"No, no, it's good. I promise." She glanced in her rearview to see Sarah's truck still behind her, its headlights looking like the wide eyes of a smiley face.

"Fine, what did Paul say?"

"That this means he can finally bring his lady friend over."

Mark clapped a hand on his leg and laughed. "That's true, you know. You'd hardly have been into me if I'd lived with my dad when we met."

"You *did* live at home when we met," Birdie retorted. "We were in school together, remember?"

"Now you know what I mean," Mark said. "But see? Good for him!"

Birdie sighed loudly, then was silent for a moment. They were near enough to her church that she could see the illuminated sign beckon from down the road.

"What now, Birdie? I promise, Guy's gonna get the help he needs, and it's going to be close enough ..."

"No, not that." She watched the sign switch to CHRISTMAS EVE 8 PM CANDLELIGHT SERVICE— 'BE THE LIGHT OF THE WORLD.'

"Then what is it?"

Birdie signaled to turn into the parking lot. She watched Sarah do the same. "Who do you think his lady friend is?"

Mark laughed again. "Birdie, when he's ready to tell you, he will."

"But what if," Birdie started, then lowered her voice conspiratorially, "what if it's Martha?"

"Then praise God! Think of how organized she'll get that house!" They laughed together at the thought.

"I do wonder who his lady friend is," Birdie said, parking far from the entrance and turning the engine off. "But I am glad he's got someone."

Mark grabbed her hand. "Me too, darling." He kissed her on the back of their clasped hands. They stayed that way for a moment.

Sarah's truck high beams flashed, illuminating the car. "Eww," they heard Isaac yell as he jumped from the truck. "Mom and dad are kissing!"

"Gross!" Nathan stepped down. The twins raced each other to the church.

Birdie opened her car door, the winter night cold taking her breath away. She grabbed her purse and followed the boys. At the church's front door, she looked back at the parking lot, holding the door open as Sarah helped Guy across the icy parking lot. Sarah had her arm intertwined with Guy's, and instead of chivalry, Birdie saw that Sarah's arm supported Guy's just a bit, helping him walk mostly independently.

Would the miracles never cease tonight?

* * *

At home, alone in the apartment, Johnny Tae searched for a box. He should've thought to buy wrapping supplies earlier, but he knew there was some Christmas wrapping paper somewhere in this place. Ara Grace had carefully wrapped a handful of items, all of which were currently stacked higher than their little Christmas tree. Even in what he knew she viewed to be her weak attempt at Christmas, his aunt was still outdoing herself on expectations.

He needed to cover the lame gloves he'd bought for her in something Christmas-y. He'd searched the coat closet, finding an old birthday gift bag with two pieces of tissue paper in it. That would have to do. He'd make up some explanation that it was Jesus' birthday, after all. She'd get a kick out of it. *And see right through me.*

Johnny Tae threw the gloves in, and tried to rumple the tired tissue paper into something cheery. It sagged drearily, bending in on itself. He'd be better off using regular paper.

The thought gave him an idea. He rushed to his laptop. Pulling up his PV on the screen, he printed it out. The pages spat out from the printer onto the floor in Ara Grace's room.

Gathering the pages, he folded each of the four pages lengthwise as if he were creating a fan. He remembered his auntie teaching him how to make a fan when he was a kid with the bulletins from Umma and Appa's church, when they'd be stuck in the airless room for hours. He used the folded paper as replacement tissue. It looked a little off, but at least it was sturdy.

Plus, he figured this way, when he told her he wanted to stay here in Triumph, he could pretend it was part of his gift. That way, she had to pull through on her end and agree it was right. Because who'd ever return a Christmas gift?

* * *

The voices of the small choir raised together to reach a high note. Though her church couldn't afford to have a separate choir director, their musician, Jeremy, did double duty for events like today. Even Martha, her ears heavy with literal jingle bells dangling from each lobe, watched for his cues as the group sang. The choir wore no robes, creating a visual kaleidoscope of colors, but their song books were all the same uniform green.

When the song ended, Guy began to clap. Paul and Sarah joined him, and soon, the entire congregation was applauding the choir's song. Birdie saw more than a few choir members blush in gratitude.

She waited until the applause faded on its own.

"Thank you, choir," Birdie said. "You know, I'm reminded that this time, each year, we get together for Christmas. That's expected. And each time, each year, we're surprised by the unexpected: angels proclaiming God's love, the Christ child resting in a horse trough, or even gratitude for the gifts we share together."

Birdie inhaled deeply, taking it all in. "Despite all we have in our daily lives, God is born, anew and again each Christmas. And that, that is the best news of all."

* * *

The final verse of "Silent Night" began, Sylvia plugging away on the piano for once instead of the organ. Ara Grace looked out at the late-evening crowd gathered. Most of her congregation had opted for the battery-powered candles, their LED lights a nearly blinding white. She spotted one lone flickering flame—Johnny Tae, his face illuminated in a candle's dark yellow glow.

He caught her eye and pointed to his candle, eyebrows raised in a big smile.

Ara Grace's mind flashed back to a daycare performance of his, nearly fifteen years ago. It was some kid song show that lasted no more than ten minutes. He had been standing nervously on the risers, looking around the crowd. Ara Grace had thought he was searching for his mom. That morning, when Hana had told Ara Grace that she wasn't going to Johnny Tae's "dumb kid show," Ara Grace had called herself sick in to school, faking Umma's voice on the call. When Johnny Tae's eyes found hers in that crowded sea of families, he had jumped off the risers in excitement and ran toward her. His teacher had reached out to stop him, then waved in recognition. "Auntie, you came!" he'd shouted as he threw himself at her legs. Ara Grace had been wrong: Johnny Tae had been looking in the crowd for her, not Hana.

The same eagerness was on his face this evening. His face was older, of course—a more defined jaw, the absence of chubby kid cheeks—but the eyes twinkling in the candlelight were still the same.

She smiled broadly, feeling tears stream down her face. He was staying. Here, with her. Things were right again.

* * *

Johnny Tae hung back in the narthex after the service. He knew the drill. Auntie would have to say Merry Christmas and good night to everyone, then they could go home together. He'd gotten permission to drive over to save them from walking back in the freezing night air. He went to Ara Grace's office and grabbed her coat, trying to busy himself while he waited.

The ruse worked. By the time he made it back, the narthex crowd had thinned out considerably.

His phone had just buzzed with a notification when Ara Grace caught sight of him. "Johnny Tae," she said, and wrapped him in a hug. The woman barely made it up to his shoulders. She pushed back and held him at arm's length, just looking at him.

Why is she being so weird?

"You got Christmas nostalgia or something?" he asked instead.

She shook her head and hugged him again. "You brought me my coat!" she exclaimed, as if it were the most wonderful thing he could have ever done.

"Yeah," he shrugged, handing it to her. "Ready to go? I've been waiting to eat dinner until you were done."

Ara Grace's eyebrows softened, looking at him again.

"Seriously, what is going on with you?" he said. *Is she exhausted?*

"Dr. Brown was at the earlier service," she said. "He told me he read your paper."

Johnny Tae's blood ran cold. She knew. This was the moment, here, now. She'd tell him she'd offered it only as a nicety, didn't think he'd actually want to stay in this hell hole of a town. He reached into his pocket for his phone, readying himself for a reason to look anywhere but at her.

"You're staying!" she squealed, and wrapped him in a hug again.

He felt himself instantly relax. "Yeah," he said. Then he started to laugh. "Yeah, I mean, if it's all right with you."

"Of course it is! I've been telling you that for months!"

"Okay, but I didn't know if you meant it ..."

She swatted him with her coat. "Stop that! How many times do I have to tell you?" She hugged him one final time. "All right, give me just a second to turn off the lights and we'll go home."

Johnny Tae realized that while they were talking, everyone else had left. He watched his auntie go back into the dark sanctuary to unplug the Christmas tree. He glanced at his phone.

He'd forgotten about the notification. It was from Instagram.

LALALAELA67: MERRY XMAS! COULD WE TALK?

Johnny Tae smiled. He hoped there would be plenty of chances to talk with Laela in the coming days. But for now, he walked beside his auntie to the car, readying himself for the stupidly short drive home.

Epilogue

Christ Candle

Epiphany

Ara Grace had to crack a smile, sitting in the clergy corner, looking around the coffeeshop. She had survived her first Christmas in ministry. Somehow, she'd powered through her version of it. Her nephew didn't hate her. She hadn't ruined everything. Receiving Johnny Tae's paper had been even more tender and sweet than she could have imagined. He liked his gifts, too. She had guessed right with the ski pass and new tech-friendly gloves. He told her he'd wanted to start skiing with Morgan this winter and couldn't wait to use the pass, and not freeze his fingers off doing it.

Nel sat on the small sofa across from Ara Grace, with Hudson and Victoria snuggled into her on each side. They were both messy and smiling. Victoria's mouth was smeared with chocolate from a filled croissant, and Hudson's lap was covered in crumbs from the bagel he was eating bird-style, pecking pieces out with his fingers. Nel wore no makeup, and her hair was gathered on top of her head in a messy bun, but the color was back in her face. She looked like herself again.

"Jacques is away on a gig for the next six weeks, so these two are my shadows until he gets back," Nel said. Ara Grace expected her to look haggard at the thought, but instead, she looked content. Nel mouthed, "Trial separation," and Ara Grace nodded knowingly.

Birdie rushed in the door, followed by a cold wind. The temperature had dropped on Christmas Day, and it was now a more typical, single-digit Wyoming winter day. Ara Grace watched her unravel her long scarf and walk up to the counter to place an order with Morgan. Johnny Tae was working the espresso machine.

"The usual?" Morgan asked. His bun was tied up neatly, and he was wearing a knit cardigan on top of his typical flannel.

"Yes, please. Tea is going to serve me well today." Birdie looked windblown, but more at peace than Ara Grace had seen her lately. "That's a very nice sweater."

"Thanks. You know, it was actually my mom's? It was huge on her, but I'm really liking the fit on me. Feels like a hug."

Ara Grace's heart swelled at the thought of Johnny Tae having such authentic, open friends in his life. She was so grateful for Morgan.

"A hug. Just perfect." Birdie grabbed her mug of tea from Johnny Tae and said, "I hear a hug might be in order for you, too. You're staying?"

Johnny Tae only looked slightly uncomfortable as he accepted the brief hug across the counter, both avoiding the steaming mug of tea that Birdie had set on the counter.

"Yeah, turns out it's not too bad here."

Birdie gave him a gentle nod, then made her way over to the clergy corner.

"Hello, wonderful women!" she exclaimed with feeling. "What a day."

"How was the big day yesterday?" Nel asked.

Ara Grace remembered that Birdie had spent yesterday packing up her dad's things to prepare him for his move.

"You know what? It was actually lovely. Lots of good chats with Dad and Paul about the stuff we were packing up. Brought lots to Goodwill, thank goodness. And a few fun things for the boys. Sarah even took some of my mom's old costume jewelry. Today was tough, though. Dad woke up confused. He didn't know why all his things were in boxes. So that's where I was just now." She collapsed into her chair.

"Oh, Birdie," Nel murmured, stroking Victoria's hair absentmindedly. "That's so tough."

"Not as tough now that we've got a plan. I feel a lot of clarity around it now. It doesn't scare me, Dad's episodes, knowing he's got somewhere safe he's going."

Ara Grace nodded knowingly. "It's all so much easier when you have a plan."

"Sure is," Nel agreed. "I've got an evaluation for this one," she tousled Victoria's hair, "in late January. It feels like such a relief to have it on the calendar."

Ara Grace sipped her peppermint hot chocolate and felt a wave of what she could only describe as warmth wash over her. She was decidedly not a sentimental person, but she could not have imagined finding such dear friends in this tiny, quirky town. None of this was easy, but they were making it.

"So, speaking of plans," Nel said. "Do we want to start hashing out Lent? Or should we bask a bit in Christmas?"

Birdie sighed. "Jesus was just born. Can we have a few moments with the baby before we work our way to Easter?" The women laughed together.

"When even is Easter this year?" Ara Grace asked. "March or April?"

"Last day of March," Nel replied automatically. "So, you can't do an Easter spin-off of April showers bringing May flowers, or even any kind of spring-has-sprung thing."

As Ara Grace wondered what the town would look like in the fresh beauty of spring, the door to the shop burst open. The robotic frog ribbited as Sarah came in, Nathan and Isaac in tow. Laela trailed behind them. Ara Grace heard Morgan ask her what was with the pipsqueaks, giving each a knuckle punch in greeting. Sarah announced loudly, glancing over at Birdie, for the briefest second, "My mom is the worst. I just wanted to hang with my brothers."

Morgan acted like these two comments made sense together. "Turns out they're pretty cool if you give them a chance. And if you have a friend like Laela who knows what to do with little kids."

Laela smiled shyly and helped the twins take off their jackets. While Sarah ordered, Laela walked over to the side of the counter where Johnny Tae was standing at the espresso machine, ready for his next assignment.

Ara Grace watched as Morgan nudged Johnny Tae, bumping him lightly on the shoulder, and told him to take five. She saw Johnny Tae and Laela pull up the calendar apps on their phones and thought she heard Laela say, "It's a date."

She thought shyly of her own upcoming date. A library date with a very cute, very fascinating sounding someone named Lex. They'd video chatted twice. Once they ate lunch together, over many miles of distance, but the conversation had felt easy.

Ara Grace hadn't told anyone yet. Not Johnny Tae, not even her good friends here now. There would be time for that.

I might love it here after all, Ara Grace thought.

For the love of Triumph.